I0551710

The
Social Event

written by Don Lively

Copyright © 2013 Don Lively

All rights reserved.

ISBN-10: 0692233121

ISBN-13: 978-0-692-23312-2

This book is entirely a work of fiction. Names, characters, places, events as well as other elements are either products of the author's imagination or used fictitiously. Any resemblance to actual events, locales, or person, living or dead, is entirely coincidental.

No part of this publication can be reproduced, or stored in a retrieval system, or transmitted in any form or by any means, electronic, mechanical, photocopying, recording or otherwise, without express written permission from the author or publisher.

Edition: June 2014

Cover design by Donna Snyder – www.rsdesign.net
Cover and author photography by Bob Snyder

To my wife.

For the elegant tenacity with which you supported me throughout this endeavor.

Thank you for believing.

CONTENTS

PART 1

THE START OF THE END

§

*"In us all is the desire to be either remembered
or forgotten for what we've done." – Kim Ishida*

CHAPTER 1

Day 127 of the fourth year A.E. (After Event)

Wind came from the west the day Kim chose to leave. Hot, thick and foul, it was a hard-to-breathe stench pushed by a listless breeze over the coastal hills and downslope into the valley. It was a day the same as any other, a day like all the rest.

From the terrace of the empty house in the hills, the house that stood above the sprawling waste of urban and suburban leftovers, Kim scanned the valley. Noticing the muted gray-brown haze of the poisoned sky had lifted, she stood a moment, regarding its gradual drift. Change in the sky, when it happened, was subtle, yet the sun remained constant with its relentless heat. The acrid humidity that came with the breeze left the taste of rusted steel in her mouth. Each breath held the mephitic sting of a dying ocean littered with the rotting carcasses of dead ships. The west wind was good.

The day Kim would move on from the valley where she had

been hiding since The Before had come. She knew if she forced herself onward, she might find peace with her demons. It could be the start of the end, the closing of a chapter in what was left of her life.

"Let's do this," she said, as if making audible noises meant something irrevocable. She had started talking to herself aloud some time ago. She needed to remind herself she was real.

Across the distance below, through the dingy haze, she could see the columns of smoke that so often streaked the expanse. They were the Social Sites. They dotted the valley out there, down around the edges where the land rose from the salty, festering waters of the encroaching bay. They were the places where people gathered, those who were left. They were the ones who would try to connect with likeminded survivors. They were the ones who tried to recruit or abduct, or worse.

The sites could be identified from miles away by the signature column of toxic black smoke that rose from fires fed with the skeletal remains of The Before. Old tires and the pervasive plastics were the dye that blackened the caustic plume, the petroleum-based remnants of a failed society. The products of a world once powered from deep within the planet's crust gave the ominous columns of smoke their strength.

These sites and the billowing black shafts that announced their presence would one day appear off by themselves, separate from the rest. They were brought *online* by one or two who felt they had something new and different to offer in the way of thought or perspective. Those who were sure their version, their view, was the right view, the superior view. Whether or not they lasted depended upon how many *hits* they received, how many would *like* them, *friend* them, *follow* them. Each site was different and each could be treacherous or trustworthy. It was always difficult to tell at first contact.

Friends. Kim was not interested in the sites, or their friends. That was the last thing she needed. Her thoughts were of another place and of other people, people about whom she had heard mentioned over the years, people spoken of in the voice of innuendo. It was a voice in the air moralizing truths that did not exist. Her thoughts were about the people of a place, and the place was the Assemblage.

These people held the influence. They had directed the current and channeled course of society's impulsive actions, its so-called social causes and beliefs. They had dammed and controlled the river, the tide of social flow, what was left of it, and that was wrong. That was not how it should be. Kim knew that now, but then, before this time in which she now survived, she did not see it. Even if she had, she had lacked courage and resolve. The river had to be free to find its natural course. It had to be free to flow wherever the landscape of individual human thought took it. She needed to free the river. Maybe then, she could be free.

She would go alone. She had been alone and preferred to stay that way. Kim was not a follower, and she sure as hell did not want to lead. The cost of being a leader had left deep, painful scars, wounds that had not yet healed. She wanted no more of that. She led only herself, by knowledge and instincts. She followed the whispers and the low words, those unsaid but known things that haunted her. She would go to the Assemblage. Maybe she would find, finally, an opportunity for achieving something positive. It was not happening there in the valley. What she had done there was far from positive. It was time to begin ending that part of her life. It was time to leave.

Leaving the abandoned mansion meant leaving the safety of the known for the uncertainty of whatever might lie beyond. The nearest house to her mansion-camp stood just over a mile away. The surrounding grounds were clear, except for the wild and overgrown vineyard that fed the meager deer population. The open terrain afforded a good view of all approaches and the valley in the distance. Those features had made it a safe place to stay.

Before the mansion, Kim lived in the server room of the place called Obyavit. What started as a hiding place had been, for almost three years, her secret shelter in the midst of the winnowing chaos of a dying population center. It was convenient from a sustenance perspective, for a while. She could move easily among the campuses of the other empty and abandoned corporate headquarters. In the various restaurants, cafes and food stores nearby, she foraged food and supplies while the usable scavenge lasted. The water from the bay eventually came, however, and reclaimed the ground it once owned a few hundred years ago. When it reached the parkway that was less than a mile from where she had been hiding, she scouted and then moved to the mansion.

As she stood there alone above that valley whose vibrancy had faded and crumbled so long ago, she began to think that she was fading, crumbling, a relic of something that had once lived long ago. Anxiety filled her, pressing out against her chest hard and tight. She turned and walked back into the mansion.

I am not old. Not by the standards of The Before, she thought. But life was harder now and the world was different.

A fit woman by any standard, Kim was of average height, slightly underfed, but strong. She could cover many miles in a day and had explored all of the peninsula, South Bay and most of the East Bay. She had learned to hunt and survive. But the elements had left their marks, and her once soft brown skin had become weathered, sunbaked, and harsh, the skin of a wanderer. Her once long dark hair was now short, gray and angry, the hair of a cast-off.

She prepared to leave. Her thoughts, her actions, what she wore and how she wore it, they all served a specific purpose: to hide herself from the elements, to hide the things that could keep her alive and to hide the fact she was a woman. Protection, from mankind and environment, and the ability to carry a lot without looking as if that was the case was what she needed. Anyone who wanted to stay cool in the new and changed world dressed light and loose, as did she. A wide-brimmed hat, which she wore whenever she ventured out, also helped to protect her some. But the raw heat and UV from the depleted ozone ravaged everything it touched, even her. These and other habits of character became her rigid life.

The trip she was planning would be a few days and she needed supplies with which to make the trip. Dried deer meat and scavenged energy bars made up the bulk of the food she carried. She stashed these in a beaten pack along with a few remaining antibiotics she was able to salvage from an abandoned pharmacy in a dead strip mall. She also brought clean water, two quarts; one went in the pack and one hooked into a loop on her belt near the small of her back. Then a hunting knife. Easy to reach, it hung off her left hip. There was a place for everything and everything had to be in its place.

Always thinking, planning and organizing, she included nothing that had not felt the pressure of her obsessive vetting process. The process she used for every project. The fact that each shoe had a small, unnoticeable, hidden pocket just over the outside ankle was not by accident. Nor was the fact that in the left shoe pocket there was an inch-long, razor-sharp folding knife. The right held two rock-hard pieces of Bazooka Joe bubblegum.

Then there were the guns. There was a time when she could never have imagined carrying such an instrument. But the world was full of dangers, and now one went with her everywhere. On this trip, she would have two. One was a Kahr PM9. It was not much larger than a pack of cigarettes. She carried it in a flexible nylon holster strapped tight to her ribcage, just under her left breast. The way her clothing hung, no one would see it there. The other was an old friend, a Smith & Wesson M&P .357, which she wore on her right hip, out where all could see. The .357 was the deterrent; the red lettered sign that declared *don't mess with me*. The 9MM was a safety net, a plan B. She carried seven additional clips that were also a part of plan B.; five in various pockets for the .357 and one strapped to each calf for the 9MM. She knew well how to use those weapons; she knew what it felt like to end a life.

Scanning across the room, she spotted the only thing that served no practical purpose in her survival, the smartphone. It was one of the most advanced in The Before, the flagship model of its time. She had been able to live her entire waking, working and social life through it, when it worked. Few phones worked now. Often there was no signal to receive, no bars to show connectivity or no power with which to keep it charged. She kept hers. She had drilled a small hole in it and had strung a thin leather lace through the five-ounce beaten piece of glass and metal. In its smooth, blank screen she could see herself, her thin, weather-worn face with its short scraggly hair. And, just as the screen, her face held a blank emptiness. She saw what she felt. The device that was once so innocuous was her millstone. It stayed with her, around her neck, so she would remember the purpose of her journey and her part in The Before; the past that gave humanity the present.

CHAPTER 2

Kim stayed out on the edge and skirted the dead suburbs. There were few, if any, people to worry about along the wild overgrown periphery. When she had been scouting and roaming the East Bay and the Peninsula, she had estimated there were just a few thousand people left. Early on, everyone evacuated in a hurry because that was what they needed to do, what they were supposed to do. It was what was trending at the time. The viral reaction of one emulating the other soon left the homes, towns and cities empty. There were the Social Sites, from where the smoke columns came. Those had people, but they were spaced far apart, on the higher ground of the urban areas, near where the bay was now encroaching. She stayed wide of those places. One person at a time was fine, but experience had taught her, no more groups.

She was keeping a brisk but steady pace as she moved south past the abandoned and burnt city of Morgan Hill. By hugging the eastern side of the wet grassy tidal estuary that extended down beyond what was once the epicenter of technology, she was able to make it safely out of the valley. The jungle was thick and shaggy along the two-lane road she had chosen. It was quiet, subtropical, hot and damp, no people or cars, no sounds. There were no birds either. This made her sad.

The birds had died first. It was much as in the early years of mining. They were the proverbial canary in the coal mine. A sad anachronism, their death was a signal that something was terribly wrong, but very few people noticed. People were too busy focusing on their collective social consciousness, as delivered to them by their various social information sources. So long as they were connected, they knew their purpose. It was only when the voice of the virtual society went quiet did they look up. Something had gone wrong. And with the blank screens came a realization, which quickly became panic. No one listened for the birds in The Before and no one could hear them in The After.

The old state highway that ran over to the San Joaquin valley stretched out ahead of her on the morning of the second day. She was familiar with the road, both from The Before and The After. Being on this connector of two valleys increased the potential for contact with another person. The plan did not call for that, not yet. Contact probably would not be dangerous. Most just wanted to connect and chat with others in order to get news and share information. Still, there were the Mechs and others like them, the ones who socialized only to harass and intimidate, or worse. Her plan was to head east, staying head-up and aware while trying to make it to the San Luis reservoir by dark.

Just as in The Before, people wanted and needed information in order to make their decisions. In The After, information no longer moved across the web of technology that physically connected friends via their electronic presence. It now moved through human-to-human contact, through people talking to people. Most information was local, seen and shared by people within a day's walk of each other. Then there was the news of the wider world, news about far-off places such as St. Louis or Chicago. This was the news brought by the Carriers.

About a year after she had found the mansion, Kim was scavenging in a dead big-box home improvement store near the swampy Willow Glen area. That was when she met a Carrier for the first time. He was passing through on his way to the dry Klamath wasteland in the north. She was either not paying attention, or was just too engrossed in trying to pry open a locked cage of specialty tools, when the Carrier walked up behind her unnoticed. He stepped out of an aisle just a few feet away and simply said, "Hi."

Kim jumped, letting loose with a high-pitched yelp as she turned and drew the .357 strapped to her right hip. Almost as quickly she yelled, "What do you want? Stay back, I *will* shoot you if you move any closer."

He took two very large steps back. Holding his palms up above his head so they were visible he said, "I'm not armed, don't shoot. Please. I'm a Carrier."

"A what?" Kim said. Pointing her weapon at the stranger's chest and determined to sound strong, she was not processing whatever it was he was trying to tell her. "Are you diseased, infected? Stay back. Just stay the fuck back away from me, or you'll not have to worry about your affliction, whatever the hell variant it may be."

Puzzled, the man who called himself a *Carrier* tried to hide his bemusement with Kim's take on his title. Distracted, he began to lower his hands. He had been in this position before.

"Not so fast, up with the hands."

"Please. Don't," he said, lowering his eyes and cringing a little, as if preparing for the pain that was about to come. "You've been out of circ for a while, haven't you? Not much contact since The Event, I'm guessing. I'm a carrier of news, of news and information. I, and others like me, others with strong memories and recall abilities, roam about gathering and sharing news and other information from the places we've been. We have markings, see?" And he slowly turned around, hands still raised, to reveal the back of his jacket where there was a crudely drawn and painted rainbow peacock with the word "NEWS" written in large black letters underneath.

Kim looked at the Carrier and was at once confused and suspicious. She recognized the emblem. She knew the association. He was right, however. She had been out of circulation for a while. She had been making a concerted effort to avoid people. Now there was this apparent messenger, this human email so he claims, standing about twelve feet beyond the barrel of her .357. Well, she thought, if he was all about sharing information, then she should start by finding out more about him.

"So, news man, since I'm a little out of the loop, why don't you catch me up. What's your name?"

"I'm, I'm Allen," he said with a nervous hint. "Can I put my hands down?"

Kim nodded, and with a short jerking motion she pointed with the .357 down and to Allen's left, where there sat a large unopened box of orange buckets. "Sure, have a seat." She sensed this might take a while.

Allen appeared to be part Anglo and part Asian, maybe Japanese or Korean. It was hard to tell. He was probably in his early to mid-thirties, tall and a little on the thick side, too. He obviously had no trouble scavenging food. His black hair was cropped short on top, even shorter on the sides and stood straight up, almost as if it were a crew cut, but not quite. He smiled a lot, but not a subservient or shy smile, more as if he was enjoying a private joke. At this particular moment, Kim decided he was not to be trusted.

"Tell me, Allen. Why are you here, in this store, in front of my gun?"

"I was looking for an adhesive to fix my shoe when I heard a noise. What about you?" Allen asked.

"You see me and I have a gun, pointed at you," Kim said in a matter-of-fact voice, trying hard to sound serious and not afraid to blow his head off. "That's all you need to know. Now tell me your story."

"Well," Allen started, looking down and toeing at a loose bolt that lay abandoned on the floor, "I'm from St. Petersburg, Florida. I lived and worked there, in The Before. I was two years out of college and working for an ad company, in sales. I was doing well, but then all hell broke loose. There was this group. They called themselves The Lamplight. They had branches all through the southeast and Atlantic seaboard. Have you heard of them?"

"Yeah, I heard of them," Kim said, trying to keep a tough demeanor. "There's a man on the radio here. He's like a blogger, like an audio blogger. He's spoken of them, and others. Have you heard him, the man on the radio?"

"Yeah," Allen replied. "He rants."

"Yeah. That's him."

"Anyway," Allen continued. "This Lamplight group, they were big in The Before. They were on the net and hooked into all the major social network sites. Nobody knew where they were based or even if anyone was in charge. If you heard of them, then you know that they claimed to be 'fair and equitable.' They said that the government was tracking and using data from people's internet activities to influence societal movements, you know, fads, trends and so on, so people would be easier to control. So that the government could manipulate their behaviors and actions."

Kim knew of these theories. The attempts to control people by using predictive analytics and big data. Some blamed it all on government spy agencies. Others said it was corporate interests trying to direct consumer trends. She had even heard groups say it was major media outlets trying to drive ratings by sensationalizing the trivial.

"I don't know how much, if any, of that was true," Allen continued, "but this Lamplight group eventually got people pretty worked up. All that angst, anger and fear they roused was starting to boil over at the same time all the other crap in the rest of the world started happening. It was as if the entire planet became dissatisfied and scared all at once. What did one blogger call it, the Earthling

Spring? Just like the Arab Spring a bunch of years earlier, only all the little people all over the planet were fed up with the people in charge.

"Anyway, when the paranoid countries in Asia and the Middle East had their little b.y.o. nuke party, that's when I hid. People were scared. Hell, I was scared. Those who didn't die in the riots when order went away began dying from weird new diseases that popped up as the air turned dark orange."

Kim knew about the death. She knew it well. "How is it you're still alive?"

"I spent the first year hiding in a theme park in Tampa. I wasn't necessarily avoiding people, I was just trying to stay safe. I think that's what saved me." Allen then observed as he smiled his secret smile to himself, "It surprised me, though I don't know why in retrospect, but when the world goes to hell no one goes to the theme parks."

"That's it? You just avoided people. You'll excuse me if I find that a little hard to believe given you just walked up behind a stranger who happened to be carrying a gun. In plain sight."

"It's different now. It's my job to seek out people now. Besides, I won't carry a gun. I just don't believe in it."

"That's either really brave or really stupid, but I admire the principle."

"Honestly, I think that's what caused all this, if you want my opinion."

"What's that?"

Allen looked thoughtful for a moment, "Principles, everyone lost their principles. Everyone started following everyone else and stopped thinking for themselves."

Kim knew what he meant, but she wasn't ready to hash that out with another person. Not yet. "So what was going on in the places you passed through? What's the news?"

"Well, let's just say that most people in most places have not been very kind to each another, and still aren't. Many people became sick too, and there was no significant or organized medical help, so most died. When I went through Atlanta, it was just a smoldering husk. The smell of death was overwhelming. But there were a few small groups scattered throughout the city. Social Sites. That's when I found the News group, on the fourth floor of some cable news network building near the heart of the city. There were eleven there at the site but there were sixty-two in the group, most roaming the country, when I joined."

Kim became incredulous, "You joined a Social Site? After all that happened you went back into that mindless herd of sheep?"

"Hey, hey, they're not all like that. There *are* some good ones. Sure, I was wary. I had some bad experiences with Social Sites, especially the small town ones, the ones with four or five people, and the others, the bigger ones that recruit." The word recruit was tinged with sarcasm. "I kept my distance."

"But you joined."

"Well, yes, eventually. They sent people. Different ones at first but, then previous people started coming back. I was able to get a pretty good count of how many there were. They told me they weren't armed and that they were all about news and information. They and their members are based there, but they go on these tours of duty. The goal, my goal too, I guess, is to cover a great distance while gathering and sharing information along the way. We set out on a route that is planned to intersect with other members, and along the way we try to meet and talk to anyone who wants to talk, and won't try to kill us. We tell people what we know about the state of things where we have been, and we ask people to tell us about the state of things where they are, if they can. Sometimes they can't, they're not allowed to talk on behalf of the group. They're just a piece, a segment, I guess, of the group they're with. All they do is listen. Only the leader talks and tells, and then only what he or she wants you to know, nothing more. Along the way though, when our path crosses with a fellow Carrier, we download our learnings to one another, and then we go back on our way. It's a way to let people know what's left, what's working, where's safe and what to watch out for. It's the internet without the wires. It's a news network."

Eventually, Kim began to relax and came to trust Allen enough to share her camp at the mansion with him for a few days. It was during those days that she learned things beyond the valley and the Bay Area were no better. There were many sites out there, some with as many as a hundred people. There were islands of functioning infrastructure too, parts of the grid that took power from hydroelectric, solar and wind sources. It was from Allen that she learned the location of the Assemblage. He described them as a group of strong minds trying to improve life for those that remained. He thought they were somewhere in the Mojave and were able to pull power from a wind farm spread across the desert floor.

She enjoyed his company. She shared with him what she knew of the current state and health of the places she had been, but no more. He was easy to talk to, like an old friend almost. They shared a few interests, and she felt a sense of hope finding someone with whom it was so easy to connect. It reassured her, somewhat, that not all of the humanity that once existed was lost.

Kim could not talk about everything with Allen. It seemed for all they shared, the reluctance to reveal their entire story was an act of omission practiced by them both. Their shattered pasts were held desperately close in flimsy containers, sealed boxes wet and dripping with their broken contents of pain and loss. They each had them, and they silently acknowledged them, but those boxes remained sealed, stored away. With time, they would dry and the wet freshness of broken memories would cake over with a tough crust. Then the boxes could be opened, their contents handled. Not yet, though. Not yet.

CHAPTER 3

It was dusk of the second day when Kim spotted San Luis reservoir. She approached from the west, using the high ground to look for others near the shore. The changed climate had supplied the once dry Golden State with plenty of water and the reservoir was full. That meant more shoreline to separate her from any others.

Down on the western shore, at a boat ramp, there was a large encampment. The familiar fire with its column of black smoke said everything she needed to know about its inhabitants, a Social Site. Kim chose to camp up high, away from the lake. She would sneak down and refill her water bottles during the night, then move on south tomorrow.

The hill she was on provided a good view of what lay below so she settled in just behind its crest, out of sight from watching eyes. The presence of a Social Site made her uneasy. She was familiar with all the sites from San Francisco and Richmond south to Morgan Hill, and knew which ones to trust and which to avoid. She did not know this one. It looked big, maybe 25 or 30 people. She studied it as best she could, until it was too dark to see. They had a collection of small boats, some with sails and some with oars. She also heard a gasoline-powered car rattling and popping in the distance. It was very rare to see a running vehicle of any type. Usable gasoline was scarce, having either degraded or been used up long ago. They must be well stocked and organized. This well-established presence worried her.

Having the high ground and a good distance between herself and the site, she flattened out a small area of the tall green grass and lay down with her head on her pack. A strip of dried deer meat and an energy bar was dinner. Looking up, she could see a few stars through the haze and as it grew dark, she began to feel almost as lonely as she had in the early days.

§

Kim sat up as if she had been jerked, drawing her .357 with thoughtless mechanical reflex. She was gasping for air and strained to look deep into the darkness that surrounded her. The blackness pressed against her eyes as if two unseen thumbs were forcing themselves into her eye sockets. What was it? How long had she slept? Was it a gunshot, or just the click of a weapon? Was the noise close? Her vision began to accommodate the darkness as she rolled onto all fours, raised herself into a crouch and began to take a defensive stance. Then she heard the grass rustle all around her. A calm voice came from the night, "Put the gun down, sister, and slowly stand upright. We don't want to have to hurt you but the choice is yours."

Doing as she was told, Kim left the gun on the flattened grass and complied. Armed figures then stepped forward out of the darkness and revealed themselves. There were four with semi-automatic rifles pointed at her; a fifth was standing behind them, without a weapon. All of them men, except one. With the four other men was a boy, maybe twelve or thirteen years old. Holding his rifle with an awkward, white-fisted grip, he seemed nervous. The rest did not.

As they held her at gunpoint, the leader of the group stepped up to examine her as one might examine an animal in a trap. "Who are you? Where are you from?" he asked in his same steady and calm tone, his eyes squinting as his head moved up and down looking Kim over. "You're not a Carrier, you're armed. I want to know why you're in our domain, watching our Site. Can't you talk?"

"I don't want anything, I'm just passing. Let me go and I'll be far gone within the hour."

Again, in the same even, almost formal manner, "Yes, I've have heard that before. Brother Enrique09, grab the weapon, remove her knife and gather that pack. You're coming with us, sister. Let us go."

The boy gathered her gun, knife and other belongings and threw Kim her hat. Another wrapped a chain tight around her waist, handcuffing her to it. They set off.

As they hiked down towards the Site, she noticed it was becoming daybreak. Barely audible, she cursed herself, "Damn it! I slept too long."

She could see out into the valley, but not far. The haze and smoke were thick. Soon the sun would rise, with its familiar red-orange disc, struggling to push light through the greyish-brown layer of dirt, soot and chemicals that hung as death's hot embrace about the planet. It was already warm. Soon it would be suffocating. She needed to think.

Moving down the grassy oak-studded hills towards the site, no one spoke except the leader, and he only gave the occasional brief command. When they arrived, she counted twenty-two men and boys, no women. This worried her. As they entered the site, she began assessing the encampment, the people and their ability to pursue. Kim was already planning her departure.

There were three forty-foot long trailers, the kind that were once pulled by diesel-fueled big-rig trucks, eighteen-wheelers that long ago traveled back and forth across the country carrying goods.

These had been converted into barracks of sorts. They sat on flattened and rotted tires next to each other near the start of the boat ramp. There were wooden steps up to a landing on each. One of the two large hinged doors was open while the other looked to be fastened permanently shut. They each had two window-like openings cut into either side and there were what looked like salvaged hoods of cars being used as metal shutters. A teenaged boy was sweeping the landing of one. He looked at her with a startled expression then quickly looked down at his broom.

Off separate from the trailers, near where the access road emptied into a large parking area, were three weather-beaten motorhomes. One was very large, the size of a bus; the two others were half that size. They too sat leveled with wood planks and jack-stands on rotting tires. The engines had been removed from each and the vacant compartments held firewood, stacked neatly, no doubt placed there to keep it dry. There were open tents and awnings with tables and a few chairs under them centrally located at the top of the boat ramp. Straight up from the ramp on an unused part of the large paved parking area, just beyond the bulky trailers, was the fire, signifying this was a Social Site. The question was, what kind?

In a green and grassy field, several horses were tied off to a long line suspended between two oak trees. They stood grazing the weeds. There were a few more horses tied near the lake, drinking and just standing belly deep in the cool water. It was quiet for the most part, but off in the distance she heard a noise. A rattling, rumbling commotion that was coming closer, yet no one seemed concerned by it. As she watched, a small faded green SUV, with no window glass and bullet holes scattered throughout, came down the road to the camp and parked next to an equally tortured-looking beige sedan. Two armed men got out and came walking over to the one that had questioned Kim.

"Brothers," said the man whose group had captured Kim, "It's good to see you safely back."

The man walking in front replied, "It's good to be back

brother Ernest17. I see you've found our traveler." As he spoke, he looked in Kim's direction. When he saw her face, and short hair from under the wide brim of her hat, his eyes went immediately to the ground. In a surprised tone, he said "A sister! Alone without a manservant, this is good. But, is she a free thinker? She is dressed like a man and unescorted, she must be. What's her story?"

"We don't know yet, brother. She's not being very cooperative. We'll secure her and wait for the Matriarch to be brought up from the women's camp." The leader then ordered two men to take her to the "box." The boy with her pack and .357 followed.

The "box" was one of two old shipping containers located a few yards past the motorhomes and surrounded by several old oak trees. Further, beyond through the trees, she could see the lake and a boat dock with four small boats tied off. They escorted her towards the closer of the two containers. As one of her captors unlocked the latch, she noticed that each door had a one-foot-square opening with an expanded metal mesh bolted over it. Across the front of both doors in large white hand-painted letters, it said "WOMEN." It was clean but bare. Inside it wore splotchy paint of varying age. It reminded her of the way cities used to try to paint over graffiti on walls and buildings in The Before. One of the men, being careful to not look directly at her, pointed her into the container with the barrel of his rifle and then secured the latch. The door clacked, echoing within the metal shell of itself. She watched out the screened opening as the men walked away, noticing the boy had dropped her pack into a metal storage box that was attached to the other shipping container about fifty feet away. The one labeled "MEN."

CHAPTER 4

This did not make sense, Kim thought as she began going over the events since being caught. They had not searched her or her pack. They almost never spoke directly to her, and only the leader, the one who called himself Ernest17, made eye contact. The rest, once they realized she was a woman, averted their eyes. There were women, but they were elsewhere, needing to be sent for. What was this place?

With her hands still shackled to her waist, she paced the length of the container, noting in her mind the location of all that she had seen along the way. Kim also considered what she had not seen and where it might be if it were here. She saw transportation, living quarters and the primary way in and out. On the hike down, she saw a few hilltop sentry posts located out away from the site. Because it was morning, she presumed that most of the members were at camp getting ready to start the day, but it was clear that there were still others out elsewhere. They had a perimeter and there apparently were scouts. The two who had returned in the SUV saw her at some point, long before she was near San Luis. Where and when did they first start tracking her? Were the scouts patrolling in other directions motorized or horse mounted? Given this site's apparent preparedness, anything was possible.

Kim was forced to conclude that she did not yet know what she was dealing with. Standing by the doorway, she began to notice more about the box she was in. The floor was clean with only a thin rusty dust covering it; this somehow seemed odd for a place meant to hold prisoners. Though the walls were a mishmash of patchwork paint, they too were clean. That was when she saw things in a few of the painted areas. Writing, scratched into previous layers of paint or into the metal itself. She leaned in close. By rubbing her finger across the thin layer of rust on the floor and then across the etched writing, she could cause the grime of the rust to fill the thin grooves of the lettering, making it easier to read.

"Do not become of the whole," it read. Underneath was a name, "Chandra," and there were more. One simply said, "Individual." Another declared, "I am not lost." Not all had names with them, but those that did, had the names of women. She had seen this kind of thing in The Before, during the buildup to The Event, when a singular voice tried to separate from the social tide. Just as here in the box, the posts that did not flow with the tide were made to disappear. Kim was certain; she needed to leave this place.

Back at the screened openings in the doors, she took in the details of what she could see and hear. It was mid-morning now, and beyond the motorhomes she heard activity and could see flashes of movement in the space between the large bus-like vehicle and the two others. She also heard the faint movements of someone nearby. There must be a guard. She could hear horses riding away, some to the north towards the highway and some to the south, into the hills above the reservoir. The SUV that the two men had come in also started, in a spluttering half-hearted and insincere way, leaving back up the access road. After about an hour, it was mostly quiet with just a few indistinct voices coming from the central area and a couple of other voices from down near the water.

Frustrated and scared, Kim paced the length of the container twice then sat against the back wall, opposite the doors. While she pondered her situation, she stared at the wall to her left, not seeing it, just thinking. Some amount of time had passed. She did not know how long. Her thoughts were drifting. That was when she noticed more writing had been painted over, but still showed through. It was very near the floor and said, "Strong women. A man's fear is your freedom, sister." Just then, there were several voices outside.

Looking out through the screened opening, Kim saw four armed men at the front of the far container. Another on top of it, over the doors. They were poised and ready to shoot anything that came out of the big metal box. Three of the men stayed back forming a semi-circle, rifles raised and ready. The fourth was opening the door and commanding whoever was in there to come out peaceably. As the door was opened a man, shackled and taking small choppy steps, came into view. He looked to be in his mid-thirties, fit and muscular, about six feet tall, black, and was either completely bald or had shaved his head. He wore a faded camouflage Marine Corps uniform. He was probably among those in the various service branches that were sent in to maintain the martial law and curfew order issued by the President in the last months of The Before, she thought.

The sleeves of the shirt he wore had been torn off, though an Eagle, Globe and Anchor were still visible on the slanted chest pocket. He had on a tight-fitting olive green t-shirt underneath; it too was missing sleeves, otherwise, the military issue shirts were in good shape. He looked strong. His size was imposing. His trousers, also well kept, were tucked neatly into eight-inch-high combat boots. His uniform was complete with the exception of its sleeves, any displayed rank or name patch, and the required headwear. As he stepped out, she could see that he had on handcuffs that were attached to a chain locked tightly around his waist. All five weapons were pointed at the man and the muzzles followed his every move, in unison. They did not want any trouble from him. After an exchange that she could not hear, they moved off out of sight past the large motorhome.

The activity across from her prison over, Kim went back to the rear of the container and sat. As she began to contemplate what she had just seen, there came a noise from the heavy metal door. The latch was released, and then the door swung open. She stood inside the box recalling the sight she had just witnessed and was afraid the same awaited her. Then, a woman's voice called in to her, "Come on out, sister. No one's going to hurt you. We want to help you. Come on out."

Stepping cautiously out of the container, Kim was greeted with a sight altogether different from what she had witnessed a moment ago. There were only two men, both back about six feet with their rifles pointed down and resting in the crooks of their elbow, their thumbs in their belt loops and their eyes down, watching but not looking. Ernest17 was also present, but he too was a few steps back, eyes also down, watching but not looking. Then there was the woman to whom the voice belonged.

She was a woman older than Kim, possibly sixty or sixty-five, exuding a motherly look but not in a modern sense. No, her mannerisms were that of a nineteenth-century pioneer woman, with the costume to match. She was wearing a light, almost white, ankle-length cotton dress with an indiscernible faded floral print over which was an apron, tied at the waist. Her hair was up and kept mostly hidden under a bonnet. *She* was the one in charge.

"Come with us," the woman said, "we will go to a place where we can talk." She then turned and raised one arm, extending it towards Kim with her palm up. She held her hand in a very relaxed manner and with a slight nod, gestured in almost a spiritual way the direction they would go.

They walked towards the boat ramp, passing tents and canopies. There Kim saw two boys in their early teens lifting boxes of dirty breakfast dishes onto a cart. The dishes were being cleared from three long tables by two girls who appeared to be sixteen or seventeen. They too were dressed in the manner of frontier or Quaker women. The girls were directing the boys in the heavy work. With deferential obedience, the boys complied.

Walking a little further, they arrived at the top of the boat ramp. There, to her left, Kim saw the Social Site's signal fire. There were two more boys, not much older than the two loading dishes, tending the fire by feeding it scavenged junk and trash. To her right she could see down the ramp to the lake and the dock. All the boats that were there earlier were gone. The only activity that stirred was another young boy making repairs to a craft that lay upside down on the cement ramp near the water's edge.

They moved across the top of the boat ramp, then left the pavement and followed a well-maintained trail past several large and twisted oak trees. After a short distance, they arrived at another tent. It was a weathered, ivory colored canvas structure with a wooden frame and a wooden floor, and wood planks that went partway up the sides. The group stopped at the entrance and the woman motioned towards the tent opening and entered. Kim looked towards the tent, then back to Ernest17 as the two men bearing rifles nodded towards the tent. Kim entered and saw only two chairs in the large space. One was in the center of the tent and appeared immovable; the other was off to the side. The woman motioned for Kim to sit in the chair that sat bolted to the floor in the center of the tent. When she started to refuse, Kim felt the end of a rifle painfully and forcefully pushed deep into the small of her back. She sat. Ernest17 handcuffed the chain around her waist to the chair while the two rifles ensured her cooperation. When this ceremony was complete, the men left.

CHAPTER 5

"Now that we are alone we can talk," said the woman as she moved the other empty chair closer to where Kim had been chained. Still standing, she spoke further, "I am Lucette02 and I am the site administrator. You, being from elsewhere, may be curious about my name. It is the account name assigned to me when I became administrator. Only the site admin can be called Lucette and only a woman can be site admin. We are a part of a network of seven sites that are called Avenging Lilith. Our site is the second. That is why I am Lucette02."

Kim learned that Avenging Lilith came *online* after the madness and chaos that followed the loss of order, when humankind was ravaging humankind and the keepers of laws no longer upheld them. This was during the time before the new diseases, the compound diseases, and the bacteria with deadly infections grew, spread and took down entire populations. That was a time when it was every man for his self, and in some ways, it still was. Unprotected, independent women did not stand a chance alone, on their own, not without staying hidden or finding *friends*. In that time, intelligent women began leading strong women. Together they protected themselves and their less strong, more vulnerable sisters. From this formative and beneficial alliance, Avenging Lilith grew.

During this lawless time, many ultra-conservative social groups in the U.S. began adopting the most severe interpretations of Shari'a law regarding women's rights. The evolution of their racial and religious hatred towards all Muslims was great, and their ignorance deep. They were the most radical of the extreme and they were emulating that which they despised. In the course of cleansing the earth of sin and bringing forth their new world order, they jailed, beat and even stoned to death independent free-thinking women who did not conform to their strict tenants of feminine modesty.

Further, packs of men roamed the streets as if feral dogs, looking for entertainment. Entertainment that usually manifested itself in the form of lawless subjugation that often ended with rape, torture or worse.

Finally, there were the loners, the spinners of manipulative stories and lies, men whose sadistic fantasies were set free when the laws stopped existing. Men who could keenly read their prey and offered whatever it was they were needing, whether that was protection, comfort or sympathy. However, once ensnared there was no escape, not alive anyway, and often not in one piece.

Avenging Lilith started as the antithesis to the predatory treatment of women who either had lost everything in The After, or who had given it all up for the sanity of being in control of only themselves. Time passed. And, as with all things, the group grew and evolved. New ideas and diversity of opinion saw the need for greater structure and organization, which led to the need to recruit specific talents. However, in the course of building a stronger group, the goal took precedence over the means and the creeping disease of paranoia germinated the seeds of distrust; if you are not with her you are against her, and Avenging Lilith began *protecting* itself from any perceived danger to its thoughts and goals, be it from man *or* woman.

"What is your name, what are you calling yourself?" Lucette02 asked. She was looking down on Kim as one might look down on a child that had misbehaved and was about to receive a lesson.

As Kim sat staring at the military style boots Lucette02 wore, contemplating the incongruity of their appearance beneath her nineteenth-century garb, she felt lost for anything to say. Looking up from under the brim of her hat and staring directly into Lucette02's eyes, Kim felt a cold determination come over her and she said in a calm but demanding tone, "Why should I tell you anything? I'm passing through with no intention of making contact and you chain me as if I'm an animal and lock me in a box? To hell with you." She knew what Lucette02 had planned for her was not going to be good and she would be damned if she would go without a fight.

Lucette02's fist was a vise of white-yellow hinges surrounded by streaks of heated pink as she slowly removed Kim's hat. Clutching it tightly, her fury remained controlled and emotionless while her breaths, rushing passed clenched teeth, momentarily kept pace with each woman's tense beating heart. Then, taking a seat in the chair she had situated across from Kim, she let her anger and the hat fall to the floor beside her. "No matter, we will get to that later," she replied calmly.

Lucette02 exuded power and self-control, and she knew it. "You are a strong woman. You would fit well here. We need women of strength. You see, this site, and the others like it, are matriarchal, they are run by a hierarchy of women, each woman having a purpose, strength, intellectual talent or specialty. We are a gathering of women, some strong as yourself, some not, who survived The Before, and the chaos of The After, chaos brought by men and their animal ways. We started as a single site, for women only, surviving and socializing from under the suffocation and masculine posturing of men. Over time, we grew, and over time, we found that there were men who wanted to be directed by women.

"You've seen the men here, the service men? They are like

pets, like service dogs," said Lucette02 with laughter that effused ridicule. "They just want to serve, stay busy, please and receive praise. They want to be good dogs. If they do not fit this mold, they are considered a threat and are put down. The female hierarchy does all the thinking for our men, and the men just do that for which they have been trained. Those three outside, Ernest17, Bradly24 and Andre03, they are my service men, my pet dogs if you will. Through them I manage all the others here."

"What about the boys?" Kim said. "I've seen boys here, boys *and* girls; you can't tell me that a child knows they wish to choose a subservient life."

"There are no children here," replied Lucette02 in her cold steady tone. "For those who wish to join, young men must be thirteen and young women must be sixteen, and all must submit to three months of mentorship and conditioning. Any kind of intimate relationship between the women and their service men is strictly forbidden. That is why there are two compounds, this one for the men and another, at the southern boat launch, for the women. The separation is not far by boat and our boatmen are skilled and efficient. But, any member that is suspected of changing their relationship status is sterilized and banished, their account is closed."

From the chair, Kim looked across to her captress, an unassuming leader of what once might have been considered a reversed social order. Some of its aspects appealed to Kim and her desire to start a new life, a life far away from the grotesquely mutated form of social interaction she felt she had somehow laid upon the planet. Wasn't this a product of that? This was what had become Social Sites, an attempt to interpose individual ideas as group think and social mores. These Social Sites had become islands of trending thought in the absence of technology.

"No relationships? How do you grow your site? There aren't that many others out there."

"People find us. The Carriers have been through here and we have a message, an image if you will, crafted especially for them. They do the rest for us. We have turned away many. Either they offered nothing useful in terms of skills or intelligence, or their motives are not as they stated. Those with nothing to offer, and are of no threat, are made to leave and not return. We utilize a treatment that includes psychological manipulation and sleep deprivation to *convince* them to go and stay gone. Those found to be a threat are dealt with physically, the severity of which depends upon the perceived danger they may represent."

"You kill them."

"Yes, we terminate the accounts of malicious threats," Lucette02 said with a grim smile. She seemed pleased, self-satisfied with her power. "Nevertheless, voluntary recruitment is not a problem. Occasionally we need to recruit by persuasion, but only when we find a highly desirable prospect."

Lucette02 paused for a moment, then rose from her chair and paced across the plank floor of the tented space, stopping at the back wall where Kim could no longer see her without straining against the metal clamps that held her in her chair. As she passed, Kim noticed in the warm stillness of the canvased space that Lucette02 smelled of Ernest17, a faded male muskiness tinged by cigar box menthol that mingled with a heavy soapy smell. Power corrupts, Kim thought, and Lucette02, the keeper of the law at San Luis Reservoir, was obviously receiving the most intimate of service from one of her service dogs. Hypocrites become leaders.

From behind Kim's back Lucette02 spoke, "We have been watching you since you started up Highway 152. We thought you were a young man, possibly a Carrier. Only after you were detained did we realize you were a woman. I received regular reports as you progressed and when I heard the report of your gender, I was intrigued. The strength and determination you exhibit make me think you are a desirable prospect."

A cult, Kim thought. "Thanks, but I'm not interested in becoming a part of your happy family," she said with disgust and sarcasm.

"I was not asking you to join, I am simply telling you my plans. We have methods for integrating reluctant prospects. Either you will integrate or you will leave here far less the person you currently are, if you leave at all. It is up to you."

Kim began to feel an icy trickle of panic slide down her spine. She needed to keep her fear locked within her. She could not let it gain the slightest hold. If it did, she knew she would lose the struggle, and that was what her entire life had become, a struggle. With control tenuously at her fingertips Kim turned her head towards Lucette02 and said, "Or to use your words, have my account terminated?"

"I certainly hope not. You seem to possess so much potential." Lucette02 then turned towards the opening of the tent, and with her thumb and middle fingers held to her mouth, she whistled in two short, quick bursts. Within seconds, Ernest17 came running in, eyes to the ground, not saying a word and waiting obediently for instruction. "Blindfold her. We are going to see how she responds to initial persuasion treatments."

Kim did not try to resist being blindfolded; she knew it was futile. While Ernest17 was performing the task given him she asked, "What about the guy in the other box, the soldier looking guy?"

From behind her blindfold, Kim heard Lucette02's voice reply, "He is another desirable prospect. He was once a member of the Marines Special Forces and his skills would prove quite helpful in maintaining our security as well as expanding our domain. He is proving to be a challenge, though. The training he received in The Before has made him very resistive, very tolerant of our conversion techniques. We have one of the best re-programmers still known to be alive. Her name is Nadeeda01 and you will meet her tomorrow. She is having much difficulty with the soldier. Nadeeda01 has never had difficulty with anyone." Lucette02 paused and moved to some other location in the room, then added, "Additionally, he is a high fraternization and distraction risk."

"You mean soldier boy has a thing for the girls? What a surprise," Kim said, responding drily from behind the cloth which bound her eyes.

"No, he has a thing for the boys, well, rather, for other men. Until we cure that we cannot put him in with the rest."

Cure that? Kim thought, incredulous at such a statement. Those two words, in that context, cause her to shudder. If that was their line of thought, then what were they going to do to her? Over the next several hours, she would glimpse the answer to that question.

Blindfolded and restrained, Kim listened as Lucette02, without cessation, droned on with a well-rehearsed litany of leading questions, psychological manipulations and deceptions, all designed to coerce information and reveal the person with whom she was dealing. It was a test of Kim's will, a clawing at the fabric of her being in an effort to snag the loose threads of self-doubt, and as time slipped by the illusion that Lucette02 knew Kim's secrets felt all too real.

"We all had our place, our part in The Before. What was yours?" Lucette02 asked.

Kim faced straight ahead, staring through the blindfold and clenching her fists tight against the handcuffs that dug into her flesh. She had run from that place, her part in The Before. She was still running. Sitting there, she felt those memories burn. As they began to come into view, they began to rob her of strength and a power of will that had taken so long to rebuild. Remembering her place meant enduring a descent into the pain and darkness of loss. Kim sat tense and silent. Her refusals were her answers and Lucette02 continued to dig.

"There was a man, wasn't there. There always is. Who was he? Who was the man that ruined your life?" Lucette02 continued. "Was he a lover, a friend, a superior, a stranger? You can tell me."

Kim's chin sank to her chest, her head hanging limp signaling resignation within. There were men, and there were women too. They were each of those things, she thought. A lover, a friend, a superior, a stranger. They were also memories, pain and guilt.

"I have nothing to say to you," Kim whimpered into her chest.

More time slipped past and Kim felt pain within and without. Steel dug into her wrists, her ankles and her waist as she pulled against the ties that held her tight in the immovable chair, and Lucette02 continued her digging into the mind, emotions and innermost self that Kim was struggling so hard to keep tightly controlled.

"You had goals; you desired something larger than yourself. All women of strength do. But someone exploited your efforts, perverted your goals." A generalization, Kim knew this, but so close to still tender wounds. Lucette02's blind probes were making vivid and near a past kept muted and distant. Control slipped from Kim's grasp and in its place she held anger and fury. Lucette02's random stabs at Kim's spirit were achieving their purpose. Any restraint Kim possessed was consumed by the fire of resentment that raged for Lucette02. Kim exploded, lunging towards the sound of Lucette02's voice, her exposed face hot, every muscle and tendon tearing out from her neck, her body raging physical.

"Who the hell are you to think you know anything at all about me," Kim yelled. "You know nothing of me. Do you think you can hurt me this way? Fuck you, bitch!"

Lucette02 could sense weakness. She could smell blood. Slow and shark-like, she walked a circle around Kim who sat heaving deep breaths, her teeth clenched, her face red, the blindfold tight and saliva blowing wet and stringy from her parted lips. As Kim continued to pant hot angry breaths, the footsteps stopped. Standing so close Kim could feel the chill of cold, controlled rage on her exposed cheek; Lucette02 slapped her across the face with brutal strength and force. Kim's entire body jerked and pulled against its bonds as the impact of the blow sent its energy throughout her body. Her head snapped and her neck strained as droplets of blood and sweat sprayed out into the room.

"Don't *ever* speak to me like that again," said Lucette02, with firm and quiet indignation, as Kim raised a veiled gaze of defiance towards the sound of the voice. Blood, snot and spittle mingled in strings of viscid rope and swung dangling from her red and swollen face.

The questions seemed endless as time crawled by. Kim could feel the heat of the welt on her face lessen as the stuffy warm air of the tent began to cool under the shade of evening dusk. The desire to give in and give up began to overwhelm her. She wanted to become someone else, anyone other than herself. Since The Event, and all that led up to it, she had struggled with her part in it, her survival and her still being here, in a world so changed.

I could give myself over to Avenging Lilith, Kim thought. She could leave behind her previous self and all that had been. So many lost so much, and she was sure she was the cause of that loss. This was the demon that made unrelenting, repellant love to her conscience, leaving her to lie naked in a fetid welter of guilt, disgust and self-loathing.

"You could be at peace with your sisters," Lucette02 enticed. "Let yourself free of the past. The *love* and protection of the sisterhood can strengthen you."

Love, this word cut Kim deep. Love brought her sorrow and hurt. Tears soaked into the heavy black cloth, making wet the mask that covered her eyes. The thought of love made her body jerk, her breathing short and chopped. Kim fell forward limp, pulling against her bonds until her wrists became purple and swollen. The thoughts that love brought to Kim eviscerated her soul.

These probing questions of The Before threw Kim's mind into war with itself. My friends, my colleagues, I led them to their end, she thought. I cannot give in. I owe them an end.

Then, as now, she somehow found deep within her a personal resolve, a handhold to grab, a hidden door behind which light and logic existed. It was the tangible thing, the force that would bring her back to the search for answers, the search that started in San Jose, the search that told her to go to the Assemblage. She knew at the end of that last hour, after the psychological molestation of someone digging at her mind and the mental depredation meant to rob her of herself, after not having been allowed to go to the bathroom and fighting hard against the pain, then finally the indignity of letting go, she knew what she would do. She knew she would leave Avenging Lilith, or die trying.

CHAPTER 6

It was still warm in the turbid darkness of the container. The deafening racket of a violent rain hammering the steel shell of her vault did not distract Kim from engineering her escape. She had been hard at work for the last two hours. With nothing to eat in over twenty-five hours, she also worked hard at drawing every bit of sugar from one of the pieces of bubble gum she had retrieved from the hidden pocket in her right shoe.

After returning to the container, she had managed to release the handcuffs from her wrists by using a one-inch-long scrap of wire she found in a corner, a party trick she had learned from an old boyfriend back in college. After freeing her hands, she had begun attacking the next barrier, the door. Kim was working on loosening the eight bolts that held the expanded metal mesh over the small square openings on the doors. By squeezing one cuff tight around the hexagon shaped fasteners of the bolts and jamming the ratchet of the second cuff in behind the ratchet of the first, she could leverage enough pressure to loosen and then unscrew them.

No one was standing guard outside. When one of the now-common summer storms moved in, everyone in the men's camp ducked into their trailers and motorhomes. The rain continued to fall hard and the long rolling peals of thunder further covered any sounds that might come as she worked to free herself. When the third bolt made a splashy thud into the wet soil on the other side of the door, she pushed against the heavy steel mesh and was able to bend it outward at the bottom corner just enough to reach her arm through and begin to feel for the handle. Relieved, she found they did not put a lock on the heavy steel latch that sat in its U-shaped rest. All she had to do was reach it, lift it and swing it outward, turning the steel bar and rotating the cams that held the door shut. Kim thrust her arm through the opening and groped at the limit of her reach. It was there, she could barely reach it. Pushing herself up onto the balls of her feet, she strained to reach farther, feeling the sharp edge of the steel door digging deep into the pit of her arm. She could just brush it with the very tip of her middle finger. No luck.

Kim pulled her rain-soaked arm back in and paced once the full length of the container, head down and teeth clenched, deep in thought. Then, turning quickly, she ran back to the doors, grabbing the handcuffs that lay tossed on the floor along the way. Closing both cuffs and making two metal loops, she stuck her arm back out into the elements and let one of the cuff ends dangle.. After a few tries, she managed to loop the latch handle with the dangling cuff. She lifted, pulled, and the latch opened.

"Yes!" she whispered. She was free.

Kim stepped out of her prison into the pelting rain. An ankle-deep stream ran past the container and heavy drops made slapping sounds against the wet earth all around her. She moved towards the small tin box that was attached to the container marked "MEN" to retrieve her pack. As she stepped across the muddy ground, fear and tension gripped her. Her breathing was fast, her mind was numb and her thought was singular. The day's events had left her sore and hollow; her wrists were bruised and swollen, and her soul was bleeding.

As she opened the steel box to grab her pack, she heard a hushed but deep voice at the front of the container, "Hey. Hey!" She froze. "It's you, isn't it? The one they caught early yesterday morning. Hey! You have to get me out of here, K? They're messin' with my head. I can help you. Hey, I'm combat trained. Hey!"

Kim stopped. She clutched her pack tight against her chest as the rain ran fast off the brim of her hat and soaked through her drenched clothes. She reached into her pack and took inventory by feel; everything was there, except the .357.

Then the desperate voice from the container came again, "Hey! I know you're still there. You haven't moved since you shut that box. Come on, man. Help me get out of here, K?" The voice, the requests, the dialog, it was half pleading and half manipulative. Kim was not sure what she was going to do.

This was not in the plan. She just wanted away from here. She did not want another person with her, trying to plan for her and think for her. "I don't need a traveling partner. How do I know I can even trust you?"

The voice pleaded back, "Look, I'm not one of them. They ambushed me as I tried to steal a horse. I just wanna get out, K? Get back to my guys, up in Sac. Come on, man. Look, I've been here over a week, I know their patterns and I know where they keep their weapons."

He knew things. Things she needed to know, should know if she expected to get out alive. He was another opinion though, another lead. He was competition. There was risk on her own and there was risk with him as a partner. What held the most risk?

"OK, here's the plan," Kim said. "We work together to get out of here, then we go our separate ways. Got it?"

"Yeah, yeah. That's fine with me, I just want outta this place. Trust me, you ain't got nothin' to worry about from me."

Kim slipped on the pack, then reached in under her wet shirt and loosened the snap that held the PM9 in the nylon holster pressing tight to her ribcage. As she moved around to the front of the container, she saw that this door had a lock.

"It has a padlock on it."

"There are keys on the side of the container, opposite the box. I hear them get 'em every time they open the door," the voice inside the box said.

In the stormy darkness, Kim sloshed through mud and water to the other side of the container and moved down the side of the steel structure looking for where the keys might be. About three feet back from the front corner, about chest high, she found a small metal box. Inside were a set of keys and her .357. It was no doubt put there by the boy who gathered her belongings. She reached up under her shirt and cinched the strap tight around the PM9, and then she grabbed her gun and the keys from the box. Moving back around to the front of the container, she pulled the clip from the weapon, checked that it was loaded, then slapped it back into place and levered a round into the chamber. At the sound of the weapon clicking into death-delivering life, the soon-to-be-freed captive called out in a deep and raspy whisper, "What the hell was that?"

"That was me reintroducing myself to an old acquaintance."

As she began trying keys that looked as if they might fit she said, "Just so you know, soldier boy, I'm quite proficient with my friend here. Until I know where we stand, we both will be keeping an eye on you." Kim wanted to sound tough.

Just then, over the splattering din of the falling rain, they both heard the lock click open. She lifted the latch to the container door, rotating it to its open position. Stepping three deep paces back, elbows locked, both hands firmly around the .357, finger on the trigger and the weapon pointed at the ground in front of the container, she was ready for whatever was about to happen.

The door creaked open and he stepped into the rain, still shackled at his hands and feet. At this closer vantage, Kim could see that he was rock solid with muscle. She relaxed only long enough to throw him the keys and then locked back into a "ready" stance. As he bent and reached to unlock the chains from his ankles, she noticed two daggers were tattooed the length of each forearm, such that if he were to make two fists and cross his arms the daggers would cross as though they were a coat of arms. He had an unmistakable warrior look about him.

As he removed the last of the fetters, he looked up at Kim in her police-like ready stance and said somewhat mockingly, somewhat jokingly, but with a warm, friendly smile, "Well, you certainly look like you know what you're doing." Then, stepping out and to the side he scanned the area for others as he said, "We're going to need more than your friend there to help make sure we get outta here in one piece. You gotta plan?"

"I was going to grab a horse and head over to the I-5, then south. You?"

"Not a good plan," he said as he lowered into a crouch. "I tried that the first time. They chased me down in their car and shot the animal out from under me. They don't give a shit about them horses. I suggest we get over to the trailers, the barracks, and get ourselves more substantially armed. I've heard them talking and they each have a weapon with 'em inside, at their bunks. But in between the trailers are small tin sheds with additional weapons. We take what we can carry then steal one of their cars and put a lot of distance between them, and us as fast as possible. You in?"

"Count me in, GI Joe," she said with a sarcastic smirk. "Hey, one more thing, what's your name? What do I call you?"

"My name is Jerome. People call me Blade. What about you?" Blade said, again in a very warm, sincere way that seemed incongruent with his massive warrior presence.

"Well, Blade, you can call me Kim."

Blade had been Lieutenant Colonel Jerome Wilcox with the Second Battalion of the Marines Special Operations Regiment. He had spent time in the second Iraq war, the Afghanistan war, the Egyptian occupation, the Mexican Neighbor Assist & Cartel Eradication Operation and two dozen other tactical operations that he could not, or would not, talk about. He would be the first to tell you that he had seen some heavy shit go down and the world was, overall, not a happy place. Nevertheless, he had served proudly for eight and a half years before he left. He felt the world was changing. And, from his perspective, the change the planet was experiencing was unstoppable, and it was going to leave an ugly mark. Before that could happen, he had left the Corps and struck out as a solitary soldier, fighting only for the country of Blade, population one, looking for the happiness he had heard once existed.

The rain was still coming in volume and the noise it made hitting everything everywhere was good cover. Blade motioned Kim to stay low and quiet. They cautiously moved off to the right, away from the largest of the motorhomes, and up under the tent closest to the boat ramp, where they paused to survey the three semi-trailers for activity. He signaled her to wait and he, in the crouched run of a trained combat professional, moved across the wet pavement to the rotted tires and rusted wheels of the nearest trailer. Scanning across the front and then looking through under all three trailers, he then moved underneath into the murky night-shadow of the makeshift barracks. Within a couple seconds, he reappeared and motioned Kim across, making gestures to stay low and move fast. She dashed across the open expanse, sliding up beside him. Together they passed under the structure and over to a small tin shed. Blade pointed to her gun and then to his eyes, indicating she should keep watch. He then opened the doors to the puny shed and ducked in.

Blade could not see anything inside the tin building that contained the armaments, but his combat training was extensive and he knew his weaponry well. Without the aid of sight, he felt his way around the contents of the storage shed and emerged with two automatic rifles and clips stuffed in all the available pockets in his fatigues. They ducked back under the trailer closest to the boat ramp and retook their previous position near the rear wheels, where the wooden steps led up to the platform and door. Blade looked at her and then pointed towards the overgrown median strip that separated the road from the large paved parking area. The tops of two vehicles were visible on the far side. They ran through the downpour and made it to the brush that crowded the island between three giant oak trees. There, they stopped and planned their next moves.

The car and the SUV sat parked beside each other in the middle of the roadway. Both were facing downhill. Cradling one of the automatic weapons he had just acquired, the other slung across his back, Blade looked at Kim and asked, "Can you drive a stick?"

"It's been a while. But I hear it's like riding a bike."

"K, here's the deal. We'll take the car. When we load up, I'll be up through the sunroof stopping anything that moves. You'll be in the driver's seat. It has no starter so you'll have to get it going by letting it roll a ways. If we're going too slow, the compression will just stop the car without firing the engine, so we'll need some momentum. Once it starts, make a U turn at the tents, then head up past the trailers and the fire-pit, and then on out. There's only enough downhill to give you one shot. You good?"

Kim stuck her .357 into its holster and nodded. She felt outside herself and started to think she was in a vivid, fast-moving dream. Adrenalin pumped through her veins like a foreign, exhilarating drug. Smiling a crafty smile, Blade nodded in return as the rain beaded off his smooth, dark head.

Side by side, they both ran towards the car, Blade jumping onto the hood then roof and finally dropping down through the sunroof and standing with his left foot on the dash and his right in the passenger seat. Kim climbed through the windowless driver's door feet first and sank into the wet spongy seat. She grabbed the wheel with her left hand and the stick shift with her right. "Ready?" She called to Blade, his backside uncomfortably close to her head.

"Ready," he answered back, barely audible over the sound of the rain sizzling against the pavement.

Kim stepped on the brake pedal, released the hand brake and turned the ignition to on. Pushing in the clutch, she stirred the shifter around until she found first gear. Working the lever into the slot, she let off the brake pedal. The car creaked and slowly the sticky sound of tires on wet pavement became audible.

As they approached the end of the densely vegetated divider strip, Kim pulled her foot from the clutch. The car jerked, the front-wheel drive tires locked and skidded, and the engine feebly coughed and sputtered. It was not responding to the throttle. It was on the verge of dying. She jammed the clutch back in as they rolled closer to where she needed to turn and head back up hill. The engine was faltering. She feathered the gas pedal. She was about to lose it. Her jaw clenched and her heart raced as she began to realize that she, Blade, her hopes and the engine were going to die.

Just then, the door to the largest motorhome flew open and Ernest17 was standing in the opening, raising a revolver, aiming at them. Her throttle and clutch work were beginning to have a positive effect when three quick reports rang out, making her ears hurt badly and ring loudly. As she contemplated death at near the speed of light, the car's engine started to find its strength and Ernest17 fell forward, landing head first in a heap on the wet pavement at the foot of the steps leading into his shelter. The shots must have been Blade's.

Kim could feel the car pulling under its own power as she turned past the tents. The three trailers came into view as she shifted to second. The doors to all three of the large semi-trailers flew open and armed men were stepping out onto the landings located at the tops of the wooden staircases. Their heads were turning quickly as they assessed the situation through the dark and rain. As she nursed the engine RPM's up through second gear she heard Blade yelling over the ringing in her ears, "Go! Go! Go! Go! Go!" Then hell-fire erupted over her head as hot brass casings rained down on her along with the warm water from the sky.

They were moving past the trailers as she floored the throttle. Slamming the shifter into the third of six available gears, the front-wheel drive car searched with momentary desperation for traction on the rain-slick pavement. Kim looked past Blade's legs and could see men and boys falling as white-yellow muzzle fire erupted around them.

Kim saw the boy that had collected her belongings, the nervous young man with whom she had never made eye contact. The one they called Enrique09. He had stepped out of the barracks with the others, holding an old lever-action 30-30 by the forestock in his right hand. He had a stunned look on his face. Suddenly, his upper body jerked back and his arms reached for the heavens, as if he were attending an evangelical revival. The rifle fell, banging and sliding down the steps leading to the platform. As Kim and the boy made eye contact for the first and only time the young man's knees buckled, the weight of his body pushing them down and out ahead of him. He was leaning back at a forty-five degree angle but his entire body was coming forward. Bending sharply at his ankles, he landed with a jarring thud upon his knees. His momentum carried him forward and revealed a blossoming red exploded chest as he followed his rifle down the steps, coming to an abrupt rest at the bottom. Kim felt nothing.

The bullets sang a single-note song as they whistled by. Kim heard five quick metallic plinks as she saw five holes magically appear across the hood of the car. Fear became strength and time had become a blurry streak as they moved passed the trailers and towards their escape. Under the cacophony of Blade's weapon in full automatic mode, she felt her chest tighten as if it were ten sizes too small to hold her heart and lungs. They reached 45 miles per hour and she took fourth gear. They were moving fast up the access road towards Highway 58 as Blade fired a few more rounds, then sank into the seat next to her as though he were a sandbag dropped from a truck. She glanced over at him to see if she could get a read on the situation. He had the two rifle barrels down between his legs and his arms crossed tight, almost as if he were giving himself a bear hug. He stared straight ahead with a serious meditative anger on his hot wet face. Without words, they fled into the early morning darkness.

CHAPTER 7

Day 130 of the fourth year A.E.

Spoken to only by the sound of the tires hissing over the rain-soaked roadway, Kim sped down I-5 for thirty-five minutes in silence as Blade, who was a motionless rock, stared straight ahead. That was fine by her. She was not feeling much for chitchat at that moment. The ringing in her ears was finally beginning to dissipate. Maybe in fifteen or twenty minutes she would be able to hear anything he might say.

Looking at the odometer, which actually still worked, Kim calculated that they were just over thirty miles away from those that would have taken their individuality and homogenized it into the uniformity of the group. Thirty miles was yet not nearly enough. She would drive until the gasoline-powered steel horse they stole either ran out of fuel or fell dead in the roadway from its own mechanical rendition of heart failure. Right then it was about distance.

After some time the rain stopped and the air began to warm. The clouded night sky began to turn battleship gray. It was becoming day and the knot of hunger in her stomach was something that she could no longer ignore. Kim reached back between the seats and grabbed her pack. Finding her stash of energy bars, she took out two and offered one to Blade. He turned slowly, giving the bar held before him a tired look. As he uncrossed his dagger-covered arms and began to reach for the offering, Kim's mind froze with uncomprehending shock. Fear knifed her through the chest and her throat constricted. He was hit. His massive black hand was covered with dark coagulated blood. She could now see his fatigues also were covered with this vital fluid.

"Shit!" she yelled above the dull roar of the seventy-five miles per hour wind that was crashing through the front of the windowless car. Looking back to the oncoming roadway, she jerked the steering wheel, swerving the vehicle back into the main driving lane of the abandoned freeway.

Ahead she saw a derelict semi jack-knifed and lying on its side in the center strip, its skeletal remains sticking halfway into the fast lane. Vandalized remnants of the wheeled box were strewn about the roadway. Slowing the car, she began scanning the surroundings. It looked safe.

She pulled up and parked on the south side of the overturned trailer, next to what was the roof. Here, they could only be seen from the south. "Damn it, Blade. Were you going to tell me?"

"No, probably not," he croaked weakly in his deep low voice.

Kim got out of the car. Going around to the passenger's door, she opened it and knelt down in the opening. "How are you?" she said with concern, actual genuine concern. Was she serious? This was something she had not felt in a very long time. It felt dangerous to begin to care for someone. Dangerous, but somehow right.

"Can you turn towards me? I need to see so I can help you," Kim said as she placed the automatic rifles onto the hood and reached for his wound.

Blade groaned, a long grimace-laden groan, as he turned and swung his feet out and onto the ground. "I don't think it hit anything serious," he said as he pulled up his shirt, exposing a ragged and bruised hole through his lower right ribcage. "It feels like it messed up a rib or two, but I'm breathing alright."

Kim reached out and began to feel about. He winced and, with a jerk of his bear-sized paw, grabbed her wrist. She felt brittle in his grip. "It went all the way through. Let me look," she said. "I'll be careful, but we need to treat this."

"K, sorry," he said, "I was pretty good with it 'til I started moving. Then you poking me kinda caught me off guard."

"I'll go easy, but it's going to hurt a bit. Ready?"

He nodded.

Kim assessed his injury, determining that the bullet entered between two ribs, may have passed through the outer edge of his liver and clipped a rib on the way out, maybe fracturing it, but she was not sure. He was not bleeding too badly but he needed patching up. She went up to the looted cab of the big-rig. Inside the sleeper, she cut the fabric headliner out and tore it into wide strips. Then she cut vinyl off the inside door panel. With the cloth folded as a pad that reached around Blade's midsection, she improvised a tight dressing made of tan-colored polyester. Placing the vinyl over the pad as if it were a half corset, she secured it with three tightly cinched cords of nylon. It looked the same as a flak jacket on sideways.

"Not bad," Blade grunted, partly from pain and partly from the corset.

"Thanks," she said, as she handed him a bottle of pills. "Take one in the morning and one in the evening. They're antibiotics."

"K," Blade said as he sat resting for a minute. "You know, I'll take that energy bar now, if the offer still holds."

"Sure thing," Kim walked back around to the driver's side and dropped into the seat. Reaching into the pack, she handed him the food she originally offered. They sat, ate and rested.

After the energy bars were gone and a water bottle had been

passed between them a couple times, Blade's curiosity began to overpower any desire he might have had to mind his own business.

"So, Kim, where you headin'?" Blade asked as he looked straight ahead, out onto the feral valley that once fed the world. "You're headin' somewhere, and you're not the same as the other survivors. You aren't lookin' to latch onto a group. What's your story?"

"No story," Kim lied. "I'm not a real people person any more, I guess."

"Right, and headin' no place in particular either, huh?"

Kim was beginning to like him but he was trying to get too close. Getting close to someone had always ended with pain. "Look, I appreciate the help in getting out of there, and maybe I am headed somewhere, but I'm traveling alone. I'm happy to leave you with the car. I had planned to walk anyway."

"You sure you want to go it alone? I mean, I got nothin' really calling me back and I kinda feel like I owe ya a favor, for gettin' me outta there and all. And for this patch job too," He said, pointing to his makeshift brace.

"I thought you wanted to get back to your guys in Sac? Besides, I don't need a man to take care of me and keep me safe," she said with a bit of sarcasm, which she immediately wished she could take back. "You don't know anything about where I'm headed or why. Do you just go around signing up for the unknown?"

"The guys in Sac aren't anything, just something to pass the time. And you ain't gotta worry about me, I'm watcha call a man's man, not so much into the girls. And... and as for the unknown, well, ain't that what we're livin' in? I mean, since the whole social meltdown? What'd they call it, the Earthling Spring? And the crazy-ass nuke parties. The world is a completely unknown thing now. Hell, look at *this* place. It's supposed to be arid and dry here but now the San Pablo Bay reaches all the way to Modesto and the valley is green all year. The world is all jacked up. I need a purpose, a reason to be, and none of those Social Sites are it." Blade shook his head and looked out into the humid haze that hung in the valley.

Kim sat quietly for a minute or two, both hands gripping the steering wheel, fingers tightening and loosening as if she were squeezing the rubber pump of a blood pressure cuff. "A man's man, huh? I never would've guessed by looking," once again not revealing the entirety of her knowledge.

"Well, we all can't be bitchy interior designers," Blade replied with his own bite of sarcasm. They both smiled and laughed, his own chuckling followed by the grimace of pain.

Sitting there in that car and staring out across its shot-up hood, Kim was surer of her plan than she ever had been. She knew that what she was doing and where she was going was for her alone. A debt needed to be paid, and in the course of meeting this obligation, she wanted to be responsible only for herself. Even though Blade would freely risk himself for a cause he believed in, she would still feel responsible because she involved him in her battle. This was what happened before, and she had vowed in her hidden seclusion of The After that it would not happen again.

"Look, I'm a loner and I intend to keep it that way," Kim said quietly as she grabbed her belongings and stepped out of the car. She then pulled the knife and the .357 from her pack and restored them to their empty sheaths on her belt. "I'll spell it out. Where I'm going is dangerous, and what I plan to do is payback for lost friends and others like you who wanted to help, but instead paid. I owe them an end. This trip I make is me beginning that, me doing that. This jacked-up world, as you call it, the crazy-ass nuke parties, the Earthling Spring, all of that came from one voice, one place and one brain. I need to settle things."

Blade's forehead wrinkled and his lips went tight and flat as he shook his head, "No way. Everyone knows there were multiple groups and many different leaders, all with different agendas, vastly different. The nukes were going to happen anyway, they just needed a reason. Hell, here in the U.S. that was the political fear mongers playin' people's ignorance."

Kim shouldered her pack, "Sure, that's what it looked like. But all those groups, all those leaders, all the top boxes in the hierarchy charts, they all were a part of a connected societal network and they all got their information from it. The network watched and told them, it confirmed for them, what they wanted to do. All of it based on what they did… and were already doing."

"What the hell are you talkin' about?" Blade responded, looking up from his seat with a puzzled, mouth-open squint.

"I'm done talking. I'm going alone. No more leading, no more following and no more asking others to do what I should be doing." She turned and started to walk.

"Hey, Kim!" Blade called as he pulled himself up and out of the cars passenger seat. "You seem pretty bull-headed about this. I respect that." Kim paused and half turned to face him as he continued, "Look, I owe you. You got me outta that nut camp, you patched me up and you gave me the antibiotics. Those things are hard to find, and you just gave them to me. They're probably going to save my life," he paused, frustrated but knowing she had made her decision. "Take the car. I'll keep the M-19's and I'll be fine."

"You sure?"

Blade nodded.

Together they pushed the car back onto I-5 and got it rolling north, downhill, for a push start. After it fired up Kim pushed in the clutch, braked, made a U-turn and pulled up next to Blade, who was standing on the centerline using an M-19, barrel to the pavement, as a cane to lean on.

"Thanks," she said, and stuck her hand out the window.

Blade reciprocated by engulfing her tiny appendage in his giant black fist. They smiled and enjoyed what had become for their world a rare human moment, two individuals going their individual ways. Blade released her hand, slapped the roof of the car and in his deep bear voice said, "Good luck."

Kim drove away, moving up through the gears and gaining speed. The sky was holding its gloomy gray-brown dinge, but the steamy rain had stopped. Her pack and hat lay next to her in the passenger seat as she headed south, the wind blowing warm through the windowless car, across her face and through her hair. She was making good time down the lonely freeway, and her thoughts of what lay ahead left her scared.

PART 2

THE BEFORE

§

CHAPTER 8

Long before Kim found herself in that windowless wreck speeding south on Interstate 5, long before The Event and long before anyone ever imagined something called The After, Kim was much valued and highly sought after. A social networking and technology company called Obyavit International, as well as many other technology firms, followed her and her work closely. Kim was a scientist, a unique scientist, and the theories she published as a young post-graduate had shown great promise. It was the controlled study she performed on the student body of the university she attended that brought the social networking industry to worship at her feet. The competition to recruit her was fierce. It was then that Obyavit first sent its recruiters to begin the process of making her theirs.

Kim was in her late twenties when the world lay at her feet. She was vibrant and focused. Her life was her work and the rest of life beyond her work just happened. At five-four and maybe 120 pounds, she gave the appearance of a studious teenaged scholar. Her flat, straight brunette hair reached down between her shoulders and was never not in motion, following her as she moved, trying desperately to keep up with its energetic owner. Her fine brown skin was that perfect shade of tan sought after by every tall blond girl in southern California. Her features reflected her heritage, faintly Mexican and faintly Japanese.

Like her father, she was an immigrant. While they both lived as citizens of the country they were in, they both lived in different countries. Kim's father, Kimihiko Ishida, had immigrated to Hermosillo, Sonora from his native Japan as a young man. Enamored of the prospects of becoming a rancher in the semi-arid Mexican state, he worked hard, battled prejudices and slowly earned the respect and admiration of his rural neighbors. It was during that struggle to adapt and fit in that he met a young woman from a nearby ranching family who was named Ramona. Mona, as she preferred to be known, admired his tenacity, strength of will and the fact that he was unlike any of the other boring and predictable boys from her part of Sonora.

Mona's parents were not eager to see their precious daughter involved with this strange young man. However, his perseverance and strong will brought him a good reputation among ranchers looking for dependable ranch hands and soon word spread among the landowners. Those qualities were Kimihiko's strengths. In time, and with the blessing of her parents, he married Mona and they bought a small ranch of their own near the sprawling cattle empire of his new father-in-law.

Not long after their marriage, Mona gave birth to their only child, Kimiko Maria. Named for her father and her grandmother, she grew to be a good ranch hand and an excellent student. She loved the outdoor life of the ranch, but her parents saw a future for her in the world well beyond the simple life of rural Mexico and encouraged their daughter's intellect in every way possible. Often that meant sacrifice.

Kimihiko and Mona sent their daughter to live with an aunt in Tucson when she started high school because the drug cartels had virtually supplanted the government, and the educational system was suffering greatly. The chance at any sort of real career, unfettered by corruption, was all but impossible, so Kim went to live with her naturalized relatives in *Los Estados Unidos*. She was an intelligent young woman, but also humble and naïve. That, and a negative American sentiment towards Mexican immigrants, pushed her into a self-imposed solitude filled only with science and math. Once she became a citizen, she pursued scholarships for college. She was soon recognized by the University of Arizona for her intellectual abilities and was awarded a full four-year scholarship. Her parents were very proud.

It was at the U of A that her ideas about improving predictive technologies first began to grow. During her post-graduate work at CalTech her ideas became functional and tangible, and they became prized by others. As knowledge and evidence of her work spread through the tech industry, companies similar to Obyavit became keenly interested.

Obyavit was the mega-darling of the tech world. It held patents on most of the prevailing technology for connecting people with people and people with data. Licensing the rights to other businesses so they too could use this technology was the same as owning sunlight; almost everyone needed it to compete, to be viable, and they paid Obyavit for the privilege.

Being a cash-strong company, Obyavit acquired businesses, technology or people whenever it most benefited them. Whether to gain control of useful innovations or to stifle competition made no difference. The goal was the same: be on top and stay on top. They also recruited, hired, courted or stole the best and the brightest talent available and paid them well. Obyavit made no friends among those companies raided by its recruiters, but it was unmistakably clear that it was a healthy, strong corporate power. It was also clear that it might one day control the world market for digital personal assistants, and more.

Kim became Obyavit's most prized catch. She was twenty-eight years old and a post-graduate who was twelve months away from completing her dissertation and obtaining her Doctoral Degree. The epitome of an academic lab rat, she was innocent of the cutthroat double-speak of the high-powered business world.

When white papers and media reports of Kim's work came out it was as if the tech world were hit by a tsunami. As potential suitors floundered adrift in the wake of what she had done, these companies quickly concluded they needed her in order to be the best, to take the lead, to own the market segment. In the sea that was social networking and web-based predictive marketing, they needed her mind to stay afloat, or be sunk to the bottom with all the rest of the failed and forgotten.

Kim liked the attention, but was ill equipped to manage those who coveted her. The aggressive media frenzy that was taking place and being reported publicly quickly overwhelmed her. The speculation surrounding who would win the prize, who she might sign with, was a trending topic. She had become a reluctant reality TV star. The whole process unsettled her; it was exciting, frightening and sickening all at once.

§

It was the start of her last year at Caltech. She could still remember it vividly. They had sent a car for her, a limo. It was so exciting, and somewhat unnerving, having all these different companies wanting *her* to come work for them. It had gotten so that every time she moved there was live streaming video feed and a dozen or so Chatters following her every step. So when the car from Obyavit came to the modest apartment she rented in Pasadena and whisked her away in quiet, private seclusion to Spago, in Beverly Hills, well, she felt glamorous.

Her studio apartment was anything but glamorous. There were bars on the one window and locks on the door. It was less a place to live than it was a place to store things. She did sleep there most nights, by herself. It held a large, steel, greenish-gray government surplus desk on one side of the main room and a cot-like twin bed on the other. She kept the place clean, having bought her first vacuum solely for maintaining her flat. The place was tired though; it had been lived in hard by many, many tenants before she had come to rest there.

The kitchenette, as it was advertised, was defined by its four-foot-long counter which held the puny sink of a wet bar. Lavishly equipped with a single cabinet below the sink and a small cupboard above, a two-burner hotplate and a dangerous looking toaster oven completed the list of amenities. The microwave was hers. When she ate at home, which was usually only breakfast, she did so standing over that diminutive kitchen sink. In the open space between the desk and the bed stood two tall bookcases, back to back, and books, folders, binders, overflowing in-trays, equally packed out-trays, newspapers, magazines and any other written note or printed matter that might hold informational value found refuge for extended periods upon their shelves. Just outside her only window, the one with bars, was a trash laden shrub beyond which was a sidewalk. That desolate sidewalk ran along a seldom-used frontage road that was separated from the noisy, crowded and noxious 210 freeway by a vine-covered cyclone fence that held a colorful assortment of plastic and paper debris. The view of the freeway, she felt, epitomized the L.A. car culture. She did not own a car. At the time, she could afford only the bus.

When Kim arrived at Spago she was greeted by a man and a woman. Both were dressed in ways that spoke power. The woman presented herself in a single-breasted jacket and mid-length skirt, flawless white blouse, understated pearls and Prada shoes. The man wore a Brioni that fit as though he were born to it.

"Wow, I feel as if I'm somebody important, and woefully under dressed," Kim said, overwhelmed by the opulence.

She had on her only suit, a dark gray outfit she had bought on sale at Macy's, and a pair of black flats she saved for special occasions. In a moment of subconscious self-consciousness, Kim caught herself brushing her jacket and skirt flat with her hand in an effort to make them look better.

With a friendly, prepared smile, the woman recruiter reached out and shook her hand, "You are somebody important, Kim. You and your work are well known at Obyavit and it is a pleasure to meet you."

Not noticing the practiced facade of her reception, she thought she said thank you, but she may not have. She was still somewhat awestruck by her surroundings.

The other recruiter extended his hand to greet her as well, "It is a genuine pleasure to meet you. Shall we move to our table? I have arranged for a place on the patio," and with well-rehearsed synchronicity the woman was already advising the maître d' they were ready to be seated.

At the table, while they ate, they engaged in conversation that contained undertones of the purpose for their meeting, but it did not seem overtly as if it were a recruitment exercise. The recruiters' tact was very much a soft touch, quite unlike the others. Kim liked the lack of pressure but it also seemed odd.

As the gentle banter moved along, she began to relax. The crisp white wine Kim was drinking took her mind off the pressures and demands of being heavily recruited. As she sat with the two employees from Obyavit enjoying a tender salmon filet, she could feel the warmth of the alcohol creeping slowly over her. It was then, during a moment of relaxed distraction, that her eyes and demeanor whispered a sense of unguarded comfort and satisfaction. Across the table, the woman recruiter reached to the side of her perfect hair and brushed back a non-existent stray lock.

That must have been the signal because the male recruiter's tone changed and the direction of the conversation turned towards business, "Your groundbreaking work in the area of Behavioral Economics is causing quite a stir among those interested in predictive analytics. Consequently, we appreciate that many in the global business community are contacting you with opportunities, very enticing opportunities I'm sure."

That was true, Kim thought, as she drifted back to the exchange. She had been contacted by a number of the big players. The Googles, Linkedins and Facebooks of the world were all in pursuit. Even a government intelligence agency had approached her. But she wasn't interested in the public sector. The private sector offered far more opportunities. She knew she was in demand and she was enjoying the excessive consideration during this competitive courtship process.

"Yes, I have been talking to a few people. There are even offers being extended," Kim said with the smug pride of an inexperienced negotiator.

The female recruiter placed her knife and fork down on either side of her plate in a manner indicative of someone schooled in proper table etiquette. She leaned forward ever so slightly, looked Kim directly in the eyes and said in a quiet and confident tone, "We hope that, given the time you have remaining at Caltech, you'll not rush into a decision. We believe Obyavit can provide you with an offer, environment, culture and lifestyle that will allow you to further your work in your field to a degree you may only have imagined thus far. Any limitations you may have experienced in the academic world will be non-existent."

"Th-that's quite a promise," Kim stammered.

She must have blinked a few times at the bold nature of this statement because Kim thought sure she saw the briefest concealed hint of arrogant satisfaction. "I suppose this is where you present me your offer package?" Kim could feel the fog of relaxation lifting. The hard light of the recruiting process was beginning to sharpen the contrasts of the world around her.

"No, no," the male recruiter offered. "This is merely a chance to introduce ourselves and Obyavit to you. Mr. Tichý will extend any offer made."

Then almost on queue the female recruiter added, "As my

colleague has stated, we are the greeters. Emissaries sent to introduce Obyavit to you and ask if you would consider meeting further. We have come only to ask if you would come to San Jose to meet with Mr. Tichý. We will of course provide food, lodging, a car and driver as well as air transport on one of Obyavit's private jets."

This brief encounter with Obyavit was progressing unlike any other. Kim was suspicious and she did not hide it well, "All this, the limo, dinner at Spago and two highly-paid recruiters just to say 'Hi' and find out if I have free time on my calendar in a week or two?"

The male recruiter, sitting with perfect posture, closed his eyes and nodded, "Mr. Tichý respects your time and believes your work is the priority. He hopes you are not in a rush to accept any offers that may be on the table already. He hopes you can find time to come to San Jose to see Obyavit International's corporate headquarters in a private tour led by him."

"Why?" Kim asked. She was sure there was more to this than she saw, but the puzzle pieces eluded her. "Why would the owner and CEO of one of the top software companies in the world want to spend his time doing your job, recruiting talent?"

The female recruiter sat back and answered. "Because, unlike the other companies, Mr. Tichý is just as you said, the owner of this company. He is not at the mercy and whim of shareholders and institutional investors. In matters of great importance to Obyavit, he personally sees to their success. He wants to personally convey to you your importance to Obyavit, now and into the future."

Kim did not know whether to feel flattered or guarded, but the heady events of the evening, and a feeling that there was more to learn, told her she should go to northern California and hear their pitch. "OK, I'll come up and meet Mr. Tichý. I can do it in three weeks."

Three weeks later, Kim found herself in a limo headed to the Executive Terminal of the Burbank Airport so she could step aboard a private jet that was bound for San Jose International.

CHAPTER 9

The corporate mission statement of Obyavit International read as follows:

"Obyavit International connects people to the life they want and need to live. We empower each individual, regardless of nation, language or culture, to live his or her social life with clarity and purpose, whether using information online or offline. Text, images, video or sound – Whatever is needed, whenever it is needed, Obyavit will bring it to you."

Obyavit International was founded by Bojanek Tichý, a Czechoslovakian immigrant from an affluent suburb of Prague. After about a year of being submersed in the American culture, and to the protest of his parents, he shortened his name to Bo. "Bojanek Tichý is a Croatian goat farmer; Bo Tichý is a *captain* of industry," he once said when asked about shortening his name. However, on the rare formal occasion he would still use Bojanek.

He had come to the United States at the urging of his family to attend an Ivy League school and obtain a dual Masters in both business and technology. The goal of his scholastic pursuits was to one day take over his father's commercial carpet manufacturing company and bring it into the twenty-first century. However, Bo loved America. To him it was a land of great possibilities, a stable platform from which to compete in the world. So he stayed, a green card ex-pat living the American dream.

Bo was a natural with technology and he keenly understood business. He was a shrewd person in many ways. In combining technology, business and people, he saw great distances into the future. He saw possibilities and opportunities that few could fathom. This future vision was nothing psychic or science fiction, it was just the way his brain worked, the way he was mapped. He was not necessarily an innovator, but he could see the prospects in anything that came before him. Ideas, concepts and personalities were three-dimensional things that could, or could not, be fitted together. He was asked once, at a product introduction press conference, what his objectives were for the future of Obyavit. Bo replied, "The people of the world are migrating their lives to the internet, the cloud, the global virtual world, whatever you wish to name it. Society worldwide uses the net to live, learn, connect and communicate. My objectives for Obyavit you ask. To own that entire market, or at least have the single largest piece, my friend."

Kim had published two papers on the use and implementation of predictive technologies, a topic that fascinated Bo. He saw her work as an integral part of his future. In an effort to secure that future, he had flown her to San Jose so that he could meet her in his offices at Obyavit headquarters.

Later, when asked by the press about this strategy of personally recruiting desirable candidates on site at the company's headquarters, he would always reply, "If you are going to play the game, play to win, and there is no better advantage than home field advantage."

On the day of Kim's visit, Bo made sure that every employee at the San Jose headquarters knew of her arrival, and of her importance. There were email briefings and short staff meetings at all levels relating the accomplishments of their guest. All employees were ordered to be warm and welcoming during her visit. There was an electric tension coursing through the entire site the day Kim first experienced Obyavit.

§

Her flight from Burbank to San Jose was exciting and strange. Besides the two pilots and the flight attendant, she was the only person on the luxurious ten-seat aircraft. Obyavit was spending a lot of money, it seemed, just to interview one person. Suitably impressed, she sat back and enjoyed the one-hour flight.

When Kim arrived in front of the Obyavit lobby, alone in the back of a non-descript black town car, two formidable men wearing gray suits, dark glasses and earpieces awaited her, ready to open the car door. She stepped from the limousine to see two fashionably dressed women and an impeccably groomed young man walking briskly from the lobby. She was greeted warmly there in the pleasant sunny expanse of the beautiful architected entrance to Obyavit International's world headquarters.

"Hello. Hello. Welcome to Obyavit, we're so glad you have come," said one of the women as she reached for Kim's hand.

The young man, probably in his mid-twenties, asked, "How was your trip? Can we get you anything?"

"No. No, I'm fine, thank you." Kim was feeling as though these three people from the lobby were almost too happy to see her.

The oldest of the three woman, the one who seemed to be in charge, stepped forward, and in a much less effusive manner, introduced herself. "Hello and welcome to Obyavit International. I am Mr. Tichý's administrative assistant. Please, call me Jan. I will be accompanying you throughout the day to ensure we stay on schedule. If there is anything you need, anything at all, please ask and I will make it happen."

Kim just nodded, not wanting to risk sounding foolish or inexperienced.

"Well then," Jan said looking at her smartphone and sliding her thumb down its screen twice. She tapped the screen four or five times successively, then looked up, "Let's head to security and get you a badge. After that we'll go to Bo's office on the second floor."

When they arrived at Bo's office the door was open, and Jan led her in without knocking. It was an impressive place, with one wall entirely of glass. At the end nearest the door was a large, very modern desk that was simply a thick sheet of glass spanning two chrome arches at either end. The entire office reflected a clean, sparse, modern feel. It was as though it were an Ikea showroom, only it contained high-end items that did not require you to assemble them yourself.

"Mr. Tichý, your guest is here," Jan announced.

Bo, who was standing at the window looking out when Kim entered, turned, smiling to greet her. He looked younger than she expected. His was the face of a hard-working technology geek: pallid skin, tired, deep-set eyes, short, scruffy hair and three days of stubble. His smile and manner was that of genuine sincerity, as put forth by an exhausted man. Crossing the room and reaching to shake hands as he approached, he exclaimed, "Welcome, Kim. Welcome. Thank you so much for coming to see us." He then proceeded to shake her hand with vigorous determination.

Concealing the jarring surprise of Bo's enthusiastic greeting, Kim reclaimed her arm and hand. "Thank you. Thank you for inviting me here."

"Good, good." Then turning to his administrative assistant he said, "Thank you, Jan. That'll be all for now. Come get us later as discussed." Jan nodded and then left, closing the door as she went. "So I trust the trip was comfortable?" Without waiting for an answer he added, "Come. Sit."

They walked to the far end of the office where there were two leather couches facing each other, and a chrome and glass coffee table between them. The table had an arrangement of Torch Ginger, Halekonia and Pink Hibiscus accented with tropical foliage, and in the middle was a cut crystal bowl with small bottles of Pellegrino. They sat opposite each other, Kim admiring the beautiful flowers and taking in the view beyond windows. Pink Hibiscus was one of her favorites.

The few people she could see strolling between the buildings of the Obyavit campus were either engaged in conversation or busily interacting with tablets or smartphones. All of them seemed relaxed and happy as they moved through the oasis below. The greenery, the shade, the trees and the grass, even the fountain with its water sculpture, were all so serene. Then she heard Bo's voice bringing her back from her brief trance, "So, what do you think?"

"It's beautiful out there, so green and lush."

Bo smiled, "At Obyavit you will be in comfort while you work. We want our people to be happy they are here, and if they are happy, they will be more creative and more innovative. You will find there are many benefits that come with being a part of our family."

Kim saw this as her opportunity to find out more about what she might expect from Obyavit and its owner, "So tell me, Mr. Tichý..."

"Please, Kim, call me Bo. We are very informal here. "

"Bo. Tell me Bo, why do you want me to work for you? How do you see me and my work contributing to Obyavit's success?"

Bo laughed a deep hearty laugh as he smiled wryly, "You get right to the point. I like that." Then, pausing thoughtfully and scratching his stubbly face he said, "My reasons are not unlike anyone else's, no doubt. Your work applied to my… that is, Obyavit's software and services will move us to the front, not only in our current business, but also in other markets and services that are yet only loosely-modeled plans. You may ultimately choose another company with which to work, but only at Obyavit will our existing platform be migrated to your architecture. Others will have you adapt to them."

This was a powerful declaration. Kim had fully expected to see her work as a subset to an existing architecture. She had already begun preparing herself for the time when the company that would eventually hire her would start pulling out only the pieces they felt were useful. In fact, she had planned to spend this last year in academia finalizing her thesis and developing methods that would allow her system's components to be modular. She never imagined a company, especially a corporation the size of Obyavit, would migrate in entirety to *her* platform.

Kim sat back blinking. Again, she was surprised at his boldness, and again she tried to hide it. Something behind her conscious thought prickled. "That's quite a statement. From what little I know of your systems, I should think that would require at least a two-year investment before there were any tangible results. No one I've met with as yet has had the stomach for that."

"I am not without the ability to understand the structural implications of a platform shift," Bo said, cocking his head smiling with humorless patience after the reply, quietly letting her know that she had come very close to insulting his intelligence. "The long-term payoff makes the costs of such an undertaking moot. That is the difference between my competitors and me; I am playing the long game. Besides, my customer base is quite dedicated. We will not lose ground."

"How can you be so sure you are not the only one who is willing to take such a risk?"

Bo stood, picking up a bottled water as he did so. He then moved towards the glass wall as the metal cap of the wet bottle faintly cracked and popped in protest of its removal, "The battle for corporate dominance is much the same as the old ways of the Cold War. Companies are always trying to know what the competition's next move will be and then be one or two moves ahead of that. They have spies, we have spies. And quietly, we battle."

As Kim sat pondering Bo's statement, Jan knocked twice and entered the room. "It's time we start the tour. They're ready for us in

Building 3."

The day would hold several meetings. Kim met an individual from Human Resources who told how much more superior their *total compensation* package was – everything held value, the vacation and health plans were obvious, but even the free onsite Starbucks was considered compensation. Kim met the Chief Financial Officer, Madeline Kresky, who conveyed to Kim, with numerous slides and charts, the financial robustness of Obyavit. Kim liked her personality and thought they could become friends, if she decided to work there. There was a catered lunch where Kim met a number of project leads who might be associated with the type of work with which someone such as her would be involved. But the most important stop on Kim's itinerary was the tour Bo would give her of the new test lab, which made up one half of the 90,000 square feet that was the new Building 3.

They entered the ground floor of Building 3 and Bo stopped. They had entered at a corner of the building and before them was a vast expanse of emptiness. On the far side was a wall that was solid on the bottom half and glass on the top. The first floor of the building was divided in half. Inside the giant room that was half a building away were many men, and a few women, putting the final touches on what was a state-of-the-art technology lab.

"This," Bo said with a flourished wave of his arm, "is a dream come true."

"What exactly is it?" Kim asked.

As Bo started walking across the emptiness towards the room's security door, he pointed in that direction and said, "Come, I will show you."

Bo waved his smartphone across a square gray sensor on the wall. The door emitted an electronic beep and slid open. They stepped in unnoticed as the contract installers continued to busy themselves with their various tasks.

Bo turned and faced Kim, "Should you choose to work at Obyavit this, all of this and another room twice this size below us, will be yours." Then Bo just stood there, hands on his hips and a proud grin, watching Kim's reaction. It was priceless.

Kim's mouth fell open and her eyes went wide. Jan, who was standing off to the side, smiled slyly. Kim knew what she was looking at. It was a lab similar to that which she had been using at Caltech, only bigger, much bigger. The equipment was newer, faster and there was more of it. She had been limited to only a few hours here and there at Caltech. Time-sharing it was called. Even then, the equipment was barely up to the task. But spread out before her were the newest versions of equipment she was familiar with, and additional equipment that she had petitioned the university to budget so the school could remain competitive. There was even hardware she had only dared to fantasize about with other technology-geek friends.

As she wandered throughout the lab, Bo following behind telling her about the complete systems capabilities of *her* facility, Kim could only think that what Bo had said was true. This place was a dream come true.

It was after the tour and the various meetings specifically designed to impress that Kim signed a letter of intent. She had decided, and she was declaring her intention to become Obyavit's Director of Technological Development, but this was as Bo expected. The tour, the meetings, the orchestrated day in its entirety, and especially the lab, had all been calculated to feed Kim's young ego. The team at Obyavit gently and stealthily attended to her professional needs, desires and dreams. Dreams she shared only with those closest to her and her work, dreams about which very few people knew. Yes, it *was* exactly as Bo expected. Because, as he said, "They have spies. We have spies."

CHAPTER 10

Obyavit grew fast. In the first two years of its incorporation, Bo's enterprise doubled in size five times. In that time, he acquired several of the startups he had partnered with in order to grow his technology. One of those acquisitions was a small software company in Berlin called IdentaTrack. While Obyavit was Bo's company, and the roadmap it followed was his plan, he always sought his Board of Directors' input and analysis on matters of growth and acquisition. Nevertheless, Bo's feelings on issues that were important to him were always detectable, but usually well controlled.

Quite some time before Kim's arrival, a great deal of Obyavit's growth was attained through acquisition. And at the meeting where potential takeover targets were discussed, everyone came prepared with data and analysis that either supported or opposed the purchase. Madeline Kresky was no exception.

Madeline was the epitome of the over-worked over-booked, overachiever. A graduate from the Masters of Law program at Stanford, her specialty was international corporate tax law. Bo's recruiting vultures had plucked her from a well-known firm located just east of the New York Stock Exchange, on Wall Street. Since her job at Obyavit was not quite as demanding as that of her previous employment, she found ways to fill that time by realizing a life beyond work. She married her college love who had stayed in the Bay Area to practice law for a venture capital firm, and together they had two children.

Madeline led the process of financially vetting any potential expansion that Bo had set Obyavit's sights on. But Bo was a bottom-line man. While others on the Board offered valuable input, it was understood that if a target could not realize a return on investment within the timeline of the framework he had set, then it was off the table.

§

"The last item on today's agenda is the acquisition of IdentaTrack in Berlin," Bo announced as he directed the Board's attention to a slide being shown on-screen at the far end of the conference room. "Madeline and her team recently flew out and thoroughly examined their financials. As you can see here, the first two quarters after purchase will be cutting it close in terms of the level of profitability I like to see. Comments?"

Rather than take the floor and discuss her report, Madeline waited for Arijit Roy to be the first to speak. He was always the first to speak, as he always seemed to be in an anxious state of restless-eagerness. The rest of the Board was politely aware of this aspect of his otherwise respectful personality and obliged this quirk.

"Well, Bo, we are the only suitors at this time and all indications are that the two young entrepreneurs are highly desirous of selling their technology. Maybe we can negotiate to a lesser figure and make profitability look better?

Arijit Roy, although in America he simply went by Roy, had come to Obyavit through acquisition. He and Nalani Rawat were both from a suburb of West Bengal and both were honors graduates from the prestigious Indian Institute of Technology Kharagpur, though Roy had graduated ten years before Nalani. Nalani had developed the technology that would ultimately become the BuyAt functionality in Obyavit's MyWorld suite of products. Roy was the business mind of the former venture. He knew well how to manage a company at the speed of technology. At Obyavit he held the title of Senior Vice President of Technology. Nalani brought her deep technical abilities to the partnership she and Roy had in India. When Bo bought their small enterprise Roy made sure he knew the importance of keeping Nalani. Bo did.

After Roy spoke, another member of the Board observed, "Yes, that could conceivably work, but there is a risk they don't bite. Then what?"

"I understand why we want their technology," Madeline acknowledged, "but why now? Strictly from a tax perspective, it is not advantageous at this time. There are pending revisions to the German tax statutes becoming law early next year. That change alone will save us $2.6 million."

"Good footwork Madeline," Bo said. After pausing for a very brief moment to consider the implications of this additional data point he continued, "When is that tax benefit going into effect?"

"Q2 next year," she said.

Bo looked to Roy and asked, "It's your project team that benefits most from this. Can you make your timeline support a push to a revised Q2 time frame?"

"Yes, yes," Roy said shaking his head side-to-side as if meaning no. Roy's head movements, side-to-side while saying yes and up-and-down when saying no, always distracted Bo, but in the short while they had worked together he had grown accustomed to it. "There are other tasks and features we can move up. When we integrate this German technology does not matter, as long as we know we'll have it."

Bo looked across the table to the head of Mergers and

Acquisitions with a questioning nod. "I think we can keep things on the hook until then. Our sources tell us that the offer we have extended is the best one on the table, and they're hungry."

Bo started gathering up his tablet and two smartphones, indicating he was ready to wrap things up. "Good. Good work, team. I don't want to lose this. Is that understood?" Then his character seemed to transform. He set a cold gaze upon the room and with a firmness that meant it would be career suicide for any who failed at the next directive, he said, "This technology is crucial to MyWorld and I do not want to get in a bidding war with some small-time software house that just wants to mess with us."

He paused as an uncomfortable blanket of silence settled on the room. All eyes looked on with full attention to his now stern demeanor. Then just as quickly as he had grown dark, the clouds parted and sunlight came back to his eyes. With a smile he said, "This is the kind of strategizing that will keep us strong. Madeline, keep us apprised of any developments regarding the pending tax law. I'll expect reports on this only if there is a change, positive or negative. Otherwise, we'll revisit this again in Q1." As everyone stood, Bo added, "Thanks again everyone," and then turned to head toward his office.

Not long after that meeting, Obyavit moved from their tiny offices in the strip mall. Obyavit had almost entirely taken over the property and all its storefronts. Cash rich and needing additional tax shelters, it had become time to grow beyond leased property. That year, Obyavit moved into the 1.7 million square feet of office space that was formerly the global headquarters of Harbinger Inc. Harbinger had been bought by three venture capital firms from its former and rather flamboyant owner Larry Flanders. Larry's highly publicized escapades in Belize had cost him almost a billion dollars to clear up and ultimately he found it necessary to liquidate his assets. Harbinger was skinned, chopped, gutted and filleted. It was sold piece by piece on the fish market of American commerce for the ROI sought by the investors. Even Bo bought a couple pieces, technology he knew would prove beneficial to his plans. Bo also had his recruiters out culling talent from the wreckage of companies similar to Harbinger. Such was the cycle of life in the valley.

Bo's long-term vision for his software and services was that it should become the de facto standard in all the areas Obyavit pursued. To that end, MyWorld and its suite of companion services remained in a state of continual evolution over the years. WhereAt, BeAt, AmAt and BuyAt, with their astounding popularity, had become just that, the de-facto standard. At that time, most of the population in North America had adopted the suite to help them manage their overloaded 24/7 lives. Likewise, adoption in Japan and South Korea was equally prolific. Europe was hit-and-miss. There was deep saturation in Western Europe and pocketed adoption throughout the old Eastern Bloc countries. Surprisingly, there was widespread use in the Middle East, though some countries in the region forbade its use by women. Bo's analysis team could see, however, that those rules were largely ignored.

Obyavit continued to avoid pursuing markets or regions that would yield a low per-user return or a high per-user cost to secure. That meant most of Africa and the "stans," Pakistan, Tajikistan and the others, were allowed to happen organically, without the aid of marketing or promotion. Bo led with a firm but wise calmness. His logic and strategies were always grounded in sound business sense and he weighed the advice of his analysts carefully before executing or discarding a plan. He could be demanding, but the reasons always made sense.

The Board had grown accustomed to his firm but fair, well-reasoned leadership. That is why the day forever known in unspoken corporate legend as *The Day of the Republic* changed things at Obyavit. The Day of the Republic was the sobriquet given to the board meeting when the decision was made to deliberately and aggressively go after the market and user base of Bo's homeland, the Czech Republic. This reference was known throughout the industry but never acknowledged in Bo's presence, even though he was well aware of the parking lot prattle and water cooler gossip. The experience, as described by those who were there that day, was akin to having been dangerously close to a powerful force that could cause terrible things to happen if it were completely unleashed. It was a fleeting glimpse of a vehement hostility.

The day had started as any other day. Bo had convened the Board of Directors in order to gauge status on the health of the business, get updates on current efforts and plan future growth. He arrived in the conference room a couple minutes after the rest. The room was located on the second floor, forty feet from his office. It was a long rectangular room. One side was a wall of switchable electrochromic glass that could change from clear to a light-blocking opaqueness at the touch of a button.

As was customary, all the windows were switched off except one closest to where he sat. The view out that window was onto the lush green commons where Obyavit employees were encouraged to further their creative process in a social, campus-like atmosphere.

"Sorry I'm late everyone," he said in his accent that was mostly Czech but hinted at a bit of Ivy-League, Kennedy-esque New Englander. "At last week's meeting you all received copies of my Czech Republic plan. I asked you to review it, then bring to me your feedback. This discussion is the extent of our agenda for today. As always, let's start with you, Roy."

Roy had the customary, and this time unenviable, task of being the first to tell Bo the Board's opinion. This time it was that the project was not worth it. Roy was the first, but would not be the last. There was a consensus. With a few keystrokes, Roy called up onto the eighty-inch flat screen at the opposite end of the room a five-year cost of operation chart overlaid with projected income. He began to speak, "Well, Bo, I ran the standard cost figures we use for that part of the world and added in aggregate taxes, fees, and other country-specific cost. As you can see, it's just not showing any profit potential over the first five years." There was nodding in the room around the table. "I tried modeling different cost-sharing tactics in an effort to leverage existing successes in the region," Roy continued. "But the Czech effort would prove too big a drain, and making it a part of other efforts in the region would put us below the quarterly margin percentages you've asked us to achieve. I'd have to advise against it at this time."

"I see," said Bo. "Is this the consensus here in the room?"

With the invitation, Madeline added, "If we can wait twelve to sixteen months, the landscape will be completely different. There will be enough organic adoption that the cost model to take the risk may flip. By then it could be a money-maker, maybe." Once again, the room of seven nodded in agreement, as Bo looked on.

"So, no one here in this room can find a way to make this work," said Bo, his tone taking an edge that often indicated frustration.

The room was silent and then Madeline said, "If we're to maintain the quarterly targets you've established, then we will need to wait."

His words chopped, his tone glinting an incredulous edge, Bo asked, "Do you mean to tell me there is no way this can be done now?"

Madeline, Roy and the rest looked from Bo to each other, then back to Bo. Their eyebrows raised and foreheads furrowed, they silently questioned each other. The discussion seemed headed somewhere new and no one was sure what was expected of them next. The assembled team had done the same exhaustive research and analysis they always had ahead of these types of meetings. The numbers did not reconcile and no one in the room had any reason to suspect, that given the facts, the decision would be anything other than to hold off.

Roy, whether out of a sense of obligation or confusion, rose to address the question that lay festering on the table before them, "We each met and collaborated closely on the analysis, as we always do. The numbers…"

"You're meeting behind my back?" Bo said as he cut Roy off

mid-sentence. The tension in his voice was rising and the look in his eyes grew distant. "Did you not sense this project was of great importance when I gave it over to you? Surely, you've recognized the pointless nature of this meeting. You should have."

Bo again looked around the room. Then suddenly, he seemed to explode.

"Are you all idiots?" he shouted at the room. His face was a Rottweiler ready to attack. His eyes held a primal anger and saliva foamed like cotton in the corners of his mouth while his entire body steeled with vibrations of shaking rage. "I own you. I own you because I know what I am doing, now and five years from now. You sold to me so I would show you the way. I own you, all of you. You are here because I bought your companies. I bought your technology. I bought you."

Bo, hammering his fist forcefully onto the table before him, declared, "We are taking the Republic." Staring with a blind, obsessed fury at everyone in the room he quieted to a tone that clearly said, if you aren't with me, you should leave, "We are taking the Republic because we can, God damn it! The cost doesn't matter. In the end that will not be noticeable. What will be noticeable is that I, Bojanek Tichý, will be the most powerful man in Czechoslovakia. As I own you, I will own the Republic. I will be known, and they will look to me, to Obyavit, to know what they want, what they should do, and when they should do it. Obyavit will be the virtual leader of their world. They will buy what we tell them to buy, they will watch what we tell them to watch, they will go where we tell them to go, they will like what we tell them to like and they will not even be aware of the invisible hand that guides them. All of you, all of you here, your short-sightedness has blinded you from what is possible. You do not see what we can do and where we must go."

Bo walked to the center of conference room, near the large windows. With a touch of a nearby sensor, the windows changed from their dark gray opaque fogginess to clear. He stood, gazing out onto the bucolic setting of the four-acre quad that spread before him.

This was his kingdom, a sanctuary surrounded by six massive two-story buildings that were Obyavit World Headquarters. His back to the room, he spoke in the unsettling tone of a man possessed, "There is so much yet to do and MyWorld is merely a weak demonstration of the possibilities. It can be so much more. In the Republic, we will prove out a new technology that will do more than simply anticipate; it will know, and then it will guide. There is out there a means to see ahead of the virtual society, and to help them. Yes, help them. Obyavit will do this. I will help the world know what it needs to do." He then turned and left the room.

At this, those in the meeting who were not immobilized by shock were gathering their papers and starting to leave. Madeline did not know it then, but his last words before leaving the room were about Kim and her work. Already he was making plans to use her advancements. This, the Day of the Republic, was not long after Kim's second paper had been published. The buzz in the valley over her had not even begun yet.

When the door to the conference room latched, only Madeline and Roy and remained. Their expressions of shock and surprise spoke volumes. She blurted out, "What the hell was that?"

Roy, whose temperament was all about minimizing confrontation, sat looking down at his hands, which were locked together, fingers interlaced and his thumbs pressed so tightly into his fists that his dark brown skin was white. Shaking his head in slow wide arcs, he was chanting over and over, "That was not good. That was not good. He sounded mad. That was not good." Roy then looked up and said, "Not mad angry, mad crazy." Roy's eyes were large and frightened.

Madeline had to agree, "I've seen him speak firmly, I've seen him upset, but I've never seen anything like that."

Roy shook his head. "He sounded possessed, like this was some sort of vendetta. Like he planned to take over the entire world."

"I agree. He said the cost didn't matter. I never thought I'd ever hear him say such a thing. He spoke as if he wanted to rule that country. What do you suppose he meant?"

"I don't know, I don't know," Roy said, again shaking his head in a way that resembled a worried prayer, eyes closed. "This does not feel good; this does not feel good at all."

They each then gathered their things and went back to their offices.

Whether the Czech Republic was a matter of pride or of ego, no one close to him at the top was entirely sure. It could have been both. The Republic was a money loser for Obyavit and went against every discipline that Bo had drilled into his leadership team over the years. Quietly, there were those who felt it was a flash of the true Bo Tichý, a driven, win-at-all-cost, megalomaniac. Three of those who were in the room on The Day of the Republic departed the company shortly after. Madeline and Roy never possessed the level of trust and confidence they once had in Bo. It was clear that it was Bo's company, and in the final analysis, what Obyavit did was completely under his control. This was his machine and he had plans, plans that would reshape the way the world moved.

CHAPTER 11

Kim was driving north on the Bayshore. It was mid-morning. Traffic was congested, but moving, when she saw her opening. She dropped a gear and punched it.

She was giving Madeline a ride into work. It was a summer day and as they sped south towards Obyavit, Kim was lost in thought around that night's coming events. Madeline was watching Kim smile an almost secret smile as she navigated the traffic. She thought how unaware Kim was of herself and her own beauty. Kim made no effort to bring it forward, it was just there.

Kim and Madeline had become friends. Madeline, having lived in the Bay Area for some time, took it upon herself to help Kim acclimatize to the region. This meant literally dragging Kim away from her lab. "Working twelve hours a day, seven days a week is not a healthy lifestyle, Kim." Not an uncommon refrain from Madeline to her new friend. The effort necessary to find and make friends outside work was tiresome, Kim thought. But she enjoyed the *family* days she spent with Madeline and Todd. "Come with us this weekend. Saturday is boys' and girls' soccer league and Sunday we're all going to the Boardwalk in Santa Cruz. It'll be fun."

"There's a Boardwalk?"

"That's what I mean. You'll come with us. You'll love it!"

Madeline also enjoyed the idea of having a *girlfriend* with whom she could do things that were not manly enough to interest Todd. "Kim, you need to get out more. I'm taking Madison shopping for school clothes. Come with us. We'll have lunch; it'll be a girls' day out."

Madeline also liked to manage the occasional introduction of Todd's single male friends to Kim. An activity Todd wished Madeline would curtail.

"Madeline, an investment banker? He is so not my type."

"He's nice, I thought sure you two would… you know, hit it off."

"We're both way too Type-A. It would just be a competition."

"Can't blame a girl for trying," and the search continued.

In the course of Madeline's social intervention, a kinship had grown between them that would weave itself far into the future.

Kim continued to exploit openings as she ushered her car down the busy freeway. The sky was clear, and warm South Bay sunlight flooded down into the two-seat convertible. A salty bay breeze swirled around them behind the windshield, whipping Kim's brunette hair into a whirling tornado. Kim's Type-A personality was in charge behind the wheel.

They were now little more than twelve hours away from seeing the results of years of research and development deployed to clamoring MyWorld customers all across the globe. As they flew down the busy four-lane, Kim's bronze face was radiant with happiness and satisfaction. Madeline shared her happiness.

Over the buffeting wind and hum of the engine Madeline shouted to Kim, "You look so cheerful today."

"It's been almost two years, Madeline. Two years," Kim

emphasized, "since I started work at Obyavit and now the worldwide launch of the next generation MyWorld is hours away. The team worked hard during these past twenty-two months. I'm really proud of them." Then, after a quick glance over her shoulder, Kim accelerated the bright yellow sports car across two lanes of traffic and onto the sweeping loop that connected the 101 with the Montague Expressway. Reaching between the seat and the door, Madeline gripped the seat as lateral forces pulled at the car and its contents.

The years of work Kim had devoted to her research, the slogging through grant applications, the begging of endowments for funding during her post-graduate work, were behind her. The payoff was near. The realization of what all those long days would be worth was only just then sinking in. The last two years of testing in the Czech Republic had been a strain, an endurance test. Now, the global launch was upon them. Finally, all the twenty-four-hour workdays and sleeping in the lab with her team was going to pay off. Kim's head was spinning. She even dared let herself imagine a Nobel.

Almost from nowhere their bliss was interrupted, "Route revision suggested, current route no longer optimal, *Beep* - Route revision suggested, there is an accident 1.3 miles ahead, *Beep*." An otherwise perfect start to another workday had been intruded upon by that familiar feminine electronic voice.

Madeline looked down and saw Kim's MyPhone wedged into a slot next to the gearshift. Her MyWorld AmAt app had anticipated she would be late if she stayed to her regular commute and was advising a change. Kim nodded towards it as Madeline reached for the device. She touched *new route*, followed by *fastest* and then tapped the search icon. As MyWorld spoke, it advised them of a new route and that they would be at their destination with ten minutes to spare. Then the electronic voice from Kim's BuyAt app added, "It has been fourteen hours and twelve minutes since your last cappuccino. There are two coffee shops on your new route. Would you like to stop to get a cappuccino?"

Madeline and Kim smiled at each other. Their MyWorld app

was always willing to feed their vices. She barked a firm "No stops," and sped on.

When Madeline and Kim arrived at Obyavit, Kim was not running late, but she was close. Now she had cappuccino on the brain. Kim had scheduled a mid-morning meeting with Bo and was pushing it to the wire.

The MyWorld global launch had been hyped in the world press. While not much had been formally released to the media by Obyavit, no effort was made to hide what was going on in the Czech Republic. Kim's development team had been running a controlled development and test effort in that country. In Prague, where use and adoption was approaching one hundred percent, anyone interviewed offered such unrestrained praise that the media portrayed the use of the pre-release version of MyWorld as an amusing fad. Many had tried to buy a configured device on the black market, but as soon as the GPS detected the device crossing the border it went blank. The planet was eager to get its hands on it.

Kim ran into the conference room at just a minute past her scheduled meeting time. Her hair, the tornadic chaos that had followed her the duration of her commute, was frazzled. She had managed to swing by the on-site Starbucks on her way to Building 1, "the mother ship" as they called it, before her final meeting with Bo. This was the last checkpoint meeting before the launch later tonight. That caffeine-driven side trip was the cause of her one-minute tardiness. The entire campus was electric.

"Sorry, Bo," Kim panted. "Had to get a cappuccino, you know how it is." Almost two years in Obyavit's lab, not to mention all the years before at Cal Tech, had done nothing for her cardio endurance, even though she managed to eke out a couple hours a week to do step aerobics at the Obyavit on-site gym. In her mind just then, she resolved to get in at least an hour a day at the gym, after the product rollout.

"That's OK," said Bo, seated at the end of the room. His feet were up on the conference table and crossed. They were the only people in the cavernous room, "If we're as ready as you say there's no reason we can't relax a bit before tonight's big event."

Kim pulled the lid off her coffee drink, blew once across it to part the foam a bit and then gingerly took a sip. "Yes, we're ready. The aggregation team has over four years of data up in the cloud and the updated Gatherers built into the last three releases of MyWorld are adding six hundred and thirty-five terabytes a day for the Analytics engine to process. At any given moment we are able to anticipate need or want with a seventy-five percent degree of accuracy," her voice slowly rising and quickening with excitement as she spoke. She could barely contain herself. "We can do this based on over two hundred real-time action criteria. Bo, it's so exciting. No matter who you are, or where you are, no matter your cultural, political or religious preference, heck, no matter if you liked blue today and will hate it tomorrow, the Intelligence engine can anticipate what you will want next, with accuracy never before realized. And, the more people who use it the better it will get. It learns, Bo!"

"And you're seeing this?" Bo asked calmly but deeply interested. "I know you theorized this, and I know we measured fractional movement of this kind in the Czech Republic. Why have I not seen this mentioned in the recent reports about the Intelligence? You know how I dislike surprises, Kim."

Kim was seated about halfway down the conference table, leaning forward on her elbows with both hands clasping the brown cardboard band around her coffee drink. "I know, I know. But that's why I wanted to talk to you today." Bo was starting to perceive the level of excitement rising in her eyes as she continued, "We hadn't seen much of a lift in the learning curve either, not until the last three weeks. Then, when it happened, we thought we had exposed a bug somewhere. The improvement in learning and predictive accuracy suddenly started showing an exponential increase. I had the entire team looking at nothing but this for the last week. Bo, it's working better than any of the models predicted. Once the Gatherers amassed the first petabyte of data, the Analytics seemed to become more efficient." Even this amazed her. With intense emphasis on first few words of her next sentence she said, "A quadrillion bytes of data, Bo. Modeling said it might get slower as it gathered more data, but just the opposite. It's as if the Intelligence engine suddenly could see the whole picture. Once that occurred the Analytics didn't have to work as hard." Kim was almost breathless again.

Bo took his feet down off the conference room table and stood. Placing both palms on the table and leaning forward with a restrained exhilaration, he said, "This means once we go live tonight, MyWorld Personal Assistant will only get better and faster at showing you what you want before you know you want it."

"Yes, I mean…" then she could feel a puzzled look smear itself painfully across her face, "Is that what you're calling it?" she said with a halt. "I mean yes, you are correct, as far as we know. We're entering into uncharted waters here, although, every indication is yes. But, is that what you're going to call it, Personal Assistant?"

"Yes, that's what I've decided it should be called," Bo replied dismissively.

"Oh! No, I like it. I guess I hadn't really given any thought as to what it might be called upon release. Back in the lab we called it Fortune Teller."

"A little clichéd, don't you think?" said Bo as he sat back down, still leaning forward with his elbows on the table, head down and massaging his neck. "It's a good thing I got marketing involved, you lab rats would've scared everyone."

Kim frowned playfully at this. She agreed whole-heartedly, the nerds were no good at thinking up product names. She was happy to leave that tedium to Marketing.

"How about coverage," Bo asked, "are we still able to achieve what we outlined in previous reports? I'm planning on saying that we'll be there no matter where you go in the world."

This was an easy question. She had been living and breathing this entire project since long before coming to Obyavit and she had mapped distribution so many times that she knew every dead zone on the planet. "We won't be able to reach the herdsmen in Northern Mali and there are huge chunks of Mongolia and Siberia that are out of reach, but we own any place with 6G," she said confidently.

Bo smiled, "Well, that's just about everywhere. Good job. I knew when I discovered your work four and a half years ago, you were changing the world. I'm glad we convinced you that Obyavit was the best fit for your talents."

"Well, there were a lot of suitors, but you understand technology. I liked that and your vision," Kim paused looking for words, "…and your willingness to devote the necessary resources."

"I saw a perfect fit. I have a vision for MyWorld and your work is making that vision a reality. This will fundamentally change how people conduct commerce, stay informed and socialize. After tonight they will not know what hit them."

They broke their meeting on that good note. From there Bo went straight to the San Jose airport, boarded the largest and fastest of the three company jets and left the country.

CHAPTER 12

"Where are we headed, Kim?" David shouted.

"Over there, that booth. The one with the giant monitors."

Kim was leading the way across the floor of the cavernous vendor pavilion and following close behind was her team, Nalani Rawat and the guys, Wafiq Doka and David Barr. They were at the west coast location for this year's Obyavit Global Summit. The four of them were the brains behind what was to become known as Personal Assistant – or Fortune Teller as they affectionately called it back in the lab. At this moment, they were immersed in the cacophonous roar of a few-thousand technology geeks, all of whom were intent on being the first outside the Czech Republic to get their hands on Personal Assistant.

David was immediately behind Kim. He was a numbers guy; statistics, predictive science and probability theory were his passion. Bo's headhunters had poached him from an insurance software company where he was the Lead Engineer heading up a multi-million dollar revamping of their product architecture. He had graduated from the University of Maryland, at College Park, with a MS in Mathematics, but found numbers were more fun when used beyond the intangible world of theory. That was what led him to software. He had developed an actuarial algorithm that became somewhat of a global standard because of its accuracy. Bo told his recruiters Obyavit needed that talent, and soon after David was an employee.

David was about five-eleven and weighed in at 163. For a guy whose chosen career involved spending many, many hours under the artificial light of a corporate big-foot building, his personal life was an apropos contrast. He was an avid outdoorsman and spent almost all his free time hiking the trails and mountains of the desert southwest. He would spend days in the arid wilderness. This, and other things about David, Kim found very interesting. She once asked, "What do you do out there for so many days, David?"

"I hike, hike and camp," he said absently as they both monitored a performance simulation in the test lab. "I have a list of famous and historic trails I want to hike. Some are hundreds of miles long, and I want to do them all."

"You do this all by yourself? Isn't that a little scary? I mean, bears and all sorts of wild animals. Not to mention any psychos that may be out there."

In the two-plus years that they had worked together, Kim had become intrigued by him in ways she could not quite sort out on an emotional level. Something about David was different and she really enjoyed just talking to him. That and the fact she could never imagine herself doing some of the things he did in his free time. The strangeness of those activities fascinated her.

David chuckled, "It's nothing like that once you're on the trail. It's during the drive there and back that I worry about encountering a psycho. The wildlife wants nothing to do with humans." He paused for a moment, then added, as if it were nothing important, "I carry a gun too, just in case."

"What, you own a gun?" Kim said with an incredulous smile, half snorting and half choking on laughter.

"Shhh! Not so loud." he chided with a sense of embarrassment. Then somewhat smugly, he added, "Yes, I own a gun. And I'm well trained in using it, in case you hadn't gone there yet."

This exchange irritated David a little, but he liked Kim. She could tell he was already letting it slide, so she quickly followed with a boost to his ego, "Sorry, I didn't mean to react like that. It's just that there is so much I don't know about you. I actually admire the fact you can do that; the long treks, camping out in the wilderness all alone and the gun. Wow!" Then after a bit of a pause she said, somewhat introspectively, "I could never imagine myself doing any of that."

"You never know," David responded in a tone that showed he appreciated the save she put forth. "Situations change and the future is full of surprises."

Then a light went on in her head, "Hey, I know it's not mountain hiking or anything, but what do you say we go walking at lunch from now on? I need the exercise and we can talk through issues and ideas from the project, you know, sort of a working and walking lunch."

David smiled, "So, this is how you'll finally rope me into those boring status update meetings you love so much. Clever."

From then on David and Kim were more than coworkers, they were friends. That was all, just friends. At this point in her life, she did not have time for anything else. It was all work for her, so she said.

Wafiq Doka was another member of the team that followed as they moved arduously against the tide on the floor of the Global Summit. From a family dripping with oil money, Wafiq had come to Obyavit from Doha, Qatar. As a child, and then young man, he had attended the mandatory government-provided education from kindergarten to high school before finding his way to Cambridge, where he became a nerd's nerd while securing a Master's degree in computer science. Although his family was well connected with the family of His Highness, The Crown Prince, Wafiq chose to live a life that was closer to the average Arab Muslim. He had volunteered in Syria before leaving for college. There, he spent two years helping to rebuild their infrastructure after a decade-long civil war. This was not always a safe undertaking. He had seen much death as militant groups struggled for their tribal pockets of power.

Thin, almost frail looking, Wafiq wore the requisite thick black plastic glasses and walked everywhere with his arms crossed. All he needed was a lab coat, which he would have had if not for the fact that David made him take it off at the last minute because, "We'll never meet any girls if you go everywhere dressed like that."

Now they were stopped in a open area on the floor of the pavilion, "Can you believe it?" Kim half shouted to Nalani. "And there are eleven other summits the same as this going simultaneously in different cities around the world. Bo sure likes a big splash."

Born third in a family of three, Nalani Rawat fell in behind her older sister and of course her brother, the first-born male. Though she demonstrated the strongest intellect of all three children, she was never allowed to forget she was the bottom child. She resented this. In college, in Bangladesh, she graduated fourth in her class. This was achievement in itself, given the high academic standards and fierce competition within her school. But for all her effort and accomplishment, all her father could muster in the way of acknowledgment was to say, "No one remembers fourth place."

Even her partnership with Arijit Roy was out of necessity in the subcontinent's male dominated society. The technology that Obyavit bought, the technology that became BuyAt, was entirely of Nalani's design. However, in order to grow her ideas and technology at a pace that could remain competitive, she needed a male face out in front. So, she partnered with Roy. He was a good man. He respected Nalani. Thanks to him, they grew fast and became a player in the predictive sales space, but the entire time she felt she was forced to work in the shadows. She saw the move to Obyavit as an opportunity to shine, until Kim arrived. She stayed optimistic, though. Silicon Valley was full of opportunity.

"I have not been a part of anything like this, before or ever," Nalani agreed in her faint but detectable Bengali accent. "Look, over there," she said, pointing to a vendor booth with five sixty-inch LED displays. All five screens were demonstrating various features of some new software. "It's another add-on app. They have not yet seen Fortune Teller and yet they anticipate it with their new apps. How can they be so sure, I wonder?"

"Leaks and spies," David piped in. "The vendors here, the ones with apps, sent spies to the Czech Republic to live during the pilot we were doing there, in some cases for up to a year. Once they found they couldn't smuggle the test devices out of the country, they just set up shop and designed their apps in place, right there in the republic."

Wafiq was nodding, "Yes, yes! But they only saw what we chose to show them." Wafiq was proud of this aspect of the Analytics, and you could see it in the twinkle of his eyes. "The Analytics are smart enough to tell a real user from someone running automated scenarios." One of his sub-teams developed the logic for discerning a real user from any non-human activity and he took any opportunity to show his pride. "We're able to prevent false magnification of data by product manufacturers who would try to make it appear that their product was better and more popular than another. My team did an excellent job of ensuring that only data caused by human action is collected."

Kim nodded to Wafiq with a sly smile, "Let's go see what these sneaky geeks were able to produce." The group then squeezed their way in the general direction of the booth Nalani had pointed out across the floor.

§

The North American location for the summit was not far from Obyavit headquarters, in San Jose's McEnery Convention

Center. Obyavit had been in negotiations for naming rights to the center for the past two years, to no avail, and as a diplomatic show of support had booked the entire center, as well as the nearby Parkside Hall, as the anchor site for their three-day worldwide extravaganza.

"Placing the Obyavit brand on a place like this, in Silicon Valley, where people gather to experience technology, would be huge." Bo once said. It instead remained named for a former mayor, a choice that forever puzzled the hardcore businessperson, given the generous sum Bo offered.

Four hours had passed since Kim and her team had arrived at the main pavilion. The start of the keynote address was now just thirty minutes away. Those at the summit in San Jose who had a ticket, all three thousand, were draining away from the vendor booths and filling Parkside Hall. The keynote had been anticipated, hyped and otherwise wrung for all it was worth by the global media for the past four months and this was literally the hottest technology ticket on earth.

Adding to the hype was the fact that the keynote address and presentation was happening simultaneously at twelve venues around the globe. Kim and her team would be on stage in San Jose and would be a part of the global presentation. Roy and Madeline were also a part of the San Jose team, but they stayed off stage, meeting only with the C-Level management of prospective customers.

Bo had flown to Dubai right after his meeting with Kim earlier that day. From there he would deliver the keynote via satellite to all the other venues. The other cities hosting the global summit and keynote presentation were London, Berlin, Istanbul, Moscow, Mumbai, Delhi, Shanghai, Tokyo and São Paulo. All the venues were fitted with a two-story-tall high-definition display and a small army of Obyavit marketing personnel. With the exception of San Jose, Dubai and Moscow, the events were held in large stadiums that could accommodate at least forty-five thousand. Every ticket at every location had been sold. This last point made Bo the happiest because, as he said, "They're coming to me, in some cases at great expense, and then paying me to sell them my product. At this point I think they will follow us anywhere."

It was midnight in San Jose when the lights went down in Parkside Hall and the five-minute intro clip with music began. The clip was pure marketing, showing happy people around the world, a cross-section of society from business professional to farmers, busy families to hip singles, politicians to reporters and educators to military personnel, all living a better, more efficient life with MyWorld and the new Personal Assistant. In some ways, Kim felt it was comical; in other ways, she truly believed the product of her hard work was really all the video said, and more.

In Dubai, just as the clip was ending, the lights came up and an ethereal feminine voice washed out over the audience. It was the same voice at all twelve locations around the globe, speaking fluently in the prevalent local language. The world would ultimately embrace this voice as their own Personal Assistant, and the first thing they herd it say was, "Please welcome Owner, President and CEO of Obyavit International, Mr. Bojanek Tichý."

Bo stepped out onto the stage and was greeted around the world by applause, whistling, stomping of feet or whatever was the appropriate expression of approval. He stopped center stage and waited for the quiet to rise.

"Thank you," he said, his words showing as translated subtitles on the screens located elsewhere. "Thank you very much."

"Welcome to this year's Obyavit MyWorld Summit. You may have noticed it's a little different this year," the audience rippled with subdued laughter. "This global debut is truly that, a global debut. Right now there are just over three hundred and seventy thousand ticketed attendees joining in at various key locations around the world, and to you I also say, Welcome!" A deafening cheer arose from the capacity crowd gathered in DY Patil Stadium near Mumbai, likewise from the forty-eight thousand comfortably accommodated in Sao Paulo's Estádio do Morumbi, and all the other stadium venues. He had already started working the crowd.

Bo was dressed casually, as was his form for these functions. He wore tan khakis and a loose-fitting short-sleeved white oxford shirt that was pressed but un-tucked and unbuttoned at the top, with comfortably worn leather lace-up boat shoes. He strode amiably across the stage, hands in his pockets, and spoke to the audience, "Well, we are about to introduce a revolutionary new product. This product, or service, or software, or whatever you choose to call it, is unlike anything you have seen before. Now, I know there are many of you who have worked hard to see it in advance, and I know there is seemingly accurate information in the press about what this is and what it will do, but let me tell you now, all that is just a hint of what is to come.

"Starting today we will see a turning point in the lives of billions, a sea change in how human social creatures live their lives. Starting today, anyone with a smartphone, anywhere in the world there is a signal, will have the opportunity to live a life more efficient, more organized, more informed and more connected than ever previously imagined. Starting today, it will not matter who provides your service, what type smartphone you have, which social site, search site, email service or cloud service you use, because starting today MyWorld will bring it all together for you anywhere, on any 6G device. And yes, for those who want or need this evolutionary convenience on a traditional computing device, we have you covered.

"You are all very familiar with the MyWorld AtSuite: AmAt, WhereAt, BeAt and BuyAt. We have heard from people around the world how this suite of services has simplified their lives and saved them time and money. The AtSuite removed the blindfold from the eyes of the connected world. But, to us it fell short. Well, no longer. Starting today, we will provide you the MyWorld Personal Assistant; a revolutionary real-time, predictive, personal needs tool. A service that can, to the degree you choose, anticipate your daily needs as you move through life...."

For another fifteen minutes, Bo went on to detail exactly what Personal Assistant could do for the average person. By the time he had finished the presentation there were 1.2 million people with the newly released Personal Assistant completely installed and another 3.5 million either queued or in the process of installing. In the four days that followed, as details of what Personal Assistant was and what it could do spread through the media, Obyavit had over 400 million of their current user base upgraded and an additional 190 million new subscribers. Personal Assistant was on track to take over the world.

CHAPTER 13

The Obyavit Board addressed many issues in the course of directing the company, but only the issue of an underperforming bottom line was taken more seriously than the issue of fear; specifically, fear that your data, your virtual life, was being collected, stored and analyzed.

Of course, there were the conspiracy theorists and the big-brother claims. These were inevitable and had long been anticipated. And so it was almost four months after the summit, following a three-week marketing blitz which showed graphically the breadth of usage worldwide, that Bo's Vice-President and Chief Technical Officer, Brad Winston, went on CNBC to address mounting data privacy concerns.

Obyavit, being a privately-held company, did not necessarily need to talk to anyone. However, a rumor was swirling that a bipartisan committee of the U.S. Senate, which happened to be looking into data and personal privacy issues, was thinking of calling Bo before them for what Senator Ron McBain, R-Arizona, called, "A friendly discussion of the topic." Senator McBain had been photographed using air quotes as he said the word friendly.

The CNBC appearance was an attempt to address public concern. While Kim and other Obyavit staff stood in front of a fifty-five inch monitor located in the development lab conference room watching a live stream of CNBC, Brad was in New York, looking forward to spinning this into a positive.

"Welcome back. I am Michael Ya. I'm joined here at CNBC Global Headquarters this morning by Brad Winston, Vice-President and Chief Technical Officer with Obyavit International, the company known for their widely used software application, MyWorld Personal Assistant." Michael was the Senior Global Business Technology reporter. He had produced several investigative pieces that focused on technology abuses and Brad was anticipating some tough questions.

Michael continued with his preamble, "MyWorld Personal Assistant is by all accounts the most pervasively installed software and service ever in the history of the world. However, its ability seemingly to know your next move, your next desire, your next purchase, has some privacy advocates very concerned. These advocate's concerns center around Obyavit's extensive tracking, storing and processing of its user's data, data that could then be used by government and private parties for purposes other than those that are publicly stated. In this exclusive segment, we hope to answer these and other important questions. Welcome, Mr. Winston. Thank you for taking the time to join us."

Brad Winston looked relaxed and confident in his un-tucked sky blue polo and denim jeans. Obyavit worked hard to maintain the image of their start-up roots. Suits were worn when the circumstances dictated; today, however, Brad wanted to present Obyavit as down to earth and of the people. He smiled a pleasant smile he had just been practicing in the nearby men's room mirror moments earlier and acknowledged his host. "My pleasure, Michael. Thank you for having me."

"Mr. Winston," Michael began, "Obyavit is currently enjoying huge global success with its recent release of the MyWorld Personal Assistant. I think it is fair to say record-breaking success. To what do you and Obyavit attribute this success?"

The real reasons for the success of Personal Assistant were many. Those that Brad would share with Michael and his audience were obvious enough. But there were other reasons, some of which even Brad did not know or understand. That depth of knowledge was limited to a need-to-know basis, and Brad was given only that which he and the public needed to know.

"Well, Michael, I think our current dominance in the portal services market space is driven by the lessons we learned with the original MyWorld service and the AtSuite of applications. By that, I mean the four widely used products we offered, and still offer: AmAt, WhereAt, BeAt and BuyAt. During the five years this suite has been available we have sought customer feedback constantly. In fact, within the past two years the application has come with a way for our customers to communicate feedback, ideas and opinions directly to our product development team. Our familiarity with the voice of the customer is not centric to a particular culture, region or nation; the sensitivity to the customer is just that, sensitivity to the customer. We have taken into account all social, ethnic and cultural aspects. We believe building that level of personalization into the user experience is what has driven, and will drive, our success."

This interview was under a time constraint and Brad's answer, whether intentionally or unintentionally, led right into the subject they both were there to address. Reporter Michael Ya seized the moment, "That brings me to the matter that has become a hot-button issue of late. Many media sources as well as government agencies and privacy advocates in the European Union, the United States and China, have raised concerns about data privacy and data gathering. The general concern revolves around the almost creepy – their word, not mine – accuracy of the predictive and anticipatory features of Personal Assistant. I guess the fear is that Obyavit cannot do that without tracking, storing and using a specific individual's data. How do you respond to that?"

Brad was prepped and ready as he launched into the company line, "Obyavit has seen the media reports and finds them to be an overstatement, if not exaggeration, of the truth. Yes, we are talking with the governments mentioned, but we have been working closely with them for some time now. These discussions are merely a formality and are not the result of any regulatory issues. The personal privacy of our customers is paramount for Obyavit and we work closely with these particular governments and their agencies because their regulations are the most comprehensive."

"Are you implying that if you can meet the requirements of these regulators you have met the requirements of the rest of the world?"

"These three are the most demanding. No other government exceeds them in their requirements."

"But what about the privacy of the individual? You have not addressed this publicly as yet."

"Yes, well," Brad started, "Obyavit uses proprietary technologies that aggregate the general activity of our customers based on where they are in the world and by language. The language aspect is used primarily to make assumptions about regional culture. We also can make assumptions based on generalized population activities over the network at the region level, service provider level, and purchase activity level via key partner vendors. Those types of general activities, in addition to news and video hits for a region or locale, are" --

Michael interjected, "So you're looking at population groups, demographics and bulk regional activities?"

"Simply put, yes. Imagine you are standing above a large city and you can see endless numbers of nameless and faceless people going about their business, buying coffee, shopping, stopping at newsstands and so on. If you are fast enough, and watch long enough, you can plot all this activity. Then, using statistics and impersonal demographics, you can, over time, begin to see patterns emerge. This is a very rudimentary explanation, but at the concept level, that's it."

Michael was not convinced and it showed in his face as he led into his next question, "OK, let's say it's that straightforward. Personal Assistant is nevertheless scary accurate. I just can't see how the degree of predictive accuracy being demonstrated by your product can be achieved based entirely on the scenario you've described."

Brad smiled, "Do you use Personal Assistant, Michael?"

"Yes, yes I do."

"And have you linked it with your social network sites?"

"Yes, of course. The degree of integration is incredible."

Brad paused and smiled at Michael's last remark. That was a free endorsement right there on national TV. How much better could it get? "What about other add-ons, ours and third-party applets? I'll guess you've found value in some of them?"

"Sure, there are some that have proven very helpful," Michael was wondering where Brad was headed with all this.

"Then you'll know that each of those add-on apps have their own data privacy agreements, as well as security settings, that explain and control the amount of personal information those apps are allowed to track," Brad explained.

"Isn't that a bit misleading?" Michael asked with a flat tone and expression.

"Well, Michael, Obyavit recognized early on that in order to establish the dynamic level of partnering needed, an all-encompassing privacy policy would not work. As far as data privacy is concerned, we only dictate that add-on apps, ours and anyone else's, meet the regulations of the countries within which we operate. It is up to each customer to read and understand the privacy policies, as well as what data is collected. Each app offers sufficient controls such that the customer can manage what data is collected."

"Many of the largest handlers of electronic user data are or have been subpoenaed to supply specific and bulk user data to the NSA and other government organizations under the Foreign Intelligence Surveillance Act. I have to imagine that Obyavit is not immune to these requests. Can you tell us the type of data requests Obyavit has received?"

"All I can say to that, Michael, is that to the degree we are required by law, Obyavit complies with those requests. We are, however, working with a consortium of corporations that are impacted by this to provide greater transparency into the issue. That said, we can't provide data not gathered." What Brad failed to mention was the ineffectual nature of the data security settings. In order to get any useful functionality from Personal Assistant you had to give away data. If you did not give up your data, you essentially got nothing useful from the service.

"Well, then, I guess that's a word to the wise: check your settings." Reporter Michael Ya then paused half a second to look for his off-camera cue, "We're almost out of time, Mr. Winston, but before we go I'd like to ask if there's any truth to the rumor that Obyavit International is in talks to bring the company public on the NASDAQ?"

Brad smiled and looked down, letting a faint chuckling spasm escape, "No, none at all. Bo Tichý believes that staying a privately held enterprise allows for a greater degree of creative flexibility. Nope, there is no IPO in the future of Obyavit."

Michael also smiled. He smiled as if he and Brad had just shared an inside joke, then turned to his guest and said, "Thank you, Mr. Winston, for taking the time to stop by." He then looked squarely into the camera and announced, "Coming up next, Carl and Jim will be looking closely at the economic impact of rising tensions between Pakistan and India as well as in the Korean Peninsula. So stay tuned."

There was a five-second pause as they both sat motionless until a voice from behind camera two rose slowly, "And… we're clear."

The two men stood and two sound technicians came over to begin removing the small microphones hidden in their shirts. Michael extended his hand, "Thanks, Brad. That went very well."

"My pleasure, Mike. We needed to get this message out and Bo appreciates your providing the opportunity." Then once again chuckling and smiling he asked, "What was with the IPO question? Where'd that come from?"

Michael smiled back, "Yeah, that. Well, I needed one unscripted surprise in there. Besides, it is a business news network. Maybe it'll distract the critics."

They parted and moved on to their respective upcoming appointments, smartphones in hand. Michael's was already telling him where he needed to be, how late he was, which way was fastest and asking if he wanted to post a comment on the interview to his social network or his Chatter account. Brad's was doing the same thing, except it was suggesting brief text messages about the interview he might want to blast out to his 2.5 million Chatter followers. Brad's Personal Assistant was also reminding him that his anniversary was next week and he had not yet bought his wife a gift, and was dutifully recommending various things she would absolutely love to receive on that special day. Personal Assistant may have just saved my butt yet again, he thought to himself. As he walked away shaking his head, he whispered, "God, I love this thing."

PART 3

THE DISCOVERY

§

CHAPTER 14

It had been almost five years since the introduction of Personal Assistant, five of the most profitable years in Obyavit's history. In that time, the world had fallen in love with Personal Assistant and Kim had fallen in love with David.

Everyone who worked at Obyavit, including Kim, had witnessed the world of the consumer and the world of commerce benefit from that which she had spent so many years of her life working on. Commerce saw value in being a resource within MyWorld; being available for the consumer so they could sell what the MyWorld user was going to buy became the new paradigm. The more social Chatter there was about your product the more often you would pop up when Personal Assistant predicted the need would arise.

Beyond the arena of commerce, the same forces were at work. At a time when the citizens of the world were increasingly distrustful of traditional media and news outlets, social media was fast becoming the channel of choice for staying on top of matters deemed important. Personal Assistant users around the globe had taken to Chatter, MyBook and other social media to report and consume events they saw as central to their daily lives. Surveys began to show that a majority of the global population, relying on the personalization and preference automations of Personal Assistant, read and *acted* upon the tailored news feeds they received. News feeds that were based on criteria determined by their personal choices and actions were directed to them through Chatter, MyBook, blogs and any other social media source that best fit their individual preference.

This did not go unnoticed. Surveys by media research firms, which were funded by Obyavit and provided only to Bo and the Board, began to identify this shift towards non-traditional media. As this shift towards short, un-vetted news bites grew, experts monitoring societal trends raised concern that this lack of direct personal involvement in the gathering of information to shape one's own understanding was alarming. Dr. Ghazali Jaffar of the Malaysian Institute of Social Economic Studies said, "The lack of individual personal effort in the gathering of information on societal events could lead to a one-sided and closed-ended view and understanding." Others concurred, agreeing that the potential for accelerated social trending, another term for actions feeding actions, seems to be very high in a globally connected social environment where filtered information was pushed at the population.

Of course, these views were counter to those professed by Bo. In a counterpoint statement via Obyavit's marketing arm, Bo was quoted as having said, "Busy people in a busy world have the right and the need to use any technology available to expedite their daily lives. Any attempts to take that away simply amounts to censorship and will bring the global economy to a screeching halt."

Bo knew he could always count on a few things. The fact that society often, and without critical thought, bought into technology as a salvation was one of those things. That, for him, was easy to predict.

§

Kim was up early. It was a lazy Sunday morning and she was sitting on the back patio in yoga pants and a jogging top holding a cup of coffee with her head cocked slightly. Her face held a contented smile and dreamlike gaze as she watched her index finger trace the black uppercase D on her coffee cup, over and over. It had been a good night and a morning run had left her energized.

David and Kim had been seeing one another for almost two years. It had started innocently enough. After a late night in the lab, wrapping up around ten, they both decided to head over to a nearby diner, one of many places in the valley that catered to the irregular hours of technology geeks. They had been working together three and a half years by then but had never been alone, just the two of them, outside of work. That night, Kim realized she wanted to know more about the man sitting across the table from her.

As the night progressed, Kim learned more about David's romance with the great outdoors. When he spoke about the open expanses of the Arizona and New Mexico desert, it was with wistful desire. She treasured how he did not try to push himself upon her, and because of that, she wanted to bring him closer. He adeptly balanced his driven inner technologist with a shy, quixotic outdoorsman. And, as he described saguaro-studded mountains in the Northern Sonora Desert, Kim drifted back to her father's Mexican ranch. She felt the warmth of the familiar with David.

Walking to their cars, Kim began thinking how comfortable she felt that evening. She realized it was not a sudden thing. Her eyes finally brought into focus something that had been slightly recognizable but distant. She was in love, and David was the guy. It was the middle of the night in a restaurant parking lot in Santa Clara and she felt warm sunlight. Three simple words floated through her, each one strumming cords of delight; "I'm in love."

"I'm in love," Kim blurted out as she and Madeline sat by themselves in a corner of Obyavit's main café a few days later.

"With who? Do I know him?" Madeline asked. "Is it Jonathon, from the BBQ a few weeks back? I saw you two talking. You looked good together."

"No, no. Madeline, I wish you'd stop doing that, those attempts to... socialize my social life. I mean, they're all nice but... Anyway, it's David!"

"David?" Madeline asked, her face going blank, her mind frantically thumbing through the mental rolodex of potential partners she kept for Kim. "David! David Barr?"

"Yes," said Kim, dreamy and lost, her eyes staring off into space.

This girl is gone, Madeline thought.

After dinner that first night, David kissed Kim on the cheek before they parted and she simply blushed. It was not about the conquered and the conqueror. David was in love too. Things moved slowly and David was respectful. His not driving towards just one objective, rather giving time towards their growing closer – almost the antithesis of his work personality – made her love for him deep. Soon they were seeing each other constantly.

David soon began sharing his passion for nature and the outdoors with Kim. He had unlocked something inside her. They spent many of their weekends and days off camping and hiking in the wilderness of the Southwest. She learned the ways of an outdoorsman quickly, how to live with what she carried and how to use what was available to survive. And it was during a trek into a southern Arizona wildlife refuge that bordered Mexico when the danger of an untamed environment made itself known to Kim.

It was in early November, Kim and David were three days into a six-day hike through the Cabeza Prieta National Wildlife Refuge. Their journey would take them within eight miles of the international border before turning east through the Organ Pipe Cactus National Monument and then on to the town of Ajo. Following a dry unnamed arroyo down through the desolate Mohawk Valley, dry autumn breezes eased south as the occasional small herd of desert pronghorn observed guardedly from a distance. The crush, crush, crush of their footsteps in the gravel was punctuated by the distant scream of a red tail hawk riding high on thermal currents. Steady, even breaths and the faint trill of antelope squirrels mingled in the parched air. Under her wide-brimmed hat, Kim took in the quiet isolation and thought of David and herself as lone survivors of some terrible accident. With him, I could survive, she thought.

David suddenly stopped.

"What is it?" Kim asked.

"Listen."

Kim turned her head and faced the same direction as David. She strained to hear but the endless pressure of a wide and silent autumnal desert was all that met her ears. Then something. A rolling echo scratching hollow across the desert floor, immediately followed by another. Gun shots.

"How far away do you think?" she asked.

"Far, but they're getting closer."

"What do you mean?"

"The first one was much fainter, much farther. The last two were closer. Follow me."

Kim and David moved along the wide gravely pathway until they found easy egress from the dried gouge in the desert floor that was their trail. They moved through the riparian thicket of jojoba, acacia and cholla for several yards, then stopped in the weak shade of several palo verde trees near the edge of the bushier growth. It was a place where they could see for miles over the stunted sage and creosote that dotted the open flats. The shots echoed again. They were getting closer.

David pulled out a pair of binoculars. In the distance he saw dust rising and soon they both heard the dull growl of heavy off-road trucks, and more shots. He and Kim were about three hundred yards west of a poorly maintained and seldom traveled dirt-covered cut in the desert landscape that posed as a road. A black four-by-four Chevy Suburban heading their direction was chasing a silver four-wheel-drive pickup. Someone in the Suburban was shooting at the pickup.

As the trucks grew closer, David put his hand upon Kim's shoulder and pulled her down as he squatted even with the brush line. More gun fire. The silver truck was now visible in the distance. A plume of reddish-brown dust billowing and drifting east in the breeze trailed it. As the black Suburban became distinguishable, the silver truck dropped out of view as it moved across the undulating desert floor. Kim knelt frozen in the heat of the November sun as David watched events unfold through his binoculars.

Moments after the Suburban dropped out of view into the same depression, the silver truck then reappeared, but something went terribly wrong. It disappeared in its own cloud of dust. David saw wheels and the underside of the truck. What looked like plastic-wrapped bales of hay went flying in all directions. The sound of large angry engines had ceased.

It was quiet for a moment as the dust cloud moved away. Then there were voices shouting, some in Spanish and some in English. In the vacant dryness of the open desert, the voices carried. As David watched, Kim listened.

"You. Get up. Get up and stand right there. Don't move." a voice ordered in Spanish.

A man stood up. He was some distance from the overturned truck, out in the desert away from the road and covered in dry brown dust. Another man, a well-dressed dark man shouting in Spanish, stood partly behind the driver's door of the Suburban with a handgun drawn. A third man, a white man with blond hair and sunglasses, stood behind the black vehicle. He shouted to his partner, "Ask him who he works for. Who's he runnin' for?"

"Who are you working for?" the man with the gun asked in Spanish.

"I don't work for anyone. I'm independent," said the dust-covered man.

David whispered to Kim, "I can only understand half of

what's being said."

"He says he doesn't work for anyone. He says he's independent," Kim whispered back.

"Geez, I forgot. You're pretty much Mexican."

"I'm American, just like you," she reminded him. Kim was not ashamed of her Japanese or Mexican heritage, but she hated the labels that most white European descendants liked to put on people.

The two men at the Suburban were engaged in a barely audible discussion when more shouting in Spanish erupted, *"Sorry, my friend, but we don't believe you. Make it easy on yourself. Tell us who you work for."*

"No, sir, I do not work for anyone. I am just a poor man trying to make a little money for his family," the lone man answered.

David leaned into Kim, "What's going on?"

"The two, they keep asking him who he's working for. He says no one. Says he's just a poor man trying to support his family."

"I bet it's a drug deal, a rip-off or something. Bet that guy in the silver truck stole their shipment."

"Really?" This prospect seemed obvious now that David had said it.

"Heck, yeah. Did you see all those bundles go fly'n when that truck rolled? Drugs of some kind. I'm sure."

"David, I'm scared. This is dangerous," said Kim, her voice rising in pitch to a shaky squeak of a whisper.

David lowered the binoculars, looked over and saw Kim, her jaw clenched and her lips a tight flat line. "Hey, no one is expecting us to be here," David said quietly. "Look at them. Watch their body language. They're watching the sky and the road for Border Patrol. Two fools hiking up a dead riverbed 30 miles from the nearest paved road is the last thing they'd look for. Just stay low and quiet." He squeezed her hand and she relaxed a little bit.

Kim eased up a little so she could better see what was happening. It was like a scene in a movie, a man standing alone at gunpoint in the middle of nowhere. Scenes like that never ended very well, she thought.

The man behind the Suburban was in a rage. Yelling and pounding the hood of the black truck with his fist he said, "I don't fucking have time for this. He's lying. Tell him I'm gunna ask him only once more, goddamn it. If he doesn't tell me, he's fucking buzzard meat."

The man with the gun turned towards his target, *"My friend, the white boy here, believes you are lying. He says you are a dead man if you do not tell us who you work for."*

As they spoke, Kim whispered the translation to David, "He says they'll kill him if he doesn't tell who he works for."

"I'm a dead man either way," the lone man responded.

"He won't talk."

The man with the gun turned to his partner, briefly cocked his head, and shrugged a shoulder slightly. That was all the discussion necessary. There was a single pop. Kim burst with a short scream. The lone man dropped as if he were a marionette cut from its strings.

David grabbed Kim and together they went flat onto the rocky desert floor. She was shaking as he held his hand tight over her mouth. Fast breaths came though her nose accompanied by a high-pitch whine that kept pace with her breathing.

"Shhhh! Shh, quiet," David whispered quickly. Then more slowly, "That's it, shhh. I'm going to take my hand away but you gotta be quiet. Can you do that?" He looked at Kim and her eyes were wide and wet. She nodded. As he peeled his hand away fast, frightened breaths and strings of saliva came forth.

"Wha… What are we going to do? I don't want to die here in a barren desert," Kim said in a fast whisper.

David held a finger to his lips then raised himself high enough to see over the brush line. Bringing the binoculars to his eyes, he could see the two men tromping about. They were gathering up the large bundles that lay tossed about and loading them into the back of the Suburban. He lowered himself down next to Kim.

"We sit tight. They're gathering up the cargo that flew out of the silver truck. Then they'll probably leave."

After about thirty minutes, Kim heard one more pop. "They're making sure the dead man is dead," David said. Then the two men did exactly as he had predicted.

It took David and Kim another four days before they hiked out of the wilderness and into the town of Ajo. They reported what they had seen to the local federal Fish and Wildlife officer, the same one that issued their permits to be on federal land. Days later FBI agents interviewed them at work and by the end of the day they were folk heroes among the nerds and techies at Obyavit. With David's help, Kim quietly researched her choice and then applied herself fully, learning how to use a .357 Smith & Wesson M&P. As she became more proficient she could not help but think she had taken a first step, but towards what she was not sure.

CHAPTER 15

Remembering an arid southwest but feeling the kiss of early morning humidity on her skin, Kim drifted back into the present. Looking past David's coffee cup and its black letter D, she noticed that the irrigation system for the lawn had recently run. The grass smelled fresh and moist ahead of what would be another unusually hot day. It must be Tuesday. She took another sip of coffee, smiled for her thoughts of David, and set the cup on the small table next to her. She picked up her new MyPhone and checked her daily feeds:

> *Kimiko's* Social World – Daily Feed:
>
> !!! MyWorld five-year *demographic usage reports* due today
>
> !! It has been 5 days 6 hours since you last called your first level friend Remy – *Call now?*
>
> ! It will be *your mother's* birthday in 11 days 17 hours
>
> ! You need to buy gasoline this morning, go *here* to see area gas prices

Jack and Sara will be at *Coffee Bean Café* at 11:30 AM

Pakistan Tests Rocket through Indian Airspace

Rocket crashes into Arabian Sea – India Lodges UN Protest

47 of your friends, 2462 of their friends and 155106 of their friends find this important

245,000 Students fill Washington Mall

Students Protest Ten Fold Increase in Tuition Costs

127 of your friends, 7874 of their friends and 488188 of their friends find this important

Scientists Forecast smallest winter ice cap ever recorded

Northern Passage to remain open all year

62 of your friends, 2914 of their friends and 136958 of their friends find this important

There is a 50% off sale at *REI* in four days

4 of your friends, 15 of their friends and 31 of their friends plan to go

14 of your friends, 122 of their friends and 672 of their friends just bought the new *MyPhone 5*

You have 14 *new friend* requests pending

After a few moments, the patio slider opened. David stepped out, a towel wrapped around his waist and a goofy smirk on his face. "Hey."

"Hey," she said back. "I was wondering if you were ever going to get up. You look like hell."

David dropped into the patio chair on the opposite side of the table and took a long slow sip of Kim's coffee. "For some reason I wasn't able to get much sleep last night," he said with a grin.

Not looking up from her MyPhone, Kim smiled. "No one held a gun to your head. Besides, look at me. I've already jogged five miles."

117

David was holding Kim's coffee with both hands as he sat slouched in the patio chair. His elbows were propped on the armrests, the cup of coffee positioned just under his nose. They were blanketed in dapples of shade and light as the morning sun made its way through the trees along the back fence. "What's going on in the world?" he asked, nodding and pointing at her MyPhone with his pinky finger.

"A lot of the same, some of it worse," she said. "A new group has formed in Europe. This one is calling itself *Nations for the Nationals*. They appear to be about expelling all the North African immigrants that fled into the EU when Egypt, Libya, Tunisia and Algeria formed the United North African Republic. What a mess."

"Yeah, that was pretty ugly," said David, as he absently contemplated the evenly cut grass before him.

"And North Korea is getting all worked up again. This time they are saying South Korea and Japan are planning to invade, but of course, those two deny it. Doesn't it seem like more and more people are working in a coordinated manner just to berate some other group or government? I mean, the human race has never really gotten along on a global scale, let alone at a national or local level, but the speed and frequency at which these networks and groups form seems faster."

"Yeah, I guess," David said, as he set the coffee cup down, not yet fully engaged in the conversation. "It could be because there are just more and more people on the planet. Then there's technology, which makes everything happen faster. Most of it's just hot air anyway. One fad blogger rants for a couple months on the topic du jour, then all his followers get bored and latch on to the next fad blogger."

"I suppose. I think it's worth studying sometime. There must be something there causing people to be drawn together. You know, connecting like that in such large numbers for such a specific purpose. It has to be something more than the addition of technology."

"Maybe, maybe not," David said. "Take what happened a year and a half ago in Venezuela. The people were fed up with the government corruption. They obviously were going to rise up at some point. Social networking just acted as a tool to expedite the process."

Kim sat forward quickly and threw David a cold stare, her jaw tight and her eyes narrow. He knew that was a sensitive subject with her and she was not about to let him off the hook just because he was half-asleep.

"Hey, don't gimme that. The media was full of crap trying to link that to the Fortune Teller. Besides, an independent investigation by the WPC exonerated Obyavit, and MyWorld. They found no connection between the Fortune Teller and the coup in Venezuela."

She sighed and relaxed. "Sorry, it's still a touchy issue for me."

"No kidding." Switching the subject for his own safety, David said, "What's on the agenda today?"

Maybe she *was* a little over-sensitive about the whole Venezuela coup and subsequent investigation by the World Privacy Counsel. That was a stressful time. It seemed that there was always someone taking a shot at the Fortune Teller, trying to portray it as Big Brother.

She settled back into her chair and tried to take her mind elsewhere by thumbing through the features of her new smartphone. It was a prototype the MyPhone lab had given her to test. As she sat there reviewing her schedule for the day and scrolling through her MyWorld app she was thinking how it was to live her entire waking, working and social life through it. It made her feel more in control of things. She looked up from the device and over to David. "I need you to gather and summarize historical performance data today."

"Is this for that five-year status meeting coming up?"

Kim nodded once, looking back down at the screen of her phone. "Yes. I still have a lot of work to do on it by next week and I need that data to finish out things. Here, I'll send you a summary of what I need."

She made a few quick motions with her thumb and forwarded David the summary.

"Thanks. How do things look? I know our quarterlies were good, but did we hit the five-year numbers?"

"Oh, yes. We hit the numbers. That's not the question. The question is by how much did we beat them? By all accounts twenty-eight percent of the world population uses Personal Assistant on a daily basis."

"I knew it was something close to that, but I didn't know what we were targeting."

"Hey, have you noticed that Bo seems a little less available lately?" Kim said, setting her smartphone down on the patio table.

"No, not really, but then I'm not a big shot like you. I don't think I even show up on his radar."

"Now, now, you're important to me," she said with mock sincerity. "Seriously though, it's like he has his focus elsewhere. He seems content to let our team run the MyWorld and Personal Assistant roadmap meetings without input or guidance. It's like he's not interested in where we're planning to take the platform."

"Yeah, I suppose he has seemed a little more distant. But why wouldn't he be focused elsewhere? The stuff we're on is in maintenance mode for the most part. Sure, we add new features and services, but that's all modular plug-and-play stuff. He's probably got some other next-best-thing percolating."

"Perhaps." But she could not let it go. "We met just the other day and he showed only a limited interest in our work. He was asking if anyone was running other instances of Fortune Teller. You know, multiple consoles, separate isolated user bases and such. I told him no, of course, because no one is. I explained that there was only the one instance of the Analytics and the Intelligence. Then he asked an odd question. It caught me off guard because it was something I had never given thought to before."

"Well, I'll bite. What did he ask?"

Kim looked at David, feeling the same puzzlement she felt when Bo first asked. "He asked how I would know if there were another instance running somewhere else in the world."

David took another sip of coffee. Then scratching his ear he said, "How would you?"

"You know, I don't know."

"Well, he probably asked because he's worried about competition. Probably wants to know if we can spy on them or them on us. We had better add that to the to-do list."

"Yeah, you might be right," she said, thinking aloud. "I don't know why that worried me so much. I'm not sure what would happen if there were another Fortune Teller console running. They'd likely start to influence each other, skew each other's results."

"You mean make their predictive qualities less accurate?"

"Yeah, yeah, probably..." Then her smartphone beeped. Picking it up and snapping back to life, she blurted, "Damn! I have to get into the office. Would you mind picking up some stuff at the store? My Assistant app says I'm running low on a few things. Your frequent sleepovers are running me out of food. I'll share out my shopping list to you."

"Yes, dear," David said. Then with a playful grin he added, "I'm liking all this sharing. Maybe we do a little more sharing later?"

"Give it a rest. What is it with you man creatures? Everything turns to sex. I'll bet you can't go an entire day without thinking of it. I'll bet you can't go an hour."

"Probably not."

Kim got up, leaned over and gave David a quick kiss on the forehead. Nodding towards the bath towel that had fallen away, leaving David completely naked in the patio chair, she said, "I'm going to take a shower. You might want to wrap that towel around you a little more securely there, Mr. Free-And-Easy."

"Yes, dear," he laughed, remaining seated while sipping her coffee and enjoying the feeling of the warm morning sun on his skin.

CHAPTER 16

Bo had begun maneuvering. For him, the time had come and the pieces were in place. Before he could move any farther however, he needed full access to Personal Assistant, Kim's Fortune Teller. He needed different people with a different purpose on that system. He needed people who would do as he instructed, without question.

Kim, Wafiq, Nalani and David were in the second-floor executive conference room just down the hall from Bo's office late on a Friday afternoon. It was their weekly checkpoint meeting but Bo was unusually late. Far more so than his usual two or three minutes.

Kim was seated across from Nalani, putting the final touches on the reports David had helped her prepare over the past weekend. Wafiq was pacing back and forth along the glass wall, oblivious to the goings-on in the commons that stretched below him. These big status meetings with Bo always made him a nervous wreck. He hated them.

David was sitting three seats away from the rest of them, casually thumbing his smartphone, reviewing the stats on the services Obyavit was providing those government agencies, both U.S. and abroad, that used Personal Assistant as an interagency tool. Nalani had a distressed look contorted onto her face as she feverishly typed with both thumbs into her MyPhone. They were there to talk about the quarterly numbers and performance stats, or so they thought.

About the time Wafiq was starting to get on everyone's nerves with his nail-biting laps along the wall of windows, Bo entered the room and in somewhat of a rushed manner said, "Sorry I'm late everyone. A 'fence mending' call ran a little long. Let's get this show on the road. What do you have for me, Kim?"

With a couple of quick thumb movements on her smartphone the flat-screen wall monitor lit up with four large graphs in each corner of its screen.

"Well," Kim said, "I have the historical performance data for the past quarter, year, three years and five years. Based on the targets set in…"

Bo cut Kim off mid-sentence and said, "That's fine. That's fine. I've already pulled all that data and I'm happy with what I see."

Bo had not made eye contact with Kim since entering the room and she had not failed to notice this. This was not like him. Another odd thing, or new thing, or different thing, she could not quite categorize it in her mind, was that while Wafiq, David and she sat attentively as if well-trained dogs, Nalani was still head down working her MyPhone. She had what appeared to be agitation, or distress, on her face. It was as though she had not even noticed Bo had entered the room.

Bo stood and walked towards the flat screen display upon which Kim's charts were showing. "Nalani, if you wouldn't mind," he said in a mildly admonishing tone as he passed behind her.

Nalani turned and looked up, holding the screen of her phone out as if to be showing it to him. She started to say with a restrained sense of urgency, "But I need to…"

"Not now." said Bo, cutting her off in a manner that was direct, impatient and just short of a verbal backhanded slap. Nalani responded only with a nod and a pained, worried look. Pulling her MyPhone back slowly and looking at it once more, she placed it and both her hands in her lap as she gave Bo another less than subtle pleading look.

"I'm up to speed on what I need to know with regards to how Personal Assistant is performing in the marketplace," Bo said as he looked up from Nalani and continued his way to the front of the room. "Since I have you all here together I think this is as good as a time as any to share with you some changes I want to make with the team. I think you'll find this shifting of focus to be beneficial to the future of our various initiatives as well as offering opportunities for the team to create new, innovative products."

David, Wafiq and Kim were looking at each other with expressions of confusion, surprise and curiosity. Nalani stared at the center of the conference room table in front of her.

"What sort of changes?" Kim asked.

"Effective immediately," Bo said, looking at her for the first time, "I want you, Kim, to lead Wafiq and David in tightly focused R&D efforts related to our Intelligent Home and Office initiative. You'll be chartered with advancing the predictive aspects of Personal Assistant into a service that will be directed at automating functions related to the security, environment, maintenance and entertainment in our users' and clients' homes, offices and businesses. You'll start by developing a strategy with Marketing. We'll meet twice weekly for status updates. Are there any questions?"

Before she could recover from the sense of bewilderment that had overtaken her, Wafiq meekly raised his hand and asked, with a quiet apprehensiveness, "What about the work that is in progress? There is an investigation into anomalies surrounding authenticity of some news-related feeds. There is also a possibility that some social groups are being created and led by a means other than live user direction."

Thinking more clearly, Kim added, "Yes! Bo, as I've been reporting this to you recently, these anomalies are worrisome. I think we are only a few weeks away from being able to identify this and put a fence around it." She sounded somewhat exasperated as she outlined these concerns.

"I'm aware of these efforts and I will be putting Nalani and a handpicked team from the existing staff to take over those efforts as well as further ongoing day-to-day management of Personal Assistant."

Kim felt as if the air had just been knocked out of her. She was speechless.

David snapped to his feet, tipping his chair over backwards as he stood. "What? You're putting Nalani in charge?" he said, unable to suppress the incredulous tone in his voice. Catching himself, he turned to Nalani and added, "No offense, Nalani. I mean, it's just that this thing is Kim's baby." Then turning to Bo he continued, "I'm just not gettin' any of this. What are the drivers? Why are you doing this?"

Bo turned to David and in a well-practiced tone of reassurance, he said, "Now David, relax. This is an enormous opportunity for you three. The home and office automation arena is huge and Obyavit is poised to dominate that space. With a strong team focusing its full attention on it, we can be the first and only provider for these types of services. Everything we do and every move we make we do for the company. Remember that."

David retrieved his toppled chair and sat back down, putting forth a face of appeasement. It all sounded as though it were so much manipulative corporate bullshit, David thought. He might have bought it were it not for those last two words – remember that. The way Bo said them, not conciliatory or reassuring; no, when Bo told David to remember that, he said it and meant it as a threat. Of that, David was sure.

Then, as if to ensure the discussion went no further, Bo took two steps forward to the head of the table and said, "Good. Kim, you, David and Wafiq turn over any work in progress to Nalani and her team by the end of the week. I don't want any hold up on you getting your attention turned towards this new assignment." Then, stuffing his hands into the pockets of his trousers he turned towards the conference room door and began to walk, "If there are any further questions feel free to set up time with me through Jan. Nalani, come with me, I want to talk further about your new assignment."

Bo left the door open on his way out. Nalani, giving a halfhearted shrug to her former teammates, followed immediately behind. David rose, crossed the room and closed the door. "What the hell just happened?" he said to Wafiq and Kim.

Kim was resentful but did not want to admit it. "I knew this day would come. It had to. It's a natural progression, David. I just wish we could have finished our investigation."

Wafiq, in his usual passive way, sat quietly shaking his head as if willing it not to be.

"Bullshit!" David said as he stormed to the opposite end of the room where Bo usually sat. "That's just bullshit. Nalani? Come on. No freakin' way. Something's up. Bo's not been the same this past year. Something is going on and I think Nalani is part of it. Kim, you said it yourself the other day and it's been bugging me since. There is a definite difference in how we're being managed by him. His relationship with us, as compared to a year ago, has changed. And Nalani, she seems to be getting more and more of his time."

Kim had her elbows on the conference table, her forehead in the palms of hands. She was speaking to the table as she addressed David, "I don't know, David. I think you're reading too much into this."

Wafiq was still shaking his head no to her words when he finally spoke. "No. No, Kim, David is correct. You have been quite busy, maybe too busy to notice. You both have been preoccupied with other matters." He paused, smiling sheepishly. David and Kim looked at each other with poorly hidden expressions of surprise and guilt. Wafiq continued, "Nalani has become Bo's favorite. She spoke of it proudly to me many months ago. I envied her. Now she is very hush-hush. She meets with Bo secretly, often, in person and on the phone."

"You seem to be well informed about what's going on at the interpersonal level here in our little family, Wafiq," David said, smiling a flat, irritated smile. "What else do you know?"

"Not much more. The team working under Nalani is not from here, not from headquarters. One is a Czech hacker and another is an Israeli hacking scientist, both of them are from their respective governments. There are North Korean and Cuban government hacks too, both of them are also scientists. That is all I know."

Kim's jaw went slack at this news. She had been taken off her project, what was essentially her life's work, and replaced by Nalani and four scientific hackers. What was going on? Why were these government mercenaries hired to come in and run their fingers through the guts of her creation?

She needed to find out what Bo was doing. Her work had potential for ill-use but they had been careful to design in guards and fail safes against attacks from the outside. This threat, if it was a threat, was coming from inside. She needed to know if she could still trust Bo.

With this final realization, a sudden resolve came to her. She would not let go so easily. She needed to know what was happening to her Fortune Teller. Standing and looking at Wafiq and David, she said in a way that both men knew not to question, "Come on, we've got work to do."

CHAPTER 17

The day Bo brought Kim and her team together to announce that Nalani Rawat would take the lead role on the Personal Assistant project was the day when the course of many things began to pivot and turn. The gears of upheaval began to spin with a speed and force that would appear unstoppable when anyone finally noticed.

The world was changing. It was becoming more unsettled, more impatient for change. A trend towards larger and more regionally focused *activist* social groups was growing. Technology advanced, and the connected society increasingly accelerated the movement of its ideas, opinions and beliefs.

Of course, there were the tens of thousands of people who liked a particular soft drink, song or charitable cause, but something more was happening. There seemed to be a recognition, even acknowledgement, among some experts that this was happening. This perception was faint among the general population, however. Society was nearing a tipping point and its grasp on independent thought was about to succumb to the pull of capricious social acceptance among one's thousands of friends, friends of friends and other network connections. An electronic social tide was rising and its flow was sweeping up everything in its path.

Bo, whose mind worked at a level and in a direction that few could appreciate, had modeled these social and societal behavioral characteristics years before. Bo knew there would come a time when a shift could be made to occur. Just over eleven years ago, four years before he hired Kim, he had theorized a time when a trending society could be led by their likes and dislikes, their fears and hopes, their values and judgments, their superstitions and beliefs. In the time since, every move he had made with Obyavit had been in support of arriving at that moment. The moment was upon him.

When Bo left the conference room that late afternoon, he was in a hurry and Nalani was right on his heels. Madeline was on her way down to accounting after having stopped by Jan's desk for information on Obyavit's printed materials vendor, but Jan had already gone home for the day. Bo was stepping into the hallway just as Madeline was passing and he walked right into her.

"Oh, jeeze! I'm sorry, Madeline," Bo was saying as Nalani, who was looking down at her MyPhone, plowed right into the both of them, dropping her phone onto the carpeted hallway.

"I am so sorry. Please forgive me." Nalani repeated as she stepped back, bowing and supplicating, embarrassment flushing her dark brown skin.

"Damn it, Nalani! Watch where you're going," Bo said before catching himself. "Well, I guess I'm guilty of the same."

As they stood there for that moment, Madeline could see that Bo and Nalani were engaged in something together and were in a hurry to leave. Over Nalani's shoulder and through the conference room door she could Kim seated with her face in her hands as if she were exhausted. Wafiq, his back turned to Kim, stood behind her staring out the wall of windows. David did not appear to be in the room. Bo was again apologizing.

"Please excuse us, Madeline. We both are late to a phone

conference in my office and are obviously distracted."

He then gave Nalani a cold stare, and with a cock of his head and the movement of his gaze, a clear nonverbal signal, directed her to pick up her phone. As she did, Madeline could not help but notice a text message in Russian, and a partially composed response, also in Russian. Nalani stood and tucked the device into the pocket of the white lab coat she wore.

As he began to turn and leave, Bo said over his shoulder, "Come along, Nalani, we're late. Have a good weekend, Madeline. So sorry for the bump."

Nalani scooted past Madeline, bowing three more apologies as she went, and then turned to catch Bo. The door to the conference room door latched shut as Madeline watched the two move down the hallway towards Bo's office.

Madeline thought that the entire exchange had felt very odd. There was a lie hidden somewhere in what had just occurred, and there was something peculiar in what she had seen in the conference room. Something had happened.

Madeline turned and began to walk. Trying to catch Bo and Nalani while maintaining a degree of professional composure was difficult. As they turned past Jan's desk, she knew she would not catch them. Madeline continued to her office, not at all comfortable with what she had just seen.

Bo entered his office with Nalani following close behind. As he sat, he pointed to a leather chair across the desk from him. "Sit," he said. It was half command, half request. He sat back in his chair and turned, looking out the windows while devoting his full attention to her. "Now that I have refocused their attention I see no reason for any further delay. Our customers are very anxious to have the services I promised them in place. Can you still meet our timeline?"

Nalani looked pleased, as though she were a student who had won the favor and attention of a teacher. She almost squirmed with excitement. Always striving for a degree of notoriety in the eyes of power, it had constantly been just beyond her reach. The most recent years under Kim had been hard. Once again, she had felt overshadowed, working hard but never getting the credit she felt she deserved. Bo saw this. He saw the frustration and growing resentment and he cultivated it to his advantage. He lifted her up, he moved her into a position among a privileged few who knew the real goal. She was finally where she wanted to be.

Sitting across from Bo, Nalani was feeling confident and sure of herself. "Yes, meeting the timeline will not be a problem. The team we've assembled is capable, and fast."

"Good. I want this in place in eight months or less. Then I want our customers to be fully trained and operational with their respective regional consoles in the two months following. I understand you are already coordinating with each government's..." Bo paused, catching himself, "Rather, each customer's representative?"

"Yes. The Russian Federation has supplied two analysts from their Federal Security Service, both experts in social terrorism. India has sent two more analysts from the Ministry of Home Affairs. Actually, they are from the MHA's Intelligence Bureau and specialize in Afghani and Pakistani socio-societal counterintelligence. Bo, the Arab League wants five trained. Five! I only found this out last night. With the U.S. and British coalition wanting four trained, I will need more staff. That is what I was trying to tell you in the conference room."

"More staff? Let me see what I can find. I'll talk to the recruitment team and our friends at Homeland Security. They will know the right people for these openings. You are careful to maintain the secrecy of these new customer engagements, aren't you?"

"Yes," Nalani said, firmly and professionally. If she were a soldier speaking to a commanding officer, all she would have needed was to add the word *sir*. "The customers do not know of each other, except of course the Americans. My assistant and I will work with their management team, keeping them apprised of the others. We will also start tracking Kim and her team when they are on site or online.

We want to know if they come in contact with anyone involved with our effort."

Bo nodded his approval, then spoke with an intensity that caused a brief and inexplicable chill to her core, "Do not underestimate her, Nalani. She may be naïve, but she is the most knowledgeable person on the planet when it comes to Personal Assistant. She *cannot* be allowed to know what we are doing; neither she, nor anyone outside the customers and your small team must ever know this new system. Understand? No one!"

"Yes, Bo. Yes, I understand."

CHAPTER 18

A few days after being exiled from their primary roles on the Personal Assistant project, Kim stopped by Madeline's office to talk through her frustration.

"Hi, Madeline. Do you have a couple minutes?" she asked, leaning half through the doorway of Madeline's office, one hand on the lever, the other on the doorframe.

"Hey, Kim. Sure. Come in."

She entered the office and closed the door behind her. Her face wore the tired look of resignation and defeat. She took a seat across the desk from Madeline.

"I just came from Bo's office," she said.

"Did you go to talk about the reassignment?"

Kim nodded, not looking up.

"I'm guessing it didn't go well." It was a safe guess.

"No. No, it didn't. Madeline, I think there is more to the story than he's telling me. I mean, he goes on about the Intelligent Home-Office being the next big initiative and wanting his best players on it and so on, but it doesn't feel right."

"I know, Kim. I get the same feeling."

"Wafiq says there are Czech and Cuban computer scientists working with Nalani; others too. He said Nalani is being very quiet about it. She won't even look at me any more if she can help it. I cannot tell if Bo picked her or if she asked. I don't think she would have done that, though. I just can't believe she would do something like that."

When Kim revealed what Wafiq had said, Madeline told her how Bo and Nalani had bumped into her in the hall right after their meeting, how she felt things were not as they seemed. "Kim, whatever this is, it's being kept from the board and the operational executive committee. I also don't know whether Nalani was drafted or what. But whatever the case, it does seem that she is involved. I can try to find out more from this end. Whatever is going on, it is doing so under the guise of Obyavit. Some activity will eventually show up somewhere. If it does, I'll find it."

As Madeline spoke, she could see Kim's forehead furrowed deep in thought. As soon as she broke off, Kim looked up and straight at her, her brown eyes clear with strength and a plan. Standing to leave, she said, "I can track them through the system. If they're building or altering something, the guys and I will find it."

"Be careful, Kim."

"We will. We'll hide ourselves in all the noise that Intelligent Home-Office project will make. They'll think we've been too busy to do anything else," she said with a crafty smile.

§

Kim, David and Wafiq made great strides in using MyWorld to interface with a proprietary environmental controls system that had been designed by another team at Obyavit. Over the following six months, they put in place a full-sized prototype of the system at PayPal headquarters. The PayPal buildings, already fed by solar power, could now sense how many people were in any room, office, hallway or indoor space at any moment. Individual user MyPhones, through Personal Assistant, had been configured to track their environmental comfort preferences. This added feature would then supply the data necessary for PayPal's environmental systems to run at optimal efficiency based on the average person's comfort, light and electricity needs. This was another victory for Obyavit, given the ever-advancing state of the global climate deterioration. "Clean and Green," Bo called it. Another big win brought forward by Kim for Bo. But while the three of them toiled quietly and under the cover of Bo's make-work project, Kim was discovering that her work, and Fortune Teller itself, was being used in ways she could not fully fathom.

Kim and the guys were secretly digging around Obyavit's systems. They had been conducting a covert assessment of Fortune Teller ever since their reassignment. They had to be careful, and that meant the going was slow. Wafiq's skills were best suited for this type of activity, but it was Kim who knew best where to look.

§

Kim sat in her office on the second floor of Building 1. It was with plaintive interest that she watched the changed weather the region was now regularly experiencing. Slow-moving thunderstorms punctuated by fierce lightning were the new monsoonal summers of the northern coastal latitudes. As the towering cumulus formations grew, then emptied themselves on the landscape below, she too could not help but feel empty, a shell of her former self. What she had found the night before had kicked the wind out of her and left her grieving. She had been sitting there at her desk, looking out the window at the lightning from the thunderstorms moving east across San Mateo Bay, since 11:45 PM. It was now 9:20 AM. Her spirit had been stepped on.

David and Wafiq were down in the lab in Building 3. They

were at their usual workstations. Engineers were nothing if not creatures of habit. Anytime the guys were in the lab, Kim could walk straight to them blindfolded. Whether now or a year from now, they would always be at the same stations. David sat near the front of the lab. When Kim finally made it down there, she went over to see him first.

Awake for over 24 hours, she must have looked in bad shape. "Damn, you look like you haven't slept in three days," David said when he greeted her. "What's up?"

Kim might have smiled on any other day. David felt the weight of that lapse hit him immediately. He knew she must have found something. He also knew she would not talk to him about it there, in the lab. That was why she walked all the way over to where he was in Building 3, no phone call, no email, no text.

"Let's meet at one o'clock," she said, not looking at him but out through the lab windows into the rest of Building 3. "Bring Wafiq. I'll be sitting at the edge of the fountain across from the Starbucks in Building 2. Eat lunch like normal." She turned and left.

Kim had been around those two long enough to understand and anticipate each of their predictable quirks. For Wafiq, normal was him in his office over in Building 1 with the door shut eating food from his homeland. Every day he ate a lunch that was prepared by a local Middle Eastern restaurant and delivered to the lobby. "It keeps me sane in this insane world," he would say.

Lunch for David was also a well-rehearsed routine. His daily ritual centered on specific vending machines strategically located in each building. These machines were selected for their content variety, high rate of turnover – therefore, they were fresh – and their proximity to his standard routes of travel. Only after they had finished their lunches, as one o'clock approached, did David go by and gathered up Wafiq. Then, they walked the shortest and most direct route to Kim.

She waved to them from her seat in the shade, a nondescript cement bench nearest the fountain. The fountain was by no means a small affair. A statement to Bo's ego, he had spent a million dollars on what most said resembled a wet smartphone. It was a twenty-foot high rectangular, black obelisk over which ran, evenly on all sides, a thick curtain of water. On the face of the obelisk, under the water curtain, was a large screen on which simulations of various MyWorld apps would display, the same as a giant MyPhone. Kim had picked the location because the noise of the water was loud. It would allow them to talk without being overheard.

"Hey," David said with a worried look. He could tell something serious was about to unfold.

Kim had met with them once before in this location. That had been just after their reassignment, six months before. They had laid out their plan as to how they would traverse Obyavit's systems and networks looking for the real reason why the Personal Assistant project, its lead and its staff, had gone dark. Since then, their meetings on this matter all had occurred well away from work and no communication on the topic ever utilized technology. David and Wafiq sat on either side of her. They all three faced the fountain.

"There's been a murder," Kim said. She had just blurted it out as she leaned forward, putting her elbows on her knees and her palms over her eye sockets, rubbing them tiredly.

Wafiq and David looked as if they had been slapped. "What!" they yelped simultaneously, trying unsuccessfully to suppress their surprise from casual observers.

"What are you talking about? Who? When?" David asked.

Realizing what she had said, and how she had said it, she sat back shaking her head. "No. Nobody. Not who. What. They killed the Fortune Teller. They replaced it. It's gone."

Wafiq leaned forward, "Kim, I do not think David and I quite understand what it is you are saying."

"Yeah, what are you saying, Kim?"

Nearly babbling, she said, "My design, our work, it's gone. Listen, whatever is out there is not the same thing that was there six months ago. Not even a month and a half ago. It's a copy, a fake, an imposter. It's been completely reworked. It acts different. It functions different. I haven't figured out just how much yet. But it's not the same Fortune Teller. I was in the code last night verifying people movement data for the prototype at the PayPal campus and I discovered that my tracks are gone. Your tracks are gone too. The coded signatures and notes I showed you how to imbed into the code, they're gone. So I started following a few routines and I found new input paths into the predictive logic and the decision-making logic. There are other new input paths also. I don't know yet what they do. I only just found this last night."

"How can that be? My app is fine, acting the same, as I would expect. I just checked on the way here," David said, not quite grasping the enormity of the situation.

"That's what I'm saying, David. From all angles, it looks fine, but that's not the Fortune Teller. *That* is not the Personal Assistant project we left six and a half months ago. It has input paths that were never there before, that were never supposed to be there."

Wafiq, always quiet and always thinking, stood and faced them as they sat on the bench, "The input paths obviously mean they want to provide it with something more than the data it gets from user actions, choices and communication. We might be able to figure out their purpose by mapping them. Trace where they come closest to, or touch, the decision-making processes we understand. But…"

Kim was starting to follow his thought process. As he trailed off she became worried. She stood and looked directly at Wafiq. "But what? You're worried about something."

"My security features," Wafiq said, frowning and shaking his head. "The same ones that kept developers from hacking the system during the Czech pilot five and a half years ago, the same ones that watch for data manipulating. It will be looking for people like us, people moving around in there."

David, finally rising from his seat on the bench, added, "But you wrote those things, man. Surely you still hold a set of keys that'll get us around undetected."

Wafiq shrugged. "If Kim says they have erased our tracks, then my keys, as you so cleverly put it, may not work. Using them may even get us detected quicker."

"We will need to step carefully at first," Kim added.

"Yes," Wafiq said. "They may already be aware that you know. The discoveries you made last night may have already been noticed."

"We probably should wait a few days then," she decided.

But David was ready to jump. She could see it in his eyes. He did not say anything then, though she knew he would protest later, when they were alone. She could see in his face that he did not think waiting was the right thing. She could trust David. He would not question her publicly. She could also trust that he would later.

They did wait before making any other movement into the system, and that proved wise.

CHAPTER 19

It was almost midnight and Kim was hidden away in her darkened house. Illuminated only by the light from her laptop, Kim was walking code that lay deep within the Fortune Teller. A sweltry rain was falling across San Jose. The fine droplets sounded as though sand were being blown in soft waves against her windows and roof. The patio slider was open and she was shrouded in a humid blanket of blackness. A viscous breeze banked and swelled about the room. Draperies moved as if they were ghosts trying to free themselves from the death grip of merciless curtain rods. In what felt like clandestine seclusion, she found the changes. Alterations left by those who corrupted her Fortune Teller. She began to see what she had begun to suspect and as she stepped deeper into the code, she stepped out of the darkness of denial.

In the weeks that followed, she, David and Wafiq carefully ventured in and out of the huge and complex system. It was not until two months later, as South Korean and Japanese public sentiment against North Korea mounted and threats of nuclear retaliation from the north loomed, did she begin to see how the Fortune Teller code was interpreting and guiding those events. That was when she saw what the new input paths allowed outside influences to do. She was horrified by the potential the system held.

§

Trying to give the appearance of just another day, Kim stopped by Wafiq's formal office in Building 1 after lunch. Together they walked across to the lab in Building 3. Wafiq went back to his workstation where he had been earlier in the day, logging in and picking up where he had left off. His lab workstation was located against the back wall. To get there, which for anyone unfamiliar with the layout might prove difficult, he had to first move through an administrative area near the lab's secure entrance where there were located several shared workstations and a few cubicles, two of which belonged to David and Kim. Beyond that, there were three large test bench areas where various hardware prototypes could be hooked into the system. Once through the front area he had to navigate a labyrinth of server racks, disk, tape and optical storage racks and switch racks, being careful to watch his step, as at any place along the way sections of the raised floor might be missing, leaving a two-foot-square hole. At worst, one would suffer a broken ankle; at best, a bruised ego. Once past the forest of racks, he walked towards the south corner, past the two loud environmental control units and into a lone eight-by-eight cube with four-foot-high walls. Wafiq had chosen this location because, "This corner behind the A/C is the warmest place in the lab… and I like the solitude."

David noticed Kim the moment she entered and walked towards her, "I found something, not sure what. I left notes for Wafiq. Let's go see what he thinks."

David and Kim wound their way back to Wafiq's secluded cubby. As they emerged from around the environmental control units, he looked up as if he were expecting them. The two arrivals grabbed chairs that had been pushed up against the wall and scooted around Wafiq and his workstation.

"I take it you've seen what I left for you?" David asked.

"Yes, I did," Wafiq said. "It appears to be a hook for delivering canned instruction sets into the system. Its location is significant because unless you're at this branch," he said, pointing to text on his screen, "it would be impossible to detect that the actions taken by the Fortune Teller were not driven by data from the Gatherers and Intelligence."

David nodded, "That's what I thought but I knew you would be able to tell for sure."

Kim leaned forward past Wafiq and highlighted a block of code showing in one of the several windows open on the large, flat monitor. "So this, from here to here. They're able to merge coded input with the aggregated data from the Intelligence. What are you monitoring in this window over here?"

Grabbing the window and bringing it forward, Wafiq said, "This is my lookout. I keep it running when I'm in their system just in case someone, or something, is watching."

"Shouldn't we be using this too?" David said, in an irritated and impatient tone.

"Yes, you should and you'll find it in your secure mail. I only finished this just before lunch. There are instructions but you both should understand what to do once you see it."

Kim brought the discussion back to the adulterated copy of the Fortune Teller on the screen, "I see where this section of code merges its input with the data stream. But where does it get input from?"

Then David said, "From what I can tell, it seems to be accepting instruction from another system. See here? There two discreet input paths right at the top. It appears one is for human input, typed, spoken, emailed, texted and such. The other appears to interface with an external automation and database. Is that what you see Wafiq?"

"Yes, David, but look here, further upstream in the code. They are monitoring what the Fortune Teller is going to do and pulling that data into their system."

"And that's how their automation determines what to send back in," Kim said, finishing Wafiq's thought. "That's where they're altering outcomes, damn it! That's where they're deciding for themselves what the user should do."

Kim's anger felt like a glowing ember resting against her sternum. She was again realizing how blind she had been to the negative possibilities. Her stomach tightened around this comprehension. As she scanned the code she had architected, she began to enumerate the many other locations in the system where these dark tentacles could intrude.

"Wafiq, go to the news feed section," Kim said, still running the possibilities through her mind.

"I am already there and yes, it's the same. So is the location section in BeAt. They are in all the key decision points. Their work is rather good. They were remarkably thorough and complete," he said with an intonation of ironic respect.

The guys were looking to her, their team leader, but she was blank, lost in dejected thought. Why? What was the purpose? *Control*, that's the purpose, you idiot...

Kim cursed her tunnel vision of a happy efficient world. How could it have reached this point so fast? When did they start working on this? For how long has this been influencing people's lives? And who? Who made this happen?

She knew Bo directed it. He probably designed it. He possessed the technical and analytical depth. But who could realize the implementation so quickly? Who? Nalani!

§

Nalani had seen Kim and her team moving about inside Personal Assistant. She had been watching for a week, in a panic, wanting to tell Bo but afraid to do so. Eventually she did tell him.

She blew through Bo's outer office with such a stride that she caused the leaves of the potted plants to rustle and sway. She was beyond Bo's door with a slam before Jan could be sure who just went by. With her back to the closed door, her fist still clenching the handle and her brown Bengali complexion looking a pale and frightened, anemic tan, she issued a breathless hiss, "She knows."

Bo, seated at his glass desk, looked up from the tablet he was holding. He was making movements with his thumb and index finger across its screen when he paused to size up Nalani. She was a panicky mess standing pale and wide-eyed in his office. "I know," he said. "They all three know. They have for six days now. They know everything."

This news melted Nalani. Her shoulders dropped and an expression of confusion sagged across her face as she stepped forward from the door.

"Sit," Bo said, in a soft and comforting tone. Nalani sat.

Bo looked towards Nalani. Not looking at her, but looking through her, as though she were not there, as though she were already gone. Then returning his gaze to the tablet he held, he said, "The last of the customers left today, did they not?"

"Yes. Iran."

"Good. And, they're all running their programs and initiatives independently I presume?"

Nalani was puzzled by this line of questioning, "Yes. There are a few questions, but the staff is managing that. Overall, the various deployments have been very successful and the customers are already realizing results. They have been trained well and need very little support."

"Very good…"

"But, Bo," Nalani interrupted, "all of this will be in the reports I will present in two days. What should be done with Kim and her team?"

"Yes, yes, that. Let's see, they made initial discovery six days ago," Bo said, as if enumerating project phases. "They each then took sections of the system and traced through it line by line every night for the next five days. They had conclusive proof, a clear understanding, earlier today. Let's see… David spotted it first at, yes, right here, 12:45 according to the log. He confirmed with Wafiq as Kim back checked. They've been watching it ever since."

The information Bo had just shared with Nalani caused her stomach to tighten. As she processed the information further, the tightness evolved into a yet unrecognized fear. He knew what she had come to tell him.

"H-how… How did…"

"How do I know? Or do you mean how did I find out?"

Nalani gave a slow unblinking nod to either or both questions.

Bo set the tablet he had been holding down onto his desk and stood, speaking as he did so, "I should think in this instance the question should be mine. You didn't just find this out, did you? You've known this for five days, haven't you?"

Nalani's eyes followed Bo. She did not move, she did not speak. His manner was changing; the frenetic intensity that she had witnessed a few months ago was evident in his expression as he moved around the desk towards her.

He began to shout, not giving her any chance to speak, "Five days, Nalani, five goddamned days. Now? Now you finally come to tell me? What were you doing? What were you thinking? Why the hell so long?"

"But, Bo, I…"

"Shut up! Shut the fuck up. You no longer have anything to say. In fact, by your own account you are no longer needed, are you? No. No you're not."

There came a faint clicking noise from the door, a mechanism of some type. It sounded as if it locked, and the electrochromic glass windows switched to an opaque dark gray as the lights came on low. This sudden change in her surroundings caused Nalani to jump. She was before a very powerful man and he was very upset.

"I gave you my trust and you've failed me," Bo continued, his voice quieting but sounding no less aberrant. "I gave you instruction that no one should know of this effort beyond the team and you have failed me. I gave you the opportunity to come to me and tell me of this breach and damn it, Nalani, you failed me. I cannot trust or depend on you any longer. You are done."

From the far end of the office, Nalani heard another noise. One of the six wood veneer panels that made up the wall just beyond the two couches, the second panel from the windows, opened. It was a hidden door, and behind it opened an elevator. Stepping out of the elevator were two men in black suits and dark glasses wearing earpieces. In what seemed as if it were one fluid, choreographed dance sequence, they moved quickly and with purpose across the room to where she sat, their shielded eyes trained unflinchingly upon her. They grabbed her firmly by each arm and proceeded to lift her easily from the chair. As she felt herself elevated from her seat, she felt a sharp pain in her outer left thigh. Darkness clouded her eyes and Bo's satisfied smile was the last thing she saw as the man on her left pulled a syringe from her leg.

PART 4

THE EVENT

§

"When it happens, they will have been led there by hope,
or pushed there by fear" – Bojanek Tichý

CHAPTER 20

Obyavit was under public siege. The sound of military vehicles and the smell of spent diesel hung in the air around the company's campus. It had been this way for a month or more, ever since the news story was leaked by a government informant.

The property inside the twelve-foot-tall wrought iron fence that surrounded the company had been transformed into a military forward operations base. It was in complete lockdown and the National Guard was shuttling employees, those that had stayed on, to and from work using well-armed, glossy black helicopters with tinted windows. They were flown to the air base at Moffett Field then driven away in nondescript vehicles to meet up with their families, who had been relocated for their safety. Obyavit's infamy had laid suspect many other technology companies as well. The ripple effect was being felt across the planet with "occupations," as they were called, occurring at almost any location belonging to a technology company rumored to have played even the smallest part in the scandal that was beginning to frighten the world.

The morning it broke, Bo immediately called a meeting of the executive staff. He needed to react, for them as well as everyone else who might be watching. Roy and Madeline, and the rest of the Board, wanted to know what it meant. He said that it was meaningless and of little consequence. Madeline thought otherwise.

The story had been reported by a Canadian news agency. A reporter from the agency had been approached in India by a U.S. government employee who was on loan to the Indian government. The informant had leaked that government entities within India had been using social media to incite anti-Pakistan sentiments. The resulting story had become a call to arms for a nervous public. A public who increasingly felt too much data was being kept on them.

So they, the many, guided by the invisible hand of the social network, formed their groups, built their coalitions and fought in unified oneness for their right to be individuals. Everything was going as planned.

§

They sat in a dank unlit room far down a narrow alley that snaked away from the crowded market in Surat. Through a half-shuttered window nearby, an illuminated curtain of dust hung in light that sliced across the table between them. With acute trepidation, they contemplated each other.

The American had chosen the tea den because it was hidden deep in the recesses of an older part of the city. A place where other Americans, whether tourists or those stationed there, would never venture. He had not considered that he and the Canadian, shiny with their pallid sweaty skin, stood out in stark contrast among the neighborhood's residents. There was no cooling air-conditioning where they met. A four-bladed fan overhead, which turned at a pace so leisurely that flies could land upon its blades, receiving a free circular ride over their intended victims, was the only respite from the oppressive heat. The air, weighted with a close, almost suffocating smell of the seldom bathed, held a musky odor, cut sweet by the many different teas that sat in open bins behind the counter. It was foreign and familiar, exotic and personal.

"You can't use my name, or anything else that would give away my identity, you understand?" said the diminutive man who looked like a small town CPA or a timid male librarian from the midwest. He was repeatedly looking back over his shoulder. "What I've seen and what they plan is dangerous. It needs to be stopped."

The Canadian reporter was walking a psychological line between nervous excitement and skeptical apathy as he sat across the table from the American. Fingering his MyPhone below the table and out of view, he had not yet turned on the recorder function. He wanted eagerly to either get on with it, or to get out of the dingy teahouse where they were meeting. He was not at ease in his present surroundings. "It's okay, it's okay, no one will ever know we spoke," he said, trying to calm the American.

"You can't say you got this from an American source in India either. If you do that you might as well plaster my name all over Fort Mead."

"We won't. If I can corroborate what you say from additional sources there will be no need to mention anything. Can I record this?" The Canadian then revealed his MyPhone to the man across the table.

"Yes, but give it to me. I'll set it, voice to text, and no voice print. You can have a transcript but you can't have my voice. I'll get it started, then we set it here," the American said, tapping firmly on the center of the table with a hooked index finger extending from his pudgy white fist. "You don't touch it until we're done, then I'll end it and save it. Got it? We do it this way or no way." When the Canadian's face betrayed his skepticism, the American added, "I'll set it to display as we talk. So you can confirm that it's transcribing. You can verify the file after, while I'm still here. Okay?"

"Okay." The Canadian handed his phone across the table.

The American placed the phone on the table so the Canadian

could see and read the screen as he spoke, "Okay. What do want to know?"

The Canadian sat back, "Well, you contacted me and you seemed pretty agitated. What has you so worried?"

"You know the Venezuelan coup that happened a few years back, and how the World Privacy Counsel investigated Obyavit?"

"Yes, I worked on part of that story for the agency. There were accusations of mass sociogenic persuasion by way of subliminal media influence, but nothing conclusive was found."

"That was the first major test, an experiment. The WPC didn't find anything because member country representatives were told not to find anything. Obyavit... Well, lemme backup. A secret part of Obyavit, a part most of their own employees don't even know about, has weaponized their MyWorld Personal Assistant app. They've adapted it to influence social direction and near-term trends. They're using all forms of social and traditional media to do this. Venezuela was their proof-of-concept. Essentially, influencing the Venezuelan people to carry out a coup was simply a demo for prospective governments."

"What?" the Canadian said, coughing as he blinked through the thin layer of sweat that had accumulated across his brow and was dripping from the dark swaths under his eyes. "How is that possible?"

"Well, you know how Personal Assistant works, right? I mean, you use it, right?"

"I use it. I know vaguely how it's supposed to work."

"Okay, so in Venezuela we..."

"Wait, wait! What do you mean 'we'?"

"I was a NSA contractor then, on loan to the DOD, Department of Defense, working in the Psych-Warfare unit. I specialize in suggestive manipulation; media based, you know. I'm not a prophet or anything. Anyway, using an isolated copy of Personal Assistant on U.S. Military computers, we mapped likely scenarios based on the Venezuelan population's propensity for action. Once the system found the outcome we wanted, we backtracked it to see what conditions needed to be in place for it to occur. When we understood what the social and political environment needed to be like to start the chain of events, we set the system loose and it guided public opinion towards those conditions."

"But how is that possible? That many people can't be that unaware. Surely there are those who could see this?"

"It's a numbers game the whole way through. We accounted for a fifteen percent skepticism rate. But, get this. Throughout the entire experiment, we saw not more than ten. Actually, it was averaging about eight and a half percent. Not enough to deter the masses from the planned trajectory. It was like leading sheep. As the system transformed public opinion, our military supplied arms to the rebel forces and counterintelligence courtesy of the CIA and Britain's MI-5."

"So how's it done? How do you influence the opinion and mindset of ninety to ninety-two percent of a population?"

"That turned out to be surprisingly easy, largely because Obyavit did such a great job at making their product so prevalent. MyWorld and Personal Assistant have become a thing people cannot live without. They're practically woven into society. The system is an omnipresent delivery mechanism. News feeds containing manufactured news articles and videos, fake social bloggers, bogus Chatter texts sent out from influential people, all this blanketing thousands and thousands of followers, friends and network connections. The system can keep all of these chats, posts and whatnot alive in the cyber-sphere just long enough to be read and remembered. Then they mysteriously disappear minutes, hours or days later. Let your mind run for a minute."

The American paused a moment, mopping sweat from his neck using a dingy gray handkerchief. He then continued, "Regional viral videos made by so-called amateurs are another means. Oh, and of course there's the old standby, fear. Gauging and exploiting regional and national fear is remarkably easy. Bloggers blog about fear, news sells on fear and people post and Chatter about fear constantly. We used web crawlers to identify and aggregate this socially documented fear. Then it's sliced and diced based on geography and other demographic data. The *customers* then feed the fear, they guide it and use it to a desired advantage. Heck, history has shown that populations are most easily managed when they are afraid and the system is adept at regulating their fears and hopes. It provides them with just enough hope to be controlled."

"I'm not following." The Canadian wanted to keep the American talking, providing more detail.

"Yeah, hope. Not too much, though. It's a balance. Too much hope and they will feel empowered. Too much fear and they give up. Oddly enough, most of how the system approaches the fear angle is based on the past successes of some of the world's oldest religions. Heh, imagine that."

"But what about influence from the rest of the world? The web is interconnected with the rest of the planet. Surely people outside a region can see activity that seems out of sync with reality?"

"That's easily enough controlled with filters and other domain name restrictions. Remember the Iranian intranet several years back, and the way China switches on and off access to anything beyond their borders they deem a national threat? Think of that on a more nuanced and refined scale," said the American. "Now, think of what it means to give that kind of power to the nations you would least like to be in control when the dust settles."

"Who's involved? Who's driving this?"

"Governments, ours and India are for sure. They both have had long-brewing beefs with Pakistan and are trying to provoke them into a cross-border attack or strike on India. The Indian government will use that as an excuse to level the place." And then, with a touch of disgust the American said, "Just like the other wars that will happen soon enough, they'll all be acts of self-defense."

"There are, uh, I mean, will be other wars?"

"Oh yes. I don't know who though, division of responsibility and all that."

"So Personal Assistant and MyWorld are a new source of delivery for a kind of global hate or international bullying?"

"Hate? Not always. But fear, yes. Fear, and enough hope to gravitate the masses to the desired solution for their manufactured fear. That is, desired insofar as it coincides with what they've been led to believe, absent any reasonable facts."

The Canadian reporter was stunned by the obviousness. The simultaneous protests and the well-coordinated news, even the timing and release of pivotal videos that inspired and united or incited and divided, when re-examined more closely there was a plausibility that could not be ignored. The story the American had given the Canadian was huge. It took time though, too much time. It had to be investigated and substantiated with fact. There needed to be evidence enough that it could not be denied. Meanwhile the wheels of the machine were already grinding away. Momentum had built and the tumblers that would unlock an unimaginable future were already falling into place.

CHAPTER 21

Things are getting bad fast, Madeline thought. She and Todd were worried about the kids. Schools were beginning to close because of shortages in both supplies and teachers. Oil prices were skyrocketing due to political instabilities and gasoline was approaching nine dollars a gallon. Food scarcities were also starting to appear as the survivalists along with other doomsayers began stockpiling vast stores of supplies in preparation for what they called the inevitable event that was yet to come.

Social media was alive and surging with a flood of speculation and rumor as media reports fed fear and anxiety. Any postings that spoke of the turmoil were automatically promoted for maximum effect. People began grouping out of fear, common cause, rebellion and dissatisfaction, anything in which they could find hope. The changes occurring – the actions transpiring – were causing each individual to seek support in the comfort of those they could trust, those they could believe. Those similar to them.

"Todd? Todd, where are you?"

"In here, Maddy. In the kitchen."

"Are you watching it? Do you have the TV on?"

Madeline walked into the kitchen and over to the island where Todd was watching the live news on a television that hung on the wall next to the walk-in pantry. She stepped up close to him, very close, and slid her arm through his, holding tight his hand which, until then, had been pressed against the cold granite countertop. "This is becoming very unsettling."

On TV, in split-screen, were live reports from the Punjab state of India and the south-central areas of Queens. In India, heavy fighting had broken out in five fronts along the India Pakistan border. Losses on both sides were heavy and several civilian targets had been hit. There were scenes of grieving Hindu women screaming over the bodies of children, hands raised, palms open. There were men gesturing violently at heaps of rubble that were once schools and temples. Additional reports from the desert region in the Rajasthan state showed a Pakistani armored unit moving uncontested deep into India. The rhetoric from the Indian government was heavy with nuclear threat.

In New York a mosque had been bombed. Social networks were ablaze with rumored reports of Indian sympathizers. The scene was antipode, hysterically grieving Muslim women facing towards the heavens asking Allah why, and angry young men brandishing guns towards the rubble, all seemingly unchecked by the noticeably absent NYPD.

"What do you think it means Maddy?"

"I don't know, it seems isolated but yet it's not. It's not good that retaliation is taking place so far from the fighting."

"It's not good that they're throwing around talk of nuclear retaliation."

As they both stood watching events unfold, Madeline's MyPhone chimed with a new alert. Withdrawing from her comforting entanglement with Todd, she tapped the screen and opened the alert. "Look at this, Todd."

It was a news feed with a grainy imbedded video showing two male figures running from the mosque moments before the front façade exploded into rubble and dust. The article said that a Chatter message written in Hindi was sent with the video attached to the editorial desk of the New York Times through an anonymous account just as the explosion occurred.

Madeline followed the news closely these days. The things that were happening around the world, and in her own country, caused her great concern. It felt as if people were all moving towards some logical destination. The way she saw it, people were uniformly unhappy. It seemed rather simplistic she knew, but there was no other way to say it, no other way to view it. People of the world were unhappy.

People in Iran were unhappy with their leaders. The leaders of Iran were unhappy with Israel. Israel was unhappy with the lack of support from their allies. The Israeli allies were unhappy with both Iran and Israel for their lack of diplomacy. It was one huge dangerous circle of fear and no one was trying to dismantle it.

There was also the circle around India and Pakistan that had once again moved itself front and center in the various media channels. The circle that encompassed North Korea, South Korea, Japan and the U.S. was yet another. They were circles of international unhappiness that involved large chunks of the world. As these circles went round and round in social media they gathered up the emotions and lives of individuals everywhere.

Outwardly, North Korea said it found few benefits in the western world's internet technologies. In that country, only the Democratic People's Agency of Propaganda had internet access. No one in North Korea beyond that particular agency and its party overseers even knew there was such a thing as the internet. A western news reporter once asked a few *average* North Korean citizens about this thing called the internet. Their answers abstractly equated it to a telephone with a fax-like capability. The Democratic People's Agency of Propaganda's knowledge of the internet, however, was deep. Their training came from China and they had learned well how to leverage social media to promote their cause.

By constantly streaming a drumbeat message of looming threat and coordinated global discrimination from their adversaries, the north peninsular nation found believers in its message in the backyards and living rooms of those who would prefer to see their demise. From these sympathetic minds grew the U.S.-based Democratic People's Support whose goal was to further the North Korean message in the west. Soon, however, exaggeration of fact, followed by all-out fiction, supplanted truth, and the situation between the north and the three-nation coalition grew into a dangerous circle of rhetoric and posturing.

There were the lesser circles too, the ones that were not considered geopolitical. Some were big and dangerous, others less dangerous but no less destructive. In her own country, Madeline saw there was now war being waged against everything. Those whose cause was not receiving the political, financial or social priority they felt it deserved were waging a war of principles. There was a war on women, a war on free speech, a war on free enterprise and a war on religion. These caused more circles to form as people found their cause and their cause found its voice. When a cause found its voice, the voice found venue, and as the venue gathered people, the people created conflict.

At the office, Madeline had seen the reported statistics. They showed activity by social groups, discussion forums, news groups, bloggers, Chatter feeds and every other means available. The numbers were showing that Personal Assistant was facilitating the circles she saw appearing. Social groups formed, followers joined and the Gatherers and the Intelligence assembled and aggregated their data. Performing the analysis inherent to its design, Personal Assistant found for its users the groups, the causes, the interests and the news that best matched them and their entire history of internet activity.

The rejection rate was astoundingly low. Trending showed that if Personal Assistant suggested, recommended or automatically subscribed someone to a group, that person was ninety-two percent likely to stay with, follow and interact with that group. People were trading critical thought for the speed of immediate self-validation. Belonging to a social group or cause had become the benchmark of friendship, an electronic stamp of social approval.

It became clear to Madeline that this grouping of people into circles was increasing and compounding at an alarming rate. At the same time, she also wondered if she were the only one to have reached this conclusion. There were few others at Obyavit who had access to the same information that she did.

As she stood next to Todd watching the news unfold, Madeline also skimmed the Chatter texts, comment posts and news feeds that were coming in with such remarkable immediacy, almost as fast as the live news happened. She needed to understand better the mechanics before she brought this to the attention of the Board.

While Todd went over to the dining table and readied the children for school, Madeline scheduled a meeting for herself. She needed to bounce her observations and thoughts off the one person who knew the most about these types of phenomena. She needed to talk with Kim.

§

Later that day across central Europe the group Nations for Nationals began a full-out assault on North African immigrants who had fled the war and strife of their homelands. Using social group pages and short hard-hitting Chatter messages, @NforN had gained support from the large populations of unemployed. The workers' unions, who had been unable to organize the immigrant labor, also joined the circle. Regional groups were organizing massive and unruly demonstrations that were causing large-scale deployment of riot police, who brought teargas and water cannons. The demonstrations in Germany, France, Belgium and Italy attracted groups of anarchists who, during what were peaceful marches on the embassies of LNAN, the League of North African Nations, began overturning cars and setting fire to them. Then, in an assault that was coordinated real-time over Chatter – #RiotsforPeace, #ChaosforCalm – and simultaneously video blogged on MyTV, the embassies were stormed and set afire. Their staff and officials were either killed or injured and the walls were spray-painted with racial bigotry. The speed and quality of the coverage by amateur video bloggers and citizen reporters was unbelievable. The situation in Europe, and by extension through the net to the rest of the world, had become extremely tense very fast. LNAN, with their recently expanded military capabilities and short-range nuclear missiles, lodged a formal protest with the United Nations. The complaint contained the threat of military retaliation if the rioting continued and the citizens of LNAN were further persecuted.

And so it went. The circles of unrest around the globe were growing fast and efficiently. Because, after all, that was what Personal Assistant understood its users wanted.

CHAPTER 22

The First Day (Day 0)

David was late. He was supposed to be down in the lab with Kim but was instead up in his office crawling out of the cot where he had gone to sleep the night before. He had been on site since the protestors showed up a few days ago. So had others. Young single nerds like Wafiq, Kim and himself had volunteered to stay so those with families could work from home until the mess outside was cleared up. There was no reason to leave. The only person he cared about was here, on site, with him.

Wafiq and Kim were down in the lab keeping the server room up and running. Somehow, Bo had persuaded the U.S. military to airlift in two huge diesel generators along with enough fuel to run them for a month if needed. The military had also doubled the number of battery backups that could be charged off the solar array Obyavit had installed three years ago during its big "green" push.

David was supposed to be configuring the monitors and interfaces for all of this grid-less power, and when he was down there he was. But he also had time to work on his own project.

While Kim waited for David, she grabbed her tablet and scanned the news. There had been four coordinated bombings since she last checked the news six hours ago. Groups sympathetic to wars, causes or conflicts transpiring elsewhere were bringing it home. This borderless global citizenry meant if Pakistan went to war with India then patriotic Indians were retaliating against Pakistan wherever the lines of national pride could be drawn.

In this morning's news Kim saw that the embassy for the European Union of Federated States in Salt Lake City had been bombed. A fringe extremist group supporting the League of North African Nations was claiming responsibility. There had been three other bombings also, including a mosque in New York. She looked up from the discouraging events and saw David just beyond the automatic security door coming towards her.

He entered the building the way they all did, by crossing the dimly lit lower floor of Building 3. Most of the lighting in the area outside the lab was off. Even though it was well into the workday, no one else was around. Only the off hours emergency lights were on. Every few hundred feet, they cast down ominous pillars of light, like transporter beams from a fleet of widely scattered invading spaceships. Moving into the building, he was guided by the glow of fluorescent light escaping through the twenty-foot-long row of wire-mesh safety glass panes that separated the lab from the rest of the building. The long wall, with its formidable windows and security door, was about two hundred feet from the outer wall of the building and its conventional windows. Building 3 was unique in that it had been built into a man-made hill and was the only building that had ground level entrances on both the first and second floors. Unique also to Building 3 was its bunker. Below the lab, below ground level, was a fortified server room. With its own power and backup power, it was designed to remain functioning when all else around it was not.

When David reached the lab door, he badged himself in and went to his workstation.

"Hey," he said as he passed Kim's cube on his way to his own. "It's noisy out there between buildings. If it's not the landing and departing of helicopters it's the loud diesel engines. The crowd out by the perimeter fence has gotten bigger too. There's a National Guardsman on a bullhorn ordering them to remain back and disperse. You know, for just the briefest of moments, I began to wonder just how long until someone tries to bomb Obyavit."

"Don't say things like that, David." Kim cringed at the thought.

"Sorry. There's nothing to worry about anyway, those guys in the green fatigues have it under control."

"Did you see the news this morning?" Kim asked as she walked up behind David. He had already seated himself at his desk. She stood behind him and discreetly slipped her hand down past his neck and under his shirt, her palm flat against his bare chest. Then, after looking around quickly, she bent down and gave him a quick kiss. He smiled. Rubbing his chest once, she removed her hand and stepped back a pace, also smiling.

"No. I overslept. I hurried straight here when I came to," David said as he swiveled his chair around so he could face Kim.

"There's bad news in western India and retaliatory bombings here in the U.S. and elsewhere. There are protests turning into riots in the EU and other countries, all for different reasons. They're organizing using the Fortune Teller and MyWorld as their primary communication network. Groups and coalitions are forming fast, online and via Chatter. Too fast. You should come back to Wafiq's desk, he's found something more."

"I'll be right there. I just need to answer a couple emails."

Kim was heading back to Wafiq's desk when her smartphone chimed. It was a meeting request from Madeline. She texted back that she would be in the lab all day and that Madeline could stop by anytime. Before Kim reached the back of the lab, Madeline replied she would be over in about an hour.

Wafiq was hunched over his keyboard, like a starving prisoner huddled over food. He had been situated in some form of this pose since six o'clock the night before. In the course of searching for clues, he found himself being chased by the automated intruder detection system. It was clear to him, *they* knew what he, Kim and David knew. What exactly did that mean?

A little more than two weeks ago, Kim had found the replacement, the altered version of Fortune Teller with its surreptitious channels for input. Since then, she and Wafiq had been trying to understand their use and to monitor the effects on outcome when whoever was using these channels fed data through them. Last night at about nine-thirty they finally recognized the purpose for the pathways. They spent the next two hours documenting their find and storing the work onto a micro-SD storage card. It was after Kim went back to her office to get some sleep that Wafiq made a new and more frightening discovery. It was a finding that no one had anticipated; but, once uncovered, seemed logical and obvious. He, being a good scientist, thoroughly documented his findings, sampling code and mapping examples. There would be no mistaking what this meant when these notes were read. He wanted to be sure of that.

At Wafiq's desk, Kim grabbed a chair and pulled it over to where she could see his screen better. "Have you been up all night?" she asked. "You should get some rest."

Unshaven and drawn, he turned to Kim. "Here, keep this and read it later," he said, handing her a micro-SD memory card clad in a protective case. "There's more going on than we thought."

"What do you mean?"

"You know how we saw the new input channels and thought there were people out there influencing the direction and suggestions?" She nodded. "Well, that is happening from several places around the world, and each source appears to have their own console. But their manipulations are not having any real effect."

"I don't follow. I mapped those into my design several days

ago. The result showed that anyone who used those input channels could direct the trends. They could move large groups of people in specific directions. They could control the trend. So, what are you telling me? I have it wrong?"

"No. No, not exactly. Look here." Wafiq swiped two screens of raw code to the side and brought forward two others. "This report and this graph show the volume and effect of the commands that came in via the new channels. The volume of input is relatively high when measured against the impact on the various trends they were intended to effect."

"In other words, for all their effort, they're having very little success. They're not changing the course of the river," Kim said, finishing Wafiq's thought.

"That is correct. We can extrapolate what was intended by the input sent via the channels and see that the trends are not responding, or responding negligibly. But over here," and Wafiq brought up a third screen showing a much larger graph and timeline, "we can see an increasing deviation from the expected. This trend line shows the expected commerce-based trajectory that would be the normal behavior for the Fortune Teller. But here, this is the actual user trends trajectory. The Fortune Teller is trending towards a news-based curve; and not just any news, but highly charged, conflict-based news. It is using reaction-inducing news it finds in blogs, videos, Chatter feeds and social network posts."

A chill fell through Kim's body at the thought. "Fortune Teller is giving them exactly what they want. The more user bias trends any one direction, the more Fortune Teller enforces the trend."

Wafiq and she stared at one another. He knew exactly what she was thinking. They both felt the grip of realization tightening around them.

CHAPTER 23

The lab's security door beeped and slid open as Madeline waved her MyPhone near the sensor. She entered and saw Kim, looking mechanical and absent, coming out from between the racks of servers. As the door slid shut behind Madeline, Kim looked over in her direction. It took a second or two before recognition moved across Kim's face.

"Hi, Kim. Is this a good time?" Madeline said.

She could see in the way Kim glanced over to David that it was not a good time. Kim wanted to talk to David. Madeline knew of their relationship, as did many others, but no one spoke of it out of professional courtesy. It was clear from Kim's expression that she wanted to speak with him, but Madeline needed to talk to her first. She would keep it short.

"Hi. Yes, now is fine," she feigned, "Let's go over here to my desk." Kim directed her over to the small cubicle office she maintained in the lab. "So, what's on your mind?"

"I know you and the team have been pretty much living on

site for the past week or so and I'm not sure how much outside news you're getting." Madeline, a competent professional, was wise enough to recognize she was venturing beyond her area of expertise. She needed Kim's help and did not want to misstate or exaggerate the facts. She proceeded cautiously.

"Maybe it's a misinterpretation of the data I'm seeing from Personal Assistant that makes me think this, but something doesn't seem right. There seems to be an almost coordinated unrest building around the world. There are circles." Madeline paused, searching for additional words. "That's the only way I can describe it. There are groups, large ones and small ones, forming around various geopolitical instabilities and other social conflicts. For example, on the way in today, I heard a social group has formed whose purpose is to coordinate a movement of civic terrorism in order to combat the industries responsible for the climate change. That's a very large number of companies spread over many countries. Yet they're doing it. They're getting the people they need, Kim, and it's happening fast. Trending reports indicate it's unnaturally fast. And remember that Canadian news piece? At first, I didn't believe it. I thought as Bo said, that it was an attack by our competitors. I'm not so sure anymore. Kim, this all can't be just a coincidence."

Kim was quiet for a long time. She knows something, was the thought that ran through Madeline's mind.

"You're right, Madeline. I haven't been off site for almost two weeks. I've been catching a little news here and there, but not a lot. Tell me more."

"Well, I wouldn't share this with just anyone but I know you're cleared to receive executive-eyes-only information. About three weeks after Nalani left the company, I began to notice a shift being reflected in the revenue reports for Personal Assistant. Product referrals were off and the social media driven purchase metrics started showing a gradual decline. At first I thought it was an anomaly, but it persisted. I started doing some digging, because these types of minor revenue contractions need to be addressed quickly or they compound themselves. It took time, but what I found was a shift away from commerce and towards a news-driven predictive response. It appears to me that Personal Assistant is switching focus, and it's getting worse. In the last three weeks, the shift has compounded.

"The odd thing is," Madeline continued, "I know Bo has to be seeing this too. He's too smart to miss it, and yet he's not said a word to me about the slipping revenue numbers. That's why I wanted to talk to you, Kim. I think there is a connection between what's going on in the world and what I'm seeing in the reports. Again, I think the Canadian news piece might be right. It might be true."

There was a long pause. Kim seemed distracted, deep in thought.

"Has Bo not mentioned the decline in the commerce numbers?" Madeline said, trying to get a response from Kim on the matter.

"How did you get on site today?" Kim asked, changing the subject. "I heard things are pretty messy outside the gate."

"I came in on a Guard chopper. Fewer and fewer people are coming in, though. Most are working from home until this blows over." Madeline wondered what this had to do with the information she had just shared. How was her commute to work that day at all related to these suspicions?

"Have you seen Bo? What's he saying now that the site is under military protection? Have you told him what you think about the Canadian news story?"

Kim was trying to make sure Madeline was genuine and not a pair of eyes for Bo. She, Wafiq and David had been sneaking around inside the systems for weeks and Wafiq had said that the automated security routines were trying to trace their activity. Kim was feeling paranoid.

"No. No, I haven't seen him," Madeline said. "It's been five, six – yes, six days since I last saw him. Even then he didn't seem present. He's here today, but he comes and goes in his private helicopter. He's been taking one of the company jets on trips back and forth to Las Vegas. The staff in finance has been asking how to journal the expenses, that's how I know." She paused for a moment, shaking her head in bewilderment. "A time like this, with all that is happening, and the man takes overnight junkets to Vegas."

Kim had decided. Madeline had been a friend to her ever since her arrival to Obyavit. If it was a trap, so be it. But something in her heart said Madeline was still, and would always be, her friend. She needed to warn her.

"Madeline, I think you should work from home. No, I think you, Todd, and the kids should take a vacation and leave the Bay Area for a while. I'm not sure this is going to blow over any too soon."

"What do you mean?" Madeline said. She was growing impatient with this game of tiptoeing around the truth. "What do you know?"

Kim felt sure that Madeline was just another worker bee; an executive worker bee, but a bee nonetheless. She could see that Madeline, just as the rest of humankind, was unaware that when viewed from a great distance, their so-called individuality was lost. They were all just bees in the hive. Each individual insect knew only their role, yet the hive moved as a synchronous unit. For so many years, Kim had known this. She had worked to use this knowledge to benefit the giant hive of which she was a part. Now something had changed. Instructions had been tampered with, code had been changed; and the hive, the network, was propagating a virulent directive madly throughout itself.

Kim leaned over her keyboard and called up her ad hoc report writing software. She recounted her conversation with Wafiq earlier, and how that had set her mind on a path to verifying what she already knew. She looked over to Madeline and pointed to her monitor screen. "See this? This is the change, the shift when commerce revenues flattened and then began to decline. And this,"

Kim highlighted another trend line, "is the news-driven predictive trend starting up. But, if I drill down into the data behind it and characterize the type of news that is being used to drive all other social activity, I see this."

The screen before them began to build out a graph that showed what type news events drew the most views, caused the most discussion and elicited the most action. The graph further showed how the high level of interest in those types of news stories drove the Fortune Teller to organize users into groups that followed these events. The events targeted religious, political, social and economic demographics, as well as many other social strata. The organization of users into groups was thorough and fast, significantly faster than the commerce-based drivers of Kim's design. It was clear that predicting and driving people's tendencies based on social and societal events was far easier and happened much faster than anyone could have guessed. While it was what people would do or think anyway, its amplification by the Fortune Teller was causing things to happen too fast for rational thought to intervene. Madeline was speechless.

"What are we going to do?"

"David, Wafiq and I need to stop this but we are not sure how, yet. We're still trying to understand what they did to it."

"They?"

"When Bo took us off new work and put us on the smart home project, he put Nalani in charge of new work and changes before she left. He also brought in a team of computer scientists from various governments. Mercenary hackers. They changed the Fortune Teller."

"The Fortune Teller?"

"Sorry, that's the lab name we use for Personal Assistant. Anyway, they've altered it, a lot, and we think it's not working as they intended. They wanted to be able to drive it externally, by giving it commands and providing it specific data input. It looked like their intent was to influence people within their countries to believe and follow their political agendas by using false news, blogs, Chatter and other media. We think the Fortune Teller is overexploiting media, real and fake, that meet a specific type of criteria."

"What are they? What type of news events is this thing choosing to amplify and build against?"

Madeline heard and felt Kim's confidence fade when she said it aloud. "Fear. Fear and hate. Religious and political extremism, class warfare and ethnic intolerance, social and environmental causes. All the things that most people quietly feel or think are suddenly becoming rallying points, and they're magnifying fast."

A switch had been thrown and the light cast out in front of Madeline. The chief architect of the most pervasive, socially influential system in the world was telling her that the thing had developed a mind of its own. This was surreal. Yet, when she turned on the television or checked her news feeds, the evidence was there.

Madeline felt a need to be in a group, but not any of those groups that showed up on the MyWorld or Personal Assistant reports. She wanted to gather her children and her husband, and stay safely together until this all was over. Her heart beat hard and fast as she fought the urge to run home, to her family, to anywhere. As she walked towards the lab's exit, she pulled out her smartphone. Before she had reached the electronic sensor that opened the door, Madeline had sent a text to Todd telling him to get the kids and meet her at home.

CHAPTER 24

Madeline could not help but think that she was witnessing Obyavit's fall. She knew that when she left she would not be coming back. The realization of this decision led her towards her office in Building 1. She wanted to gather some personal trinkets, family photographs, a couple of small, special gifts and a few other things that held meaning, all of which she could carry in her briefcase or the backpack she had left hanging on the coat rack.

Building 1 was minimally lit and similarly staffed. The part of the building where she had entered, on the first floor, was a vast expanse of cubicles, all with four-foot-high walls. She could see across a hundred or so of these little eight-by-eight work hovels, less than a quarter of which were populated by employees. Why had they come, she wondered. Was it dedication to their job, personal responsibility? That was in part what had brought her in today: a dedication, a responsibility. But what now?

Madeline took the stairs up to the second floor. Her office was past Bo's reception area. Jan was not at her desk outside Bo's office when Madeline walked by, but she could hear a voice inside Bo's office. It was the head of Bo's personal security detail, his bodyguards. He was asking Bo what he wanted to do. Curiosity getting the best of her, she stopped just beyond the half-opened door and listened.

"We need them. Are they down there?" she heard Bo say in his unmistakable Americanized Czech enunciation. His statements were followed by the electronic ring of a MyPhone.

"Hello?" Bo said. "Yes... Yes. I know... I know... Yes. I know it's not working... Yes. I can fix it. There is a team here that knows it better than anyone. I will get them involved... I am sorry, very sorry... No. No, it is unexpected... Please, there is no need... Yes, the other team on my end has been disposed of. They will not be talking to anyone... Yes, the team, dead... No, it is not working any differently for any other country.... Yes, that's right... No! Please! Give me time, I can fix this. I beg you. Yes. Hang on, just one moment."

As Madeline listened, she heard someone walking towards the half-open door next to where she was standing. She stood frozen with fear, her hands clenched, knuckles turning white. The faint carpeted steps grew closer.

Madeline knew from what Kim had explained in the lab that Bo was referring to Kim, David and Wafiq. She could probably explain away her presence there, outside the door, she thought. Nevertheless, if caught, she was not a good liar. As she turned to take a step, the door closed and latched behind her. No one appeared in the hallway. Madeline moved quickly down the hallway. She needed to warn Kim.

Once in her office she closed the door. Making sure she heard it latch, she reached into the pocket of her suit jacket and took out her company MyPhone. Somewhere deep in the list of hundreds of contacts she touched the icon that represented Kim.

"Hello?"

"I think they're coming for you," Madeline said. She found

herself whispering with a breathy urgency. "I was passing his office and I heard him ask one of his personal security staff, the lead, I think, if 'they' were still down there. I'm sure he meant you."

"Are you sure he meant us?" came Kim's voice, clear and precise.

"Yes, I'm sure. I am very sure. He then spoke to someone, someone who had his private cell number. Government I think. They know it's broken, that it's not doing what they want. He was almost groveling. I've never heard him talk like that."

"Whoever it was has power. He doesn't bow to just anyone."

"Kim?"

"Yes?"

"Kim. Kim, I think they killed Nalani. I think the story of her disappearance while visiting India is a lie, Kim. He said that the team that did this, the first team, would not be talking to anyone, any more. Then someone on the other end said something, and he responded by saying, yes, dead. It was how he said it, Kim. I really believe she's dead."

There was a long silence. Madeline could hear only faint, short breaths.

"Kim?"

"Yes. Yes, I'm here."

"Kim, you guys should get out of there."

"What about you? What are you going to do?"

"I'm leaving. There's only one thing I need here, then I'm on the next chopper out. You should do the same."

"Thank you, Madeline. We will."

"Good luck, Kim."

Madeline ended the call and turned towards her desk. Scanning its surface, she saw the one thing in that large office of hers without which she could leave. Hanging from her desk lamp by a delicate gold chain was a pendant, a small heart and a key dangling within it. Her son Todd Jr. had made it in summer camp. When he gave it to her he'd said, "Here, Mommy. Now you have the key to my heart."

She brushed away a happy tear and unceremoniously grabbed it from its place of prominence.

Heading the opposite direction, away from Bo's office, she again took the stairs down to the ground floor. Stepping from the stairwell, she noticed there were several members of the finance department hard at work in the dimly lit building. To the right she saw that the office of the Director of Finance was brightly lit and the door was open. One last duty before I go, she thought.

She walked over to the office of Bill Harding and knocked twice on the open door while trying to take a relaxed stance in the opening.

"Oh! Hey, Madeline! How goes it?"

"Hi, Bill. Oh… I've had better days, and I've had worse," although she was thinking today was probably the all-time worst. "Listen, Bill. With the mess outside the gate and the strain on those trying to come in every day, I think we ought to send everyone home. Tell them to take some hardware and plan on working from home until things quiet down. You too, Bill."

"Wow, ya sure you want to do that?"

"Yes. Something tells me it's going to get worse before it gets better."

"Okay. I'll spread the word. Although it's not much better anywhere else. I here there's a huge protest up in Benicia at the Petro-China refinery. Something like eighteen hundred people."

"Well, I think it'll be safer in the immediate future to not be here with what's going on out there," Madeline said, pointing her thumb over her shoulder towards the direction of the front gate. "I'm headed out. Goodbye, Bill. Take care of yourself."

As she started to turn and leave she noticed Bill's expression change from his usual light casualness to a faint anxious look of concern. "Yeah," he said tentatively. "You too, Madeline. Take care."

Bill knew she had just told him something, something other than what had been said. Madeline could tell by the way his forehead wrinkled that this suggestion to send everyone home suddenly did not seem so odd. Bill understood. Madeline smiled weakly and left.

CHAPTER 25

Kim had persuaded herself that all the talk the guys made of foreign government contractors and political espionage was their male imaginations running wild. She told herself the boys needed that in order to keep it interesting and exciting. At the same time though something in the back of her mind told her she should worry more, be more suspicious, that things were not adding up right.

Kim had trusted Bo. His faith in her science was her real-world validation. Until Bo came along and seemingly put his belief in her, it was all lab theory and white papers. But the pieces were falling together and the picture was becoming whole. The events of the morning led her to only one conclusion. She felt used.

After she ended her call with Madeline, she went back over to David's desk where she had been reviewing what Wafiq had found.

"We need to get out of here, now. Burn whatever you can onto this storage card. I'm going to get Wafiq. I'll be right back."

Kim's sudden change in demeanor struck David with alarm. He knew this woman well and he could see she was having trouble holding it together.

He stood and held her by her shoulders, close and gently, bending to look into her downturned face. "What's wrong? What was that about?" he said, his voice hushed with concern.

"That was Madeline. We need to get out of here right now. They're coming to find us."

"Who? Who is coming?"

"Bo. Bo and his security goons." Then, for the first time ever, she let emotions she had so mastered and controlled rush to the surface. David pulled her close.

"Nalani. He's killed Nalani," she sobbed into his shoulder, shaking in his arms.

"Kim. Kim, look at me." As he held her close, his arm around her in a protective embrace, he bent and put his face next to hers. Placing his hand on her cheek, he brushed away pooling tears with a tender sweep of his thumb. "How can you be sure?"

Kim was afraid if she tried to say anything she would come apart further. She waited. Then, looking down but not seeing anything, she began to gather herself back together. "Madeline overheard Bo in his office just now. He said he got rid of the previous team, Nalani and the team they put in place after he took us off. Now they want us. They want us to fix it because it's no longer in their control and there's no one left who can do it. No one knows it as well as we do." Then suddenly, with clarity, it came to her, "David! We need to kill it, not fix it."

Kim stood straight within David's embrace. Looking into his eyes, she pulled him close, not saying anything, and held him tight. With tenderness and gratitude, she brushed her hand across the side of his face, tracing his ear with her fingertips, looking deep into his eyes. The wordless exchange held them in that moment protected from the world around them. Then, the sounds of the lab equipment slowly intruded and the reality of their situation overran them. "We need to go."

David nodded in agreement.

Sitting down at his workstation, David hurried to copy down code, files and documentation. Kim gathered her composure and made her way back to Wafiq's desk in its hidden recess along the back wall. She found him, as usual, hunched over his keyboard. "We have to get out of here."

"I know," he said almost matter-of-factly.

"You know?"

"I've been monitoring movements of MyPhones here on site for the last week. Paranoid, I guess. I've been tracking them by their GPS identifiers, so no one can tell I'm watching. Oh, and I've been sniffing out Chatters that have certain keywords in them. Listening, as it were. Bo's security staff has been Chattering back and forth about us and now there are five of them in Bo's office with him. There is hardly ever five of his security in one place unless something is going to happen."

"Can you tell when they're headed this way?"

"Yes. They're headed this way."

"Good." Then she paused, feeling somewhat stunned. "What?"

"Three of them, they're headed this way."

Just then, David joined them at Wafiq's desk. He reached out and handed Kim the micro-SD card, "Here's all the stuff we'll need to take down the Fortune Teller. Is everything OK?"

Kim looked at David with a suppressed urgency. "Bo's security goons are headed this way."

Wafiq stood up from his workstation, powering off his MyPhone as he did so. "They've just exited Building 1. We need to disappear."

Looking at both Wafiq and Kim, David said, "It'll be close, but I think we can exit the lab, staying low, below the cube walls, and make our way to the north exit. It's just a quick dash up the hill to where the Guard choppers are ferrying people in and out."

Wafiq smiled, then said, "I have a better idea." He reached over and rolled his office chair out of the way, then stretched his leg under the desk and stepped down onto an almost unnoticeable metal bracket that stuck up from a small gap that separated the two-foot-square tiles that made the raised false floor in the lab. He then bent down and moved the large floor tile to the side to reveal a crawl space. "I have it rigged so I can pull the chair back over it."

David looked down at the dark hole in the floor much in the same way one might look at an abstract painting. He knew there was something tangibly good there, but it wasn't making itself clear to him. "What the heck is that supposed to be?"

"It's a way to hide and escape, unseen. We can move around under the floor, to other places where we can exit. We can also get to the main duct that takes warm air from the computer room below." Then looking somewhat embarrassed and bashful, he added with a stutter, "I-I found all this in my spare time."

David and Kim exchanged looks that seemed to say, what the heck, it's as good a plan as any. David then looked back at Wafiq and said with a smirk, "You are a lab rat. Aren't you."

"I say let's go."

Wafiq, pointing to Kim's MyPhone sticking a quarter of the way out of her jeans pocket, said, "You have to turn off your smartphones or else they'll be able to track us once we're beyond the firewall of the lab."

David and Kim reached for their phones, David patting himself in an exaggerated manner. He then said, "Shit! I left my phone on my desk. I'll be right back."

Taking one last look at the screen on his desk as he directed Kim towards the opening in the floor, Wafiq called after David, "They are very close, my friend. Hurry!"

Kim turned off her MyPhone and looked up at Wafiq as David disappeared through the racks of equipment heading towards his desk. Stuffing his smartphone back into his jeans pocket, Wafiq turned to face her. "You and David will go first and I will close up the floor behind us."

At his desk, David reached into the pocket of his light jacket, pulled out his smartphone and turned it off. The more they had uncovered about Fortune Teller the more David's paranoia had begun to spike. About a week before the protests began he had brought in one of his handguns. He felt then that something was building. If the top blew off, he wanted to be ready.

He began digging through layers of papers and other documents, tossing them out onto the floor in his frantic search. "Damn it! When I don't need it, it's in the way. When I need it, I can't find it," he said to no one as he pawed trough the artifacts of his office life. Pausing for just a second, he remembered the flimsy plastic pencil drawer. Giving it a quick pull, the entire tray came loose from the desk and spilled its contents across the floor in front of him. As the sum of collected minutiae bounced and scattered, he saw the small caliber pistol skitter under the desk. Bending to grab it, he heard the familiar triple-beep of the security door.

In the back of the lab, Kim looked up at the wall clock that hung overhead. Just over a minute had passed when she said to no one in particular, "What the hell is taking him so long?" It was at that moment an electronic triple-beep tone came from the monitor at Wafiq's desk.

"The door. They're here." Wafiq said. He looked alarmed and pale.

Holding the pistol, David turned and began taking large fast strides towards the pathway that led back to his friends. He saw a large unknown person in a dark suit step into the lab. David did not see that there were two more people following close behind the first.

Kim could feel her adrenaline rise as she waited for David in the back of the lab. The primal instinct of flight was setting in. Suddenly she heard a loud and explosive pop and the simultaneous crashing sound of shattering material. It was coming from the front of the lab.

As David took another long stride, he saw in his periphery an explosion of sparks and flashes that occurred almost simultaneously with loud explosions of a kind that sounded familiar. Time sped and slowed for David. He thought he heard a shout or a command or something from behind him as he saw the first tall rack of routers and switches grow nearer. He heard a loud pop or crack to his rear and saw the six-foot-tall smoked Plexiglas door of a gear rack move closer, then explode and shatter. He could not process what had just happened. But just as the confusion of the exploding rack of network gear began to solidify in his mind, he heard two more pops that were accompanied by whizzing, zinging noises very near him. In the distance, opposite the direction of the loud noises, he saw fireworks, flashes and showers of sparks. Looking back, towards the garbled voices and popping noise, he saw another kind of flash and sensed searing pain, as if the two were one. He felt airborne; it was as if a giant unseen fist hit him square in the chest, lifting him from his feet and sweeping him from his intended path.

Kim and Wafiq looked at each other with fear and shock. Almost without pause, there came two more pops and across the lab they saw fluorescent bulbs exploding, raining glass and sparks from the ceiling. Then there was a fourth pop.

Those are gunshots, David thought with puzzled amazement as he violently fell backwards into another nearby rack. Given his location in the lab, he knew it to be the rack that held all the swappable hard drives containing the geographic test data, and he remembered that he was supposed to start a backup on that data two hours ago, but had never gotten to it.

I have to get Kim to safety, was the only thought he could hold. Catching himself with an outstretched hand, he held onto another rack in the next row. It was slippery and hard to grip. Either his hands or the cabinet, he could not figure out which, were covered with a slick wet substance. Holding his chest and losing focus, he gasped for breath. So much was in his mind, so much he wanted to give voice to. But foremost was that Kim should go. She should go.

Wafiq and Kim both took two steps towards the back row of equipment racks so they could see up the passage that led to the front of the lab. What Kim saw ripped her with ruthless anguish.

David had been shot in the chest. As she watched, he slammed backwards into a rack of storage devices, his head shattering the flat-screen display mounted at the top. He was struggling to keep his feet. Blindly, he steadied himself with a blood-soaked hand, his other palm splayed across a mass of red wetness covering his chest. Their eyes locked. Silently, his lips formed the word she heard without sound, "Go."

In his tired, desperate gaze, she felt him leaving her. Everything inside her drained away: her hope, her love, her reason. She felt all this and more leave as she felt David leave. He then fell forward, flat, hard and empty, onto the floor.

Wafiq grabbed Kim by the shoulders and shook her with one sharp jerk. When he saw that she recognized him, that her vision and attention were with him, he said, "We must go. Now."

He then pushed her towards the opening in the floor.

CHAPTER 26

They lay flat and quiet in the two-foot space between the lab's false floor above and the solid sub-floor below. Wafiq was frightened. Kim was lost.

"Stop! Stop shooting! Stop shooting!" Bo said, yelling at the security detail.

Above them, they could hear the men on the floor inches above them. Kim was numb, vacant in her thoughts, an empty shell.

The armed men, who were running as they entered the lab, now walked slowly in different locations. One made his way to where David lay on the floor. The other made a wide loop of the surrounding area. He then moved towards where the other was mechanically assessing the state of their target.

"You stupid idiots, have you no brains. I need him and the others alive. Damn it!" Bo's breathing was fast, but not exhausted, from running across campus and through the maze of cubicles.

"He had a gun," said one of the suited men.

"Damn it! Is he alive?" Bo asked.

A suited man was crouched next to the crumpled, bloodied body of David Barr. Methodically he probed and evaluated his quarry for the degree of injury inflicted. He looked up at Bo with a flat professional gaze and said, "His left shoulder and lung are pretty much useless, his pulse is barely readable and, well, as you can see, he's lost a lot of blood. He's dead, he just hasn't died yet."

Wafiq looked sick in the faint light that leaked into the space where they hid. It was taking every ounce of his determination to keep from audibly gagging and retching. He clenched his fists and his jaw as he strained to hold back the bile that pressed against the back of his throat.

Bo, looking down at the floor, shaking his head and pacing, was silent with thought for a moment. Then, moving past David's motionless body much as a crime scene investigator might gingerly step past evidence, he made his way to the back of the lab, along the apparent path David had been headed.

"Where was he going?" he wondered out loud. Walking back past four more rows of equipment racks he met the other suited member of his personal security detail and asked, "Anything?"

"Nothing. But this man here, he knew we were coming." Directing Bo's attention to the screen on the desk the man continued, "He was tapped into the private tracking system. The one we use. He must've been expecting us. He was keeping an eye out."

"There are two others. We need to find them." Leaning down to the keyboard Bo entered the information necessary to show him the location of the two he desired. Nothing appeared.

"Their MyPhones must be off. They're not showing up," said the guard at Wafiq's keyboard.

The guard who had been examining David came walking back to where Bo and his partner were standing. With a nod towards David's body, he asked, "What would you like us to do with that one over there?"

"Reach out to our friends," said Bo. "See if they can discreetly deal with a package we need to be rid of. Tell them to hurry. Maybe we can still salvage something from this mess."

One of the men stepped aside and began making a call while Bo began to walk back towards the entrance of the lab. Bo moved a few paces away to make his own call. The fact that the other two men were present was obviously of no concern. When he finally reached the person he sought, it quickly became a one-sided conversation that bordered on an angry rant. He sounded desperate as he reviewed the situation and his available options.

"Hello?... Damn it. It's all gone to hell. The Chinese government called only a short while ago and chewed my ass for delivering a failure to their doorstep. They were counting on this altered version of Personal Assistant as a tool to rein in the middle class. Instead, their damned population has become more organized and more outspoken than ever. Even the National Police are seeing defections.

"…What? No. No, they got away. Well, Kim and Wafiq got away. We have David, but he's useless… No, he's dead… Yes, dead. My security detail became suddenly stupid," said Bo, with obvious disdain. "I need to go. I'll be in touch."

He finished venting and started walking towards the front of the lab. "I'm going back to my office. Contain this and then see me there," he said over his shoulder as his security detail began to clean up the mess.

Walking back between buildings, Bo was lost in desperate thought as he reviewed the situation and his available options. He had promised his other clients he would fix it. The North Koreans, the Iranians, the European Union of Federated States and, most importantly, the U.S. Government all were breathing down his neck. However, it was the Federal Government he needed to placate first. They were the reason Obyavit had not yet been overrun by the raging mob that surrounded the site. They were also the reason that the CEO's and boards of other Silicon Valley consumer technology firms were being held at bay. It was they, his industry brethren, who wanted to see his head on a pike. The world was railing against them too, thinking that they also were a part of Obyavit's scheme to control their decisions, choices and direction. They were not, but the Department of Defense was grateful for the diversion. He knew that the military presence was only here protecting what was left of Obyavit until he secured his technical resource and fixed the problem.

But the problems were mounting. The undesired results of Personal Assistant were expanding exponentially. Entering his office, Bo switched on one of the twenty-four-hour news channels. He checked his secure message app and saw that three urgent messages had arrived while he was dealing with the mess in the lab. One was from the Indian government, one was from the Department of Defense, and one had been sent to him by the European Union of Federated States. As he read these messages and their urgent demands, which bordered on pleas, the television spoke of coordinated and unprecedented acts of civic terrorism.

CHAPTER 27

Wafiq and Kim stayed between the floors, motionless and quiet, until those who were there, and the others who came to meet them, had gathered David and left.

When the lighting in the lab above shut off due to lack of human movement, Wafiq pulled from his shirt pocket a small, thin MP3 player. On one side was a screen and he could use the light it emitted as a means to see his way through the blackness of the passage within which they hid.

He turned it on and the dim glow shown on Kim's face. Her eyes were closed and she looked asleep. As he extended his hand to touch her arm, her eyes snapped open and looked directly into his. Her gaze startled him. It was different. She acted as if she were a robot, mechanically following instructions. This worried him.

Wafiq was concerned and hid it poorly. He was carrying a heavy sadness for Kim. He knew of the affection she held for David. He knew she was hurt deeply now, yet she did not cry, she did not rage. He worried because he had seen this before.

He could not help but think that the corruption and selling of the Fortune Teller was turning into another hopeless war for power, like so many other factional conflicts he had seen growing up in the Middle East. This one too would be socially relevant and societally righteous because Fortune Teller would insure every user would hear or read what they needed in order to make what they wanted to believe come true.

As Wafiq motioned to indicate the direction they would go, Kim nodded mechanically. He squirmed and turned on his belly, then crawled into the darkness that was lit only by a faint electronic glow. After about a minute, they came to a stop in front of a rectangular sheet-metal box. They had come to one of the four exhaust ducts that took away enormous volumes of warm air from the computer room that was below the lab. Wafiq crawled around to one side of the large object and grabbed the two handles of the inline-filter access panel. As he removed the awkward cover, an endless rush of warm air began blasting past them into the space they occupied. Next, he reached through the opening into the large duct and, with a little bit of jiggling and a little bit of force, removed the large square filter that blocked their downward passage.

Twisting to face her, Wafiq motioned Kim closer. Stretching to move his head beside hers, he said in a voice just loud enough to be heard over the buffeting of the warm air banging against them, "You go first. It is about four feet to the bottom. There is a horizontal duct, like a T intersection," and he made a T with his two flat hands. "Lie flat and slide to the right, that way," he pointed the direction he meant. "I will follow and then we will go to the left. I will lead."

Kim nodded. She contorted herself around and entered the opening feet first, easing down until her feet touched, then pulling the rest of her body in. Warm air rushed upward all around her. The torrent made her clothing flap and billow and her hair stood straight up, moving wildly. She then disappeared from Wafiq's view as she crouched and slid flat into the adjoining duct. Wafiq then backed his way into the river of air. Once inside he reached out and pulled the filter into the duct. Maneuvering it upward over his head, he wedged it into the space above him such that it would not move or come loose. He then grabbed the access panel and pulled it into place.

Crouching down, Wafiq directed the faint light of the small electronic device he held towards where he expected to find Kim. Then turning away from her, he moved down the blustery air duct for a few yards before coming to a grate through which bright light poured. Sticking his fingers through the small square openings, he held tight and gave it a quick jerk. It came free. He maneuvered the grate through the opening it had once filled and let it drop to the floor beyond. He then lowered himself through the opening and into the underground computer room. Kim followed.

"Are you okay?" asked Wafiq, concerned for his friend and the obvious shock she was in.

Kim nodded that she was. She was not. How could she be? She knew what was happening around her, she was processing that. She acted when she needed to act. She seemed functional in every aspect, yet she was not there.

Love, like the corruption of the Fortune Teller, was something Kim had never looked for, something she never expected to find. Now David was gone and she was hollow, empty, except for the love that she had for him. She had been stripped, emptied, then pried open and shaken. Everything in her had fallen out and been rifled through. Only her love for him was thrown back inside, to rattle around and be large in her hollow, empty self. So, she nodded yes when asked if she was okay.

"Good. We'll be safe down here for a while," Wafiq responded to Kim's nod. "There will be no record of us entering and there are no sensors or cameras down here. There is no reason for anyone to come down here unless there's a mechanical failure of some kind. Follow me to the back over here. We can get into the security system using fake IDs I set up last year. We can access every security camera and microphone in Obyavit from here."

Again, Kim nodded. *There is no one else here, he must be talking to me,* she thought.

They were standing in front of a console. Mounted above it were four very large flat-panel monitors. Wafiq swiped his index finger diagonally across a small pad, and the four large screens each blinked to life. As they stood in front of the consoles they heard a low muffled thud, and then all the lights blinked off for less than a second. There was an audible change in the pitch of the background hum given off by the equipment that ran constantly in the room.

Kim and Wafiq looked at one another. A knowing surprise swept across Wafiq's face. Kim turned and looked up toward the front of Building 3 as Wafiq said, "We've switched over to backup power. Something bad has happened."

CHAPTER 28

Pacing the length of his office, trying to gain some sense of control over the situation, Bo switched his MyPhone over to the office hands-free system and spoke out the name of his Defense Department contact. The events unfolding around the world might seem disconnected, but Bo knew they were the same event. The fact that human social nature could be so easily exploited was amazing, even to Bo, who had been exploiting that fact for years.

When the person on the other end of Bo's call answered, the first thing he heard was a loud and angry voice demanding to know, "What the hell have you done?"

"This can't all be Personal Assistant, General," Bo exclaimed. "It's too fast, too widespread."

"My analysts say otherwise, Bo."

"I can fix it. We can stop it, turn it back."

"It's too goddamned late for that. Do you see what's going on? Are you watching this on the news? Goddamned Iran has launched chemical weapons into Israel. There's a fucking gas cloud the size of Alaska drifting east and expanding as it goes. Israel has retaliated with nukes. That part of the planet has just been sterilized. You gonna fix that?"

"Just a little more time, General, that's all I need."

"We're pulling our people out of your headquarters in the next few minutes. The President will be issuing an order of martial law for the entire country within the hour. We expect to see incoming intercontinental missiles, either by accident or on purpose, and we'll have to respond. There's already rioting and looting in Chicago, New York, Miami and Baltimore. You're on your own."

"What about the other project? What about protection from the other governments?"

"You sold it to North Korea, damn it. You *gave* it to the Czech Republic. Did you think we wouldn't find out? You're goddamned lucky we don't just bomb the fuck out of you right where you stand. You go. We're done. You're on your own."

"I can get it fixed, I can make it better. When can I contact you? I know it can be fixed. I know we can get control of it."

"Are you not seeing what's going on?" the voice from the Defense Department shouted with incredulous anger. "The goddamned world is committing suicide by social network. That damned Personal Assistant of yours is encouraging them because that's what suits their preference. There's going to be nothing left to control." And the phone went dead.

Bo stood for a moment staring blankly at the news.

The General was right. Personal Assistant had seized on every cause worth fighting for and had set its followers to fighting for it, on a grand scale. Chatter and news feeds were encouraging everyone to support a movement – #youaremorallyright, #keepupthefight – even though the world was collapsing around them.

Bo issued another command into the empty air and the sound of a phone buzzing filled the room.

"Yessir?" It was Bo's chief of security.

"It's time to execute the evacuation plan. Get the usable assets and the security team to the jet at San Jose International. Then, I want you to meet me here in two." The line closed.

Bo reached down and swiped through screens on his phone two or three times, then made his third outbound call.

A digitally disguised voice came from the speakers in Bo's office. "Where are you?" it demanded, filling the room with its presence.

"I'm still in site. Getting ready to head out."

"Did you get them? Kim and Wafiq?" Beyond the digital encoding that held it tight, the voice sounded strangely accented.

"No."

"What?"

There was no tonal change; the mysterious voice had been digitally castrated.

"They are nowhere to be found. I have all my men looking for them."

"Why did you kill David?"

"I told you, it wasn't supposed to go that way. What's done is done. I'll tell you more when I get there. There is going to be a delay in getting you your resources. You'll need to improvise until we can turn them up."

"You are not making it easy, Bo."

"I'll see you in an hour." With the call ended, he picked up his phone and put it into his pocket.

As he surveyed his office one last time, the hidden door in the far wall came open and Bo's chief of security stepped out. He walked up to Bo's desk, while another man from security waited at parade rest three steps back. Bo stepped over to the windows. The chief followed, standing beside Bo, taking in the view.

"We're ready when you are, sir."

"What a mess," Bo said, more to himself than to the other two men there with him. Then turning to his chief of security and clasping his hands together in front of him, as if the short meditative pause had refreshed him, he smiled wanly and said, "Well, let's be off, shall we?"

Bo was stepping through the door onto the roof of Building 1 with its twin helipads as the first chopper was lifting off, angling up and away, showing its belly and runners as it blasted warm humid air towards him. He shielded his face from the prop wash as he looked up into the drab grayness of the hot cloudy day.

Bo's helicopter was just starting to spin up as another gray-suited man, with sunglasses and an earpiece, came towards him from the aircraft. He shouted to Bo over the increasing whine and buffeting of the helicopter, "What should I tell the team at the airport, sir?"

Before Bo could answer, a powerful explosion echoed from the front of Building 1. The building trembled. Bo's chief of security reached out and grabbed him by the elbow to steady him. Two more explosions followed, one near where the fence meets Building 3 and the other at the back of the campus near Building 5.

It was a windless day and the American Flag, visible beyond the roof, hung limp on its stanchion. Then, black smoke began to rise into view across the roof at the front of the building, and the rush of air cast off by the ever-increasing speed of the remaining helicopter's rotor blades began to swirl the smoke as it cleared the top of the parapet. Then there was gunfire.

Rifle fire erupted all around the grounds of Obyavit. Military automatic and semi-automatic weapons were everywhere, and small arms fire answered back. The suited security chief held Bo's elbow in a vicelike grip and ushered him to the waiting chopper. The doors were being pulled shut as the aircraft broke with the surface of the roof and elevated itself with speed. Moving up and out in an arcing path, the banking chopper gave Bo a clear view of the gaping, charred blast mark where the main gate once stood. There were dead soldiers strewn about inside the fence line, and dead protesters strewn likewise around the outside. People were pouring into the grounds. Many were armed but most were not. The National Guard troops had taken up defensive positions and were picking off the protesters as they poured in. Obyavit, and who knew what else, had fallen.

From the front right seat, the chief of security turned around and waited patiently as Bo regarded the battle that was taking place below. Feeling the eyes of someone upon him, Bo raised his gaze to the face of the man whom he had put in charge of his safety. This man, expressionless, asked again, "Sir, what should I tell the team at the airport?"

"Tell them, The Assemblage."

PART 5

THE AFTER

§

CHAPTER 29

Day 58 of the first year A.E.

Kim and Wafiq were no longer living. They were surviving. They were trying to make it in the aftermath of The Event, in the time that had become known in shorthand as The After.

As Kim and Wafiq had watched from their underground bunker, exploited human tendency and socially engineered bias spun across the landscape, leaving devastation and destruction in its wake. Flash-mobs became flash-battles, friending became allying and social networks became social alliances. As momentum built and governments and groups with their spurious causes could see the power and impact of their social movements magnify, there formed great certainty their causes were the just causes. Each version of each truth became for its followers the single, the only, the one truth.

The darkness of war and wretched struggle fell across the continents, and ideologies pitted themselves against one another in the forum of physically destructive social debate. Unlike in the time of The Before, when the social exchange that took place was considered extreme as the language turned abusive, the debate of the time ending in The Event saw exchanges of a cataclysmic kind.

As the debate of war raged, great clouds containing the exhaust of those exchanges began to wander, dispassionately releasing their toxic content onto an already withering planet, where it was recycled into vapor to be released again somewhere else. Virulent diseases grew and spread as technology was abandoned for basic survival. Those that remained carried on the debate in new forms, without the technology they once felt so vividly was necessary. It was in this aftermath, The After, in which they did not live, but they survived.

§

During the darkness of the early days, Wafiq pulled Kim back from a precipice. She had gone completely dark for over four months after David's death. Her body was a hollow shell within which no one lived. Speechless, motionless, vegetative, Kim existed to the degree that her sympathetic and autonomic nervous systems functioned. She ate if Wafiq fed her and bathed if he washed her. Modest and devout, Wafiq stayed strong, and treated Kim with dignity and respect.

Slowly Kim came back. First, she began caring for her own most basic needs. But guilt, rage, torment and grief seethed within her. After many weeks of inert existence, she finally spoke to Wafiq. Her first words were just two.

On a day when nothing extraordinary was expected to happen, Kim sat motionless in a chair staring into space. Wafiq, at the consoles, was working to locate the perfidious Fortune Teller instances that were living across the web, so that he might plan their deaths. Kim stood and faced him. Startled, he saw immediately that her eyes were not empty, that she was there that moment, with him. He stood calmly and returned her gaze.

"Thank you," she said.

They were simple, heartfelt words that touched him deeply. He wept with joy. He knew with those words that she had begun her journey back.

Kim continued to struggle, as did the world outside. She had become a very different person. She lacked the confidence she once had and ultimately all decisions fell to Wafiq. To strengthen Kim, mentally and physically, he built into their new lives as much routine as possible. Twice weekly, they ventured out into the world above them. At first assessing the state of order and society – there was no order and chaos had supplanted society – then later scavenging those things necessary to survive and stay alive. He also set up a regular work schedule where he and Kim would devote time to surveying the remains of the broken infrastructure upon which the web of the world's network depended. These and other things gave order to their lives as turmoil continued to spread outside.

They worked together in their bunker, over the net, to hunt and kill any Fortune Teller installation they could find. Sending out automated kill-bots, these robotic automations wandered the broken global network following apparent dead-ends to remote and often tenuous connections where they found hidden islands of computing power. Hops were made, paths were traced and code was obliterated. It was a war of its own kind.

Through the simple act of surviving and the slow work of finding and killing rogue Fortune Tellers, Kim regained herself, though it was a fragile grip at best. The act of surviving and foraging in the gaseous pollution of The After was less kind to Wafiq, however. New infectious diseases born from the fallout of war, and the pollution of a society dismantling itself, found their way to many, and Wafiq was one.

Day 202 of the first year A.E.

Wafiq's eyes were upon Kim as she wandered slowly along a bank of servers that had ceased functioning about six months ago. She was battling a decision out of herself.

Wafiq watched as Kim struggled to commit to decisive action. She did not want to fail and for her, even in the most mundane of daily activities, there would always lay the possibility of some form of failure. It may not even have been an important decision. Maybe she needed to go to the bathroom, and lacked the will to go to ground level and do it. Whatever the case, the decision would be made for her soon enough. For now, she thrashed about in the wallow of her indecision.

Lying on the cot spent and exhausted, a thin film of sweat on his forehead, Wafiq began to say something. Instead, he burst out in raspy coughs intertwined with the thick wet gurgle of phlegm. Groaning punctuated the lulls in between his painful attacks. Kim stopped pacing and looked towards him. She was helpless with concern and tried taking a tentative step in his direction, but was unable to commit. Wafiq's coughing stopped.

He looked up from the cot. "I see I have your attention." He spoke in a hoarse, breathy voice. His smile was twisted and pained. "What are you thinking? What is it you want to do?"

She mentally withdrew the step she had not taken and just looked at him. With her eyes, Kim pleaded for help but he knew better than to offer, or ask. An angry flame had erupted between them over that, some time ago. Enough time had passed since that vented passion that he knew she would come forward when she was ready. He decided he would rest and wait.

After Wafiq fell asleep, she stopped pacing and went to a console across the room to check the power levels and charging efficiency of the batteries. Above average. It must be getting light up there, she thought.

She then called up each of the eight cameras that were built into the concrete walls at the top of *their* building, outside. It was light. Good.

Kim looked over at Wafiq again to make sure he was still asleep. He was. Crossing to where they kept supplies and weapons, she began to prepare for a trip beyond the building and the grounds of Obyavit. It had to be done.

She put on the Kevlar vest and the belt with its collection of burglary tools first. These were for protection and access. Then the gun, her old semi-automatic Smith & Wesson .357. She wore it on her right hip, out where all could see. It too was for protection. Next was a bottle of clean water, stuffed into a pack. The pack would also be used to bring back what it was she was heading out to get. The last things she put on were the protective goggles, the breathing mask and a heavy wide-brimmed hat. Finally, she picked up the prox card that would get her into the stairwell that led up to the secure door and the lab.

Moving across the room towards the stairwell door, she heard Wafiq's low, croaky voice, "Kim! Where are you going?"

Wafiq propped himself on one elbow, barely able to hold himself up. He had lost so much weight. Weight he did not have to lose. The infection was winning. His time was short.

Kim stopped and turned to face him. A mistake. She did not want to have that conversation. She was afraid if she lost her momentum she would give up and give in. "I'm going down to Valley Med. You need medicine and all the drugstore pharmacies around here have been looted and trashed."

"It's an eleven-mile round trip. It's too dangerous."

She wanted to go over and comfort him, but she could not. She would lose momentum.

"You need a specific medicine. It's not anything the addicts or the antibiotic hoarders would recognize. I have the best chance of finding it at Valley Med."

"How can you be sure? There is nothing to worry for anyway. Yes, the Doctors at Valley Med say one thing, but I know my body. I just need to rest."

"There's still enough of the net left that I can see what's happening out there. You know as well as I, it's not just a bug. You're not the first or the only one to get this. What you have is new, and bad. People are dying from this."

Dying... Death... Dead... As she said the word, Kim could feel her grip, her momentum slip. Another notch jerked and clicked away from her. She tried to ignore it, knowing that fear lay in wait for her there.

"There are other doctors out there, Wafiq." She tried to reason. "They're sharing and recording their knowledge in their medical blogs."

Not all of what she had just said was true, though. Sure, there were some doctors still around and yes, they had figured out the disease Wafiq and others like him had was new. But there was no cure, no magic drug or pill. The discussion on the net, and the recent news during her last journey to Valley Med, the last medical professionals to see Wafiq before he became too weak to travel, had been that his best hope was to be kept comfortable and pain free. She could not tell the truth to her dying friend. She wanted him to feel hope for as long as possible. Somebody should.

"Bloggers? You're reading... Now you are listening to bloggers?" he said with biting contempt.

"Listen, I don't have time for this." Her frustration was building, her momentum and courage were waning. "You're running out of time and I'm losing daylight. Stay here, rest, and I'll be back." She turned and walked over to the stairwell door.

"Kim! Kim, it is too dangerous by –"

She was through the door and gone before he could finish his sentence. He was alone.

Kim had started venturing beyond the fence line of Obyavit by herself only recently. They had always ventured out as a team. It was just safer that way. She was going a long way in one day, only the second time she would be gone more than a couple of hours from the site. Five hours outside was a long time.

Hiking the San Thomas would be safest. Lafayette Street was faster, but it was too near the airport. Being near the airport was not good. The Mechs owned that. They had seen them once, from a distance, and hid in fear. The staff at Valley Med had warned them of the Mechanized, or the Mechs, and the airport... Yes, that was where they saw them, during the month-long big burn. They had guns. The big guns left behind when the military fell apart and went away and the Mechs took their place and filled the void.

The Mechs caged their women. If they caught Kim they would not kill her, not right away. She would kill herself first, rather than suffer the repeated rapes and beatings within which their perverted minds found pleasure. She would not die on their terms, not like that.

Reaching the top of the stairwell, Kim closed the self-locking access door and moved through the still-secured lab area. Using the prox card, she activated the battery powered security door. The thick door had been shot, beaten, rammed and pried, but still held and still functioned. In The Before, the blast-proof building core and over-engineered lab enclosure seemed like overkill. Now they were glad for it.

As the door slid open, Kim paused in the opening and surveyed the ransacked wreckage. She looked for looters, or worse, before stepping out. Carefully, she moved across the waste of broken cubicle walls, the debris of what had been the QA Department, to the tall beltline of open framework that once were the windows of the building's exterior wall. At the far end was a hole that had held the double doors leading to outside. An "Exit" sign hung dark by an electrical wire, swaying in the breeze that moved through the windowless space. Again, she stopped and surveyed what was beyond.

Suddenly, Kim dropped flat and hid. She thought she had seen movement in the nearby brush of the overgrown campus. Her .357 already drawn, she looked through the sight of the weapon, scanning the area until she found her target. It was a white-tailed deer, a doe grazing near the empty pool of what was once the fountain. She let out an audible sigh. The doe bolted.

Moving towards the buildings across the way, she passed under a canopy of the overgrown and unkempt trees. Nearing the front gate, the char and destruction of the blast that had occurred so long ago was still plainly visible. She paused and looked up. The sight above her was another reminder of the desperate time in which she lived.

It had happened just after the military disbanded, when the word came that two dirty bombs made from Cold-War era warheads had been detonated in Washington D.C., burning the heart out of America. The demoralization of the nation led to the collapse of the government and any hope there might have been that order and law would soon return. One night not long after, a group calling themselves Help U.S. – pronounced "help us" – turned every flying American flag they could find in the south Bay Area upside down and re-flew them. As defined by the United States Code, it was a signal. It was the sign of dire distress and meant to signal there was extreme danger to life or property. Wafiq and Kim chose to leave the flag that flew above the crumpled front gate as they found it, but they both agreed it was indeed true. The situation had become extreme and dire.

CHAPTER 30

Day 196 of the third year A.E.

Maddy was working in the garden the day she first began to feel she was ready to put her painful past behind her. It had taken almost three years to get there.

She had been placed with the harvest crew while there were no illnesses or injuries that required her in her capacity as village nurse. Maybe it was the unusual clarity of the air that day or possibly the calming effect of having her hands in the dirt, but the pain was far less that day and the weight on her chest was lifting. She felt it might be okay to let go.

Looking across the rows of damp lettuce, kale and chard that were ready to harvest, she found herself unable to suppress a smile. Across the two-acre communal garden her son, Todd Jr., who had just turned seventeen a few days ago, was looking and acting very much in love. The sight of him and Rashaunda filled her with an unexpected rush of warm, simple happiness, a feeling that had been hard for her to find until recently. Their affection for each other gave her hope.

Todd was happy when he was with Rashaunda, and she too beamed with the joy of young love. They had been together since a month after his sixteenth birthday. Just the other day he had said that she might be the one. He was very serious.

He saw his mother across the field as she watched him and a flush of embarrassment fell across him, but not for any other reason than the fact that he knew how much she loved him. Todd grabbed Rashaunda's hand and they walked around the edge of the garden to where Maddy was cutting bunches of leaf lettuce and stacking them neatly into a rusted Radio Flyer.

"Mother, may I go for a hike today? Rashaunda and I want to go to the top of Sugarloaf Mountain," Todd said, pointing north to a prominent nearby landmark.

"Have you asked Rashaunda's parents? What do they say? And your work, and chores, what about those?"

"All of my chores are done and the orchard boss let the crew off because all the ripe fruit is in. He wants me to come in early tomorrow, to help with distribution."

"And Rashaunda's parents?"

"Rashaunda's father said that so long as you knew and we were back an hour before dusk it was okay with him," Todd said as Rashaunda nodded in agreement.

"Then enjoy yourselves."

"Thank you, Mother."

"Thank you, Ms. Maddy." Rashaunda said as her dark eyes sparkled.

"Be careful."

"We will."

Maddy watched as they walked north, still holding hands, talking and laughing, the giant wind turbines that provided electric power turning lazy and slow in the distance. It lifted her heart. She wished Todd's father were there with her to see his son.

Then the pain and sadness started to creep in. She wanted so badly to hang on to that moment of happiness that had just been gifted her.

When the bombs went off in Washington lawless panic broke and spread uncontained throughout the country. Later that same night L.A. was lost, and so too was lost the safety and comfort of the life she knew. The martial law order from the President evaporated once word of the bombings spread. The National Guard troops could not contain the rioters, the police were used as target practice and the Army isolated itself along with the remaining Air Force at Travis Air Force Base.

The cities burned.

It was chaos.

Day 5, A.E.

"Maddy. Maddy!" Todd called to his wife as he came bursting into the house, sweat was soaking the t-shirt he had been wearing for three days. Worry carved his face and fear owned his eyes. Madeline felt the heat of terror radiating from her husband.

"What is it? What's wrong?"

Pulling back the breathing mask he wore whenever he went out he said, "Maddy, the Guard is pulling out, they're leaving."

"What? What do you mean? What about the martial law?"

"Maddy," he said, bending forward exhausted at one corner of the granite-topped kitchen island, "Washington has been bombed."

"No." She began to wilt. "No."

"It happened early this morning. The Capitol building and the White House are burning and the whole of D.C. is contaminated with radiation. The nation's capital is dying."

Madeline's legs would no longer hold her. She collapsed back into one of the nearby kitchen chairs. Her arm fell heavy and without life onto the table next to her and she stared blankly at the floor. Absently, her other hand found its way to the side of her face where it moved flatly up over her hair, coming to rest on the back of her neck. She looked up and said, "What does this mean?"

Shaking his head, Todd said, "I don't know, Maddy. I don't know. The military is falling back to its bases, protecting only itself. Honey, the general public is on its own."

Just then, several shots rang out not far from their house and seconds later a tan SUV sped recklessly down the street. They looked at one another, each knowing what the other was thinking. "I'll get the kids," Madeline said, as she moved towards the stairs.

Todd said, "I'll pack the minivan. We'll go to Mom's ranch in Taft. It's a small, quiet town. It'll be safe."

Todd decided to skirt the metro area as much as possible. The roads were filled with traffic heading south. It was moving and it was orderly, but tension and despair filled every car. They were not the only ones who knew that the urban areas were becoming unsafe. As they drove, Todd and Madeline could see the towers of black smoke rising out of the city.

It was nearing midday and the typical afternoon thunderheads were building over the eastern mountains. The black smoke from the city was colliding with the white puffy cumulus, bleeding into the pristine volume and turning the bottoms a putrid gray. It was as if the clouds were being poisoned by an invading cancer. Madeline knew they would likely hit a storm or two in the central valley, once they reached it. She contemplated what the rain might contain when it finally fell.

It was just after two o'clock when they reached Gilroy. The kids had dozed off and she sat quietly as they journeyed south, thinking of what the future might hold. The traffic had eased, though there were still many cars on the road. Todd looked across to her. "We should gas up here if we can." She nodded.

Cell service was sporadic. Anti-technology guerilla groups, extremist offshoots of organized efforts protesting companies like Obyavit, had been targeting cell towers for the past several months. Their mission was to "rid society of the dehumanizing plague" that social networks and handheld devices had caused. In the process the world was becoming smaller and smaller as smartphones went dark in the spaces that stretched between urban and suburban areas. As they neared the small city that lay ahead, Madeline turned on her smartphone. Her BuyAt app showed there were five stations with gasoline in that town. The app also told her that three of the stations had their own private security details. Private security was good because they maintained order in the long lines that were present at all gasoline and quick-charge charging stations that managed to be open for business. Todd queued up at the Fast-Serve on the south end of town. They were sixty-fifth in line to buy gas that was priced at $18.72 a gallon that day.

As they left the coastal valley and began to cross over to the vast and smog-filled San Joaquin, Todd let Madeline drive while he tried to keep the children distracted by going over school lessons. Most of the traffic was headed east, towards the valley. It was light but steady. The air outside was hot and becoming more humid, yet they drove with windows down and air conditioning off in order to conserve fuel. Ahead, she saw the building afternoon storms she had anticipated earlier.

"There's a storm ahead, Todd," Madeline said. "It looks like we'll be hitting it as we get onto I-5."

"With luck we'll pass through it quick," Todd hoped aloud.

The rain came hard and heavy when they caught up to it. It was a sooty rain that ran in grayish streaks as it pounded the minivan's windshield. Who knows what it might contain, Madeline thought.

The damaged planet with its unusual and unpredictable weather, and monsoon storms so far north, had been strange enough in her lifetime. Now, the recent wars and their catastrophic bombings had caused the once white cumulus clouds that formed in places they had never before to turn orange, brown or gray with chemicals and pollutants blasted high into the atmosphere. It made her sick with sadness to think of the world that would be left for her son and daughter. It just made others sick.

It was dark now and the rain was miles and hours behind them. She began to notice a steady increase in northbound traffic and in the span of fifteen minutes the opposing lanes of I-5 went from nearly empty to a solid stream of lights. Being careful not to wake the sleeping children, she reached across to Todd and with a gentle nudge whispered, "Todd. Todd, wake up honey."

"Wha? What is it?"

"Look. Look over there."

Rubbing his eyes and groping across the dash for the cup holder with the water bottle, Todd slowly became coherent, "What's going on? When did that happen?"

"In the last ten or fifteen minutes."

"Where are we?"

"We're close to Buttonwillow, just a few more miles."

Todd leaned forward in his seat, looking up through the windshield into the night sky. Blazing in a descending high-altitude sweep, he saw three flaming streaks that could only be rockets of some type. They were headed west. Two of them were well out in front and a third followed behind.

"What are you looking at?" she asked as Todd gazed mesmerized into the sky.

"Rockets, Maddy. Rockets."

"What do you mean?"

"Three rockets. They're very high and headed west. They are probably near the coast right now they're so high up."

"Ours?"

"I guess," he said. Then after a pause he added, "I hope."

Madeline drove and Todd watched the flaming dots for another minute as they grew smaller, moving from east to west. Then he saw three more appear, faint and farther off in the west near the horizon.

They etched the dark sky with blooming trails that marked their inbound path. They were heading toward Los Angeles, or maybe they were headed towards the other three fiery bright dots Todd saw first. After a moment, it became clear that they were opposite but the same, mirror images converging, headed towards each other.

The two lead rockets turned and began to give chase. The singular trailing dots of each set were still very far apart, still converging. They each seemed to have a match, a predetermined twin for whom they were intended. Two now followed two and one raced towards one. It was with that realization that a truth Todd did not want to know suddenly hit him.

He turned. In his face Madeline saw that hope was leaving him. The four dots, two chasing two, grew more and more defined in their approach to the west coast. Then, the merging dots of light that were the third and trailing rockets of each triad met, bursting into a white and painful explosion of raw, unrestrained sunlight.

"Todd!" Madeline screamed, "What was that?"

Time slowed as Todd turned to her and yelled, "Stop the van, Maddy. Pull over. Now!"

The children were startled awake and her little girl was screaming. Madeline was still trying to process the blinding distant flash when the confusion of Todd's commands and the piercing screams of her youngest child caused her to freeze in a brief moment of sensory overload. In that time, that brief, splintered fraction of time, the two flaming dots that came from somewhere so far west it was called east began dragging their white billowy arcs towards earth. The two dots whose mission it was to intercept, the two that arose from flaming holes dug deep into a desolate prairie somewhere within the heart of America, tried desperately to catch their targets. That did not happen.

When the two incoming bombs detonated themselves exactly

one kilometer over the L.A. basin, the flash that was seen from over a hundred miles away by Madeline's family blinded her. Acid had been thrown in her eyes and all sound was blotted away.

Madeline floated weightless and disconnected in an unconscious dream-state. She could see her arms and hands, her legs and feet, but they moved slowly and were distant. Beyond her there was nothing. It was not dark and it was not light. It was not far and it was not near. Then there was the rush and a roar of quiet darkness leaving. She felt heat and pain, she smelled plastic and dirt, and she tasted blood and water. She heard a voice. "Mom. Mom. Are you okay? Mom."

There had been a passing of time. Maybe it was seconds, maybe hours. Madeline did not know. Todd Jr. had climbed out of the wreckage of the overturned van and had done what he could for her. There was nothing to be done for his father and sister. She lost half of her family along the side of southbound Interstate 5 the night Los Angeles was erased. She blamed herself for losing control of the van and plummeting into a dry irrigation canal at 70 miles per hour. Someone else would have done it differently, she told herself. Someone else could have handled it better…

That night beside the interstate, next to a crumpled and torn minivan, Todd Jr. grew to be a man. Maybe he was already and Madeline had not noticed. He helped her through the darkness of loss and the deep, deep depression that followed. He more than once stopped her from taking her own life, and each time she was grateful. It was he who found the haven in which they now lived, the social group known as the Serrano Wind Farmers.

Her life was a shattered collection of painful memories, but Madeline found strength in her son, Todd. The mountain people of the wind farm *friended* them, recognizing her wounds as their wounds and her loss as their loss. They all had similar stories and they all gave her support, peace and safety from the ghosts of the burnt world below.

CHAPTER 31

It had taken a little longer than Kim had planned to reach Valley Med. A new social group appeared to be setting up their site on top of the overpass she would usually have used to cross the 101. Not wishing to engage them, she detoured.

The smoggy haze was not as thick that day and when she reached the hospital, the sun's faint but discernable disc was high overhead. The medical center was a fortress. Pock-marked barrier walls and the scars of bullets and blasts spoke to the past and the present. The medically trained and their supplies were desperately needed everywhere and there were those who would just as soon take, as wait in line with the rest.

Outside the perimeter wall of the hospital was a city of camps and shanties with sick and dying all around. Most had been seen and some amount of care had been provided, but there was nowhere else to go so they stayed and waited until they were eligible to be seen again. Kim felt as if she were a circus oddity as she walked through the camps, approaching the first checkpoint. Being healthy and strong made her stand out. The lines to get in were short that day.

She was used to the procedure and the surroundings. A few years ago, before the military left, Valley Med had been fortified by a double ring of blast walls and was a temporary military hospital. Since then the remaining doctors, nurses, support staff and guards had formed a group whose mission it was to help those who needed and could be helped. The hospital was the hub in a network of all the smaller clinics and medically trained persons who operated within a day's journey by hike or horseback. Valley Med itself operated as a self-contained village within their walled compound. They called their group V-Med-Net.

Kim and others who were hoping to get in to see someone queued themselves next to an iron post that had on it, high above the ground, a wireless P.A. speaker. Also on the post was a bullet-riddled sign dictating what one must do and how one must act in order to not be shot by the guards that were present inside the walled compound. There were large-caliber automatic weapons moving slowly back and forth at various levels on all sides of the seven-story building that rose before her. On the roof, snipers watched those waiting and those moving about further back. Two men with binoculars and radios also roamed each side of the building near the top, scanning the area and talking into their microphones.

Above Kim, the speaker on the pole crackled to life and the hollow tin-can echo of a woman's voice said, "Will the next visitor in queue please proceed to check-in."

When her turn finally came, Kim followed the zigzag path that led through a series of offset cement walls into the 30 feet of open space that separated the outer eight-foot blast walls from the inner twelve-foot Bremer walls. Above, a guard with his weapon shouldered and sighted upon her, followed her movements through the maze and down fifty yards inside the buffer zone to check in. When she reached the steel door, she stood and waited.

After about two minutes passed, the door slid to the left into a hollow cement pocket and revealed the reception room, a five-foot square bunker with a hinged steel door at the far end. Kim entered. As the thick outer blast door slid shut, she turned and faced a window over which had been welded a cast iron grate from a storm drain. Two heavy metal straps, attached with large bolts that passed all the way through the thick cement walls, held the window grate from the outside. The straps would ensure the steel grate would likely stay in place should someone detonate themselves inside the "reception area." Below the window was a small stainless steel chute, about one foot square, that emptied into a plastic bin, which was beyond any normal human's reach. A camera watched, also out of reach, in the corner of the ceiling.

A male voice located out of view commanded in a forceful monotone, "Place all guns, knives, explosives and anything that can be used as a weapon into the chute. They will be returned upon departure."

Kim immediately recognized the voice and through her breathing mask called out, "Bjorn?"

"Kim?"

"Yeah."

Remaining out of view Bjorn continued, but in his normal and friendlier voice, "Hey, how's it goin'? You OK?"

Kim began disarming herself, placing her tool belt, holster with its .357, and the backpack down the chute. The goggles and breathing mask she left on. Responding to Bjorn she said, "I'm doing OK. It's Wafiq, he's in bad shape."

"Sorry to hear. Well, we'll catch up on the other side. Gotta complete the procedure, though. You know the drill."

After she had dropped anything that could be used as a weapon into the chute, she raised her arms straight and high over her head, palms forward, then faced the exit. To the thick steel door she shouted, "Ready."

She was accustomed to the procedure and knew what would happen next. First came the slow, heavy metallic sound of the bolt disengaging. Next, the door was flung open violently, latching with a loud steel clang on a clasp that caught and held it completely open. Kim walked out to the familiar sight of five M-19's intently trained upon her. There were two each to her left and right and one directly in front, up on a second-floor balcony. She took ten paces to a red X that was painted onto the cement and stopped.

From behind, a female guard, probably former Army, came up and began the pat-down procedure. This step in the process was so vigorous and so thorough that it felt obscene. Kim had noticed on previous visits she had made with and for Wafiq, that when the person entering was an otherwise healthy, semi-fit woman, this female guard's body searches were far more invasive than necessary. Ordering her to raise her arms and stand with her feet wide apart, the guard roughly ran her hands up the insides of Kim's legs, lingering and squeezing unnecessarily. The men behind the rifles, which were still aimed keenly at her head, smiled as the invasive guard stood behind Kim with her hands on Kim's parts. Reaching around, she then held Kim's breasts, cupping and squeezing them as if they were her own and she were admiring them. She obviously did this for them as well as for herself, Kim thought angrily. Pulling Kim's hat from her head, she wrung it as if it were a wet towel as she stepped around in front to get another good look at her latest cheap thrill.

"You're done," she said as Kim lowered her arms. Displaying a smug grin and body language suggesting she was too good for Kim, the guard flung Kim's hat at her and went back to her station where a male guard, who was also on pat-down duty, stood. He too wore a creepy smirk. Kim did not complain. It would do no good.

After they had completed the procedure and it was determined that Kim was no longer a threat, the M-19's were put to rest and Kim was allowed to enter the hospital building.

"Hey, Kim. Sorry 'bout that, but ya know how it is." Bjorn gave a weak shrug. "We gotta keep the docs and the staff safe."

"If you weren't a friend I'd tell you to go screw yourself," Kim said through clenched teeth as she slapped her hat back into its proper shape.

"Hey, I said I was sorry," he said, trying to defend himself. "If it's any consolation, they didn't treat you any different than anybody else." Then quickly changing the subject, Bjorn asked, "So what's up with the little guy? Is he OK?"

Kim and Bjorn walked together towards what had once been

the hospital's emergency room entrance. Bjorn was a former National Guardsman. He and fifteen other military personnel, who were due to be discharged, had stayed behind when the Army and the rest pulled out. The presence of trained guards allowed the hospital staff to focus all their available attention on the masses of sick and dying. The need for medical attention and treatment resulting from the lawless chaos after The Event, not to mention the chemicals and other atmospheric fallout, had become so great that few were getting the help they needed. Without the paramilitary guard the hospital would be overrun.

Those first fifteen ex-military formed a group and called themselves SecureMed. Bjorn became second in command under the Lieutenant Colonel. The group now numbered a very well-armed and well-trained eighty-five. They managed the security and safety of over two hundred and fifty medical staff along with all the patients and other visitors within the compound walls. It was one of the safest places in the entire Bay Area.

As Kim and Bjorn made their way towards the pharmacy, they passed many sick people on stretchers and gurneys lining the hallways. This was a common sight and was mostly unnoticed by anyone, except for the fact that none of the staff removed their breathing masks. You never knew when someone might cough in your direction. Kim had left her mask on also but had pulled her goggles down around her neck inside the dimly lit hospital.

"Yer still lookin' good, Kim. The air, water and whatever else is out there hasn't gotten you yet." Bjorn was hopelessly attracted to Kim, but he knew his chances. Nevertheless he remained gently persistent.

Kim responded to the complement dully, "Thanks." She was still pissed about the search, but it was waning.

"Whaddya here for?"

"Buprenorphine."

"Pain. Is he hurtin' a lot?"

Kim just nodded, not looking over to Bjorn.

"What about treatment meds? What'd the docs say last time he was here?"

Still not talking, Kim and Bjorn came to a stop. She shook her head once slowly, looking down toward anything and nothing, and squeezed her eyelids shut, but she could not stop the one tear that escaped. Bjorn saw it hit the ground.

"Damn it!"

Kim looked up, off into space, not towards Bjorn. She just wanted to keep it together, get what she came for and get back. "There's a chance he could pull through, they said."

"That's good, right?"

"A slim, very slim chance."

They were quiet for a moment, and then they started to walk again. "Look, I don't want to talk about this now. Okay?"

There was a long pause as they walked down the corridor. It was crowded with equipment, patients and staff. Looking at the floor as he spoke, Bjorn confessed, "Sure. It's just... Well... I like the little guy."

Not looking anywhere in particular, Kim replied, "I know. Me too."

CHAPTER 32

The sun was one hand above the western hills as Kim began the journey back to her one and only, her last friend, Wafiq. It looked as if she was going to be out after dark and she did not like that. As she hiked up Bascom Avenue beyond the 880, her mind wandered back to some of the news and rumors Bjorn had shared with her. He heard that the Mechs had repaired a couple of cell antennas around the airport. They were using Chatter to communicate amongst themselves during their patrols. He had also heard they were receiving news feeds and other MyWorld features, though Bjorn had called it *stuff*.

"Yeah, Kim, they went around and scavenged or stole almost every smartphone in a seven-mile radius. They put a bounty on any working MyPhones that are out there. Heard they ended up with fifty or so. You know, with MyWorld still working. Now everybody wants to friend the Mechs, be a part of their social alliance, just so they can get a device with MyWorld still running. They're all a bunch of junkies, the Mechs and their followers. Strung out on meth and

MyWorld."

She had heard six or eight months ago that the Mechs were cooking meth in terminal one. That was how they assured loyalty: allegiance by addiction. The MyWorld news caught her off guard. If MyWorld is functioning, then that meant there was a Fortune Teller out there. She and Wafiq were sure they had destroyed them all. They had spent so many months in their bunker hacking what remained of the net in a relentless search. They deployed automated bots that roamed and listened all across the globe. The bots would have reported back if a functioning Fortune Teller were out there. There had been no reports. She wanted to get back and tell Wafiq.

That there was even a remote possibility a Fortune Teller might be out there frightened her. Enough damage had been done. The killing of any remaining instance was her priority, her obsession. Instead of turning towards the San Thomas and staying wide of the airport she decided to save time by taking the short route, the Lafayette.

Kim worked her way north, jogging at a decent pace and covering good ground. As her route took her nearer the airport, she could feel the eyes of the Mechs' drug-addled lackeys watching her. Word had no doubt reached their base that there was fresh meat in their territory. She kept herself alert for sound of their approach. When she reached the intersection where the El Camino crossed her path, a tangled wreckage of several cars and trucks blocked the way. The vehicles were the remnants of a panicked rush to leave. They lay heaped upon themselves, on their sides or roofs, fused together in a frozen state of perpetual collision. A frantic exit that left in its wake crumpled steel and lives.

Kim slowed to a walk as she assessed the blocked roadway. The sun had just dipped below the Santa Cruz Mountains and dusk was settling across the valley. The hulks and shells that choked the way appeared to form an almost solid mass that stretched from a looted liquor store on the southwest corner all the way across to the sidewalk and a fallen traffic light at the northeast corner. Beyond she saw a decaying quick-lube oil change shop that looked recently lived in. She moved towards the side of the street where an opening would permit her to pass without climbing over the rusted corpses that blocked her way.

Kim had taken a few steps forward when two men and a girl stepped out of the back of an overturned delivery truck that lay about twenty-five yards away. Kim was exposed and vulnerable in the middle of the street. She froze. Is that where they lived? Kim wondered.

The first man stood about six feet tall, was very thin but muscular, and his torso and arms were covered with angry tattoos and sweat. The cargo pants he wore were covered in grease and torn.

He held a pole. It was about four feet long and had a large noose at the end, similar to the kind that was once used to capture stray dogs. He stared at Kim in a half-crazed stupor. His teeth, the few he had, were black and dark yellow and his shoulder-length hair was knotted and matted. Missing patches exposed sores and pustules that covered his head and neck. He wore no shoes.

"Yer in Mech country, mister." he yelled, throwing his head back and chest out as if to exude a sense of strength and power. "You'll need to pay a toll to go further."

Kim almost spoke, and then stopped. With her gear on, the hat pulled down low over her short hair, the goggles, breathing mask and her Kevlar vest over the long-sleeved shirt, any femininity she might have shown was hidden. They think I'm a man, she thought. They'll keep their distance and stay cautious.

These men were not Mechs. Kim could tell this immediately. They were the unpredictable drug-stoked minions of the Mechs. They scavenged, scrounged and traded their finds for meth so the Mechs did not have to dirty themselves with such endeavor. They were the peasants that lived outside the castle walls.

The other man, the one with the girl, moved towards the outfacing chassis of the overturned truck. Its underside was exposed, axels and drivetrain on display and the fluids that once powered it now merely varnished dirt stains on the pavement. He was almost identical to his cohort except shorter and with no hair to cover his open head sores. The girl's hands were tied and she followed the second man at the end of a leash. She was maybe sixteen and wore a dirty pink t-shirt and baggy teal-colored shorts with the word "Sharks" emblazoned in an arc across her backside. He tied the leash to an exposed cross-member on the underside of the truck and then took up a position about fifteen feet from the one who had spoken first.

That man, the one who seemed to be in charge, again yelled out to Kim, "We don't want no trouble, ya hear? Ya just leave off that there pack in exchange for yer safe passage and ya can go."

Kim did not intend to leave the pack. It held badly needed relief for Wafiq.

Suddenly blinding pain shot through her. Kim had been struck in her Kevlar covered shoulder with such force that her upper body torqued, twisting at the waist and causing her to bend forward, shoulder first, as if a baseball pitcher, her left arm and hand flailing wildly. Her feet remained planted.

It was not a bullet. There had been no sound. Quickly recovering, Kim drew her .357 and held it with both hands, elbows locked, arms fully extended as she spun sideways, pointing the weapon at the new aggressor to her rear, then back to the two who were blocking her forward path. She repeated this checking motion until she was satisfied that no one was attempting to move any closer.

Looking to her rear, Kim saw that the new addition to this equation was a boy. He was a smaller version of the two men, a few tattoos, sweaty grime and open scalp sores. He could not be more than twelve years old. He had a woman's leopard-print purse around his neck and brandished a lethal-looking slingshot. He held it poised and drawn tight, aimed directly at her.

Surrounded.

"Hey, hey, hey. Whoa, whoa, whoa there. There ain't no need for any shootin' er anything. Besides, ya fire off that thing and all yer gunna do is rile up the Mechs. They'll be here fast if they hear a gun. And they's got their own guns. Bigger guns than that thing," he said gesturing with slight backward nod of his head, a toothless grin and cocky smirk screwed across his welted, pockmarked face.

Kim watched the two men and the dangerous boy as she inventoried her options. She could probably hold them off at gunpoint, but the boy and his purse filled with ammunition meant he could inflict pain and injury from a distance. She did not want them to get close enough to use that noose either. She had not yet had to kill another human, if that was what you called these people, though the potential that it could happen had entered her mind. She had practiced often with her weapon and was a confident shot. However, the line one had to cross to kill another human was something she had not been forced to consider seriously. Not until now.

Kim had killed a feral dog once. Even that was an emotionally hard-fought decision. She had let herself be cornered by a roaming pack one day as she hiked back from a scavenging trip. She had been lost in thought, foolishly not paying attention to her surroundings. No doubt tracking and watching her for a while, the dogs began to chase her. They herded her into a schoolyard and pushed her into the high fenced corner of a ball field where it appeared they had cornered other animals before. She stood cornered on the remains of past kills, gun drawn and frightened with barking death in her ears. The pack leader, its eyes filled with fire and its teeth laid bare, paced low in front of the five others, never taking its eyes off her. It tested her several times, coming in and slashing open her knee as the others howled and barked their approval. She fired. The animal flipped backwards airborne with a screaming yelp, landing amongst the skittering and scattering pack, a hole the size of a fist in its mangy ribcage. The others ran. Leaderless, they were lost. With her back to the fence, she slid down into a ball, her knee bloodied and torn. Her entire body shook, and then she threw up.

She was saddened with triumph and tormented with relief. She was proud and disgusted. She had taken another step closer towards the savagery that was survival in an uncivilized world, and something inside her said, if you need to, you could do this again. In the corner of an abandoned playground, as a warm, dirty brown rain began to fall, Kim felt a wretched sense of accomplishment.

CHAPTER 33

"What shall we do, what shall we do?" said the leader of the three tattooed and grimy meth addicts in his scratchy singsong voice. No one addressed the girl. She seemed oblivious to the events going on around her. Content to wait patiently, crouched up against the greasy underside of the hulk to which she had been tied, sniffing the air and scratching herself. She was feral.

"Ya haven't fired that gun at us and I thinks ya won't," said the one who did all the talking for the three. "Ya know, mister, I read me some psychologist books from The Before. I learned that ya can tell a lot about a person in their body language. And though ya have that gun there, and yer makin' a threatenin' pose and all, I can tell you don't really want to use it. Do ya?"

Standing there, staring at this foul animal and considering the accuracy of his observation, a ball bearing whizzed past Kim's head and almost hit the man who was charged with the leashed girl. "Damn it, Stump. Watch wha-cher doin' ya dum-ass."

"Sorry."

This set fear and anger deep into the pit of Kim's stomach. If I don't hurry up and do something I'm going to be the victim, she thought. I do not want to be the victim.

They were the same as pack dogs, she observed, a leader and his otherwise aimless followers. Kim tried to picture the one talking with a fist-sized hole in his chest. Then she asked herself if she was okay with that. She was.

Kim turned. Raising the already pointed gun slightly and holding it firmly, she leveled it with her shoulders. She cocked her head to the side, and behind her goggles, she closed one eye tight, sighting the weapon into the leader's chest. She could feel her anger build, and her fear dissipated. Around the gun, she felt every tendon, muscle and fiber fill with tension and heat. She was at the edge of an abyss. She was ready to jump.

At that moment, a moment when her life seemed destined to change, Kim was haunted by a memory, a memory disconnected, a memory from a regretful past. For reasons she could not fathom, as all other sound drained away, the sound of a chime rang pleasantly in her head. She began to feel a sense of emancipation as she prepared to deliver death. The chime came again; it was a sound from better times, a sound she associated with happiness, it was the sound made by MyWorld when a news feed update arrived. Then, as if being pulled backwards through the barrel of a gun, its slick, polished surfaces and grooved riflings spiraling away from her, she realized the chime was not in her head at all. It was coming from the scabby-headed leader's cargo pants. Oblivious to the fact that he was about to receive a slug from a .357 into his chest cavity, he began fumbling through his various pants pockets.

"Hang on, hang on. Just one minute," he said as he produced a MyPhone.

Kim experienced a sense of dismay. Did he not grasp his position, his nearness to death? Was he so sure of his assessment that he could nonchalantly attend to his MyPhone? That was what led the planet to this broken state, humanity's obsession with anything but humanity.

Wait…

He has a working MyPhone. It's receiving feeds. It's true. MyWorld is still out there, still running.

The leader looked up to the others with him. "Come on. We gotta go. Now!"

The boy called Stump hollered across from his location, his slingshot raised high and pulled taut. Nodding towards Kim he said, "Can I take'm out? Lemme take'm out."

"No! Let's go." the leader barked in return. Then, turning to the other nearest him, he added, "Get the girl and come on."

He put his MyPhone back into his filthy, baggy pants and turned to leave, almost forgetting about Kim. Then he stopped and turned back towards her. "Looks like ya got lucky there, mister." He then ran off towards the airport, the others in pursuit.

Kim's arms hung limp at her sides as they disappeared into the darkness of the night that had fallen. She was having a difficult time believing what had just happened. Holstering her pistol, she rubbed her painful shoulder where she had been struck by the ball bearing. Then remembering her surroundings, and the darkness, she began to run north towards the 101. When she reached the overpass where the Lafayette rose above the 101, she stopped and reached in under the bulletproof vest, pulling out her own MyPhone.

She kept it with her not because she thought she would ever use it, but because on it she had saved pictures of David and herself in better times. She turned it on when she was sad and needed to see him, and turning it on only made her sadder. Now was different. She needed to see if it was true. Was there an instance of MyWorld still out there, a rogue copy hiding itself, running undetected by the web crawlers she and Wafiq had deployed?

She powered on her phone. The screen blinked and then displayed a calendar and clock. The day and time it reported were from over a year ago. It had not been connected to a working network since then and she had not bothered to manually update the date-time function. She stood and waited. Nothing. No bars.

She dropped her arms to her side in frustration and looked up to the clouded sky. She could remember a time when the freeway over which she stood would have been a seething congested artery of commerce at that hour. Now there was nothing but quiet. No cars commuting, no planes landing or departing, no dull rumble of a living city. Just the dampened, muffled silence of a hot humid night. There were not even any bugs or birds to make the noises of nature, nothing.

Then the sensation of thousands of dull pinpricks exploded within the palm of her hand. The phone was vibrating. Kim raised it so she could see the screen. Four bars of reception. She had not seen any reception in ages. The clock and calendar had updated, and when she saw the date, she was surprised.

She and Wafiq had stopped tracking time in the conventional manner. They had set a program to randomly change the clocks and calendars on the servers they used at Obyavit, the ones that still ran, so they would be reminded less of the passage of time. But there, in her hand, was proof that a 6G cellular network had been brought back to life. She brought up her MyWorld app and tried to login.

Error: Invalid User ID

She tried again and received a more useful message: Invalid User ID – User does not exist – Create an account?

It was a completely new instance of MyWorld. She would need to setup an account. As she began the account setup process, the muted quiet of the warm, humid night was broken by a distant rumbling clatter. Kim looked in the direction from which the noise was coming. The airport.

Though she was up high on an overpass and only a quarter mile from the end of runway 12R, tall trees blocked a view that would have let her see what she already knew; the Mechs were headed towards her, up the main runway.

"The meth heads told them," she said to the heated night air. She stuffed the MyPhone into her pocket and began to run north towards the Montague Expressway.

Kim knew that if she could put some distance between herself and the 101 they would not follow. They never went beyond their territory perimeter. Gasoline and diesel were in too short a supply. She had made it just over a quarter mile, to where the Lafayette began to run alongside some railroad tracks, when she realized that the Mechs were still coming. They were not stopping at the 101 as they usually did. "I have to hide."

On the right was a burnt-out neighborhood, remnants from one of the big burns. On the left were large flat industrial buildings surrounded by a dense row of overgrown trees. Kim ran across the tracks. After fighting her way through a brush and tree line, she sprinted across the weed-sprouted parking lot to a huge single-story building. She found a roll-up metal door that had been pulled off its track on one side. It hung open and twisted like the lid of a sardine can. Climbing over unidentifiable debris, she ran deep into the building.

As Kim moved amongst machinery, she splashed through puddles releasing an acrid smell of rot and solvent. She was searching for a place that would be safe but afford her enough of a view to see the area around her. Outside, the noise of salvaged Joint Light Tactical Vehicles left behind by the Army and National Guard, vehicles now used by the Mechs to control their territory, grew loud and then stopped.

There were voices, but she could not make out what they were saying. Then the talking stopped and after a few seconds of silence, she heard the sound of chains and metal. They were doing something to the door through which she had entered. One of the trucks roared back to life. What followed was the sound of straining steel and a deafening crash. The large roll-up door was pulled from the opening it once covered and dragged back into the parking lot. There were whoops and cheers by several men. Now she could see them gathered in the weak gleam of the night at the opening where the door had once been. There were six.

As they gathered, she could see their unmistakable profiles silhouetted. They were strong, well-armed men. They wore a uniform of tall lace-up boots with belted tan khakis tucked into them. Their shirts, neatly tucked, were dark olive, long-sleeved button downs, buttoned all the way to the neck. On the right shoulder was their insignia, a gold machine gear on a black background with a red lightning bolt passing through the gear, the Mechanized. They were the exact opposite of the grubby and infected meth heads she had encountered earlier. These men were brutal, bloodthirsty professionals.

CHAPTER 34

Kim had chosen to hide in the maze of catwalk that hung up in the metal rafters of the giant building. Crouched behind a large piece of machinery that was probably part of the building's long-dead ventilation and cooling system, she panted quietly as sweat ran down her back. The edges of her short-cropped hair stuck wetly to her neck as she tried to control her breathing and processed the situation.

Two men, obviously the leaders of each vehicle, were standing together, each holding dim light-emitting objects. Other men were gathered round also, peering down at the weak light. They were talking and pointing in her general direction. As Kim watched, she saw two of the men walk back to the nearest truck. One opened the driver's door and reached in. He was doing something that did not require getting all the way in the large armored vehicle. The other walked around to the rear of the beast. Then together, they pushed it up to the doorway so that it nearly filled the opening. She knew that the Mechs were careful not to burn fuel unnecessarily, which is why they seldom ventured beyond the boundaries of their territory. The man at the rear of the vehicle then climbed up onto the roof and maneuvered a large round object that was mounted in a yoke. He upended it so it appeared to face her. It was hard to tell from such distance what it was.

Then suddenly and unexpectedly, Kim was blinded by light that was as bright as the sun. She ducked and rubbed the pain from her eyes. A shot was fired from a high-powered rifle and a round pierced the width of the large mechanical box that shielded her, easily passing through both sides and whatever was within it. A round hole with its flowering petals of steel bloomed six inches from her knee. She could hear them speak

"Private! Put another round up there, three feet to the left this time."

"Yes, sir."

As the rifleman sighted, Kim's math- and physics-trained mind quickly calculated what the order meant. Instinctively, she rolled to her left three feet, just in time to see another small steel flower bloom right where she had been crouched.

The young man at the floodlight called down, "Sir, I saw dust and debris fall."

The man to whom all the others seemed to defer replied gruffly, "That could be from the round striking shit up there, Private."

"Sir, I saw movement."

"That could have been a goddamned rat, Private."

"Sir, yes sir."

"Lieutenant."

"Major?"

Irritably the Major ordered, "Confirm location, damn it."

The Lieutenant was again staring intently down at his device, swiping and tapping, making sure his readings were correct. Looking up, he replied in a subservient tone, "Major, if all systems are functioning properly, I confirm the target's coordinates are within three to five feet of where Private Zhong is placing rounds."

Kim hiccupped a panicky gasp. She had forgotten, it had been so long. They are using DT, the device tracking abilities that are built into MyWorld Enterprise Release. A function that had been sold by Obyavit to corporate customers who wanted to track company-owned assets. "My MyPhone is on. They're tracking me," she whispered to herself.

Fumbling for her smartphone, she was just about to power it off when she stopped. Looking around, she saw that a catwalk leading away from her remained in the shadow cast by the bright light. Kim quickly moved away from her place of hiding, following the catwalk and scanning for options. A second later, another flower bloomed out from the steel. She was not there to see it.

The Lieutenant, holding out his MyPhone to the Major as if to show him something, said, "Major, the target is on the move."

"Damn it! Take your men and fan out in that direction tracking the target. I'll take Zhong and Kulwinski and do the same in this direction. Go!"

Kim moved down the catwalk with speed and stealth, assessing options for escape as she went. She had been in this building once before, a long time ago, but her memory of this place was faint and she was beginning to think her plan was futile. Below she occasionally heard the noise of metal falling or being pushed about as the squad tracked along behind her. She was deliberately heading for what she thought was the center of the building. It was there that her plan, if it were going to work at all, could begin to play out.

After about a hundred yards of zigzagging among the rafters and staying shielded from view behind air ducting and HVAC units the size of pickup trucks, Kim found what she was looking for. Suspended from the ceiling was a small room with catwalks entering from each of its four sides. From her position, she could see the little ladder that extended from the top of the suspended box-shaped room to the roof of the building. Sprinting the short distance across an open and exposed length of catwalk, she collided with the flimsy door of the room, breaking it from its frame. The noise alerted the Mechs down below. She heard distant shouts.

"Over there."

"I have it. Move left."

Kim hurried to climb the ladder, her foot missing a rung twice in her haste and jamming her knee hard into the rung above. At the top was a hatch that opened onto the roof. The latch was corroded and stuck. Reaching to her tool belt, she removed her hunting knife and began to pry at the latch. The knife broke as she levered against the latch and fell from her hand. Kim cursed as she watched it fall and bounce aimlessly across the floor of the little room below. Running out of time, she felt around her tool belt for something else that could serve as a prying device. Then, looking up at the latch, she saw that it had broken free. Pushing open the hatch, the warm outside air fell past her. She took a deep breath, pulling the sweaty breathing mask from her face. Once on the roof she closed the hatch behind her and ran in a straight line to the wall opposite where the Mechs had left their vehicles. She stood there for a few seconds and powered off her phone.

The Mechs continued to search methodically inside the building just below where she had stood up on the roof and turned off her phone. Running across the building, she scanned in all directions for a ladder rail going up and over the edge of the roof. She saw it, next to two large pipes that came over the wall and ran off across the roof.

Descending the ladder, Kim found it ended about ten feet above the ground. She climbed down to a crouch, then let her feet off the bottom rung. Hand over hand she let herself down until she hung from the last metal bar. Letting herself drop, she hit the ground and felt icy hot pain shoot from her right ankle to the back of her skull. She rolled, gritting her teeth to hold in the pain, squeezing her eyes so tight she saw white and green flashes of light as tears of agony crept from the corners. She was afraid she had broken her ankle.

Kim rolled onto her back and sat upright. Looking around and seeing nothing, but the weed-covered parking lot and the faded graffiti on the walls, she tried to stand.

"Son of a bitch!" she hissed.

It was not broken, but it hurt like hell.

Her only instinct was to get away. A quick glance to the left, then to the right, provided bearings. She began to move towards where the Mechs had parked their trucks. She was limping badly and could not move very fast. I am nothing but wounded prey, Kim thought.

She came upon a dumpster that had been overturned long ago. Its contents of plastics and metal were the only things that had not rotted and disintegrated in the years of exposure to heat and rain. From the mess she pulled a length of plastic pipe. Shoulder high, it would serve well as a walking stick.

Able to move faster, she limped off through the thicket of overgrown landscaping and into the darkness. Kim stayed to the edges and urban night-shadows, leaving the Mechs to chase about in the abandoned building, shooting at noises, shadows and each other. Within an hour, she had worked her way back to Building 3 and the Obyavit campus. She needed to talk to Wafiq.

CHAPTER 35

Conserving what little energy had been gathered from the hazy sun, only two afterhours lights were on and a thin luster scattered across the underground room. Wafiq was asleep in the chair that sat in front of the surveillance screens. He sat wrapped in a blanket breathing slow unconscious breaths while waves of bluish glimmer from the unblinking monitors of the console bathed him in a cool glow. The night-vision cameras around the site's grounds showed nothing but the stagnant stillness of repetition. Wafiq had been waiting for Kim all afternoon, but exhaustion and his faltering body conspired against him. He had fallen into dreams.

Limping in without waking him, Kim took off her gear and put it away. Then, sitting on her cot on the far side of the server room, she gently inspected her injured ankle. It was swollen, painful and grotesquely hued in shades of burgundy, blue and black. She would not be venturing far for a while. Now she wanted to wake Wafiq. She had medication and pain pills he needed to be taking, and she wanted to talk.

Grabbing onto whatever she could, Kim heaved and hopped as quietly as possible over to the surveillance console to settle into a chair next to Wafiq. She grabbed his shoulder, squeezing it softly while shaking him lightly, "Hey. Hey, wake up."

Kim spoke in the soft whispery voice of a mother waking her child. She did not want to startle Wafiq. He might roll himself out of the high-back office chair that was serving now as his cot.

"Hey. Come on, little guy, wake up. Wake up."

In a startled spasmodic convulsion, he jerked back and sat straight up, "Kim. Kim!" He was gulping air and seemed at first not to believe it was her, "Oh great and wonderful Allah. You are here. You are okay."

He held her hand as tight as his weak muscles would allow. A tear ran from the inside corner of his eye, beside his nose and down to his upper lip. Wiping it away, he smiled with a shy embarrassment as he gazed up with his dark brown eyes. He was glad to see her and she could feel it.

"What happened?" Wafiq asked. When Kim did not answer right away, he rubbed his eyes and glanced at the clock on surveillance monitors, "You were out there too late, in the darkness, after sundown. That is dangerous."

"I stayed too long talking to Bjorn. He says Hi."

"That was foolish and dangerous, Kim."

"I know, I know, but I'm here and I'm okay. Listen, the reason I stayed so long talking to Bjorn is he had heard that the Mechs were using Chatter."

"What? Wait, how is that possible?"

"I know. He said they repaired a couple of cell sites, and have been on a mission to scavenge all the available smartphones in their area. Their scabby-headed followers are rounding up the devices and being paid in meth. He says they're getting news feeds, Wafiq."

Wafiq, still in the chair where he had awoken, slowly shook his head. "How is that possible? We have been scanning, literally crawling what is left of the web. There is nothing out there. We would have seen it."

"Maybe."

"What do you mean, Kim? What maybe?"

"There are ways to hide. Ways to tunnel or remote VPN. There are ways for them to watch us and always stay where we're not."

"So you believe it is out there, you believe the rumor." It was not a question; it was a statement of what he was observing in her.

"Yes! Yes, I sa…" and she caught herself.

Yes, she believed it. She had seen it, but she could not tell Wafiq, not yet. Tomorrow, after they had rested. Getting into it now would not be productive. He needed to get better. Even if his chances were less than she would like, she was not simply going to expect that only bad things would happen. She would fight for him, with him. Besides, if he knew the entire story he would protest her leaving the safety of their hiding place again to investigate her newest finding. He needed to save his energy to fight the sickness and infection that was ravaging him. Kim finished her thought with words that were less disturbing than the truth, "Yes. I believe there is another one out there."

Wafiq shivered as he pulled the blanket up tight around himself. His eyes were red and tired and his once warm complexion was hued a yellowy tint. His sick body wanted to drift away to sleep but he kept forcing himself back.

Kim stood and eased herself over to Wafiq's char. Holding firmly onto its high back, she said, "Pick up your feet."

"Why?"

"We can work on this tomorrow. You're going to your cot. Pick up your feet."

He hugged his knees, and with a slight limp, Kim spun the chair a quarter turn and started to push it across the tiles of the computer room floor.

"What is wrong? Why do you limp?"

"It's nothing. A sprain. I'm okay." Kim lied.

"No, no, you're not okay. You limp badly. What happened?"

Kim did not want to get into a conversation that would lead to her having to relate the evening's events. Neither of them could lie very well to the other, but Wafiq had a way of wheedling the truth out of her. She tried to change the subject. "Why were you asleep in this chair? You should have gone over to your cot." Her voice hinted of motherly nagging as she took a couple more steps, trying unsuccessfully to hide her limp.

They moved past a row of racks that held wide flat components, some blinking and winking their lights, others dead, their cold lifeless corpses still hanging dutifully, awaiting repair or recycle. She wheeled him by the muted clattering and scraping noises emitting from the hard drives of the storage servers, and into the eight-by-ten-foot cubicle he had built for himself in order to preserve his modesty. It was sparse. His cot sat along the far wall, next to it a filing cabinet on top of which sat two water containers, several prescription pill-bottles and an e-reader containing his electronic copy of the Quran. Two more filing cabinets sat across the way. Those held more clothing. Rolled neatly on top was his prayer rug. Kim pushed the chair up next to the cot. "Need help?"

With a groan, he let his feet down to the floor. "Thank you, Kim. I can make it," and he sat himself heavily onto the cot. She sat down next to him.

"How are you? You seemed troubled when I woke you earlier. Dreaming again?"

He looked down, shaking his head imperceptibly from side to side. "Yes."

"Wanna talk?"

He looked over to her again. He did and did not want to talk. His jaw was clenched and the pulsing tightness on his face was an expression of intense anxiety. His mouth started to form a word then he stopped, biting his lip, his brow knitted tightly.

"It's just us, Wafiq. It might help to talk."

She could not believe the hypocrisy that had just left her

mouth. She talked of nothing, had not tried to resolve anything, since David had… Her feelings were locked up tight. Nothing could get in and nothing was getting out. Whenever Wafiq asked her if she wanted to talk, she would leave. He had been so kind and generous and she had been cold and silent. Now she had the gall to ask him if he wanted to talk. He did.

"Kim," he said, "when you woke me just now, I felt fear in my chest. I felt an overwhelming desire to get away, to flee. I have had this feeling, this dream, before. It worries me, Kim.

"In my dream, I am running," he continued. "Running hard. Yet, there is no sense that my legs are moving. I am floating. Standing upright, I move without strides but with a frightened and panicked heart. Everything I move past in my flight, my surroundings, is recognizable but disordered. I flee past the fountain where the obelisk is dry, cracked and surrounded by burnt sand and charred trees, a fire that was. I move through the main gate of the Obyavit campus and into the streets, but not San Jose, the streets of my home, the streets are of Doha. The city is empty, the winds of the Arabian Peninsula blow stiffly towards the Persian Gulf and the sky is brown with sand. As I move through the city, I come to the water's edge. I stop. I am standing in the middle of a six-lane boulevard, at an intersection that is familiar yet unfamiliar. I tremble, feeling trapped and unable to move. Looking down I see that my feet are gone, my ankles disappeared into gray filmy water and a mass of twisted cables bind my legs together. A bloated animal carcass floats nearby."

He pauses and Kim could feel him grow tense. "Beyond the water's edge is more city, but it is no longer Doha, it is San Jose. The air is dark gray and thick with smoke that rises in columns from throughout the city, and the city is flooded. I seem to know that it has been, for many years. The salt water has killed the trees and plants, the buildings are rotted and falling, and far beyond in the deepening brackish water of this city you are walking away, Kim. You are leaving and somehow I know this. You are far and becoming farther, leaving me. I yell your name in one long call but you continue away, walking slowly in waist-deep water. You do not hear. I call again. But as I call, I know you will not hear. I sense that though I have heard my voice in my head, I have not heard it in my ears. All my breath has left me and I can call no more. The sky is getting darker and I am losing you and I cannot breathe."

They sat for a while and let time pass.

"I will not leave you Wafiq," Kim assured him. "I will be here, and we will cross through this together."

Wafiq's demeanor was one of despondency as he sighed weakly.

Trying to take Wafiq's mind off his troubling dream, Kim brought the conversation back around to her discovery, "Look, I know me saying there's another Fortune Teller out there may seem a little obsessed, but I know there's another one out there. And, well, you know how I feel about that."

"I know."

"We'll start after it tomorrow, then."

"Yes. I have some ideas."

"Okay. Thanks."

With a peaceful sadness, he slowly closed and then opened his eyes.

"Take your medicine. I need you strong," she gave a tight, uncomfortable smile. A smile that hid her true feelings and protected her, a little, from pain.

Kim reached for the pill bottles and carefully transferred one of each into Wafiq's cupped hands. He took them with some water. Then, as she rose, he lay back onto the cot and tried to muffle a cough that shook him throughout. She traded the water bottle she carried for the empty one on the filing cabinet beside his cot and turned to leave. At the opening to his cube, holding onto the two-inch-thick wall, she turned to look back. He had already fallen asleep.

She did not know it then, but that would be their last conversation. Wafiq went away that night, quietly and peacefully. To his god Allah and his reward, as he would often say. She tried to provide him a traditional Islamic funeral, though she was unsure of which prayers were appropriate. She did not ascribe to any religious beliefs herself.

Kim picked a prayer that her heart told her was right. She then buried his bathed and shrouded body next to the dry fountain with its giant stone smartphone. His body facing the Qibla, she carefully poured three handfuls of soil over her friend, recited the prayer she had selected, and then covered his body, which lay among the overgrown trees and wild tall grass of the Obyavit campus.

She had always held hope that the doctors were wrong about what eventually became Wafiq's ultimate end. Truth and hope were vastly different things however, and in the world in which they tried to live, hanging onto thin films of hope as if they were the only possible outcome had proven foolish. With Wafiq gone, she was left alone to assess her place and map her journey. She knew the enemy, but now she was not sure it was worth the fight.

PART 6

THE VOICE IN THE AIR

§

CHAPTER 36

Day 211 of the first year A.E.

Kim knew Fortune Teller was still alive, somewhere. It was fully functional. It was probably running on some kind of private network. She had spent the last few days chasing it. Turning over rocks and breaking through walls, all on the net, with no result. It must see me, she thinks. It must detect me, work around me, or work me around it.

When Kim turned on her MyPhone, the battery icon screamed yellow; it had stopped holding a charge. When it did manage to connect to Fortune Teller, the Mechs spotted it immediately. They scrambled their patrols and roamed the streets, ranging out and away from the airport, aiming directional antennae to all points of the compass searching for her signal. Going online, hitting the network with her smartphone while in the safety of the underground server room in Building 3, had become too risky. The

Mechs would turn what was left of Obyavit into rubble if they suspected there was someone there using a MyPhone. She had taken to hiking far from the campus before turning it on. And she stayed connected for five minutes at a time. Not long enough.

Day 92 of the second year A.E.

Four hundred and fifty-seven days had eroded into the past. Kim spent most of that time living in an emotional cesspool that was the pit into which her guilt and depression drained. She repeatedly returned to the fact that what she thought was her great contribution, her great bestowal, had turned out to be the tool leaders of societies used to move cooperatively into the abyss; and since this discovery, nothing had happened to encourage her to think otherwise. No bridge to a believable hope had appeared. Kim began to think no such bridge existed. While in this hopeless drift, she began to consider a path that was permanent and absolute.

Kim carefully looped a heavy cable around a large and sturdy conduit that crossed the server room above the white ceiling tiles. She made a noose at one end, and tied the other end to a heavy rack of equipment nearby. Methodical in her usual analytical way, she tested it with bags of dirt to make sure it would hold. It would hold. It was there. Hanging. Ready.

Waiting patiently and poised for service was a chair. On its base were five wheels, all of which rolled easily and effortlessly. It was firm upon which to stand. It would roll far when kicked away. Often she sat across from it contemplating, imagining and trying to decide.

The world was still changing, at least the world Kim could see. Once, when exploring the peninsula and up the Bayshore Freeway to San Francisco, she saw and learned much. Bay water was creeping further inland during high tides. It was turning the urban landscape into a watery, putrid mess that filled the air with the smell of ocean brine and decomposing broccoli. And there was no fog. There had not been for years. The sun, when the deadly smog was thin, burned hotter than an opened hand slap. The days were long.

Kim was gone from her Obyavit hiding place for months on this trip to the city. But she was unsure of exactly how long. The years no longer had months and the months no longer had seasons, but the weeks had days and the days were whatever she made them.

Eyes burning and throat raw, the air had the taste of metal and was the color of a hazy sunset, all day long. The hills to the east, across the bay, were not visible. Kim was trying to tell if the noxious haze that had settled across everywhere was caused by chemical and radioactive particles in the air, or if the already damaged atmosphere was simply giving up. Her measurements revealed an airborne radiation that was much higher than in The Before. She had started measuring only recently and compared her readings to data she had found in the ransacked library of a nearby community college. There were non-lethal traces of Phosgene oxime, Sarin, VX and Hydrogen Cyanide detectable in the air. The amount and ratios varied with the weather and were most concentrated for a few days after very windy conditions. She tried not to travel or be outside much after a wind day. It was these airborne contaminants that were the cause of the great sickness that took Wafiq.

Walking north from San Jose, she saw that the giant hangar at Moffett Field had fallen. It was crumpled as if it were an enormous burnt wad of sticks and paper. It had been caught in one of the many big burns that erased swaths of the abandoned urban landscape. Surrounded by a black liquid char, the hangar remnants stood reflecting in an onyx sheet that smelled sharply of a wet fire pit. Chemicals cast purple, violet and auburn trails across the surface of the black sheen.

Farther on, Kim encountered a small group of scholars and scientists. They had barricaded themselves into Hoover Tower on the Stanford campus. While scavenging a nearby library for information on the chemical compounds she had found in the air, Kim heard movement. There was a man, he could not have been more than thirty, trying to sneak out after being trapped by her arrival, so he said. He was scared and so was Kim. She almost shot him. She drew her gun and in a moment of blind life-preserving reflex yelled, "Don't come near me, you dead fuck, I will kill you now!"

When Kim yelled, the man immediately fell into the fetal position and cried for his life, "Don't shoot. Don't shoot. I don't want to die. Please!"

She did not shoot. "Who are you?" Kim demanded.

From the huddled ball on the floor a muffled voice said, "I'm a geoscientist. I study dirt particles. I don't have a gun. Please don't shoot."

Kim talked to him from a distance. She was nervous but stayed calm. He collected himself and seemed embarrassed. Soon they were standing with just a table between them and finding out more about each other.

"You're new around here," observed the scientist. "I don't recall anyone speaking of someone like you."

"I'm from San Jose. There are others? Other people you talk to?"

"There are a group of us over in Hoover Tower. University faculty of different disciplines. We're mostly scientists, but there's two campus police and three from the medical center. You're quite a hike from San Jose. What brings you up here?"

"I'm seeing what's left. Going to the Golden Gate then back south. I saw the campus and thought I'd see if the library was still intact. I want to understand better the effects of the various airborne particulates, the chemicals and gases."

"That's some pretty ambitious reading," said the young scientist somewhat arrogantly.

"I have a Doctorate in Social Economics with degrees in Mathematics and Physics as well," Kim replied defensively. "I think absorbing a little environmental chemistry shouldn't be too much of a strain, sand man."

He smiled. He liked her wit.

The young scientist took Kim back to the tower, where the others were. A sniper up high in the tower and a guard at the door held her at a distance, at gunpoint, quizzing her for over fifteen minutes on physics and mathematics. Though she had told the one from the library she had her PhD, the others wanted to be sure. There were seventeen of them, and Kim learned a lot during her stay.

"We've been tracking the rise of the bay waters and have been able to project what we think will be maximum rise," said one who went by the name Addison. "It's based on historical tidal records and the calculated known quantity of polar ice at a specific point in time."

This interested Kim because of the location of the Obyavit campus.

"We predicted a max tidal flow would be realized in about three years," Addison estimated.

"Your calculations, if they hold true, mean I'll need to move from the place where I'm staying in a year or two," said Kim.

"Yes, that's very likely depending on your elevation."

They also shared data that showed airborne chemical compounds were decreasing but the radiation was remaining steady. She asked if they understood the weather, but they said they had no atmospheric scientists and anything they would posit would only be educated conjecture.

After five days, Kim began heading north again. The Stanford group told her of the social group phenomenon and that they were studying it. She told them of the few that were around San Jose and that she knew enough to be careful about becoming known to them. They agreed and offered that it seemed the more organized a group appeared the more dangerous they were, in most cases. Kim knew this already.

She thanked them for keeping her safe. She was grateful for their company. As much as she had come to detest the thought of socializing, she found her stay with them had lifted her spirits and given her a kind of faint hope.

There were people along the way. Not many, but some. Most were loners. Kim traveled in the open, always trying to keep a defensible space between herself and others. Looking and watching, she made an effort to try to anticipate encounters and vanish when she spotted another. She wondered how many saw her and did the same.

Kim stayed on the higher ground west of the El Camino Real. The bay water reeked of industrial waste and human death, and the breezes from the west were the only thing that made it tolerable. To stay safe, she took to sleeping on the roofs of shopping malls and sprawling warehouse stores. Sometimes she would be awakened by a gunshot or scavengers that were in or near where she had laid camp. Never did anyone venture to the roofs of the buildings they looted. She always felt safest spending her nights atop the largest buildings and near the center; more chance to know someone was coming before they were upon you.

San Francisco was the most populated, the most peculiar and the most dangerous. Kim approached the city around the east end of Mount San Bruno, staying high enough to avoid the stagnant waters and low-tide muck that had settled over the flat bottomlands of the industrial parks on either side of the Freeway. She followed the hills around to a place she remembered as being called Visitation Valley. As she approached, she heard rhythmic drums in the distance and saw smoke rising from the old Candlestick Park stadium. From high on an overgrown hill west of the giant structure, she found that the ancient landmark had become a small town. The complex was surrounded by water. Below her hidden vantage, there was a moat, a bog of standing water, between the stadium and land. Open bay lay in all other directions.

There were hundreds of small boats, canoes and sailing skiffs either moored at the base of the stadium where it rose from the water or milling about, traveling to and from the distant bay. There were larger floating structures also. They were lashed together in rows and looked as fingers reaching away from the stadium. It was very much a smaller version of the Bangkok floating market.

From the hill, she could see into the huge structure. The playing field was flooded. The water reached many rows up into the lower seats and was a cesspool of garbage and filth. There was obviously no tidal circulation occurring in there. Just beyond the water and in the upper levels too the seats had been removed, and makeshift dwellings had been constructed on the stepped slopes. It reminded her of the hillside slums of Rio. Smoke from cooking fires hung in the huge bowl-like structure until it had risen high enough for the breeze to take it away. It was a giant cauldron full of life.

On its outer shell the zigzagging stairs and pedestrian ramps bustled with people coming and going. Some carried vegetables, fish or other kinds of meat, no doubt acquired below at the market, and others carried salvaged or scavenged goods that she could not make out. The rhythmic drums she heard were at the highest points on the stadium structure. There were three groups of drummers located at evenly spaced intervals around the stadium's uppermost reaches. They seemed to be playing off one another in what she could only describe as a pulsing circular chant. It was hypnotic and comforting. Maybe that was the purpose: keeping the town's people calm.

The next day Kim set out for the Golden Gate Bridge. She stayed close to the wooded areas and hilly streets where trees and vines had begun transforming the sloping terrain into a true urban jungle. In the center of the city, high on a hill, stood a giant three-spired radio tower that was painted red and white. It looked to be almost a thousand feet tall. With a curiosity that was overpowering, she went towards it to investigate.

As Kim grew closer to the giant steel structure, she heard many voices. It sounded as though there were a hundred or so people there. They were standing in a large arc around one of the massive legs of the tower. Kim was careful to approach cautiously. She wanted to see what kind of group this was. It was not a social site.

There was no fire. It was a town meeting, she thought.

Standing at the back of the crowd, Kim could clearly hear one voice talking, or preaching, over the gathering. She was distracted by the immediacy of her surroundings and the pulsing rush of blood in her ears. It was when the voice stopped that she realized how tight every muscle in her body was. You need to breathe and relax, she told herself with a long exhale. You can do this, just breathe and relax.

The others there listening were dressed somewhat similar to Kim, long-sleeved shirts and long pants with hats, breathing masks or goggles, or both. Everyone was dressed for being out in the UV. Feeling brave and thinking she would not stand out, Kim walked into the crowd. It felt strange to be so close to so many people. Since Wafiq left, she had been avoiding people.

In a low muttering clamor, the many voices were commenting to one another, seeming to agree with the preaching voice.

"He is right, you know. The senders of the waves should be killed," said one.

"Yes, yes. His training from The Before is indisputable. The brain-damaging effects of cell phones is what brought us to this," agreed another.

It was as if the quiet mob had gathered to watch and hear one of those television commentators with extreme and outrageous opinions validate their views. From a platform about one story above the assembly was the voice, a shoeless man in ragged black shorts and black t-shirt. He was pacing back and forth across his stage holding old dead smartphones in each of his clenched fists.

The man on the platform was yelling and cursing. His face was red and spit flew from his mouth as he spoke. "The destruction of humanity was brought from the heavens on radio waves. This tower is our reminder of how humanity's addiction and dependence on the wireless device, devices like these I hold in my hands, can and will destroy us," he screamed, holding the smartphones above his head with outstretched arms.

The crowd murmured in agreement as Kim heard the angry voice on the platform spit out the words, "Those from The Before who brought this down on us should be found and removed from the living society."

As Kim moved towards the front of the crowd, the angry and raving man then said something that made the bravado of her stepping into the crowd melt away, "The ones of the place called Obyavit gave you this life in which you suffer. Their Personal Assistant drove the world to its near death through the manipulations of fear and the incitements of hate. It is they who carry the debt. It is they who should account and pay."

Kim froze as the mob cheered an angry cheer, raising baseball bats and crossbows, golf clubs and rifles. She felt as if she had been accused, picked from the crowd and singled out. She had stepped into a snake pit.

No one in this crowd suspects my history, Kim thought in a rush of panic. No one here has any idea who I am. Yet, a chill of fear swept through her as her lungs seemed to reach for air, her chest heaving, her vision that of a tunnel.

I have to get away. I need to leave, raced her thoughts.

Kim eased herself from the clutch of the gathering, backing into the woods and disappearing. She ran down the hillside falling and stumbling, afraid and desperate, escaping from no one and nothing, but needing to escape. The many voices had trailed away behind her; yet she ran, down off the wooded hill, down through the collapsed row houses. Down a never-ending street and down to the edge of the land.

Fueled by her fear, she had run all the way to the ocean's edge. There were no voices when she finally stopped, there were no others at all. Just the ocean crashing onto the remnants of a civilization that had been washed out to sea, only to crawl back onto land drastically changed from the experience. After climbing over great heaps of tangled plastic, large broken objects with writings from far-off places and the disintegrated detritus of a crumbling society, she dragged herself into a severed bow section of what was once a luxury yacht. Hidden, she collapsed.

It was then that Kim looked at her guilt and her fear for what they were. She had let these things of her own making strip her of confidence. She had made them an entity, beyond her and within her. She let them steal her courage, keeping only for herself shards of insecurity. There in the mangled and broken remnants of luxury, she looked out across an ocean and assessed.

I'm out of the bunker, she thought. I'm above ground in the hazy light, away from the hole that's becoming my grave.

Kim was discovering a new reality, but she needed to be cautious, not afraid. She was one of them, a survivor from The Before now living in The After. No one had chased her. She had chased herself. Her mind bled fear and she ran. She had been caught in a self-destructing cycle ever since the discovery, ever since she learned of Nalani's fate, ever since David had been taken and ever since Wafiq left. She was chasing herself and running from herself. It had to stop.

§

Kim never made it to the landmark she had set out to see, but she did find and cross a bridge. She crossed a bridge that led her from a very dark place. She was not happy, but she was no longer without hope. Inside herself she held optimism that the society of humanity would try to recover, and that they would succeed. Her travels had opened her eyes and her contact with others had shown her the resilience of humanity, good and bad.

In the wreckage of a boat that smelled of dusty mold and dead algae, Kim, a shell hiding in a shell, sat at the edge of a continent. A continent that sat on a planet, which was itself at the edge. It was there that she realized she had a reason, a purpose. Her purpose was exactly what the voice on the platform had said: to remove from society those who brought this down on humanity.

It was with this resolve that Kim looked up to the rope that hung above the wheeled office chair that sat in the darkened end of the Building 3 server room. She realized that she had decided. She had decided to take the rope down and put the chair away.

CHAPTER 37

Day 334 of the second year A.E.

Water fell from the sky and the looted wreckage of what remained melted further as the hand of indifference worked the slow process of reclamation. The rain was a new thing. Until a week before, it had not rained since day 61 of the first year. Almost two years without rain; then it came, a steamy deluge of biblical proportions. It was the kind of wet heat reserved for the southern Mississippi valley in the summer, only it was winter.

The dry period was hard for the survivors. The makeshift farms and group cooperatives were unable to produce. Many starved. Kim taught herself to hunt, but she was not very good. Game was scarce. Often, she spent days roaming the eastern slopes of the Santa Cruz Mountains looking for anything. She was not the only one.

Tired, weak and very thin, Kim had taken a coyote and three wild dogs since taking to the coastal mountains to hunt. One needed to be very hungry to eat wild dog; she was very hungry. She hoped the rain would continue.

Before the drought and famine forced her to conserve herself, Kim had made it as far as Richmond in her exploration of the East Bay. It was a chemical wasteland up there. The smell of unchecked petroleum was present in the air as far south as Oakland. Time and the corrosive salt air had eaten away at tanks and pipelines. Their contents spilled out, turning the ground black with a volatile sludge. Two of the giant tanks burned as if enormous replicas of those canned burners used by caterers to keep food warm. The flames danced yellow, releasing long plumes of oily black smoke that rose and followed the wind until it melted into the brownish-gray skies.

Kim wanted to cross into Marin, but the western end of the Richmond Bay Bridge disappeared into the bay before reaching shore. It was better that the journey north stopped there. From the toll plaza, she could see the smoke of a social group's signal fire rising from the San Quentin prison, which stood near where the bridge would have made landfall. Her mind raced with dangerous ideas of the type of social group that would call a federal prison home. She turned back south.

Near a dwindling reservoir in the hills above Richmond, Kim came upon a small group of people tending a struggling garden. She had seen only four loners in all of the lowland urban area between Berkeley and the bridge, but it was in the hilly oak forest behind the cities that she found the lake and the people who lived near it.

Making her way through the dry scrub, pine and oak, Kim heard in the distance the sounds of metal against rocky dirt. She came to the edge of what was once a lakeside park and picnic area. There were seven people. They were working in a garden at the edge of an area that could have once been a soccer field. Further in the distance, across an area of decaying asphalt that once was a parking lot, stood a large building that looked habitable. Kim stayed hidden for as long as it took the sun to move one hand across the sky. I'll reveal myself only if I'm sure it's safe, said the voice inhabiting her head.

There were two women, two men, two girls and a baby. Their relationship to one another was not clear. They were all different. From a distance, none looked related by blood.

The men were occupied digging a deep trench. Each of them had a shotgun within arm's reach as they worked their shovels at a casual pace. One was older, tall and thin with curly gray hair and glasses. The other man was shorter with close-cropped black hair and was younger by several years. He was a substantial man, solidly built, with large tree trunks for legs and strong thick arms. He was shirtless and his brown torso, front and back, arms and neck were covered with ominous gang tattoos. The two men were engaged in a friendly conversation as they toiled in the hot sun, often breaking into laughter or head-shaking chuckles as they flung dirt from the hollow in which they stood.

The two women and the oldest girl, probably twelve or thirteen, were drawing water into small watering cans from a nearby tank and carefully watering various plants and seedlings. One of the women was older than all the rest. She was black with short gray peppery hair cut close to her scalp and worn in tiny tight knots. Her shirt was billowy and white with its sleeves rolled to above her elbows and neatly tucked into a loose pair of worn jeans. She moved with a fluid confidence and purpose, almost gliding, as the other two followed. She was clearly in charge, and the behavior of the rest made that evident.

The second woman appeared out of place. She looked to be in her late twenties, though it was hard to tell. She was unmistakably Scandinavian. Wearing khaki dungarees, a lightweight denim shirt and tan work boots, her clothes fit well without being baggy or tight. Standing easily over six feet, she was the tallest of the group and wore her yellow-white hair tied back in a long thick braid that hung to the small of her back. She bore an intensely focused look in her eyes and on her face, almost stern. She performed every task with the determination of a Nordic warrior, smiling with pride and self-satisfaction each time she completed her assigned responsibility.

The oldest girl had brown hair. She looked like millions of other suburban girls whose ethnic background was indeterminable. As she worked near the older woman, they talked back and forth. The gray-haired matriarch seemed to be teaching the girl about caring for the garden. The other girl, who was much younger, sat in the shade against the wall of the nearby building caring for a toddler that crawled about energetically inside a makeshift pen. They all seemed to have a job or a role, and they continuously chatted amongst themselves as they went about their work.

They behaved as a family tending to the work of survival. It was this familial feeling that led Kim to believe it would be safe to reveal herself. Rising from her hiding place, she decided to let them know of her presence.

Kim pulled down her breathing mask and goggles so they hung around her neck and stepped out of the trees and tall dry grass. She was just beyond the end of the soccer field, opposite from where the two men were digging. She took a few steps in their direction.

The men shouldered their shotguns. "Hold it right there, man. Don't come any closer or we'll spray you with lead," shouted the dark stout man with the tattoos.

The older woman grabbed the young teen firmly by the arm and moved swiftly towards the building, their watering cans rolling behind them in the dirt. The tall blond woman sprinted in long silent strides to the house where she scooped up the baby and the younger girl, carrying them both effortlessly through the doorway and into safety.

Kim raised her hands high over her head and showed them her palms. "I'm alone. I'm a Walker. I've come from San Jose and I'm on my way back. I'm an individual," she said in an even, reassuring tone. She wanted them to know she was not a part of a group or site.

"You're a woman," said the older man with a sense of realization.

Kim, her hands still raised, let out a short audible laugh as she said, "Yes, I know."

The stout man slapped the older on the shoulder and sarcastically complemented his partner's keen observational skills. The two women and the oldest girl peered out the doorway, snickering at the remark.

They continued shouting across the distance, both sides assessing potential dangers. Soon they moved closer, but still far apart, Kim's hands lowered and on her hips, the two shotguns pointed at the ground. After another fifteen minutes or so, the two men and Kim were within several feet of each other and the women and children were no longer hidden. Instead, they were watching attentively from the porch of the house. After almost twenty minutes, they all came to feel comfortable with each other. They invited Kim to sit with them in the shade of the porch of their house, which overlooked an emaciated reservoir.

They continued to talk for many hours. Kim told them who she was and where she was from. She spoke the truth to them but she left out many things she did not want to share. She told them about her trip up the peninsula to San Francisco, about the social groups she observed and other pockets of people she had seen. When she asked how they were able to survive intact through the great sickness. They all looked at each other sadly.

"Except for the baby, we were all loners at one time or another," said the older man, whose name was Yitzhak. "We call ourselves the Snowball clan, because we started as two loners finding each other, then the rest were picked up as time rolled on."

Although they seemed happy, they all had sad stories of loss and separation, or worse. The oldest man, Yitzhak, was a gastroenterologist in The Before. "I had a beautiful wife and two wonderful boys," he said. "I lost them to the sickness that was everywhere about two years ago." The sickness that took Wafiq, Kim thought but did not mention. "I had been working with a few other healthcare professionals. We were close to finding, if not a cure, at least a treatment, something that could buy some time for those that were infected. One day, I had to leave my family to walk to the hospital that I had been working with so I could get a specific combination of drugs. My wife and children were exhibiting symptoms. I was going to try an experimental treatment on them. I was desperate." He paused and took a deep, sighing breath.

"On my way back, I ended up being out after curfew and was picked up in a sweep by the National Guard. They took my medicines and held me for ten days before they processed and released me. I pleaded and begged them to let me go so I could save my family, but my words were ignored. When I finally made it home, I found my wife and two boys all lying peacefully together in the master bedroom. They had been dead for a few days. My wife was holding a note that said, It's okay, we know you tried. We love you always." He sat silent, wiping his eyes with the heels of his open palms.

That was when Anita, the oldest one, spoke. "I had seen Yitzhak every day for three weeks as I passed through the Jewish cemetery on my way to visit the graves of my grandchildren. I knew why he was there. I saw the freshly turned dirt near where he sat, rocking and saying prayers. I was living near the cemetery, in an abandoned house I had taken as my own. I wanted to be near my grandchildren. When my son and daughter-in-law lost their children, they buried them and then joined the mass exodus to the mountains. They said it would be safer there and the temperatures were cooler. I didn't want to leave. I couldn't believe it would be any different, especially since just about everyone in the Bay Area was going up there. I wanted to stay with the grandchildren, so I did. After three weeks of seeing Yitzhak, I knew he was not leaving the graves he was near. I decided he needed me to help him. You see, we shared a bond of pain and loss. He needed me and, I guess, I needed him. Eventually I convinced him to stay at the house I had taken."

"She saved me," Yitzhak said, as he reached over and held Anita's hand, giving it a gentle squeeze and shake.

"We lived as mutual friends for almost a year," Anita continued, "caring for our families' graves and keeping our memories of The Before alive between us. Then one day, as Yitzhak and I were scavenging food supplies from a nearby supermarket, we heard the loud crash of store shelves falling near the back of the market we were in."

"We became scared for our lives," Yitzhak said. "Not knowing what to expect, Anita and I grabbed what we could hold and started to leave, in a hurry. But, just as we reached the doors, we heard a child's cry come from the direction of the crash. Anita, compassionate soul that she is, convinced me we needed to go see, so we did. That's was how Emma and Lila came to be with us."

Emma and Lila had been living on the streets and hiding in the buildings of the mostly empty suburban area to the east before being found by Anita and Yitzhak.

"They probably would still be out there on their own if Lila, the oldest, had not climbed up on the shelving to see who else was in the store that day," continued Anita. "Lila was eight then and Emma was just five. Lila had become pinned. The six-foot-tall shelving unit had fallen when she reached the top. It landed across her thighs and broke her left femur.

"Lila was amazingly brave for being in so much pain," Yitzhak said. "Not a sound or a tear. Emma, on the other hand, felt helpless and frightened. She began to whimper at first, but by the time Anita and I made it back to them, Emma was in a full-on wail."

Lila was standing to the side of Anita, so close they touched. A family bond had formed, Kim thought, as she said to Lila, "What happened? Why were you and Emma alone?"

"A long time ago," Lila started, "when the Army men came to do the policemen's job, my Dad boarded up all the windows and doors, like when a big storm like a tornado comes. The Army men were trying to capture a bunch of other men who were doing bad things. The bad men never wore shirts and had no hair and had pictures on their skin called swat-stickers."

Yitzhak added that she meant swastikas.

"One day," Lila went on, "the Army men chased the bad men into our neighborhood. There was a lot of shooting and explosions and my dad told my mom and us to get into the special room he made in the ground under the bedroom closet, but the bad men were already trying to get into the house and were pulling the boards off the windows. My dad began shooting at the bad men as my mom was putting us in the underground room. My mom told Emma and me to wait there and not come out until she came back, but she never came back. We waited there a long time. We slept twice and ate two dinners before I decided to go against what Mom had said. When we got out, the house was broken everywhere. There were holes all over and stinky brown goo was all around on the floor and dried on the walls."

As Lila related the girl's story, Emma, looking pensive but brave, sat next to the tall blonde woman who was named Britta. Britta was soothing the baby by rocking as Emma listened and comforted herself by gently holding onto the baby's wrinkled, pink foot with her small hand.

Anita told Kim the girls continued to look for their parents, hiding from others, until she and Yitzhak found them in the supermarket. "Yitzhak set Emma's leg. And knowing the fate that had doubtlessly found their parents, along with the fact that he and I had lost our families, we decided to form a new family and take care of the living while trying to let go of the dead." As Kim was listening to Anita, Lila had moved over behind Yitzhak and draped herself over him, reaching her arms over his shoulders and holding him in a piggyback-like hug as he sat.

Oscar, the other man Kim had met earlier, said that he and Britta were the newest to the group, having joined Anita, Yitzhak and the girls only in the past year and a half.

"I grew up in the flatlands of Oakland, north of the coliseum," Oscar told Kim. "I got involved with the Norteno gangs when I was eleven, and by the time I turned fifteen I was doing all the things expected of me, like drug runs, boosting cars and standing lookout for the others. I was doing time for accessory to murder by the time I was sixteen. But prison gave me time to think. When I got out, I volunteered with Catholic Youth Outreach, trying to keep other kids from the same mistakes.

"It was hard," Oscar said, "because by then, things were getting crazy with all the social networking between gangs. The gangs went social so they could expand their territories beyond the few blocks of turf they held in urban areas. First, they went into nearby middle class neighborhoods, but then it spread into the suburbs and other communities, taking over where less violent gangs were. Those skinheads the girls saw, they probably came outta that. By then, the National Guard were all over the place bringing down the martial law in a way the police never could, by using military type raids and big guns."

Oscar paused for a drink of water. As he twisted to reach for the bottle that Britta was passing him, Kim saw the word *Fruitvale* written in gothic script around the back of his neck. There was a thick scar running diagonally through the *F* and the *R*, leaving a pinkish-white eraser mark across the two letters. He had felt Kim's gaze and when he turned to meet it, Kim looked down. He was used to this. He continued with his story.

"I was detained and beaten more than once by the Guard. I fit the profile: Hispanic male, gang tats all over my body, arms and neck. I started wearing long-sleeved shirts and staying low. Spent almost a year up near the university, only coming out at night, and staying away from the Guard. After the Guard pulled out and everyone started leaving, I went back to Oakland and tried to find family. But no one I wanted to find was there, and those that were there I wanted nothing to do with. That was back when everyone was sick and dying. I decided then to go north. The heat and smell of death there in the city was too much, and there wasn't much left to scavenge after the fires. I made it up near the Concord airport when I came across a bunch of National Guard that were acting real crazy.

They had stayed behind and were following the direction of some deranged officer that had gone all Colonel Kurtz. They said he was godlike. They were rounding up people and doing sick and depraved things. They're still there, but they're not coming out as far because they're getting low on fuel."

That was when Britta, who had not spoken at all since Kim's arrival, looked up from the baby and said in a clear, grateful voice, "Oscar saved me."

He shrugged and almost looked embarrassed. At first glance, Oscar looked menacing, but the more he talked the more Kim saw the kind and giving person that lived beneath his tough exterior.

Oscar continued, "I was only going to hang around the airport long enough to see if I could sneak in and boost a truck. I had spent a day watching their routine. On the second night, when I saw the afternoon patrol return, I saw Britta. She told me that they found her hiding in a mall. Those animal bastards beat her pretty bad, and did other things too. They tied her up and threw her in the back of their truck so they could share her with the rest of the sick freaks at their base." Oscar went silent for a moment as he sat with his hands on his knees, his fingers clenching and relaxing repeatedly, his jaw tight, and his breaths slow and angry.

"That wasn't right, what I saw when they dragged Britta from that truck. She wasn't a person to them. They dragged her out and threw her into a cage meant for a large dog. I don't know how to explain it, but inside me I knew I had to save her, even if I got killed trying."

"Oscar saved me," Britta repeated. "The men there drank themselves blind when they got back. They were in a nearby building being loud. Oscar just appeared and pulled me from the cage. He cut loose the plastic ties on my wrists and ankles. I had no clothes, only a filthy towel. I was cold. I was dead inside. They had done things and I was bleeding. Oscar wrapped me in the shirt he was wearing and led me away into the nearby hills."

"I thought he was just another one that wanted to hurt me,"

Britta explained. "I had given up trying to fight. Doing that would only prolong things. But he spoke softly and did not look at me, just my feet. He all but carried me until we were safe. I couldn't stand or walk for three days. Oscar brought blankets and food. He even asked permission to help me clean up." When she said that, the menacing tattooed Oscar blushed and looked at his feet.

Britta went on to say that she became pregnant from the attack and Oscar, with his strong Catholic beliefs, had supported and protected her ever since.

"About the time Britta was seven months pregnant a lone walker passed by and told us about a hospital operating in Berkeley," Oscar said. "We were headed there when we came through the valley, here. Yitzhak and Anita approached us. Yitzhak explained that he had medical training and that he could help us. Anita said they needed another strong hand on their farm. So we stayed."

After the stories of changed lives, conversation drifted to the mechanics of living. The men showed Kim how they had rigged a solar panel along the south side of the building the year before and how the electricity it generated was stored in a set of batteries inside the house. They talked of the drought and gardening, scavenging and survival. They agreed that it was hard to trust people since The Event, but Kim sensed there floated near the surface a kind of hope.

As darkness settled, they sat around an electric lamp in the center of the main room. Happy in each other's company, it was a setting reminiscent of the way a nineteenth-century pioneer family might spend their evenings, Kim thought. It was then that she learned of a new person.

The family had a small radio with a hand-crank, and every so often they took turns winding the handle for one or two minutes at a time. Through this cooperative effort, they could listen to the broadcasts of someone calling himself Radio Man. This man on the radio seemed to have knowledge about things happening beyond the Bay Area, yet he seemed to be broadcasting from somewhere near the Bay Area. He often referred to small things that most might not notice, as if they were small clues. Things near San Jose, and in the mountains to the west, were vaguely touched on in a way that hinted of their existence or location, things about which Kim knew. There was an odd familiarity in what this broadcast voice said and the way it thought.

As she rested with the Snowball Clan, listening to Radio Man broadcast his thoughts and observations, Kim's mind began planning her next scouting expedition. First, there was some detective work to do.

CHAPTER 38

Day 158 of the third year A.E.

The rain that started so many months ago continued. Clouds came and water fell without end. Sometimes it was hard and torrential, collapsing buildings and uprooting trees, and other times it was a hot heavy mist that stole away the air before it could reach Kim's lungs.

Water had flooded into the open and unprotected ground floor of Building 3, seeping down into the underground bunker. There was little left to damage, but new smells of mold and mildew began to invade her space. It had become difficult to charge the batteries under the weak light of the gray skies. Kim's routine had become one of trudging through contaminated runoff searching for anything edible and cleaning the mossy growth from the solar panels on the roof. When the sun finally returned, she hoped the weather would get back to something close to normal. Whatever that was.

Kim figured she would have to move before the year was out. The rising sea was pushing the bay closer each month. The high tide was now six blocks away and lower ground in the surrounding area was starting to flood with incoming tides, threatening to cut off her access. The Obyavit campus was becoming a shrinking island.

When there was good weather, Kim would scout the hills to the west. The need to relocate to safe, higher ground was no longer something she could put off. She found several potential places. Large abandoned houses and a few commercial buildings in the nearby hills were at the top of her list. As the days of rain decreased and the return of a hazy sun increased, she moved faster and committed to moving away to a new home soon.

Kim scavenged a radio after returning from her trip to Richmond. She was listening to the Radio Man broadcasts and his ominous ramblings. He felt near. She also had built a radio direction finder, an RDF, out of components she liberated from a nearby aircraft instruments repair shop. The shop was within the Mech's territory. It was dangerous, but they did not seem to be very active during the last month of rain. Kim wanted to find this person called Radio Man.

The RDF pointed her to a location high in the mountains to the west. She had not been able to venture too far, though. The rain, dense growth and steep wet slopes were too much. She attempted to follow the highway up into the mountains but encountered an impassable gap where a bridge once crossed a creek. The bridge was at the bottom of a deep ravine and the earth where it once stood continued to move, sliding down the mountain in wet and slimy house-sized chunks.

Radio Man did not broadcast all of the time, but there was a pattern and predictability to the transmissions. He began each of his four daily hour-long programs at 7:05 and 1:05, AM and PM. Without fail, he was always there.

He mostly wandered benignly, but sometimes his thoughts and topics relating to the past took the tone of a sermon. He would talk of Personal Assistant and Obyavit, saying things like, "Obyavit went forth and explored the land to gather the best scientists and developers, and the scientists showed the people the fruits of their labors and said they could bring riches and happiness to the users of their labor. But the people could not change. And those that disbelieved the benefits of technology spread rumors that the words from the corporations in the valley of silicon were lies and that the bestowal of riches and happiness were untruths. They said that we as humans would not be able to grow in the soil of technology and that the corporations were giants that no user could defeat.

"So the users of technology began to ask, are we being led by the Personal Assistant to our own death?

"And the knowledgeable and the trained said, no, they had used the Personal Assistant in many different ways and the riches and happiness were true, and by using the tools of the social network, we could advance our causes and protect our power…"

The underlying subtext of his orations were the same. He would tell whoever was listening that the makers of technology should not be blamed, that technology by itself was harmless. "Nay, technology did not kill the people, start the wars and launch the death into the sky," he preached, "people did."

Exhorting that only social networking via technology can help people, he talked of groups that abandoned technology and the danger such ideas posed. "Following social trends as guided by technology has done great things for its users; and yet, there are those who would reject its use and disbelieve its power. I have seen the benefit of this technology and it is good. If we use the technology, allowing it to guide us, you too will see the benefits. We have no reason to be afraid, the technology is on our side, and those without it do not stand a chance."

He said he had answers. He said he could help anyone who wanted his help. He said he could make the hard life of the present easier. He never said how, just that people should continue to listen and hear him out.

The voice of The Radio Man haunted Kim. It felt as if he were talking to her. She tried to shake this off as being starved for conversation. She did not want anyone to be a part of her, or she of them. Those who she felt safe approaching were happy to talk. Even apparent loners wanted social contact, acceptance and friends, just in small and managed doses. The people that remained still wanted to be liked; they just wanted to feel they controlled the terms. Radio Man would broadcast his message to any ear, but he had conditions. He wanted you to like him, but you had to do so completely, and on his terms. She somehow knew that when, or if, they met, they could not be friends. She still listened to him rant, preach or just talk at least three times a day. She looked forward to the start of his show, the part when he said, "Welcome to the Assemblage."

While survival had become Kim's primary activity from day to day, it, along with every other aspect of her life, had to compete with a past that continued to haunt. Who or what was Radio Man, and what or where was the Assemblage? The voice from the airwaves attached itself to bits and pieces of her. At first, she did not recognize this. However, as the days of the A.E. accumulated, she became sure that her discovery of this entity was not accidental. And if not, then why?

CHAPTER 39

Day 296 of the third year A.E.

The smell of black algae filled the air and streaks of green moss marked the walls randomly where water had begun to seep into the server room. The high tides were still blocks away, but the underground water table was pushing against the walls of Kim's subsurface bunker and water was leaching through the concrete. It was time to leave. She took very little with her when she left Building 3 for good. Only gear that could keep her safe and keep her fed, and her MyPhone.

Kim had found a house in the hills. Actually, it was a mansion. It was very large and had many rooms, eight of which were bathrooms. None of them worked. There was an underground storage area which was stocked with enough survival food and supplies to last her a few years. Whoever lived here was not only wealthy, but was also prepared for the worst.

Below the balcony of the room where she had set up camp was a swimming pool that was catching rainwater. It was her private source of fresh water; she did not have such a ready and nearby source in the valley. She used the chlorine tabs from the survival supplies in the house to ensure it was clean enough to drink.

To the west was a small vineyard, and open space covered in tall grass was all around the rest of the property. There were also fruit trees, all dead, victims of the long drought. Much to Kim's surprise, there were deer. Several deer roamed together with their young, coming into the overgrown vineyard to nibble the grapes. She planned to go back down to the valley to find a hunting bow and arrows that could take large game. Using a gun would attract attention Kim did not want.

She spent three months scouting the area. Trudging around in a two-mile radius repeatedly, she searched vacant buildings, under culverts and bridges, and through dense wooded overgrowth. The only human tracks she saw were her own. She felt safe there. She could probably grow old and die there, she thought.

The room where Kim made her camp was her new home. She used the master suite and two nearby rooms. A balcony provided wide views east across the entire valley. There was a telescope. When the weather was good and the hazy smog thin, she could scan large sections of the valley floor. There was so much more water down there now. Fat fingers of the brownish-green bay surrounded the airport and reached south beyond downtown. The bay appeared to be twice its size. It truly was amazing.

From her camp, Kim began tracking and logging the Social Sites she spotted with the telescope. There were seven. The farthest was near Fremont, east of the 680 in the hills. The black smoky fires they used to draw attention to themselves were easily visible. A pillar of smoke still rose from the airport. The Mechs. They represented the worst the new society had to offer. Governing with brutality and fear, they were the remnants of a hate that would not die. As much as she was able, she tried to study their hierarchy, their miniature apelike society. They were tribal, but with a stratified, military structure.

There was a leader. Below him, the group subdivided. There appeared to be a fighter class, those who protected the group and went out to secure territory that was of value. There was also a worker class, whose members did not necessarily fight unless there was an overwhelming need. Mostly, the worker class provided the supporting infrastructure for the group. They prepared food, repaired the vehicles and weapons, and when a valued new territory had been secured the workers came in and stripped it of all that was useful to their group. That was the other reason Kim needed to leave the valley. It was slowly being stripped by the Mechs of any useful salvage.

She turned on her smartphone occasionally, for one or two minutes at a time. It was much safer to take such risks since she had moved. It only held a few more minutes of life in its battery. Since arriving at the mansion, she had not been able to charge it.

As soon as she started receiving a signal, she saw the Mechs begin stirring with activity through her telescope. An ant nest sensing ground vibrations. They were still connected, and they saw her when she hit the net. They could tell she was to the west but with GPS deactivated, the Mechs could not get an exact location. The MyPhone would try to reactivate GPS every time Kim connected but when that failed, the system would then attempt to triangulate her location. The limited number of towers – only two within range, their signal very weak – and her mountainside location limited accuracy to only five miles. That was still too close for comfort.

Why do they concern themselves with me, Kim wondered.

Kim wanted to find and kill the last instance of the Fortune Teller. But she found she could not do much from the frontend of the app for the random few minutes she was safely able to be online. She noticed, though, that something about it had changed. It was operating in what seemed to be more of a listening mode. She ran a logging program in the background when she was online once, then dumped it to one of several tablets she had scavenged in her travels.

It seemed to be observing those who chattered across the net, as if it were in some sort of learning mode.

Kim also saw a few new groups among the online social networking sites. Some user I.D.'s represented many people under one login. That must mean there were very few working MyPhones. The groups and I.D.'s originated from large inland metropolitan areas, almost no coastal cities. They all were desperate, all asking for military and government help.

"St. Louis needs civil engineers and will offer safe harbor to those who are credentialed as such," read one such message. It seemed they were trying to rebuild.

Others sounded more desperate, "Sioux Falls needs help. Please, please send help." Phoenix simply said, "We are being overrun by them. May God be with you." It was scary, the things they said were happening. Surely it had not degenerated to what she saw online, had it?

Day 63 of the fourth year A.E.

Someone else was in the mountains. Maybe multiple people. They were working for, or with, Radio Man. Kim was sure of this. While tramping through the mountains with her RDF, she found the place from where Radio Man was transmitting. Well, from where the voice she listened to came. The Radio Man broadcasts were being retransmitted into the valley from a repeater tower far up in the mountains behind her camp. She should have guessed. The signal received by the tower was itself a retransmitted signal. She should have guessed that too. There was no way to tell how many hops it made before getting to the antenna she found.

In a clearing atop a nearby peak, there was an area with an unobstructed view of the entire South Bay. In that clearing on the bald mountaintop, with its thorny barrier of thistle, was a collection of radio and microwave antennae that were used in The Before by television and radio stations. A few looked like they might still function. Others were suffering from corrosion brought by the acidic air and rain, those serving as a trellis for invading creeper vine. But the solar and wind generators were still in working order. They sat charging banks of batteries, some of which were viable. Most of the batteries were oozing lumps of toxic waste.

One antenna was in remarkably good condition. Too good of a condition. It had been maintained recently. Within the last few months, at least. The vine and thistle were cleared back from the base and a nearby solar array. The thought that someone was working for Radio Man made Kim's skin crawl. Who could be doing this?

At first, she did not go looking for Radio Man. She liked the company. It was a voice that would talk to her and not ask for anything in return. It was hard staying isolated. But then Radio Man's monologues changed. His rambling soliloquies on the nature of earth's new societies and the clumping of ideologies into small human social groupings became more pointed. Then he began delivering a more antagonistic message. It was a message similar to the early buildup that occurred in The Before. It was a polarizing discourse that acted as water to the seeds of hate. It was a message of me or you, us or them, Kim thought.

"You people have spread lies about me far too long," he raged. "You cannot talk such that I cannot hear and you cannot have both the individual and the group. Now I swear by my own being that I will give you exactly what you want, exactly what you deserve.

"You will die in a barren desert, and your dead bodies will cover the ground. You have insulted me, and none of you deserves my guidance and direction. None of you deserves to see into the glass. I will send you and your anger away and you will roam blind without me. You will all die here in an empty waste.

"I have given you the means to live more easily and in a more informed way," he said. "You think you are in control? You were in control in The Before and you brought destruction upon yourselves. Those who have the glass and follow will be safe."

When Kim discovered she was hearing a retransmitted signal, she felt sick with disappointment. She set fire to the transmitter. Hauling gallons of paint remover from the valley over several days, she set fire to the top of the mountain. Her fear was that, whoever Radio Man was, his message would only revive the destructive social mindset that had given the survivors what they now had. She was determined to stop it.

As she hiked down from the antennae mountain, she could hear the low thumps of the large batteries exploding and the high-pitched hollow creaks of the metal framework bending and collapsing in the fire. As the towers fell and the mountaintop billowed black smoke, Kim felt a sense of satisfaction. She had acted.

It troubled her, though, that someone had performed regular maintenance of the transmitter. Who? When? She told herself it no longer mattered because there was now nothing left to maintain. She made sure of that. The airwaves were silent. But two weeks later the Radio Man's voice was back in the air. Only the direction from which the signal came was different. The signal came from far across the valley, from high atop Mount Hamilton. Kim felt frustration. It would take many days away from camp to find and destroy the source. And when she did, where would the next one be? There were retransmission sites all around the Bay Area. The pursuit could be endless.

Not long after the Radio Man transmissions restarted, Kim met a News Carrier named Allen. She had been in the valley scavenging tools when he came up on her from behind. There was confusion at first, but Allen turned out to be a valuable source of information. He told her of how things were elsewhere. He was a good person. They talked for a few days and then he went on his way.

Before he left, she asked him about Radio Man.

"Have you heard of the guy who calls himself Radio Man? He transmits at regular intervals. I can tune him in later, if you like."

"I know of Radio Man," said Allen. "I've never met him, but I've heard his voice."

"What do you know about him?"

"I know he broadcasts from a place that was once a large social site, possibly the largest. It's a dangerous place now, a place where strangers are unwelcomed. I passed near it once, maybe within ten miles. I stayed away. There was a strange feeling there, electric."

He knew its name and its location. He called it the Assemblage.

Day 94 of the fourth year A.E.

"You can't control me, god damn you," Kim screamed as she threw the radio from the balcony of her mansion-camp. It fell, crashing onto the cement decking around the pool below, shattering into unrecognizable pieces, big and small.

She knew who he was and she knew what he was saying. It was a different voice, maybe it was digitally altered or entirely synthesized, but the message was the same. It was an old message. It was the message from The Before and from well before that. It was an infectious message. Those that heard it, those that listened, became infected, diseased. They heard but no longer thought. They believed they were coming together. They believed they were part of the larger group. What they did not notice is that free thought was lost and that the individual was slowly absorbed. Kim saw it in the valley, in the groups and the reasons they gathered. She heard it when she talked to the ones she could trust. She read it in the graffiti and the tags that covered the rotted cement walls and collapsing buildings. They all were lost and looking for the trend. Radio Man gave them words and the trend came to be. It worked because he spoke what others wanted, or needed to hear. The trend was created and the followers followed.

Over four years had passed since The Before turned into The After and became The Now. Memories faded. The Fortune Teller had told them what the trend was in The Before and they followed to their destruction. Kim saw it, but did nothing, nothing of substance. Radio Man was the new Fortune Teller.

"Am I the only one who sees this?" she asked the air as she stood leaning against the balcony rail, her elbows locked, her head hanging limp and tired. "This is all a part of his plan. It hasn't stopped."

Kim resolved to get to the Assemblage. Kim knew what needed to be done. She knew why. It read like a ledger of accounts due. Nalani, who was somehow caught in his plan by ambition Kim never recognized or rewarded. David, who wandered into his path and saved her by the accident of time and place. And Wafiq, who suffered the results of her own inaction and the destruction of a plan gone wrong. Wafiq had given her the means; he stayed long enough to show her what needed to be done when the time came. The MyPhone she wore around her neck would be her payment. It was time to begin the ending. It was time to leave.

PART 7

THE END

§

"Deny all you wish, but we live and die for others." – Mother

CHAPTER 40

Day 130 of the fourth year A.E.

Kim was grateful for the accidental alliance she and Blade had, if only briefly, and somewhere in a dark corner of her mind she wished she had not been so stubborn about completing her journey without him. She could still picture him standing in the middle of southbound I-5, leaning his big frame on an automatic rifle, reaching for one last wave as she drove away, turning to face what lay ahead. We are now *friends*, she thought.

Kim drove the car as far as Wasco before it finally seized in an overheated and convulsing fit of mechanical epilepsy. Pushing in the clutch as the lurching spasms began, she let it coast as far as it wanted, as far as it would. The spent machine rolled out, unwinding itself down the weatherworn pavement until finding the place it would choose to die, and there it did. She grabbed her gear and started walking. Ahead lay Bakersfield, then the Tehachapi. After that? Well, that was yet to come.

The San Joaquin valley once fed the world with its endless orchards and croplands. Chemical-laden runoff had turned it into a fermenting bog that freely released a rancid smell of rotted earth and slimy, decayed crops. The blanket of stench hung thick around her. She tried to maintain decent progress, but the thought of tainted air filling her lungs over and over unsettled her.

The car allowed Kim to make up the time lost at the reservoir getting to know Lucette02 and the people of Avenging Lilith. Her skin cooled and her scalp bristled at the thought of what might have been. I should have been more alert, she thinks. I've grown complacent in the South Bay. I knew the groups and I had a few friends, a network.

In San Jose, Kim could move with relative ease. Sure, there were unknown factors, the Walkers and people like the Carrier, Allen, who would pass through now and then, but they were not many or often. Most times, when a Walker came through, word would spread and the human networks would quietly reverberate with fear and excitement. Now she was the one about whom the network hummed. "The low voices are chattering about me. I'm the Walker," Kim whispered to herself.

Approaching the old State Route 99, Kim saw people walking on the great highway. Not many, maybe three or four. They were not together, not traveling with each other. They were just more Walkers, some heading north and others south. As she came closer to the old highway, she saw more. She could see they were maintaining a set distance from one another. They were pacing themselves and not closing the gaps they had established.

The highest ground in the surrounding area was ahead. It was an overpass that connected the two-lane road she was on with the freeway. Kim crested the manmade hill and saw there were Walkers evenly dotting the dual concrete pathways into the hazy distance, in both directions. The ethereal sight held her. They were lost souls mournfully drifting on a solitary trek to some unknown place in the distant miasma of a destitute society. I am them, she thought.

Kim filed in on the southbound track and slowly the space between her and the others to the front and back adjusted. There was an awareness, but no acknowledgment. They were together, but apart. This suited her. She felt no desire to speak to anyone.

The pace of the Walkers on the 99 was slower than she would have liked, but she adapted. Not wanting to stand out and trying to relax, she watched those on the northbound track, looking down if anyone became aware of her prying eyes. She wanted to see what they carried and what they wore, whether or not they were armed. Everyone she saw had a weapon of some type.

In two days, Kim had made it through Bakersfield. While there, she scavenged and bartered for additional food and clean water, and confirmed her chosen route through the mountains was passable. She began the climb into the Tehachapi after a night camped in a valley that lay within the northern reaches of the once famous Tajon Ranch. The passing day brought a warm wind and thick clouds that drifted heavy and low. Bad weather gathered as she hiked an old freeway into the high country.

Years of neglect and intense storms brought by the new climate had tortured the old asphalt snake that wound itself over the most southern tip of the Sierra Nevada. It was at times buried or broken and progress was slow. Buffeting winds had started to rise out of the valley, pushing and shoving Kim forward while rending limbs from trees and scrub with a belligerent force. The canyon was funneling the air up the rising elevation and the intensifying gusts were turning dangerous.

Seeing a large culvert, Kim skidded down the embankment to its opening. Bending slightly she ducked into the darkness for shelter. As she reached around to remove her pack, she heard the metallic scrape of wet stone on metal. Leaning in a bit and squinting, she peered deeper into the corrugated steel tunnel. In the dim circular backlight of the opening at the opposite end, she could see a black silhouette taking the unmistakable posture of a hunter sighting game.

She was the game.

A male voice came hurtling at her. It was a shriek, pitched high and sharp, fast and trembling. "Why are you here?"

The question was wet with panic and terror. A cold wave fell through Kim's body. Death was near. "The... The wind," she stammered.

Standing motionless and stooped in the large steel tube, she instinctively reached her arms out from her sides, palms facing forward, fingers extended. There was a terror in the silhouette's short fast breaths. The light breeze moving through the passage towards her reeked of musky, sweaty dirt and stale urine. She looked down at the water that bled thickly past her boots, then looked back at the profile in the dark. He was relaxing, slightly.

"Yer... Yer not him," he whimpered in a soft relent of realization. Then, his thin voice falling away to a whisper, he asked, "Where are you from?"

"I'm a Walker. I come from San Jose."

He slumped against the side of the culvert, sliding down the rippled steel wall and crumpling himself into an upright fetal position, his rifle dropping across his feet into the water. Inert with fear, Kim waited. Bent, standing in an awkward hunched position, tension gripped her body and pain knotted her cramping calves. She reached around for her Smith & Wesson, removing it slowly as she watched the sobbing wretch convulse and shudder. "Are you OK?" she said in an attempt to distract.

He spoke into his knees, his face hidden, "I'm... I'm sorry (sniff). I... I thought you were him."

Keeping her weapon on him and thinking there were safer and less interesting places to ride out a storm, she turned to check the weather back at the opening through which she had just come. The wind was intensifying and debris was crashing into the exposed end of the culvert. Deep metallic thuds of wood colliding with steel reverberated through the hollow in low sonic thumps. The likelihood of personal injury inside the steel tube had greatly diminished, while the likelihood of the same on the outside had risen significantly. How quickly fortune changed. Kim decided to stay and get to know her new acquaintance.

Traveling out of San Jose had been as if traveling into a darkness. She had imagined the world beyond the Bay Area. She even had her suspicions corroborated by Walkers and such. But the further she walked the darker the world seemed. There was humanity, she had seen it in Blade and others before him, but there was also malevolence. She questioned if the routine of her existence in San Jose had caused her not to see the world as it really was. That had happened in The Before. She was too head-down, too involved in her own world. There certainly was no reason to think it would not happen again.

Human frailty was the weakness that kept us from perfection, Kim reflected. Our inadequacies, whether invented or gifted by others, kept us wanting for something more, something other. Was that what the one she was after wanted, an unachievable perfection? Or was it ego? Did the blinding light of hubris cause him to think he could master the social tide? How could anyone think such a thing was possible? History has proven humankind thrived when free will was at its most chaotic. Anything less was the theft of inertia.

"Who is he?" Kim asked. "Who did you think I was?"

Nothing but sniffling, mouse-like sounds and the dull hollow thrum of the storm came from the darkness further in.

"Hey! You! Who is he? Who did you think I was?" Kim repeated.

The crouched whimpering shell began to reach down for the rifle that lay partly submerged in the deepening stream of water at his feet.

"I wouldn't do that. I have a gun aimed at your head." And she did. As he had come apart, she had come together. He retracted his hand, never looking to confirm Kim's claim.

"He is mad," said the crumpled man, his voice muffled and hollow as it passed from his downturned face to his feet, then bounced down the steel-walled cave to her tense and reaching ears. "He is angry and he is impassioned. His madness is dual. He is a soul consumed, an artist deranged by a vision so strong and so clear that he cannot manifest it adequately."

"You've not answered me."

"I don't know who he is. I just know... he is."

Kim was frustrated; she was getting nothing useful from his game of words. Looking towards the open end of the culvert, she again contemplated leaving, putting distance between herself and the unpredictable hermit balled up before her. But it had grown even darker and more turbulent outside. It was midday, and the round of sky that was visible beyond the confines of the metal cave revealed a dark veil of grey. Marble-sized drops of warm brown rain began to pepper the exposed metal where the steel tube protruded from the sloping earth outside. The space within began to rattle with static. Soon the trickle of water at her feet would be a torrent. He was looking at her when she turned back.

"We can't stay," she half shouted. "Runoff will flood through here soon."

He nodded, his face showing that he knew this well before she did. Still sitting, he pointed to the opposite end of the culvert and began to rise. Standing in a stoop, as tall as he could in the space, he pushed his rifle a few inches up the side of the corrugated tube with one foot and nodded towards it, asking with his eyes if he could retrieve it. She saw something in his face she recognized, something human she could trust. She nodded and holstered her .357. His eyes became soft, friendly, appreciative. He motioned and she followed.

They made their way up onto the abandoned mountain freeway. Big hard drops pelted and stung their bare skin; they were soaked in less than a minute. The noise of the wind and rain enveloped them. The sky was dark and peals of thunder rolled overhead. They moved without speaking; trying to communicate would be useless. They jogged east, along the painted white line that traced the edge of the roadway. After about half a mile they rounded a gradual curve where two ancient oak trees had fallen. Just beyond the tangled mess was an off-ramp which led to a solitary, abandoned Chevron station, its white and blue exterior turned gray and green with age. They made their way in and to the back where the cowardly man, or someone, had been camping very recently.

He set his rifle lengthwise on a store shelf that contained a collection of toiletries, personal items, and a coffee cup that said World's Best Dad. "You can use the ladies' room to change into some dry clothes. I'm going to change in the men's, then build a fire." His voice was calmer.

More thunder rolled across the sky as Kim looked around and assessed her surroundings. "I have only what I'm wearing, but thanks."

"There are women's clothes in there. About your size, might be a little big. You're welcome to them."

This unnerved her a little, "Do you always keep an extra set of women's clothes around?"

"They were my wife's. She won't need them. It's a long story." He turned and disappeared into the men's room.

Kim came out of the women's restroom. She had found a baggy blue t-shirt that said "Cal" in yellow script letters and a pair of women's Levi's that were about two sizes too big for her thin frame. Kim was barefoot but still had her small, hidden pistol strapped to her ribcage. Holding her wet clothes, she asked, "Where can I put these to dry?"

There was a fire burning in a makeshift wood stove that had been improvised from a fifty-five-gallon drum. He pointed to a line behind it where the wet clothes could dry. Seated, he had prepared coffee in a saucepot and was taking in the drying heat of the fire while sipping the hot liquid from a cup he held with both hands.

"Hello," he said in a voice that had a slight Mexican accent. Kim was struck by the marked difference in his appearance and demeanor from when they had first met.

After hanging her things on the line, she took a seat on an

overturned bucket across from her host, setting her .357, which was still in its holster, on the floor next to her naked feet. "So, where can a girl get a cup of coffee around this place?" she asked with a tight smile, feeling him out. She wanted to see if he was still the edgy wreck from earlier.

Retrieving a cup from a nearby shelf, he filled it from the pot that simmered on the crude stove. Staying a respectful distance, he handed her the cup, which she took using the hand furthest from her weapon. Kim still did not trust him.

"Listen," he started, "I was a little out of sorts earlier. I have these times when things become a bit overwhelming. And, well, you caught me during one of those times."

Thunder cracked loud and close, rattling the windows at the front of the station. Kim sipped her coffee. Then, looking down into her cup, she continued where she had left off in the culvert. "You never did answer my question. Who is *he*?"

CHAPTER 41

Mankind, for as long as history can remember, has tried to impose itself upon itself. There have come from this battle of wills many successes, advancements, improvements and discoveries. All of these had to find their way from dark to light, from one to many, before they were recognized for their value, before history could look back fondly upon the wise craft of the human mind. Likewise, there have been failures in this epic struggle, when the will of mankind led from the illuminating light of benevolence to the surreptitious darkness of avarice, when value was perceived or received by very few, if any at all.

So was the course of the Fortune Teller. An idea germinated under the light of advancement and cultivated in the field of cooperation, only to be sold in the marketplace of greed as an accelerant to rapacious desire. This was what Kim carried on her journey inland. This premise propelled her towards the one for whom she searched.

"He is the CEO, the one in charge," said the man, as he sat

hunched across from Kim, gripping his cup tightly.

It was shadowy in the back of the abandoned Chevron station. Light from the fire within the primitive stove escaped through the seams and gaps around the improvised access door. The glow of a crisp orange line danced across the length of his face as a scratch in a movie might dance across a screen just before the film pulls loose and flaps round and round on the bottom reel of a projector. He was oblivious to everything but his thoughts.

"He gives the orders and the rest carry them out," he added.

"The rest?" Kim asked.

"There are about one hundred and fifty or so followers. They see him as a mystic. They believe he can tell them what they need to know."

"I'm not sure I understand what you mean." She was sure she knew exactly what he meant. She wanted to hear it from him, from someone who had trod ground closer to her target.

"They're lost people. They come from all over seeking to find themselves. They heard the words from the man on the radio, that's what brought them. That's what brought me."

"You were there?"

"Yes, I was there. I ran away, escaped."

"Is that why you thought I was him? Is he coming?"

He began to finger the cup he held and fidget his feet imperceptibly. "There are stories. When the first followers came, he required that one's commitment be without end and be divided with none. He wanted your soul, but he didn't say that. The followers that were already there, the ones who protect and defend, are completely devoted. They do his bidding without morality or fear. A lesser loyalty means death. The followers keep the compound secure and keep it running. They believe him godlike and for that he keeps them alive, until they are without use."

"What made you leave? Surely, you must have felt as they did when you first got there. What changed?"

He shifted his weight as he sat in the dim light. He was a man preparing a confession of the most painful kind. Without looking up, and seeming to search the three words upon the cup he held for some deeper meaning, he continued, "The clothes you wear, they were my wife's. We owned this station in The Before. After The Event, we would offer aid to the Walkers and other survivors who passed. Some of them were headed to him, to be followers, and they would speak of what they heard, and talk of purpose and reason. Over time, we too became dissatisfied with what there was left in The After. This was three years ago, three years ago today."

Kim began to understand. For him today held significance. She had such days.

"We wanted purpose and reason," he continued. "We wanted to contribute to something larger. So we packed up our two-year-old son and enough supplies to get us there on foot and headed east, to the military base near the shallow lake called Rogers. Two and a half days' walk from here."

"Is that where it is, at the old Edwards base?" Kim had heard from the human network that was the place. That was where she was going when she stumbled across the man who sat before her. She wanted to be sure, and at that moment it seemed there could be no more accurate a source than him.

"Yes, there. Edwards," he said.

Kim was nervous and her mind raced. I'm getting close, she thought. I need to know as much as possible before I get there. I need to be prepared. "What happened?"

"When we arrived we were herded into a hanger. There was food. As we ate, they closed the giant doors and locked them. A voice spoke to us over loudspeakers and told us we would be held there for orientation. Orientation he called it. It was brainwashing."

His voice began to crack as he wiped his eyes with a free hand. "They kept us locked up in there for fifteen days. There were videos on giant screens and repetitive recordings of indoctrination. Hate and fear. Many could not take it, while others gave over their will to him. The weak were berated as non-believers. The verbal abuse turned physical, and by the end of the week you were either the beaten or the believer. There was no middle ground."

He began to sob, heaving with an emotion that seemed to tear at him as he spoke. "We could not believe. We wanted more than what remained in this used-up world. But we knew what we were being told was not right, not the way men and women, the way humans should be. Not what *we* should be. We tried to get out. We pounded on the giant doors and begged, and then we were beaten, beaten and beaten. Our son was ripped from my wife by two young men, thrown to the ground and stomped. She was killed trying to save him while others held me and made me watch."

He stopped speaking and sat quiet, head down, wet droplets splashing silently at his feet. Wiping his eyes and clearing his throat, reaching for strength and composure, he told Kim the rest. "Then I was beaten and left for dead. At the end, when it was over and the ones they called the true followers stood over the bodies of those who would not, the doors were opened." He stopped and sat quiet for a moment. Then, shaking his head in a kind of distant disbelief, he continued. "The dead were scooped by backhoes and dumped into long trench-pits that held so many other rotting bodies. This man, he had those that failed his test dumped into composting pits that would produce methane for power. He had a use for every volunteer that arrived, follower or not."

Kim sat there, stunned by the rawness. What am I headed into, she wondered. She looked at the man whom she no longer thought of as a coward and asked, "But you're here. How?"

"I crawled out of the pit at dark. I walked throughout the night across the desert. My ribs, upper arm, shoulder and jaw were broken. I was covered with blood, mine and that of others who had been piled upon me. I passed out in the middle of nowhere in the darkness, believing I died in that hangar and only then, in the desert, had I found my grave. I woke the next day in the town of Mojave. There is an old woman there that few know about. She healed me and others like me, before and since. One or two a year, she said.

Those who had escaped with only a fragment of their lives."

"And you came back to this place. This place of memories."

"It's all there is. It's all I have. My wife and son are alive so long as I am alive, and so I remember them, talk to them and keep them, one day at a time. Some days are harder than others are. Today was a hard one."

He paused for a moment and Kim left him to his thoughts. She wanted to ask more. He did not move or make a sound for quite some time. Then after several minutes had passed, he picked up right where he had left off. "I also warn those who I think will listen. I try to save the ones that I can see won't make it through the orientation. The ones that are determined to become a part of the Assemblage I leave to their destiny."

The Assemblage. There was no doubt; he was talking about her destination. Kim felt an involuntary shock jolt through her. "That is where I'm going, the Assemblage."

This man seemed to think this over for a moment, as if making sure his response was measured and thoughtful. "You don't come across as a follower. I don't picture you as a part of a collective consciousness," he finally said.

"I'm not. I'm going to put an end to it."

CHAPTER 42

The next day came quietly with muted light. The storm had run itself out the night before, but the sky still held firm the dense clouds that were common as one moved further south. Earlier the man at the Chevron station resupplied Kim with water and a few more shells for her Smith & Wesson. As she pulled on her pack, hat, and adjusted her goggles to her face he announced, "I'm going with you."

"No, you're not. I'm doing this alone."

He reached down and grabbed a pack that was heavy with supplies, and as he straightened himself he defiantly slung his rifle over his shoulder. "You need me. I know the place. I know what to expect."

"I've had the conversation already. What I plan to do is payback for lost friends and others like you who wanted more, but instead lost it all. I owe them an end. This trip I make is me doing that. All this around us came from one voice, one place and one mind. I intend to settle with him. This is between us, no one else."

Kim started walking out of the Chevron station.

"Thanks for the supplies and the dry place to sleep," Kim said over her shoulder as she moved past the lifeless gas pumps on her way towards the eastbound on-ramp. She could hear footsteps not far behind. He's really starting to piss me off, she thought.

Kim stopped, planting her feet on the cracked pavement of the intersection at the head of the on-ramp. "I'm going alone. No more leading, no more following, and no more asking others to do what I should be doing. Is that so damned hard to understand?"

He had stopped when she stopped. He was a few yards back. Under the bill of a ball cap that said "Dad" in white letters, his face showed a sense of urgency. He said nothing.

"Damn it!" Kim said, as she marched off down the on-ramp.

They traveled up and across the high valley where the old town of Tehachapi still stood. It was thinly populated, and men on horseback patrolled miles of high, electrified fence that surrounded a section of the town on the northeast. The man who was still following Kim, the man whose name she never asked, the man she never intended to meet in the first place, was about a hundred yards back. He had described this group at Tehachapi the night before. He said they were a commune of friendly people and that they drew electricity from the wind using the turbines that covered the east end of the valley. He also told her that approaching the west gate might get her in and further supplied, after a few minutes of questioning and a thorough search. They too wanted rid of the CEO and his predacious followers, but had no stomach for bringing any fight.

Kim gave the village a wide birth, staying to the edge of the low pine forest that skirted the high-desert plateau, making sure not to be seen by anyone. By day's end they were at the bottom of the mountains and the desert was spread out before them. In the distance, toward the town of Mojave, she could see the familiar black column of smoke marking the presence of a social group. She moved south off the old highway about a mile, but stayed to the high ground so she could keep both the town and the road in sight throughout the night. Having found a good place to camp, she began clearing the area of rock and brush so she could sleep somewhat comfortably. Her shadow from the old Chevron station did the same just a few yards away.

His presence irritated Kim. She understood his motivation. She just wished he had become motivated with someone else. Our reasons are almost identical, she thought. He had sought something better and it turned against him. He knew loss of the most painful kind, the closest kind, and he felt helpless when it happened. His world had been taken from him. In him, she saw herself, the part she was able to control and hide with years of practice. In him it was still fresh, still near the surface. Her scars were his wounds and her determination was his anger.

Kim stood looking over at the man who was hunched on the ground, chin on his knees, arms tight around his shins, lost and staring out into the vast, dark desert below. Then she called, "Hey. Come on over. Bring your stuff."

He grabbed his pack, rifle and hat and hurried over to where she stood, approaching with a pleading look on his face. He stood there holding his belongings in a haphazard fashion, as if he were a small boy trying to help clean up.

"OK, here's the deal," Kim started in her strongest no-nonsense tone. "We do this together but I give the orders. This is my project. You're free to suggest alternatives to any plan and I'm free to accept or disregard them, without discussion. We look out for each other, we cover each other and we work towards carrying out what I've set out to do. Got it?"

"Got it."

"Anything else?"

"Uh, well, I'm Diego. What should I call you?"

"Call me Kim."

"Kim." He paused and then asked, "Is that your real name, your whole name, just Kim?"

"It's what you can call me." That was all he needed. That was all anyone needed.

"Okay."

"Now set your stuff down and get below the brush line. I don't want to be seen."

As they sat there in the desert among the creosote and yucca, Kim began to concider what she needed to accomplish when she found him, when she found the Assembler, Radio Man, the CEO or whatever else he might call himself. She knew who he was, his real name. That was who he would always be to her.

§

The next day they made their way back to the old four-lane highway and started down towards the town of Mojave. Ever since they had gotten a few miles past Tehachapi something had been eating at her. It was not anything prominent in her mind, just a feeling. Something was different. It was not until she had relented and allowed Diego to be her traveling partner that her mind was free enough to finally notice: they had not seen a single Walker since Tehachapi.

They hiked on at a steady pace. She looked over to Diego, who was walking with his eyes on his feet, deep in thought.

"Hey, we're alone," said Kim.

"Yeah, so."

"I mean, we haven't seen another Walker since the top. Not since the wind farm. Doesn't that strike you as odd?"

"Yeah, I guess so. When I was here last, there was a steady stream of Walkers. I guess we should've seen a few, at least."

"It doesn't feel right."

They continued without talking for another mile before Diego added, "We'll ask around in Mojave. We can ask what kind of traffic they've been seeing."

The sky was solid with clouds, and the wind coming off the mountain increased as they hiked down the miles-wide alluvial fan that dumped them into the vast western Mojave Desert. The town grew larger as they neared. The black smoke from the social group's signal whipped into a vortex as it hugged the earth, beaten and blown by the wind.

About a mile outside of town, they saw the skeletal remains of three people lying face down in the center divider. Diego and Kim moved by without stopping. The shredded and bleached clothing revealed that much time had passed since these individuals had fallen. They had next to them the disintegrated remains of packs, the contents now just a pile of weathered belongings that had long ago seen better days.

"You will die upon a barren desert," Kim said, more to herself than to Diego.

"What?"

"Huh? Oh. Nothing, just something I heard once."

When they reached the edge of town, suspicions that had begun to form from afar were proven true. Mojave was abandoned. They stayed to the main street, Business Route 58, and what they saw made them uneasy. The town had been raided and ransacked. Entire city blocks had burned and the remainder had been looted. Whatever happened had occurred some time ago, maybe a year. There were bodies, but they were nothing but dried flesh on bone and bleached rotting cloth half buried in miniature drifts of desert dust. They all seemed to have been fleeing. They lay as if they had died while running, while trying to escape. They seemed to be heading towards the mountain, all running *away* from the direction Diego and Kim were headed. The two released the safeties on their weapons and held them ready.

They had not spoken since entering the town. Walking slowly, they scanned for movement and took in the Pompeian scene of frozen panic and death. At the center of town, near where the route forked south and east, they both could see the source of the smoke. The wind was blowing it low and across the road. It was not far from them.

Diego pointed towards the smoke. "That's the Sheriff's Department. It's coming from there."

"How do you know that?"

"The old woman I told you about, the one who saved me. She lives there."

"I'm not liking this, Diego. Something bad happened here."

"Yes, but someone is feeding that fire. A person or people are still here. We can find out what happened."

"Let's spread out. We're too easy a target standing together like this. I'll take the north and you take the south."

They moved east towards the source of the smoke. The Sheriff's Department stood alone next to the road. There were vacant lots on both sides of a parking area to the rear and the road crossed in front. Kim signaled to Diego that she was going to move off to her left and circle around the back. He nodded and motioned his planned path to the front. Nearing the back of the building, she could see the signal fire. It had been fed recently. Nearby lay piles of scavenged wood and tires. She noticed several fresh boot prints leading to and from the fire in the fine dirt. They were all from the same pair of boots.

So far, it seemed there was but one person. Kim moved towards the building, taking cover behind the rusted and burnt husks of patrol cars that lay dead in their stalls, just as the rest of the dried corpses that littered the town. Making a running break for the building, she slammed against the cinderblock wall near the back doorway. The door was partly open, cracked just a few inches. She gave it a push. It creaked on dry hinges as it opened, revealing a long hallway with a door at the far end and several open doors on either side. Just then, the door at the far end opened halfway and in it stood Diego, his rifle held at arm's length. He was motioning for her to come.

Moving towards him, Kim looked into the rooms that were off the long hallway down which she walked. Some were bunkrooms for sleeping, their bunks not used in so long that dust had settled upon the neatly made beds. Another room looked to be a medical examination room. It reminded her of a doctor's office from The Before. Across from it was a room that was intended for much more serious medical treatments. This room resembled a makeshift operating room. But, just as the others, a layer of dust said that it had not been used in quite some time.

As Kim reached the end of the hallway, Diego pushed the door open and stepped aside. She followed his eyes across the room to where, seated in an old leather recliner, wearing tan work boots and the olive green jumpsuit of the Kern County Sheriff's Department, was an old Native American woman with long gray hair. She was smiling. She was happy they had come.

CHAPTER 43

"This is Mother," said Diego.

"This is your mother?"

Kim was out of breath and Diego's statement confused her. The adrenaline that had pumped her emotions and senses to the edge just moments before, as she approached the building not knowing what to expect, was fading. Her mind still held tight to the danger it had sensed as she approached the building. Where was the danger?

"No, no. That's what she's called. People call her Mother."

The old woman smiled and slowly nodded once. Walking across the room, Diego knelt down on one knee in front of the old woman. She was thin, sun parched, weathered and ancient, yet her presence was one of strength and endurance. He reached out and cradled her wrinkled brown hand with its contorted arthritic fingers. "How are you, Mother? How have you been?"

Again she nodded, only this time her eyes closed and stayed close as she spoke. "I have been alone, Diego, my son." A slight tremor shook her. She opened her eyes and turned her face back towards Kim. "Who is the daughter you have brought?"

Diego placed the old woman's hand back on the armrest of the leather chair, where it seemed to find comfort. He stood. "This is a Walker, Mother. She is called Kim."

The old woman's obsidian eyes grew strong and alert. Her body became tense. Her arthritic hands gripped the worn leather of the padded armrests. She pulled herself forward, sitting straight up, strong, a look of recognition on her aged face. "Kim. Kim from San Jose. Kim from Obyavit. You are that Kim?"

Kim's mind became tangled in chaotic thought, momentarily out of sync with events. She had never seen this woman before. She had never been anywhere near this part of California before. Staring at the old woman, she tried desperately to place her. Nowhere in her memory did this person exist. A mask of bewilderment fell over her face as she looked to Diego, then back to this woman called Mother. "Yes. But... how?"

"He expects you. He said you would come."

Dazed by these words, Kim felt as if her insides had been blown out. She looked within herself for answers, but emptiness filled the places she searched. She leaned back onto a desk. Could the old woman mean what she thinks? After so many years, how can this be? Paralyzed by the thoughts that raced through her mind, Kim looked back to her. "What do you mean? Who expects me?"

The old woman leaned back, the leather of the chair creaking. She closed her eyes and, as if seeing the past play out upon the inside of her eyelids, she raised her worn face and began to speak. "I worked on the base. He had come many times before the countless wars that caused the bombs of sunlight to fly. Then, he came in his helicopter for the last time, and stayed. He had built giant flat buildings, each covering many acres, each of two floors, except one. In them, he put hundreds and hundreds of machines that could think like people. The entire base devoted itself to these machines and their comfort, their wellbeing. When the machines could think well enough, we were all given one of these."

The old woman reached into a large pocket on the side of her left pants leg and revealed a MyPhone. It was in near perfect condition, and it appeared to be more advanced than the one Kim wore on the tether around her neck. Without seams, no plastic or metal on its surface, it looked similar to a thin rectangle of onyx. It appeared solid, futuristic, indestructible. With the hand that retrieved it, Mother presented it to Kim.

The old woman continued. "We were told that the black piece of glass would guide us. That it knew what we wanted, that it knew what was right and good. It did not. People began to live in the darkness of the black glass and gave up the light of the human-to-human ways. I saw this. I saw the people stop questioning. The words came to them so fast that they took no time to know if it were true. They just believed. They shared these words among themselves and never asked from where they came. They meant well but they were weak. They became blind and were led."

"But what about you," Kim asked. "You say you saw this. What gave you the sight to notice this and not end up like the rest?"

"I drove for his helper. I drove the car of the one who helped him make the machines tell the people the lies that looked like truths. She spoke of the original builder, the one who first created the machine they called the Fortune Teller."

Again, words from the past were being uttered aloud. Words known by dead people were coming to life in the air around Kim.

She was so tightly strung with tension that her body ached from the emotional force it held over her. She listened to the old woman speak. "She said the one called Kim would come and that they were ready. She said they had left the one they called Kim in San Jose, in a place called Obyavit. The one in the car said that Kim did not know what was possible, and did not know how strong the Fortune Teller was."

"Who said this? Whose car did you drive?"

"She was of your time, your generation, and her skin was dark brown, like mine, but she came from very far away. She called herself

Nalani."

"Nalani? She's alive?"

"I was sent away from the base long ago. She was alive when I left."

An even larger picture of deceit began to reveal itself. As Kim groped to comprehend the new information she had received, Diego asked, "Mother, what happened to Mojave? Are there any others here?"

"There are no more. It was near the end of the great dry period when it happened. All those at the base, all those who followed the words from the black glass, went mad. They threw down the glass and came to the west, to Mojave. The people here in this place wanted to help them, but they would not be helped. The glass had shown them that any but their kind were a danger. Their guns tore holes in the town and the people. Some tried to fight, but their death was then made worse. The people of this place ran into the desert. Some may have made it. Most did not. The followers wanted freedom, they wanted to choose their own direction, but they were unable to live without the words in the glass. They became wretched and pitiful. They fought among themselves and they killed one another. Some wandered into the desert. Very few went back to the base, very few."

"…None of you deserves to see into the glass. I will send you and your anger away and you will roam blind without me," Kim quoted softly.

"You have heard the words," Mother said as her black eyes regarded Kim. "You have heard the words of the one who speaks through the air."

"If you mean Radio Man, yes, I've heard him," Kim replied.

Mother just nodded as if she were piecing together her own mysterious puzzle.

"How did you survive, Mother?" Diego asked.

"He let me. He kept me alive so that I would wait for her," the old woman said as she turned her head towards Kim. "I stayed here, in this building, and the angry ones never came here. The words on the glass told them to do this. In the time that they read the words, it told them over and over that Mojave was the place of their enemy and that this building did not exist. They acted as if it were not here."

Pacing the room, shaking her head, Kim was overwhelmed. "This doesn't make sense. This is unreal. You said he *let* you survive. What do you mean?"

"I was told to wait for you. I was told that you would come. I was told to help the ones that were allowed to escape and that one of them would bring you to me. I was told to send you to him."

Diego was struck by Mother's revelation. "Allowed to escape? What do you mean?"

"Your memories were given to you. You were selected before the orientation. You were chosen because of where you lived. He knew that this one would likely come by way of Tehachapi. There were others along the many possible ways to get to here, but he knew it would be you who brought her."

Now it was Diego that could not process what he had heard. So much of his life since he lost his wife and son had been pain and anguish. Was it real? "What do you mean, my memories were given to me?" he asked in a halting voice.

"You came alone. You were made to sleep…" As she spoke, Diego saw flashes of memories he never knew he had, phantasmal recollections of a forgotten past. He saw himself in a dark room strapped to a table. There were needles in each arm and fluid-filled tubes ran from them. He was forced to watch scenes of horrible deaths and listen to words spoken of a life lived not by him, a life that was filled with pain and sadness. Things were done to him; only now did he begin to remember. He reached to his scalp and suddenly knew that the horseshoe-shaped scar was not from an injury but from a scalpel. As this new reality took hold, he began to hear the old woman's voice again. "…and now I am to send on the woman called Kim. Alone."

The old woman, still seated in the leather recliner, revealed a police revolver. In what was a slow fluid wave, she brought it around and shot Diego through the arm as he tried to jump. As he spun to the ground, the old woman's aim followed. In a moment of blind instinct, Kim drew her .357 and shot the woman in the chest.

Diego lay screaming in pain. Kim stepped quickly across the room and took the gun from Mother, whose collapsed frame lay shrunken in the blood-soaked sheriff's jumpsuit. Kim knelt beside the big chair, gently pushing the woman's gray hair aside, cradling her head. "Who? Who are you sending me to?" she whispered.

"He has many names. When I was there he called himself Bo."

CHAPTER 44

Diego was weak. He laid on a cot in the back of the sheriff's station. Sealed army rations within reach, he rested where she had left him. He was sedated and bandaged, and far from the danger into which she was headed. Even in his pain, with a hole through his deltoid big enough to stick a thumb into, he insisted on coming. "Just a day and I'll be ready," he said, wincing and squeezing his eyes so tightly that his temples turned blue.

Kim lied to him. She had told him they were three prescription-strength Tylenol tablets. Actually, they were three hydrocodone. As he drifted away into a pain-free sleep, she wrote a note of thanks. And as she moved deeper into her desolate self, she moved east into the lifeless desert, seeing only death before her.

It was late in the day. The wind continued to beat the wild sage and twisted Joshua trees as she hiked the highway towards the old Edwards Air Force Base. The darkness of night would be upon her soon. That was of no matter. She was using the momentum of purpose. With each stride closer to her destination, her resolve grew.

Time and miles passed. As she turned off the highway onto the road that covered the last few miles, the sky became black as clouds boiled low overhead. The fast-moving air brought the smell of moist dirt and wet asphalt. Rain was not far away.

From some distance, Kim could see a few lights spread sparsely across a wide section of the landscape. A mile farther, as she crested a slight rise, a row of closely spaced red lights appeared. They blinked in unison. She had arrived at a gate area. It was a place that had the look of a highway toll plaza, and all lanes were blocked but one. What daylight there had been was gone, and it was completely dark except for the blinking red eyes that stared out into the nothingness of the desert beyond. She stopped feet from the open lane, her body illuminated by the pulsing red heartbeat. Turning and scanning back in the direction from which she came, she could hear only the sound of the wind scrubbing the earth, but there was something more. She saw only the desert surging red towards her, then receding back into darkness, then repeating. She could feel something more. She felt someone out there.

Kim moved through the gate and into the streets of the sprawling complex of the base. There was no trace of activity. Offices and buildings were without occupants. Their appearance said they had been for a while. There was electricity here and there, but power lines were down and damage from previous storms were evident. Continuing past smaller buildings, she moved towards a central area.

It was an island of bright light, and the sky glowed of windblown dust in the phosphorescent night. Dirt and debris clouded the sky-bound light. Plastic bags trapped on fences and in wild sage popped and shuddered against the gusting wind. As Kim wandered, a strange sense of familiarity came over her. The buildings, the streets, the walkways; she had not been there before, yet she felt as if she had.

Ahead was a building, its shape familiar. Drawn to it by an unknown gravity, Kim stopped a few feet from its entrance. Sand blew across the cement walk that was as wide as a roadway. Under a stark portico, large cement planters held dead shrubbery and plants. Paper and other discards were pressed by the wind against the floor-to-ceiling glass wall, behind which lay an empty lobby. The thick automatic glass doors were stuck partly open. Gasping with shock, she said aloud, "It's Building 1! It's Obyavit."

It was not an exact copy of the San Jose campus, but its likeness was unmistakable. Kim moved to the glass doorway and entered Building 1 through the vacant lobby. Spacious and open, it was covered with a layer of silt that turned the horizontal surfaces a chalky brown. Climbing a staircase the same as one she had traversed so many times before, she ascended to the long hallway that led right to her office. The door was closed. She never kept her door closed. Grasping the lever to open it, she hesitated. A flood of memories came washing over her. The long days and nights, working all hours to meet a deadline or achieve a milestone. Her eagerness to advance her ideas, to turn thought into action and action into a product. She was so young then. It all seemed simple and uncomplicated. She was so certain her work would advance humanity. She pushed opened the door.

Older, with chopped gray hair and a sun-worn face, Kim saw herself reflected in the window across the office as rain started to slap against the glass. Looking at the space, Kim felt that it was hers, and at the same time, that it was not hers. It looked the same, but her things, the bits and pieces of her life that had slowly accumulated on her desk, shelves and walls were not there. This was just a copy of her office, she thought. Just as Diego was made into a copy of someone else with his false memories, so too was this building a copy of something else. All this to fool and deceive, just like...

Kim turned and left that room, almost running towards Bo's office. As she moved through the reception area and through the partially open office door, she drew her .357 and held it before her. She entered, hoping to find the one she had come to see. She did. He was there.

It was exactly the same. Seated behind the same glass and

steel desk was Bo. Kim walked over to the desk, contemplating the conclusion that was before her. This was not what she expected, not how it had played out so many times before in her mind. She collapsed into the chair that sat across from him, setting her weapon down on the desk, the barrel pointed directly at him.

"What were you thinking when you started down this path?" she said. "Did you have some sort of vision? A dystopian society weakened by war and hate, longing for direction and guidance that *you* would provide? You exploited the weaknesses of an overstimulated and over-distracted society. Almost no one noticed, until it was too late. Even me. And now, now nothing is left. I wish I knew what you had hoped to accomplish. I wish I knew, damn you." She slammed her fist onto the desk. The .357 jarred on the glass surface of his desk.

As she sat, angrily staring out the huge glass windows into the wet black night, Bo sat quietly across from her. Kim was never going to find out, not from him.

Bo had left long ago. He was dead. His desiccated remains slumped in his chair, a finger sized hole in the front of his exposed skull. He had been dead for quite some time. Any secrets he may have had, any answers he might have given, had died with him.

§

Building 3 that sat intact and a part of the greater incongruity that was the duplicate Obyavit campus. And in the time it took to cover the distance from Building 1, Kim's hat, pack and outer gear became soaked. She stopped to catch her breath before going in. Once again, she felt the presence of eyes off in the darkness. This awareness had been with her since dropping out of the mountains, but it was making her uneasy. She peered into the dark wet curtain, but she could see no movement that was not caused by the wind or rain. She entered Building 3.

The Building 3 she left behind in San Jose to the rising bay waters was a looted, trashed, decaying shell. The windows shattered and the interior gutted. Her last months there were shared with the rats and raccoons that had established prolific colonies amongst the rotting debris. Where she stood now was a well-lit place that made her feel younger and older simultaneously. Anger began to rise within her.

She looked out across the neatly arranged sea of cubicles towards the lab. It was like some disparate dream. Passing those little walled workspaces, she felt at home and out of place. The contents of the cubicles were different, but the layout of the entire floor was the same. Walking back to the lab, the irony that she could have navigated the maze with her eyes shut and not bumped a single wall was not lost. As she approached the lab, the familiar security door slid open. This caused her to jump back. It was unexpected. She brought forward the Smith & Wesson.

Inside the lab near the front, where Kim expected to find it, was her other desk. Her lab desk. Then she turned and saw where David would have sat. An invisible hand reached into her chest and crushed her heart. She began to weep. The hidden box that held the secret pain burst open, and she did not fight it. She was tired of carrying the box, of keeping it hidden. In that moment of time, in that place in space, she grieved for her lost love. It tore at everything that held her together. It made her stronger.

CHAPTER 45

The Last Day

It was when she noticed the muted silvery light of the overcast dawn that Kim realized she had been lost in her own memories too long. She did not want to let go, she did not want to come back, but she was all too aware of what it was she had come to do. Placing her weapon in its holster, she began assessing her surroundings. The servers, hard drives and network equipment in the rows of racks that stretched from near where she stood to the furthest reaches of the lab were all running. Stepping over to a console, she entered the commands necessary to execute a diagnostics script. The systems were functional. With a few more carefully chosen keystrokes she found what she had been looking for, the last running Fortune Teller.

From around her neck Kim removed the MyPhone she had been wearing since she left the valley, and from it she extracted a small micro-SD card. She pulled a nearby chair up to the console desk and set to work.

Kim inserted the micro-SD card into a small slot on the side of the keyboard and began by familiarizing herself with the instance running on the system. It had been almost two years since she last moved through a complete and running Fortune Teller. She wanted to be sure it was as she expected. It seemed that it was. The changes she saw were minor.

"Wait, what's this?" she said audibly.

Scrolling up onto the screen were huge blocks of new code and procedure calls. They had replaced key decision points. They all referenced the same thing. Kim could not make sense of it. As she started indexing the code, she heard footsteps approaching from behind. In what had grown into a learned reflex, she spun around and drew her weapon as she snapped to her feet, sending the wheeled office chair flying.

"Stop! Stop," came a calm and familiar voice. "Drop the gun."

Kim was stunned. Frozen. She stood slack jawed, eyes transfixed.

"Drop the gun," the voice coaxed again softly.

"Nalani?"

"Yes, Kim. It is me, Nalani."

It was. Kim knelt to set the gun she held onto the floor, her eyes fixed on Nalani the entire time. She stood then for a moment taking in the person who was before her. It was Nalani Rawat, older and showing the wear of a life lived hard, but it was her. Time had treated her as it had treated Kim. Her dark brown face looked tired and aged beyond her years. Her hair, still long and full, was mostly gray. Only yesterday Kim had learned that Nalani might still be alive. She had not expected to see her. Kim halfway did not believe the story, and yet there she stood.

Nalani was accompanied by two dark, thin, muscular men. Both had shaved heads. On the left side of their bare chests, they displayed a large tattoo of a four-armed black Hindu goddess wielding knives. It was Kali, the liberator of souls, or the goddess of death. The similarity to what Fortune Teller had become was not lost on Kim. Each of the shirtless men held an automatic rifle.

Kim took a step back. "You're still alive," she said with disdain.

"Yes, alive and well, relatively speaking. As I'm sure you know, life has been a bit more challenging since The Event, as it's popularly called."

"What is this? This copy of Obyavit. Why? And you." There were a hundred or more questions flashing through Kim's mind. Her scientific curiosity was overwhelming her.

"This?" Nalani said as she waved one arm, gesturing broadly to the surroundings. "This was *his* idea. He brought many from Obyavit when the Assemblage went live. He said the transition would be easier if the environment were the same. So he built *this*. He bought the entire airbase and turned it into an industrial complex. All the other businesses and buildings are also his. All just cover to hide the Assemblage. It was from here that we ran my Radio Man, a ten-fold improvement over that thing you called Fortune Teller. It was my Radio Man that we sold to the governments that wanted control of their populations' mindset."

"So it was Fortune Teller? It wasn't a person, that Radio Man?"

Nalani let out a laugh of ridicule. Her two thugs grinned stupid smirks of satisfaction at each other. "Are you for real? No! No, it wasn't a human. And it wasn't your precious Fortune Teller either. That pathetic thing could not come close to what I've been able to do with *my* Radio Man. Your code was a good base, I will give you that, but the real power was in manipulating the mob mentality. Fortune Teller was a glorified shopping list. What I have built is a controller of free will."

"But it didn't go too well, as far as I can tell. You lost control, if you ever had it. You underestimated the lengths those in power will go to stay in power."

"Yes, well, there are always setbacks and unforeseen outcomes when deploying a system of this size. You know that, Kim. We learned that not only the followers needed to be controlled, that was the easy part, but the leaders needed to be manipulated also. You see, the system needs to nuance its feedback to the customers, the owners and administrators. We focused all our effort on moving the masses but neglected to understand, and control, those whose reactions determined the next step in the manipulation of the social cycle."

What Nalani said made sense, but Kim knew human response was too dynamic and too complex a system to be completely anticipated and controlled. Kim also knew that Nalani had to be stopped. The system had to be wiped. Looking down at the console next to her, she began to consider her next move. "You keep saying 'we'. Who's 'we'?"

"Ah, yes. That would be our former employer, Kim. That would be the former Bo Tichý."

"Yes. I guess you could say I, uh, ran into him up in his office on my way here. What happened?"

"We had a disagreement in terms of project scope and direction, you might say. He wanted to use it to build what he called the perfect city, here in the desert. He was using the airwaves, those Walkers called Carriers, and what was left of the net to recruit followers. They would hear about his promises of purpose and self-worth and would come here in droves. He attracted the weak-minded, pathetic souls looking to belong. Losers that weren't accepted by any of the other social groups that were popping up out there. He wasn't building a perfect city. He was creating just another social group. We could do so much more with the system. I pleaded and argued. I even built a proof-of-concept. I showed him how, with the right changes, it would be possible to do what he had set out to do. But he changed after The Event. He was a weak and hollow shell. I had to give up on him. He forced me to."

"So you killed him?"

"I didn't want to. It wasn't part of my plan. As I said, we had a disagreement. You see, we knew you were alive. We knew you were in San Jose, even at Obyavit for a while, but our agents were unable to pin you down."

"Your agents?" Kim said, indignant with surprise. She had settled with the idea that Bo knew she was alive. But this, the fact that they had people looking for her, it made the skin on her scalp creep, like when an unseen person is uncomfortably close and their unwelcomed breath falls across your hair.

"I first saw you on the net, code tracking what you thought were Fortune Teller instances. I also saw your MyPhone a few times, early on. I was sure it was you. Especially once you started killing off instances. You made things hard for me, Kim. I had to stop my work on Radio Man and spend time cloaking and camouflaging the code. When I saw you, I also noticed several paramilitary groups forming around the Bay Area. The Mechs, I believe they called themselves. They were using MyPhones to communicate with their patrols and their satellite sites. I managed to enlist them with an early version of Radio Man. They had reported seeing you, but you were remarkably elusive. When Bo found out you were alive, and that I was tracking you, he became furious. You were his pet, you know. He liked you best." Nalani said, almost spitting the last two sentences out.

Kim felt an uncomfortable flush pass over her. Nalani saw this and it seemed to empower her ego. "Yes. I think he was jealous."

"Jealous? What do you mean?"

"Oh, Kim. Please. You know what I mean. Everyone knew about your little thing with David. Killing David didn't seem to bother him so much, after it was done." Nalani was trying to hurt Kim when she said this. She knew it would be painful, so she took the opportunity to exploit the weakness. "I think he wanted you all along, but you were too in love and lost in your work to notice."

Kim's anger was building. It was becoming difficult to keep herself in check.

"Anyway," Nalani continued, "When Bo found out I was tracking you and trying to lure you here he called me to his office and threatened me. He said he didn't need me. He said I was a distraction and that I was deviating from the plan. Me, the one who made his system work. He needed me. I told him so. Then I shot him where he sat."

CHAPTER 46

Nothing was as it should have been. Bo was gone, dead. and Nalani's thugs were ready to shoot at the hint of any nervous twitch. Kim asked herself, why am I even alive?

"What do you want?" asked Kim.

Nalani moved across the space that separated the two and sat next to the desk that would have been Kim's in another life. "I need you to look at some code. I have improved your Fortune Teller, but there is one function, one key operation, whose capabilities seem to elude me."

"You want me to code-walk your work?"

Nalani's face turned hard. Her eyes narrowed and her jaw clenched. "There is nothing wrong with my code," she screamed. The sudden change in tone brought the two gunmen a half a step forward and their aim at Kim's chest became tense and deadly. Despite Nalani's ego, there was still an insecure person sitting before Kim. Kim could use this to her advantage.

"No, no, that's not what I mean," Kim surrendered as

Nalani's fists tightened. "I meant like before, when we had the team, the more eyes the better. We turned out some great stuff as a team. Is that what you want?"

Nalani let out a single heavy exhale. "I need a code-monkey, and you are going to be it. There are only a few people left here and none can code." Nalani was starting to relax again. "I will generate the models and you will code them. You'll keep your work in the code vault, and I'll review it nightly to ensure you are not just wasting my time. You will be accompanied throughout your entire day by your two new friends here and your nights will be spent in a cozy little cell designed especially for you."

"What happened to all the rest, the staff, the followers?"

"Another setback, if you will. After Bo was out of the way, I implemented the next phase. The phase I showed him. The phase he ignored. There were unforeseen reactions by the test subjects. Free will began to aggressively reassert itself, and attempts to counter it led to a fear-flight reaction."

"How many test subjects, as you call them, were there?"

"Everyone. That is, everyone except a few of my elite guard, the development staff and myself. Everyone with the new MyPhone."

Kim reached into her side pocket and pulled out the black glass Mother had handed her back in Mojave. "You mean one of these?"

Nalani reached across and took it. "I see you've found one. Aren't they beautiful? So sleek and sexy. Where did you get it?"

"A dead woman in Mojave. She called herself Mother."

"She's dead? That's too bad. I had grown to like her when she was here. How long has she been dead? Could you tell?"

"Not long. Pretty recent, I'd say."

"Hmm. That's a pity," Nalani said with a careless wave of her hand. "Anyway, the followers, that is, the user test-subjects, fought. They fought each other, they fought the guard, they fought anyone and everyone. It was the antithesis of social grouping. Users formed small family units of two to five, or just singular, and grew more suspicious or resentful of anyone not a part of their unit. At first it wasn't violent, but before I could apply changes the killing started. They used their MyPhones to record and share gruesome acts of violence perpetrated upon one another. This sharing of images acted as an accelerant, each trying to outdo the other. Soon it was a race to kill before being killed. The development staff tried to escape, some to Barstow, others to Lancaster or Mojave, but the followers went after them."

"I saw Mojave. It's a dead city."

"So is Barstow. Lancaster and Apple Valley are war zones. But enough of this gloomy talk. Much has been learned from these earlier versions. That is why you are here. We have a system to build."

Kim sat back down at the desk, half facing Nalani, half facing the console. As Nalani continued talking about future plans of a society engineered by artificially controlled social interactions, Kim looked over at the two gun-toting goons that stood nearby. They were obviously bored with the technical talk. Their attention was elsewhere. As Kim positioned the keyboard so she could begin typing, she ran her finger down the outer edge opposite Nalani. She wanted to reassure herself that the micro-SD card was still in place. Kim then turned to Nalani and asked, "How is the environment laid out? I'll need access to the libraries and various run environments."

"You'll use the lead developer profile," Nalani said as she began walking Kim through the process of accessing the system. Though Kim feigned being out of practice, she very quickly saw the many similarities between the environment at the Assemblage and the one the Fortune Teller was brought to life in at Obyavit. Too many, in fact.

Nalani continued to take Kim step-by-step across ground she already knew by heart. "And when I've approved your code, you will move it here. It will then be staged for release into the test environment, which is almost an exact replica of the production environment and, as you know, can only be accessed by passing through three progressive and encrypted security levels."

It's now or never, Kim thought as she brought up a command line window and typed three short instructions, then hit return. As Nalani continued talking, she glanced over at the keyboard and glimpsed a small green LED located next to the escape key blink several times. Then, on the screen, thousands of lines of executing script began streaming by so fast they were unreadable. The cooling fans of three nearby servers became audible with the high soft sound of fast-moving air as their RPM's dramatically increased. The machines had begun working hard, very hard.

Nalani jumped to her feet. "What did you do?" She moved around the desk, grabbing the keyboard and shoving Kim back. "What are you doing?" she demanded.

Kim stood and moved backwards two steps. Slightly off balance, she reached backwards and caught herself on a nearby cubicle wall.

Nalani was frantically typing commands into the console, her desperate efforts having no effect. She picked up the keyboard and ran her fingertips along the side, then pressed a small button that ejected the micro-SD card.

The two guards became very alert as their boss became more animated and upset. They held their weapons tightly. Nalani was pinching the micro-SD card, holding it up at eye level so everyone present could see it.

"What in the name of hell have you done?"

A sense of relief washed over Kim. A strange and peaceful feeling settled into her and she realized that nothing else mattered any more. She had completed the task. She had reached the goal. The script was running and it could not be stopped. As she watched Nalani rage, she began to think that maybe, just maybe, she could talk long enough, say the right things and distract them. She would get them to focus on the system just long enough to get her .357, and then she could settle the debt in full. The last of the bastard Fortune

Tellers was being put to death, but Kim wanted its creator dead too.

Going with her instincts, Kim spoke, "In the years since I last had my chance, I had a lot of time to think about how I should have acted differently, Nalani. I realized that there are moments when pragmatism and deliberation lead to time lost. I learned that there are times when intuition, when gut instinct and moral certainty are one's truest guide. What have I done? I've acted as I should have long ago, I've initiated a system wipe. I'm cleaning up the mess I made. I'm giving back the act of personal decision making to the individual. No more aggregating behavior, no more subliminal control and no more influencing sociogenic actions. People will be free to think on their own and not be followed by a building full of data that is supposed to already know what they should think or do. That's what I've done. I've set loose a process that will force humankind to think for itself."

"You... stupid... bitch..." Nalani growled, her jaw clenched tight, tendons and muscles leaping from her neck. "Your little script or virus or whatever hack you've cobbled together will not get through the security and other anti-intrusion systems. Even if it gets close, there are automatic quarantine bots that will attack it and the sequester servers will detach. Nice try, nerdy girl. Too bad though. I really thought you would come around, given a chance, but now I cannot trust you." Nalani then reached around to the small of her back and pulled out a semi-automatic handgun.

"You seem to have forgotten one very important thing," Kim said.

"One last desperate gasp, eh, Kim?"

"Why not? There's nothing left for me to lose."

"Okay, I'm feeling generous. A few more words before I put a bullet through your chest can't hurt." The two shirtless guards again smiled with hyena-like satisfaction at each other.

"You told me earlier how Bo went to such lengths to replicate Obyavit, saying how it made the transition easier for those who came along. Well, as soon as you let me into the system I could see that the exactness of similarities between this Obyavit and the original went far beyond the surface. I designed the development, test and production environments, and Wafiq designed the security layers upon which you now so desperately depend. Nalani, I built, tested and retested that kill app for almost four years, in an environment exactly like this. I feel confident it will complete its task. In fact, if you look there on the monitor you can see for yourself. It's done."

The last thing Kim heard before the explosive sound of a gunshot filled her head with silence was Nalani saying, "Go fuck yourself." The last thing Kim felt was a kick to the chest so powerful that her lungs exploded and a searing pain knifed straight through her heart. The last thing Kim saw as her head and body were sucked into a violent spin was the windows separating the lab from the sea of cubicles beyond exploding inward, towards her.

Am I dying, Kim asked herself. She was not sure. It was dark, quiet, and without pain, but that did not seem to matter. She was happy. Fortune Teller was dead and she was at peace.

CHAPTER 47

Blurry. The diaphanous orange glow of sunset from underwater: warm, peaceful, out of focus. Voices speak…

"Whaddya think?"

"We wait."

"How long, Boss?"

"As long as it fucking takes, that's how long."

"I'll tell'm."

"K, I'll be here waitin'."

K? K is something…

Exhausted…

Black…

§

Dark. Submerged in sounds. Clatter, roaring, banging wood and metal. Voices yell above a clamorous blanket of natural chaos…

"It's a bad one."

"When will the lights be back?"

"Not sure. They locked the turbs. The wind, it's too much."

"If you hear anything report to me immediately."

"Will do. Say, Boss?"

"What!"

"Yer lookin' terrible, ya need sleep."

"When things look better I'll fucking sleep. K?"

"Yer the Boss."

K? K is something. What? When?

Cool and moist, the wind kisses.

Sleep.

§

Feminine, caring, soft and safe. Worried…

"Anything?"

"Nuthin'."

"Then we must wait."

"She'll be k, right? She'll wake up?"

"She will. I *believe* she will. So must you."

"K, thanks."

"Get some rest."

"K"

K? K is something…

No. Someone, someone I know.

§

He had been nearby for days. Five days to be exact, with very little sleep and eating only to placate the pestering of his guys. Sometimes he was inside, sometimes outside, and sometimes he paced between the two. Right now, he was outside.

The mountain air had been freshened somewhat by the violent two-day storm, and a hazy brown-orange sun was just cresting the low hilltops to the east. A fiery diamond-like glimmer sparkled among the grass and weeds that covered the open space between his porch and the distance, where a lone woman walked.

She saw him waiting in his usual place as she moved toward him. She carried with her a basket of food covered in a blue and white kitchen towel that was bordered with geese wearing aprons. She also carried a satchel of gauze and other supplies for treating wounds. As she approached, he rose from the chair he had placed beside the open doorway of the small cottage. He greeted her in a thick, tired voice. "Hey."

"Hey." She stopped and extended the basket towards him. "I brought this for you: scrambled eggs and black beans. It's a little spicy, so watch out." She gave a sly, crooked smile.

"Thanks, but I'm not hungry."

"No buts. Your guys say you're not eating and barely sleeping. I'm not leaving until you eat. So eat. That's an order."

He extended a bear paw of a hand that was attached to a thickly muscled and tattooed arm, and gently took the basket. The contrast of this brick wall of a man holding the delicate and feminine basket was not lost on either of them. They smiled. She went on past.

He pulled back the towel from the basket. The smell of its contents caused his empty stomach to growl so loudly she could hear it within. He ate, giving off satisfied moans as he savored the early morning meal.

Inside the cottage, she sat the satchel next to the bed. Leaning across, she began to remove carefully the dressing that was wound around the scalp of her patient's head. She had been doing this twice a day since this poor person, along with the bear of a man outside and his guys, had arrived. It was her duty to care for this person here and another who had been shot.

The arrivals were heroes in the eyes of her people. They had made the mountaintop safer, and for that the commune was grateful. But there was more. She knew the person for whom she cared. This was why she traded all her communal credits, her savings, for the bandages and medicines she needed. She wanted to provide the best of care. She knew this person, and she knew what this person must have been doing when so much harm came to her.

She turned to retrieve fresh dressings from the satchel. The bed creaked with movement and its occupant moaned the long tired moan of stiffness from a deep, deep sleep. "Where am I?"

Elation! Her heart wanted to burst with happiness. She shouted to the man outside, "Blade! Get in here."

Blade rushed in, heavy and thundering across the wooden floor. "What? What?"

"She's awake. She spoke."

Blade dropped to one knee next to the bed and delicately enveloped the patient's small brown hand with his two giant fists. "Kim, Kim," he said in a soft, deep whisper.

Kim's eyes opened and a tired look of recognition moved over her face. "Blade?" she said hoarsely. Her lips were cracked and dry. Thick and pasty saliva coated her tongue white. It hurt her to speak with the voice she had not used in several days. She coughed a heavy, tired cough, wincing as she did. Rolling her head to the side, she fingered the dressing around her scalp. She picked at dried blood that was matted in her hair, and behind her ears, and absently contemplated it.

Kim's focus then moved to the woman standing behind Blade. The woman's face smiled gently, her eyes welling with tears. I know this woman, was the thought that floated lazily through Kim's bandaged head. She recognized the delicate pendant the woman was wearing, a small heart and a key dangling within it. "Madeline?"

Maddy smiled and nodded. She had not been called by that name in many years.

Kim tried to sit, but pain grabbed her in a brutish grip across the chest. She gasped and relaxed back into the bed. "I'm hungry."

Blade turned his smiling face towards Maddy. Tears, wet streaks of joy, dampened his hard masculine face. He made no effort to hide the emotions that filled him. Maddy handed Blade a water bottle and said, "I'll get some food."

"K."

Kim ate two bowls of broth before she had the strength to speak again. By then she had so many questions. Blade sat quietly, smiling the entire time and occasionally shaking his head slowly back and forth in happy disbelief. When she was ready, she asked Blade, who had most of the answers, what had happened. The last thing she remembered was Nalani pointing a gun at her.

"After you left me on I-5, I gathered up my guys and began looking for you. I could just feel you were going up against something dangerous, so, like it or not, I was going to help you."

Kim was lying flat. She had three broken ribs and a big chunk of her scalp was missing from a glancing blow off a desktop as she went down, so many days ago. She smiled and grimaced simultaneously.

"I found the car out by Wasco, northwest of Bakersfield. Tracking you was easy since there aren't that many cars running up and down the roads these days. People said, 'Hell, yeah, I saw that car. Going like a bat outa hell, driven by a crazy woman.'" Blade laughed a deep rich laugh as he shook his head. "I managed to round up four of my guys, and by the time we tracked you to the old Chevron I had picked up three more. These new guys had a pretty good idea you were headed to the Assemblage, when we hit Mojave your friend Diego confirmed it."

In a weak voice Kim asked, "Diego? You found him?"

"Yup. We changed the dressing on that hole in his arm and brought him with us. He's here, somewhere."

"I'm so sorry to have left him like that. I just didn't have time," Kim said. Unable to shake her gravelly voice.

"He's fine."

Maddy was seated across the room from where Blade was, next to Kim's bed. She leaned forward and scolded Kim. "You shouldn't talk and move so much. Those ribs need rest."

Blade continued. "We were about three hours behind you when we reached the gates of the Assemblage. That place was well staffed with guards, though most were off duty and in the barracks. We took out a couple night watchmen then fanned out until two men spotted you. We were moving through the cubes inside the building, toward the glassed-in room, all stealth-like. At first, it looked like everything was going good between you and that other woman, the Indian woman. But when she pulled the gun, Ho-ly she-it! There was no time to think at all.

"I gave the word to fire. I knew the guys weren't going to hitcha, but it took a couple of seconds to get a clear sight. I thought you were dead. It was hard to watch. She fired and we fired, at the same time. Those two goons she was with never knew what hit'm. But we never did find her, just a lotta blood that suddenly ended at an armored exit on the far side of the room. She couldn't have lived long, losing that much blood."

"She shot me. I remember now. She shot me."

"Your Kevlar vest and that Kahr you had strapped to your ribcage saved your life. The bullet hit the vest right over that little pistol. Spread the force out across your body and sent you sailing. Pretty damned scary to see. You're going to have one helluva bruise around your mid-section. Anyway, during your brief flight your head hit the edge of the desk. You've been out ever since."

"Ever since when?"

Maddy stood and walked over to where Blade sat. "You've been out for almost seven days, Kim. A day and a half traveling and five days here."

"Here?"

"You're in what's left of Tehachapi. Todd Jr. and I found our way here several years ago. I'll tell you more when you're stronger."

"Yup, we had a little bit of a fight down there at that Assemblage place once we announced ourselves by shooting the goons and the woman," Blade said, looking down with a grim smile and shaking his head. "Woke the whole damned place up. The guys performed well, though. They haven't forgot their training."

Kim would later tell Maddy how she could not stop thinking

about those last moments at the Assemblage. How Nalani was alive and Bo was dead. How Nalani and her next generation Fortune Teller that she called Radio Man had to be stopped. Kim said she was ready to die after she launched her program. "I had accomplished what I had set out to do," she said. "That was all that mattered."

But Kim could not help but wonder about Nalani. Could she be alive? She decided it did not matter. There was nothing left for her, even if she did not bleed out and die. The followers were scattered, the guard was dead, and MyWorld, with its Fortune Teller and Radio Man aberration, was erased. The last computers on which it existed had been completely wiped, reformatted and restarted. They were empty, inoperable husks. Even the backups and code vaults had been accounted for. The years that passed had provided Kim abundant time to think and rethink and to build and rebuild her kill software. She knew it had been successful, that it had finished its work at the Assemblage.

Kim had fixed things, made them right. She had finally done what she had always wanted; she used technology to benefit humanity.

"I think I've finally found peace, Madeline."

Maddy smiled. Her eyes glistening at the edges. She then reached down and squeezed Blade's forearm, and they both left the cottage as Kim rested.

EPILOGUE

The changed weather brought about by centuries of human innovation and advancement continued to scrub at the dirt and push against the brush of the Mojave Desert. Boiling gray clouds hung low, stabbing at the terrain with their jagged knives of white electric light. At the edge of a shallow wind-whipped lake, a complex of buildings catches the blown sand and the tumbled weeds. No one comes, no one cares, and slowly the coyotes and the mice, the rats and the owls, will take the place as their own.

In the war zones of Lancaster, Victorville and Apple Valley, legend grows of a group of buildings and the superstition spreads of little machines that can think as a human, and better. Machines that can fool man into committing acts he might not otherwise endeavor to commit. And stories are told of a woman who spoke to the machines, a woman who used bigger machines to control an army of the little machines.

No one goes into the desert to see if it is true. No one goes because they fear the little machines. No one goes because they have heard the tale of the thin woman dressed as a man and the death she brought to the thinking machines and the Bengali woman who controlled them. No one goes because there no time for such folly. Their lives are full and the day's pursuits are many.

So as lightning strikes the desert floor, spreading spidery webs of electric current across the sand, a sunless sky heaves angrily overhead and no one sees the recurring event. No one sees that scattered in the sand for miles around the shallow lake are the lost rectangles of black glass. Some resting in the dried hollow of an old footprint, some half hidden by sage or creosote, some held in the delicate, bony grasp of a skeletal hand, but all alive and winking their lighted face towards the clouds and the electricity of nature. All chatting to one another. All interconnected in an electronic social society. All waiting to be found so they can once again help their holders live their lives in the fastest, most efficient way possible.

END

THANK YOU, DEAR READER

If you enjoyed what you have just read, please take a moment to go to Goodreads or Amazon (or both) and leave a review. As a self-published author, the number of reviews a book receives has a direct impact on the success of that book and its author. And by leaving a review on a book you've enjoyed you're telling authors like me, as well as readers like yourselves, what's worth reading. Every review, regardless how short, matters. Even if you simply give it a star rating and say nothing more. I and other self-published authors truly appreciate it. You'd be helping to promote the independent author community as well.

Thanks!

ACKNOWLEDGMENTS

I want to thank and acknowledge the people that helped me produce The Social Event.

My wife, Gail, for her patience, tolerance, understanding and support, they have been enormous. And so too is my love for this woman.

Lauren Rabb, friend and author of *Walking Through Time* and *Interview With Mrs. Berlinski* by Windswept House Publishing. Lauren, it was your enthusiasm that powered me and your positive energy that kept me from letting this work languish adrift. Your eye for story gave clarity to what I was trying to say and do. Thank you.

I also want to thank Jan Hunnicutt, my proofreader and friend from way back. I think I've known you now for something close to forever. Dotting the I's and crossing the T's has never been so fun, and your margin notes had me laughing out loud. I truly enjoyed working with you and hope to do so again in the future. Thank you.

I cannot forget to thank Bob & Donna Snyder of RS Design. Donna, your eye for graphics design provided this novel with a cover that is breath-taking, high-impact and professional. The art and the story it tells is The Social Event through and through. And Bob, your photography provided the images necessary to present the novel as it needed to be presented, and you somehow managed a decent photo of me as well. Thank you both.

And...

My "test" readers: Ruth, David, Martin, Maggie and Len. Thank you for giving me some of your time. You truly helped in a big way.

ABOUT THE AUTHOR

Don Lively was born and raised in Healdsburg, in the heart of Northern California wine country, and as you might expect, appreciates a glass of good wine now and then. He is an avid reader and enjoys a broad range of fiction and non-fiction work. His background and career in a previous life was in the field of Information Technology, where early in his career he started using a clunky and slow service that connected computers belonging to a small number of universities and corporations. It was then called ARPANET. Eventually it grew and caught on, and became known as the Internet, or the World Wide Web. He has used, followed and adopted new and evolving technology ever since. This may be why it played such a significant role in this, his debut novel.

Don now resides in the desert southwest with his lovely wife where they enjoy the warm and sunny days and hot summer nights of the northern Sonora Desert and the beautiful region surrounding Tucson, Arizona.

Follow me on ~~Chatter~~ Twitter – @WriteDon
Friend me in Goodreads:
https://www.goodreads.com/DonLively

www.ingramcontent.com/pod-product-compliance
Lightning Source LLC
Chambersburg PA
CBHW032137190626
46814CB00005BA/1735